PRAISE FOR
A Queen in Hiding

"This is a solid beginning to an ambitious saga of magic, intrigue, and heroism." —*Booklist*

"Kozloff sets a solid stage with glimpses into other characters and nations while keeping the book together with a clear, propulsive plot. A new series starts off with a bang." —*Kirkus Reviews*

"This series opener is literary, ambitious, and epic in scope." —*Publishers Weekly*

"A deft and exciting beginning to what I am sure will be a really gorgeous saga of a girl coming to terms with her destiny." —Melanie Rawn, author of the Exiles trilogy

"A breathtaking start to a new fantasy series that abounds in magic, backstabbing, and war. This is your new epic fantasy fix, right here." —Beth Cato, author of *Breath of Earth*

"Sweeping in scope and unabashedly epic—Kozloff has written an instant classic here. I can't wait for the next one." —Auston Habershaw, author of *Iron and Blood*

THE
CERULEAN
QUEEN

Sarah Kozloff

TOR

A Tom Doherty Associates Book
New York

THE CERULEAN QUEEN

Copyright © 2020 by Sarah Kozloff

All rights reserved.

Edited by Jen Gunnels

A Tor Book
Published by Tom Doherty Associates
120 Broadway
New York, NY 10271

www.tor-forge.com

Tor® is a registered trademark of Macmillan Publishing Group, LLC.

The Library of Congress Cataloging-in-Publication Data
is available upon request.

ISBN 978-1-250-16896-2 (trade paperback)
ISBN 978-1-250-16895-5 (ebook)

Our books may be purchased in bulk for promotional, educational, or business use. Please contact your local bookseller or the Macmillan Corporate and Premium Sales Department at 1-800-221-7945, extension 5442, or by email at MacmillanSpecialMarkets@macmillan.com.

First Edition: April 2020

Printed in the United States of America

0 9 8 7 6 5 4 3 2 1

to Dawn,
who believed in this the most

TALENTS REVEALED

Remove your cloak and boots, weary traveler,

And rest. For you are not fully returned.

Land, walls, or brooks don't guarantee welcome,

And a nation—or a family—must be earned.

PART
ONE

⁓

Reign of Queen Cerúlia

THE FIRST DAYS

1

Alpetar

Smithy woke early with a feeling of deep unease. While General Sumroth had gone on with thousands of his troops to the shipbuilding center, Pexted, pursuing his plan of vengeance against Weirandale, Smithy had stayed in Alpetar with the refugees in Camp Ruby, situated where the Alpetar Mountains slid down into fertile plains.

Camp Ruby, the first of four camps established along the Trade Corridor, lay closest to the Land.

He strode out of his tent into the dawn air, gazing northward in the direction of his homeland, as he always did. He saw fingers of smoke far away and read these as a sign that FireThorn yawned and stretched.

Around him the camp stirred as the other exiles from Oromondo woke and began their days.

Pozhar's Agent stoked his nearby fire, adding coal and blowing up the flames with a hand bellows. He had no real forge here and he missed the high, cleansing heat. But he had his hand tools and he used this outdoor fire to soften metal and shape it as best he could whenever one of the Spirit's children approached him with a commission.

As if conjured by his thoughts, a girl of about twelve summers appeared, a little slyly, thrusting out at him a tin kettle with a broken handle. Smithy examined it closely.

"Aye," he told the girl-woman. "Come back tonight."

But instead of leaving immediately she lingered by his fire, mesmerized by the flames. And the fire reflected in her eyes, making them glow red.

"You like my fire?"

She nodded. "It makes me warm all over."

"Good. Make sure you come back for the kettle yourself. I will have a small treat for you."

Smithy realized he had found another; this girl made three Oromondo children who harbored a spark of Pozhar in their souls. He would tend these flames cautiously, to see if any of the children would grow into new Magi. The death of those Eight more than a year ago counted only as a setback, not as the end of the reign of the Magi.

Smithy walked to the camp's communal kitchen area and asked a baker for a bowl of bread dough, which she gave without question. When he returned to his tent, he reached under his flimsy bed for the canister he kept hidden. He used his thick fingers to add large pinches of volcanic ash to the glutinous material. After mixing in the additive, he set the bowl to rise in the warmth of the stones ringing his fire. Later in the day he would bake biscuits—it didn't matter if they looked misshapen or got singed—which he would offer to the three prospects. The ash did not contain as much Magic as cooled lava, but it would serve. These children would gain the Power, abilities that demonstrated their devotion to Pozhar and illustrated the Spirit's might and majesty.

That fool Sumroth believes that because the Eight past Magi perished, he will rule Oromondo. But he would rule as all dictators rule: for himself. Only Magi will keep the Land of the Fire Mountains for Pozhar. I will aid General Sumroth in enacting retribution against Weirandale, and then the Spirit will deal with his pride and blasphemy.

The fire he sat by rose higher than the fuel he had given it should burn. In the crackle of the flames, Smithy heard the voice of his master.

The witch's spawn has returned to Weirandale.

Smithy pounded one fist into the opposite palm.

What can I do, Mighty Pozhar, to stop this?

You can do nothing, Smithy. But I have other servants. Tend your flames and keep watch over my children.

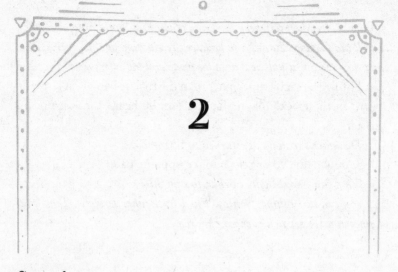

2

Cascada

Ciellō and the dog, Whaki, set out from the Sea Hawk inn in the
pearly dawn light. Both felt too restless to stay inside the lodging
house environs a single moment longer. Despite his remonstrance,
the dog had been whining and scratching at the fence gate throughout Ciellō's morning exercise routine. He could hardly get Whaki to
wait while he scrubbed and dressed.

Together, man and dog surveyed the empty streets of the capital
city. Last night these same streets had been crammed with townsfolk celebrating some wedding amongst the gentry by feasting at
squares where soldiers roasted pig—carving off generous slices—
and poured hard cider into whatever vessels the citizens proffered.
Street musicians played while people danced and cavorted, happy
with the free victuals. When night fell, fireworks set off over the
harbor bedecked the sky in patterns of blue and white.

Ciellō had partaken of the pork and Whaki had scarfed down
dropped tidbits until the fireworks started; these sent the dog into
paroxysms of terror. So the Zellish bodyguard had taken him back
to the Sea Hawk and coaxed him into a nearly closed wardrobe to

muffle the noise of the explosions. By the time the men with whom he shared the room returned, dead drunk, in the wee hours, the fireworks show had concluded, and Whaki—exhausted from his fright—snored loudly under Ciellō's bed.

This morning the thoroughfares stretched deserted except for the loads of rubbish strewn about and a few unconscious drunks curled up on their sides.

In Zellia, after a fete, the mayor would hire the poorest of the poor to sweep up the refuse. Ciellō wondered if that was the custom here. Certainly, street sweepers needed to clean these streets; their disarray offended his sense of order.

Ciellō allowed the dog to lead the way. This morning Whaki didn't detour to sniff or eat the meat scattered on the ground. His nose stuck high in the air and he loped onward without wavering. Whatever was bothering Whaki this morn, Ciellō knew it had to do with the woman he guarded. Whaki rushed up the streets so urgently that Ciellō, supremely fit as he was, had to struggle to keep up.

The white towers of the Nargis Palace, perched on the top of the hill, flashed in the morning sun, and grew larger as they approached.

Regent Matwyck had tossed and turned the whole night through, disturbed by the rich fare of his son's wedding feast, and—more than he would care to admit—by the image of his intended, Duchette Lolethia, lying murdered in Burgn's chambers.

The hole in her throat had gaped with an almost lewd intimacy, and her blood had soaked the floor black. A small quantity of this blood had stained his shoes and the side of his doublet, both of which he tore off with disgust and ordered his valet to burn, even though they were new and quite costly. Even after washing his hands three times he still felt the touch of her clammy palm in his own.

Although the Regent knew he had no cause to feel guilty—*he* had not killed the girl, nor ordered it done—an unease lingered, perchance because of how angry he had been when she failed to appear for the wedding and the banquet. Lolethia's murder—while it explained her absence—did not really douse his fury. Even if she had not, after all, purposely missed the grand wedding, he could conjure no innocent explanation as to why she had gone to Burgn's chamber.

Giving up on sleep, Matwyck pushed aside his bed-curtains and rang for his valet. His head pounded so that he poured himself a glass of wine while he waited for the man to appear.

"No word yet from the Marauders who went after Burgn?" he barked when the valet entered, carrying his fastbreak tray.

The man shook his head.

Matwyck was not surprised. It really was too soon for them to have caught up with the muckwit and returned. He would have to think of the proper way to punish the man once he had him in his possession.

"Fetch Heathclaw and Councilor Prigent," Matwyck ordered as he sat down to his food. Undoubtedly, he was the most put upon of men: after all the time and treasure he had lavished on the wedding his son had run off early, skipping the capstone events, and then that damn minx Lolethia had gotten herself killed. And when Prigent arrived, he would bring the latest expense receipts and wave them under his nose.

His valet dispatched a guard with his requests, received a pitcher of wash water from a chambermaid, and started to lay out an outfit for the day.

"Not brown, today, you shitwit," Matwyck corrected. "Black. And I'll need a circlet of mourning."

The valet nodded, replacing the offensive clothing with black silk, and pulled a box of accessories out of the wardrobe. Matwyck gave upon moving the food around on his plate and crossed to his washbasin, waiting for the valet to pour the water and hold a towel. When the man started to sharpen his razor, however, Matwyck shook his head—his unshaven appearance would show the court just how little he cared about appearances in the midst of his grief.

Matwyck had dressed in fresh smallclothes, trousers, hose, and boots, but he still had his sleeping shift keeping his upper body warm when Heathclaw and Prigent bustled in together. Both of them looked hastily prepared, as if they had been roused earlier than they had expected. But why should they loll in bed when there were so many things to attend to?

"Lord Regent," they murmured as they bowed.

"Prigent, I want a report by midday of every remark the visiting gentry make," Matwyck ordered. "Get our people amongst the servants to write everything down. Everything about the wedding and the unfortunate events concerning the duchette. They will chatter like magpies during fastbreak and I want to know who says what.

"And Heathclaw, I want you to take three guards and summon Captain Murgn."

"Where should I bring him, Lord Regent? Is he under arrest?" Heathclaw raised his brows.

"Not yet. We don't know if he was in league with his cousin in this crime, and he's been extremely useful to us over the years. Take him to my office. We will let him dangle for a while before I question him.

"Now, what do you have for me?" he asked, because both men had lists and leather portfolios tucked under their arms.

Prigent, distressed over how much it would cost to feed the visiting noble folk, wanted to talk about how long they would be staying in residence.

"No, you idiot," Matwyck cut him off, "we *want* them to linger where we can keep an eye on them. We need, however, to provide entertainment tonight, something fabulous that will wash away any negative impressions. Perchance the Aqueduct or Peacock players could be induced to give a private performance? Bring me a list of possibilities in an hour.

"And what is already on my schedule for today?" Matwyck turned to Heathclaw.

His secretary consulted his list. "Mostly formal farewells and a few 'private meetings' that dukes have requested—these are probably requests for loans."

"The farewells are so tiresome," Matwyck said, steepling his fingers. "The carriages are never ready on time and the guests themselves are worse, and thus I'm forced to stand in the entry hall making empty conversation while the spouse or insipid offspring makes excuses."

"Perhaps you'll be able to directly glean information about the gentries' reactions to—recent events?" Prigent offered.

"Hmm," Matwyck assented with a grudging nod. "Who's specified a leave-taking time?"

Heathclaw consulted his list, "First up, at ten o'clock, is Mistress Stahlia and her dependents, though I hardly think *they* are worth your time, Lord Steward. I could represent you, if you so desire."

Matwyck slapped the table with his hand because so far this morning he had forgotten about the Wyndton sister. His suspicions about her mysterious appearance and his memory of her judgmental eyes came rushing back.

"Fetch a brace of guards," he ordered, "I want to examine that wench right away."

Gunnit had been in Cascada a moon, often stealing away from his page duties to serve as liaison between Water Bearer and her allies outside the palace. Yesterday, he saw Finch—no, now he had to think of her as "Cerúlia"—from a distance: she was strolling in the garden as he hustled out the Kitchen Gate with a note. He had longed to run to her, but Water Bearer had told him that his errand was urgent.

His job today had been to unlock and unbolt the West Gate two hours before dawn. He took down the crossbeams that held it shut.

As soon as he poked his head through he saw more than thirty people waiting in the shadow of the stone wall in dark garb.

After they slipped into the grounds, however, they paused—each tied on a sash and reversed their capes. In the brightening sky he saw they wore black trousers, black shirts, dazzling white sashes (elaborately knotted), and blue capes sparkling with silver thread. Three of them, including Captain Yanath, also wore breastplates and helms so polished they caught the fading starlight. Gunnit's mouth fell open at their splendor.

"I take it you like the cloaks?" Yanath asked him. "My wife—she's such a clever fabricator—she's been working on them for moons. Uniforms matter, especially when you need to impress. We are the New Queen's Shield, or whatever we're going to be called, and anyone who crosses us better drought damn know it."

Yanath turned to a woman with a peeling red nose to whom he seemed to defer. "Ready, Seamaster?"

She, in turn, surveyed the men behind them. "Don't let your mace clatter," she said to one with very bowed legs. Then she nodded at Gunnit, "Lead on, lad."

Moving at a gentle lope Gunnit shepherded the troop across the grounds. The soldiers clutched their weapons so they didn't jingle as the boy weaved them through the deeper obscurity of shrubs and trees for over an hour. By the time the white stone of the palace loomed before them, the sun had just risen.

Palace guards, positioned in a loose formation, much looser than the nightly cordon created by Matwyck's Marauders, kept watch. Yanath gestured to his followers—singing arrows struck two guards who stood in their immediate way and slicing daggers made sure they didn't cry out. The New Shield pulled the bodies from where they tumbled, hiding them under nearby shrubs. Then the captain had everybody double over into a crouch while moving to reach the shelter of some hedges, then crawl on their bellies to a small, unremarkable door through which footmen usually brought firewood into the Great Ballroom. They paused, taking deep breaths and passing around water bags.

Gunnit whispered to the captain, "Wait. There will be a signal."

"What kind of signal?" Yanath asked.

The boy had no idea, but he placed his confidence in the Spirits. "We'll know it," he answered with conviction.

They waited. Everyone had already readied his or her weapon.

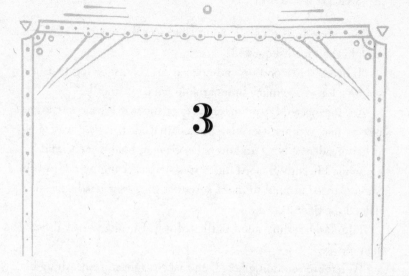

3

Although she had stayed up late conferring with Nana, Cerúlia woke when the tanager that had befriended her jumped on her windowsill to report that fewer red-sashed guards ringed the palace because last night a large troop had galloped off to the west. The princella sent the bird out again with instructions to tell her as soon as the nighttime sentries had been called in for the day.

Then Cerúlia dressed in her trousers and shirt, strapped on her dagger, and stuffed her hair into a black beret Nana had found. She noted with approval that her nursemaid had also managed to scrub nearly all traces of the ink out of the pant leg.

"It's just me," came Nana's voice muffled by the hallway door. Cerúlia unlocked it and let her in.

Nana carried a tray of tisane and scones, and she entered with a man following close on her heels.

"It's quiet as a crypt out there, what with everyone sleeping off all the wine they drank last night," Nana reported. "Your Majesty, this is Hiccuth. He's worked in the stables since you were but a tiny babe. You can trust him."

"I'm your servant, Your Majesty," said Hiccuth in a voice that choked back tears, bending his knee.

"No, none of that. I am in your debt," Cerúlia replied. "Have you brought the rope I requested?"

"Indeed." He stood up and opened his coat, showing that he'd wound a long rope many times around his wide middle.

An unexpected tap on the same door made everyone startle and look at one another. Cerúlia checked that all her hair was safely tucked inside the beret and drew her dagger, holding it behind her leg, while Hiccuth grasped the horseshoe pick hanging on his belt. Nana glanced around to make sure that they were ready and then opened the door a crack.

Tilim and Stahlia stood in the hallway. Cerúlia swiftly ushered them inside.

"What are *you* doing here?" she asked, aghast, resheathing her knife. "You ought to be sleeping safely on the other side of the building."

"*She,*" Tilim pointed at her nursemaid, "told me you are in peril. I'm not a child: I stabbed an intruder in Wyndton a few months ago. I intend to protect you, no matter what you're up to."

"*Nana!*" Cerúlia reprimanded. "And did you involve my foster mother in this too! She's no business being here—she can't fight."

"No, she's not to blame," said Stahlia, with her hands on her hips. "I woke up when Tilim tried to tiptoe out of our suite, and I forced him to tell me where he was going. I don't understand what's happening, but I will not be left out!"

"This is a dangerous morning. Perilous to all," Cerúlia protested. "I would not have you injured. In fact, I *forbid* you to get involved."

Stahlia folded her arms in a gesture that her daughter knew too well.

In exasperation, the princella tugged on the edge of her beret again. "There's really no time for an argument. If you must participate, will you follow my directions without question?"

Stahlia and Tilim nodded solemnly.

"All right, then. I need to get inside the Throne Room. The

guards have strict instructions never to admit a young woman, so I have devised an unusual route for myself. But I need all the ground-floor doors to the Throne Room unlocked for allies who will be joining us. So, your task is to force the palace guards to unlock these entrances. By dagger point if you have to."

"By dagger point? That's a terrible idea," rejoined Stahlia. "Why don't we just *ask them* to unlock this room for us?"

"Why would they do that?" Cerúlia asked, irked that Stahlia was countermanding her very first order.

"Because the room is full of tapestries, and last week, when we first arrived, Lord Matwyck promised me I could study them," her mother answered matter-of-factly.

Cerúlia paused and paced a few steps, considering. "This is help-ful. So—you couldn't sleep late. You want to study the tapestries and show them to your son. Then Nana, you and Hiccuth come along after one door has been opened and set about freeing more entryways."

"Here, eat this." Cerúlia passed Tilim the second half of her scone and Stahlia her cup of tisane. As Tilim crammed the whole portion into his mouth and Stahlia sipped her tea with a small frown holding back her questions, Nana handed Cerúlia two small hourglass pendants that she had borrowed from a cupboard in the lesson chamber.

The princella hung one chain over Stahlia's head and one over her own. "Look. These both count ten minutes. We'll turn them over together on my signal. You must get the Throne Room un-locked by the time the sand trickles all the way through."

The tanager skidded onto the windowsill and ruffled its tail os-tentatiously.

One sees no red guards outside now. A big feline awaits thee.

"Sorry, that bird is my signal; I need to leave now." Quickly, Cerúlia kissed Nana, Tilim, and Stahlia on their brows. She could not just stroll down the Royal Stair, so she led her little group out into the corridor and down the hallway to an arched opening that faced into an inner courtyard. She then drew the wooden shutters.

After glancing around for a suitable anchor, Hiccuth tied his rope around a torch sconce but held the bulk of the pressure across his wide back, letting the free end drop down through the hallway window. Nana stood in front of him, blocking him and the rope from the view of anyone happening to walk their direction. Stahlia and Tilim copied Nana's action on Hiccuth's other side. Cerúlia pulled on a pair of leather gloves that had been tucked into her belt, crawled out on the sill, and turned over her timepiece, motioning to Stahlia to do the same.

Then she grabbed the rope with both hands and feet, hanging high in the air.

Her heart was thudding so hard she thought it would burst out of her chest.

She had seen sailors on the *Misty Traveler* rappel down the ship's hull, inspecting it for damage. The action looked easy when they did it, but Cerúlia immediately discovered that her upper body had nothing like the sailors' strength. After a few bad moments when she collided with the wall and wondered if her arms could hold her, she raised her legs and placed her feet to brace herself against the wall. She bounced away, slithered down several paces, kicked off with her feet again, and slithered again. She landed in an untidy thud on the ground.

Seeing her safely down, Hiccuth retracted the rope.

With the blue tanager leading the way, Cerúlia disappeared through an arched doorway, heading toward the rear of the palace and the catamount who lingered outside, ready to escort her to his tunnel.

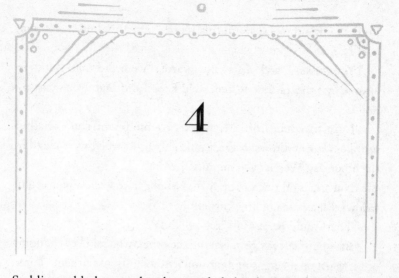

4

Stahlia could almost solve the puzzle behind all these bewildering events, but whenever she started to understand, her mind skittered away and her thoughts refused to cohere.

Besides, she had no time to ponder; to reach the Throne Room from the fancy chamber where Chamberlain Vilkit had lodged her foster daughter, one merely walked down the corridor and then down a very grand staircase.

The Throne Room of the palace was an enormous chamber ringed by entrances on three sides. The East Entrance, with high double doors of elaborately carved walnut, constituted the formal entryway, while the north and south walls formed the long legs of the rectangle, punctuated by a series of single doors that opened into different annexes and stairways to galleries. To the west, the Throne Room backed onto the palace grounds.

As they approached this historic hall, Stahlia noticed the guards on patrol. Trying to appear nonchalant, she walked up to the East Entrance, Tilim hanging back behind her. The guards watched her approach with neutral expressions.

"Good morn to you, men! I am Lordling Marcot's mother-in-marriage, Stahlia of Wyndton. Lord Matwyck told me that I might study the grand tapestries in this room. I am a weaver, as you may have heard."

"Yes, missus," said one of the guards, "we heard that. But to let anyone into the Throne Room, we'd need Lord Matwyck's permission."

"I just told you, Lord Matwyck gave me permission"—Stahlia wrinkled her eyebrows in great puzzlement—"when we walked by the other day. Weren't you on duty then?"

"Not us," said one of the men. "Might have been a pair of our fellows. I'll ask around the corners."

"That would be so kind," said Stahlia.

One guard left his post, leaving the other, who had keys hanging at his waist on a ring, standing impassively in front of them. Tilim, feigning reluctance in front of this audience, started complaining under his breath, "Mama, I don't want to see these tapestries; all my life I've seen scores of 'em; why are you dragging me around to see more?"

The first man came back shaking his head. "No luck on that side; let me just try the other for you, missus." He disappeared around the southern corner. Although Stahlia actually rued each tick, she tried to appear relaxed. She took advantage of the situation to smooth Tilim's hair and pull his sleeves straighter; though she knew he would hate such fussing, at the moment he couldn't complain.

The helpful guard came back with an older man who boasted an impressive mustache.

"I am Athelbern, the sergeant on duty. How can I be of assistance, missus?"

Stahlia repeated her story.

"Oh, aye. I was here on the East Entrance when Lord Matwyck walked by with you, and I overheard him. It would be best, however, if the Lord Regent was here with you now to give permission."

"*Really?*" Stahlia asked with polite disbelief. "I believe the lord and all his visitors are sleeping in after the late-night festivities. Us country folk, you know, we rise with the roosters no matter what. No lie-a-bed for us, as I'm sure there's no such luxuries for hard-working guards like you." She spoke faster and put a bit of pleading in her tone. "I feel kind of low, what with my daughter leaving me, and I thought, 'This would be a perfect time to look at the tapestries.' Do you mean I have to wait for Lord Matwyck—or even, by requesting to see him, wake him up?"

"I don't know, missus. I only know my standing orders," said Sergeant Athelbern.

Stahlia stole a glance at the sand seeping through the timepiece.

Nana had been loitering nearby, sitting on a bench with one shoe off, rubbing her bunion, pretending not to watch the interaction out of the corner of her eye. Now, she popped on her shoe and strode over.

"Milady," she said, addressing Stahlia with a term of higher respect than the guards had used. "Can I assist you? Is there a misunderstanding?"

Sergeant Athelbern apprised Nana of the situation.

"Oh, Athelbern, don't be such a lackwit. Since he has already given this lady permission, Lord Matwyck will be mighty wroth with you if you bar her entry. 'Tis not only the proper but the polite thing to do with such a distinguished visitor."

"Nana, will you bear his wrath?" asked Sergeant Athelbern.

"Aye, but get moving now. She'd be in and out before anyone even rises if you'd just step lively."

Ponderously working his big key, the sergeant unlocked the East Entrance.

And with that, Stahlia and Tilim made their way inside.

Stahlia looked around, gasping at the room's grandeur, clearly visible even without lanterns because of the morning light streaming through the stained glass upper stories.

They had entered the Throne Room on a mezzanine level. This low walkway stretched the whole circuit of the room, providing an opportunity for visitors to inspect the magnificent tapestries that hung on the wall. Five broad steps led down to the polished marble on the ground level. A dais, two-thirds of the way down the length of the room, rose above the floor. A small-sized empty throne, shimmering silver arms and legs with blue upholstery, stately in its simplicity, sat beside a large, unhewn pillar of rock. Water arced down the front of the rock, hitting a golden basin with a continual splash, and the basin overflowed to a pool on the dais in a solid, shining curtain of water.

Without warning, three tan-and-white mountain lions, each about the weight of a deer, raced toward their tiny group. They came so close that Stahlia could see the black rims all around their blue eyes and the brown markings on their foreheads. Although they made no noise or threat, Stahlia shrank away.

"Don't be frightened," said Athelbern. "They never come up here on the gangway. Just ignore them." And indeed, the cats stopped underneath them, looking up at the intruders, and just twitched their noses and whiskers.

"Now here," the sergeant said, proudly indicating a tapestry to the left of the doorway, "is one of the real masterworks. 'Queen Chitta Instructing the Glaziers,' this one is called."

Stahlia pulled her gaze away from the beasts to look at the tapestry. Though her mind churned with the day's mysteries, the weaver in her came to the fore. "Oh! So marvelous! Look at the sense of depth! Look at her hair. Who was the artist?"

As Athelbern started to answer, Tilim tugged on the back of her pendant chain to remind her of the time, then, with his hand on his scabbard, quietly moved directly behind the officer, who had started to discourse about the tapestry.

Suddenly, the catamounts raced away, coursing as fast as water through a broken dam in the direction of the opposite end of the room.

A fourth catamount crawled through a swinging portal in the

floor, deep in the recesses of the hall. The beast was followed by the figure of a woman in trousers and a beret, who rose to her feet, brushing off dirt. Stahlia sighed with relief that she had fulfilled her commission in time.

Then all four mountain lions leapt at Wren. Stahlia's satisfaction transmuted to terror for fear that the beasts intended to injure her. She couldn't stop a small shriek escaping from her throat.

"Hey! Hey you! What the—!" Athelbern called out.

To Stahlia's astonishment, Tilim pulled his sword and pressed it into the sergeant's back, just at the level of his kidney. "Stand still and shut up," he ordered.

Stahlia stared, paralyzed with dread, but the catamounts did not harm her foster daughter. One rested its oversized, fluffy paws on Wren's chest; she had to brace herself with her back leg to withstand its weight. Wren scratched the lion behind its ears and caressed its white chin and throat, and the overgrown house cat closed its eyes and butted her hand with its head. It smelled her mouth and licked her chin with a long pink tongue.

The other three beasts surrounded her; they began rubbing their heads against her legs; one side of their face, then the other, or they sniffed her boots. Their black-tipped tails rose almost to her shoulders; these coyly wrapped and twitched around her. Their rumbling purrs were so loud that Stahlia could hear them wafting across the empty hall. Wren reached down to pet each of the adoring animals in turn. As she kept her head bent, the black beret she wore fell to the floor.

A river of shimmering hair tumbled out of the hat. Hair the likes of which Stahlia had never seen before—hair she had often imagined and tried to capture in her tapestries. Hair of shades of blue-green. Hair the color of a blue tanager's feathers.

The catamounts pushed their faces through her hair—they drank in its color. As she continued to stroke them, one batted at her hair with a paw. When she straightened up and tried to move forward, the mountain lions impeded her progress; one lay down right in front of her and rolled over showing its belly, while another elaborately stretched out its front shoulders and a third wrapped its two front legs around her side. Stahlia heard her laughing at the animals' antics.

At that moment, the bells started to chime. First the bell in the palace church where Percia was married yesterday, then a bell farther away, then all the bells around the city, joining in joyous chimes.

Stahlia's hands flew to her cheeks, but instead of being shocked into silence, words poured out of her.

"*Birdie* is the Nargis heir! *Birdie* is the princella. Oh, Waters! I made the princella clean our chicken coop!" she cried to Tilim and the sergeant.

Stahlia absorbed the scene: the tan cats fawning over the newly revealed princella, the beams of light refracted through the stained glass ceiling winking on the floor, and the tumbled blue hair lying against the white shirt. The cascading water on the dais, flowing first in a waterfall and then in a solid curtain. In the midst of her astonishment, she tried to memorize every last detail.

"Oh, Nargis! What a tapestry this scene would make! 'Cerúlia and the Catamounts.' *This* will be my greatest creation."

5

A close-by church bell broke the early morning silence with a single chime. *Ding.* Then again. *Dong.*

"Go!" shouted Gunnit, as bells throughout the city picked up the reverberation, so that the first bell spread from one church to another, throughout all of Cascada. DING, DONG; *ding, dong*; ding, dong; DING, DONG.

Captain Yanath and Shield Pontole rammed their shoulders into the small wooden door, breaking the latch in their first attempt. The corps dashed through the small entry, Gunnit bringing up the rear. They sprinted across the large ballroom, where the leftover disarray from yesterday's party flashed at them from the mirrored walls, heading for the nearby Throne Room. Ahead, the boy heard shouts and the clash of swords.

A furious combat between palace guards and the New Queen's Shield commenced both around the exterior of the Throne Room and inside the hall. Gunnit saw Pontole struggling to overmaster a burly soldier, their swords crossed in a stalemate between their chests. Pontole broke the standoff by butting his enemy in the forehead. A mariner swung a mace that shattered the sword arm of another guard. Branwise already had a bloody nose, but he hacked the legs out from under a foe. In moments the Throne Room guards all lay dead, injured, or on their knees with their hands in the air, taken by surprise by the fierce attack. Nonetheless, reinforcements—many in various states of dress—poured in by the score, brandishing their weapons as they came.

Nana had told Gunnit that the palace boasted more than two hundred guards; the troop he had just ushered in hadn't a prayer of defeating them by force. They needed reinforcements.

Gunnit slipped into the Throne Room through an open side doorway. Around the room, blue capes crossed swords with white or red sashes; he was surrounded by the clash of metal on metal, grunts of effort, and shouts. A sword that had been knocked loose from someone's hand flew through the air, and Gunnit ducked. He ran after it, picked it up, and, steeling himself, cut the ankle tendon of a nearby palace soldier from behind.

In the midst of all this mayhem, Gunnit spied Water Bearer. She held a kitchen knife at the throat of a soldier who stood very still in her grasp. And Nana was not the only person using an improvised weapon: Gunnit saw footmen brandishing pokers and maids swinging brooms. The palace workers had joined the fray. Were they the needed reinforcements? The fight was so chaotic, he could not tell which side a given servant favored.

Called by the bells, scores of people of all stations continued to scurry into the Throne Room, including administrators and gentry. The gentry appeared mostly in their nightshifts, thronging above on the first and second balconies. A few soldiers appeared on the balconies too, including archers who took advantage of their strategic height to skewer the New Queen's Shield whenever the surging combat gave them a clean shot.

Heedless of all the chaos around her, Cerúlia walked to the central dais, flanked by four mountain lions. She climbed up the six steps.

At that moment, Lord Matwyck, half-dressed, burst through a

door onto the second balcony. "Shoot her! Shoot her!" he shouted. "A fortune to the man who shoots her!" An archer near Matwyck aimed at Cerúlia, but his arrow flew wide. The lady seamaster with the New Queen's Shield raised her own bow, and an arrow blossomed from the enemy archer's stomach.

Gunnit saw Lord Matwyck wrestle the bow from the dying man.

"Shields!" Gunnit yelled, pointing at the danger.

The instant Matwyck turned back to face the floor, Pontole let fly; his arrow caught the lord in the meat of his thigh. The Lord Regent bellowed and staggered from the blow, but held himself upright by grabbing on to the gallery's banister.

There, thought Gunnit, *that was why the Spirits sent me here.*

Cerúlia now stood next to the Fountain and the Basin.

She raised her hands over her head and shouted, "Cease!" When the fighting continued, the four catamounts roared as one, a horrific noise that echoed off the walls.

The fighting paused, midstrike. Two or three hundred people stared at the small figure on the dais.

"Though I have gone by many names, I herewith claim back my true identity," she called out in a ringing voice, stretching her arms wide. "I am Cerúlia, the daughter of the late, brave Queen Cressa the Enchanter and the heroic Lord Ambrice.

"I. Am. Your. Queen."

A chorus of shouts rang out, but Gunnit couldn't tell if the speakers were joyful or dismayed.

"I order all of you to cease this fighting."

An under-footman yelled, "But yesterday, you was a village wench from Wyndton."

Another voice yelled, full of reproach, "If you're the queen, where have you been all these years?"

"Yes," shouted a man Gunnit recognized as Matwyck's secretary. "No one should accept her just at her word. And even if . . . Well, Cerúlia deserted us, while the Lord Regent kept us safe."

"Listen," Cerúlia commanded. "After Matwyck the Usurper tried to assassinate my mother, I kept in the shadows, hiding from him and his powerful allies. I grew to maturity in Androvale. As Fate would have it, I was sheltered and protected by the very Wyndton family this palace feted yesterday.

"I was forced to flee the Eastern Duchies when the Lord Regent's hunt for me came too close."

She turned to address Matwyck directly and pointed up at him on the balcony. "Your relentless pursuit caused the death of my foster father, Wilim, the peacekeeper of Wyndton, who—once my mother's Enchantment weakened—sacrificed his own life rather than betray my secrets. This is just one of the multiple crimes I will demand you answer for.

"Since I left the realm," Cerúlia continued, her voice growing stronger with each sentence, "I have pursued retribution. I traveled far and fought Weirandale's enemies.

"I will hide no longer. I have come to take my rightful place on the Nargis Throne."

"She's a fake!" Matwyck yelled. "A fraud in a blue wig or colored hair. An imposter. A witch."

"Not so!" contradicted Water Bearer, her voice squeaky with outrage. "*I* know her. She is our own princella, finally returned to us." Faces turned doubtfully from one speaker to the other.

"No! No!" shouted Matwyck. "Will you listen to a doddering nursemaid? *Shoot her* before she poisons your minds with more of her lies." He gathered his strength and continued in a reasonable, persuasive tone. "Everyone in this room knows me; I have governed well. Everything I've done, I've done for Weirandale. She is a stranger, tainted with foreign ways—some inexperienced *female*—I am your rightful ruler."

"Really, Matwyck?" Cerúlia asked sarcastically. "But you should know, if you are a faithful regent, that the hallmark of a true Nargis

Queen lies not in her hair," (she deliberately tossed her long hair over her shoulder) "but in her Talent."

"Ah!" shouted Matwyck. "But Princella Cerúlia was never Defined, was she, Sewel?" He pointed at a small, well-dressed man standing amidst the chaos on the ground floor. "She never went through a Definition! Sewel! Tell the truth, now!"

"Alas," the man called out. "'Tis true she was never Defined—"

"Ah, Chronicler Sewel," Cerúlia interrupted, inclining her head. "It is nice to see you once more. Do you *now* recognize my Talent?"

"Aye, Your Majesty," he said, and he knelt. "And I pray you forgive my earlier ignorance. Thou art Cerúlia the Gryphling."

"What?" Matwyck shouted. "What kind of Talent is that?" With purposeful mockery he forced himself to laugh and looked around, inviting others to join in. "No one even knows what that means. This is not one of the recognized Royal Talents. Note, my friends, that this imposter doesn't even claim to be an Enchanter or a Warrior. Did I hear you correctly? Did you say, '*gryph*ling' or '*piff*ling'? This *piffling* girl, and her band of—of—overdressed mercenaries, have caused a great deal of ruckus and a great deal of unnecessary bloodshed this morn."

His voice deepened and grew stern. "I demand that you lay down your weapons and surrender to the proper authorities. You are under some sad delusion, so you will be dealt with mercifully, I give you my word. Order will be restored."

A duke shouted, "This breach of the peace is a scandal. If this woman has a claim, let her come before us and the Circle Council will judge her story. Only an imposter would assault the Throne Room by force!"

Watching the room, Gunnit saw doubt creep into some people's eyes. Gentry on the balconies shouted comments supporting Matwyck. Many palace guards gripped their weapons with renewed intent.

Instead of answering Matwyck or appealing to the onlookers, Cerúlia remained silent. In fact, she closed her eyes.

Then she motioned with her hands as if she were conducting the musicians who had played at the wedding feast yesterday.

First, the crowd in the Throne Room heard the dozens of dogs in the palace kennels. Every dog began to howl or bark. But the kennels stood some distance away, and while the noise surprised everyone, it struck them as more curious than distressing. Then, every horse in the stable started a frenzied neighing, a sound so loud it penetrated the building, especially when it was accompanied by a tremendous clatter, as if the horses kicked against their stalls. The next moment, a flock of birds of all kinds—hundreds, maybe *thousands* of birds—landed on the stained glass roof of the Throne Room in a crashing wave, blotting out the sunlight with their numbers. They sang, cawed, shrieked, and tapped the glass with their beaks as if they would break it. Finally, the four mountain lions within the hall jumped up to the dais. At this point no one could hear their roars, but their wide-open mouths and claws slashing the air presented a terrifying sight.

People shrank from the noise in terror, putting their hands over their ears. All had a sense of the tremendous army of creatures—an army capable of destroying every person in the Throne Room, every person in the palace—controlled by the slim woman with her eyes closed and her arms raised. If any still harbored doubts that this woman wielded a Talent granted by Nargis, such doubts fled.

Cerúlia moved her hands again with a flourish, and the roar of the animals abruptly cut off. The birds lifted off and light streamed back in.

The abrupt silence was equally awe-inspiring.

Someone standing on the balcony took advantage of the moment to situate himself behind the Lord Regent and deliver a mighty shove. As watchers screamed, the lord teetered at the balcony railing, tumbled over, grabbed at a vertical baluster with one hand, held on for a moment, and then lost his grip, hitting the marble floor with a stomach-turning thud.

Cerúlia regarded the crumpled man for a moment. Then she raised her gaze to the balcony.

"Whoever did that, you have done us no service. You may have deprived the realm of the chance to learn the truth about the assassination attempt on Queen Cressa and the full extent of the Lord Regent's treachery."

A guard close to the crumpled figure exclaimed, "He's alive." Another voice called, "Where are the healers?"

Cerúlia displayed no interest in her injured enemy; she was intent on a different goal. She looked around the room. "Is there a Brother or Sister of Sorrow with us?"

"Brother Whitsury is nigh, Your Majesty," called out Water Bearer. "It's fitting. 'Twas he who officiated at Your Naming when you was just a wee babe."

Gunnit recognized Brother Whitsury, slim and serious in his gray robe, from all the messages he had furtively taken to the abbey. The Brother pushed his way through the crowd and climbed the six steps. He walked to the Dedication Fountain.

From centuries of Weir lore, the crowd knew the rituals of a Dedication. With a collective sigh of satisfaction, everyone knelt, one knee on the floor, the other leg bent at the knee, hands resting on the bent knee, head bowed low. If members of the crowd still supported Matwyck, they feigned devotion so as to blend in.

Gunnit alone—who was not a Weir, who served another Spirit—stood erect, intent on observing every detail of the ceremony.

Brother Whitsury placed both of his hands in the spray of the water that spewed over the enormous, jagged quartz rock. He took the water he had gathered and trickled it over the young woman's head, saying, "By this anointing with Nargis Water I pronounce you Queen Cerúlia of Weirandale. Do you Dedicate your life to the welfare of the realm and to the security of its citizens?"

"I do Dedicate my life," Cerúlia answered.

"Do you Dedicate yourself as the champion and protector of all Weirs, young and old, lowly or high, poor or wealthy?"

"I will Dedicate myself," she vowed.

"And do you Dedicate yourself to safeguarding her Waters, the Waters that grow our food, quench our thirst, and grant us life?"

"I do Dedicate myself, from now until I perish."

Then Cerúlia walked over to the waist-high golden Basin that continually caught the flowing water and continually let it overflow its rim. She plunged her right hand into its swirling pool. She pulled out of the water something small and shimmering.

This was a piece of Nargis Ice. The new queen held it aloft for a long moment, showing it to the hushed assembly. It flashed in the sunlight that shone through the stained glass. Gunnit saw a figurine that was part eagle, part lion, hanging from delicate threads.

Cerúlia handed the symbol to Brother Whitsury; he fastened the transparent chain about her neck. The figurine nestled in the hollow of her throat, shimmering slightly, lighting up her face.

She turned her body slowly around on the dais, facing first east, then south, then west, then north, so that all the people in the Throne Room could see her wearing her token of Nargis Ice. A majority of guards flung down their weapons. Quite a few people, including Water Bearer, began to weep.

The church bell began chiming again, now with a continuous peal, and the sound echoed slowly through the room and throughout the city.

As Cerúlia turned around once more, her eyes happened to meet Gunnit's. His heart soared at the expressions of surprise, recognition, and happiness that swept across her face. She brought two fingers to her forehead in a jaunty salute.

But out of the corner of his vision, Gunnit, who was practiced at keeping an eye out for threats to his flock, saw an arm that extended from a shadow on the second balcony behind her nock an arrow.

For the second time that morning he screamed a warning. "Watch out!"

Cerúlia startled at his shout, but the arrow was already in mid-flight. It struck the newly anointed queen, who fell down with a muted cry.

At that same instant Gunnit registered a dog barking loudly and the acrid smell of smoke.

6

Tilim thought himself fortunate that Sergeant Athelbern of the palace guard, whom the boy had frozen with a sword point poking his kidneys, turned out to be one of those guards who quickly dropped his sword and bent his knee when Cerúlia revealed her true identity. Tilim trembled with relief, because otherwise he would have had to kill the man in cold blood.

He would have done it, he could have done it (he was almost sure), but he was glad he didn't have to.

Tilim, who had never been enchanted by Queen Cressa, and who had always thought his foster sister magical, was not as dumbfounded by Cerúlia's revelation as his mama, whose face looked anguished as events unfolded before them. He placed a hand on his mother's shoulder when the queen said something about Lord Matwyck being responsible for his father's death.

When the queen dropped from sight, struck by an arrow from above, Tilim was already running toward her. He fell in with several blue-caped soldiers, but they had to push onlookers and combatants out of their way, whereas Tilim wiggled through small openings, so he got there first. The catamounts had formed a protective circle about her, and Brother Whitsury crouched at her side, holding her up against his knee. The arrow stuck out of her upper right arm, but Tilim saw little blood.

Tilim took her left hand, and she smiled at him. He thought he was going to have her to himself, but suddenly a yellow-haired boy, not quite as tall as he was but stockier, showed up on her other side. Around them, Tilim became vaguely aware that fighting had broken out once again.

Wren—no, Queen Cerúlia—addressed both boys. "Tilim and Gunnit, I didn't want to do this, but it seems we must.

"I want you two to run and unlock the kennels. Let loose every dog you can find. And while you are at it, free the horses too. And then open every door in this blasted building so that the dogs have full access."

Just after she said the word "dog," a large, white-patched face thrust itself into the huddle of the three of them and licked her chin.

"Hey there, Whaki," she greeted it.

The yellow-haired boy interrupted, his voice urgent. "There's a fire. I smell smoke."

"What?" The queen half tried to sit up, grimaced, closed her eyes, and grabbed her arm.

"Move out of the way," a man's voice ordered.

Looking up, Tilim saw a stranger in a black-and-white outfit, his hair—some locks the most outlandish color—in intricate braids.

"Foolishness," the stranger said to the queen, "to leave me behind! Look at what has happened!"

"Sir!" said Brother Whitsury, aghast. "You address the Queen of Weirandale!"

"Queen? Ah, I see the hair blue and pretty piece of ice." Meanwhile, his dagger had cut through her shirt where the arrow protruded, and his long fingers gently explored the area. "Truly, what I see is foolishness."

A sword entered the tight circle of people gathered around the queen's supine body, and its point moved straight to the stranger's throat. Following the sword upward, Tilim saw a soldier in a blue cloak, shining breastplate, and bright helmet. The dog growled.

"Drop your dagger and back away," the soldier ordered the stranger.

Tilim's sister opened her eyes. "Everyone, let's not fight one another. This is Ciellō. He's been my bodyguard for half a year. He will do me no harm except chastisement. Who are you, Shield?"

"Your Majesty, I am Captain Yanath, I served Queen Cres—"

The stranger, this Ciellō, interrupted. "She is injured. Later we will make the introductions." He swooped the queen into his arms with one hand under her back and another under her knees. "Lead me," he ordered the soldier. This captain and another blue-caped guard clustered close to Cerúlia's form and moved quickly in the direction of the East Entrance, the dog at their heels.

Tilim stood up and saw that some of the blue capes had bunched tapestries together as if they were ropes and were now climbing up these priceless artworks to get to the first-floor balcony. Fierce fighting raged there between gentry loyal to the old order and the soldiers. He wouldn't want to be the tapestry climber if Mama got ahold of them.

He turned to the yellow-haired boy, who wore the uniform of a page boy. "Introductions later, I guess. Do you know where the kennels are?"

The two boys pushed in the direction of an exit, but in struggling through the crowd Tilim crashed into the broad belly of stableman Hiccuth.

"Come with us!" Tilim shouted. "We're on an important mission."

Hiccuth hustled with the boys to the kennels, where the dogs were barking and growling loudly, jumping against their pens. Though wary of setting them free, Tilim followed his orders. The dogs broke up into packs of four or five, streaking toward the building, noses to the ground.

The yellow-haired page said to Tilim, "You've got the dogs well underway, right? I've gotta go see about this fire." And he ran off toward a wing of the palace from which smoke had started to billow.

Meanwhile, Hiccuth began to turn the horses loose into a large fenced paddock, so Tilim sprang to help. The horses milled about, nervously rolling their eyes, intermittently breaking into wild, short spurts. They made no attempt to join the fight, but neither would they be penned up, easy at hand for anyone seeking either to flee or to gather reinforcements.

The boys had thrown open a few doors on their way out; now Tilim and Hiccuth rushed back to the royal residence, opening any barriers dogs pawed or growled at. Already they could hear the results of their efforts, because the packs set themselves on the new queen's opponents.

Brawls spread all over the central structure, into outbuildings and the grounds, as people tried to flee and the dogs chased them down, grabbing their ankles or leaping for their throats. Armed men turned to skewer the dogs with swords or daggers. Women desperately climbed on furniture while dogs lunged up at them, sometimes connecting with flesh, sometimes just rending the air with their gaping mouths. People—and dogs—died.

Tilim witnessed a pack corner one man dressed in a servant's outfit. The man raised his hands up high and knelt down in a gesture of submission, reminding Tilim of how a beaten dog shows his belly. The dogs then held back from pouncing; they just watched him with sidelong glances, their ruffs high and heads low.

"If you lay down your weapons and give up, the dogs won't attack!" Tilim started running about screaming at the top of his lungs. Others took up the call. "Throw down your weapons! Surrender to the dogs!" Men and women, guards and gentry, realized that fighting back meant being mauled to death. They capitulated.

Escorted by watchful canines, Tilim led people who gave in to the stable and locked them in a horse stall.

Hiccuth copied his lead, but just as Tilim realized that the task of locking up all of the Lord Regent's confederates was too big for the two of them, Chamberlain Vilkit appeared.

"Yes, yes," the chamberlain said, rubbing his hands. "We will use this stable as a temporary jail: it has several advantages in that it is large enough, away from the fire, and water is handy."

He organized three dozen staff members to search the palace and outbuildings from top to bottom. They brought in captives who had been hiding in the far reaches of the building such as the pantries, the storerooms, the root cellar, and the attics. So Tilim and Hiccuth stationed themselves at the stables, gathering weapons, searching each prisoner, making sure each stall had water and straw, while Vilkit set up a cask as a temporary desk and neatly wrote down their names and catalogued any injuries.

"Vilkit, this is horseshit! Tell these cads and curs to release me!" hollered a muscular man wearing the jacket of a palace guard, embroidered with much braid, but no trousers.

"Captain Murgn, how nice that you are alive when so many of your men are dead," replied Vilkit.

Another man had the physique and pallor of a person who worked indoors, not a military man.

"Hostler! You know me!" he protested.

"Indeed, Councilor Prigent," answered Hiccuth. "I've curried your white-stocking mare a thousand times. You've never thanked me and never learned my name."

"Let me loose, man. Fetch me my mare. I'll reward you well! You know I'm good for it."

"Aye," said Hiccuth. "I know you've siphoned off a fortune from the royal treasury. In you go, now."

"Vilkit!" The man appealed to the chamberlain. "At least find Vanilina. When I last saw her, she was fleeing the dogs. I don't know what happened to her. For the love of Water, man!"

Vilkit regarded Councilor Prigent dispassionately. "If we find her, I'll let you know."

More prisoners arrived—some sullen, others weeping, quite a few injured with dog bites or sword cuts. Vilkit's crew of servants returned to do another sweep of the building.

Vanilina eventually turned up in the grip of two footmen; she had been hiding in her maid's quarters under the bed. She wore only her nightshift, but still she dripped with jewels. She screamed as if they tortured her when Hiccuth and Tilim relieved her of her seven rings, five bracelets, and two necklaces.

Regarding her intently, the chamberlain said, "Vanilina, I'd hate to order these men to strip you. Give up the rest."

"I gave you everything, you impudent wretch!"

"Van-i-lin-a," said Vilkit, in a warning tone.

Leaning on Vilkit's cask, Vanilina slid off her shoes, each of which was so crammed with jewels Tilim wondered how she'd gotten her feet inside.

"That's not all," said Vilkit. "Where is that ruby ring you show off so often?"

It was hidden in her trussed-up hair, as was a ring of sapphires.

"That's all, I swear," she said. Vilkit didn't completely believe her, but he turned her over for locking up.

Hiccuth fashioned bolts for each stall, but they didn't have to worry much about escape, because the palace dogs had taken it upon themselves to patrol the aisles and watch the stable's doorways.

Tilim walked down the corridors regarding his prisoners (many of whom had been rude to his family during the wedding week) with no little satisfaction.

Several of the stable's new residents began coughing, and Tilim realized his own throat felt dry and scratchy. He looked up and realized that the fire had burst out into wicked flames, with smoke darkening the bright morning overhead.

7

Cerúlia allowed herself to relax as Ciellō, guided and escorted by shields, carried her to the Queen's Bedchamber and laid her on her uninjured side as if she herself were a piece of precious glass. Nana and Stahlia miraculously appeared close behind them. Everyone's face looked grim.

"Perhaps mine will be the shortest reign ever," Cerúlia joked with gallows humor. The arrow hurt a great deal, but she had no intention of dying.

"Hold still, damselle," Ciellō said. Using his sharp dagger, he cut off the arrow's head where it protruded through the back of her arm. Whaki leapt up on the bed from the other side and began licking her ear, which was annoying, distracting, and very sweet. Stahlia crouched on the floor beside her face, trying to shoo the big dog away.

"Prepare yourself," Ciellō warned.

Cerúlia reached for Stahlia's hand.

"One, two, three." He yanked the shaft of the arrow out. Cerúlia screamed at the pain but managed not to pass out. Nana had grabbed a cloth to stanch the bleeding.

"Now I need the things to sew," Ciellō said to the women.

"Oh, no! If there's going to be any sewing, I'm the one who'll do it," said Stahlia. "*You,* whoever you are!—and *you,* guards! Get out of here! Go outside and watch the door or do something useful. Nana and I have her under our care now. *Go! Get! Shoo!*"

Such was Stahlia's forcefulness that even Ciellō backed down. As the crowd of men left the room, Cerúlia called after them, "See to the fire! Ciellō! The fire!"

"Hush now. Let me get a good look at your injury, Birdie," said Stahlia, sitting on the bed and peering closely at the jagged arrow wounds, front and back. Nana already had water and soap at hand.

"Shouldn't we send for a healer?" Stahlia whispered to Nana, talking over Cerúlia as if she couldn't hear and didn't matter.

"No. You just need something to disinfect it," the patient managed to insert through clenched teeth.

"I've got a nip of brandy in my room," said Nana. When she returned with the flask, Stahlia hesitated.

"Go ahead," Cerúlia encouraged, although when the alcohol hit the torn flesh, she screamed lustily. Whaki whined in sympathy.

After too many long moments the burning sensation lessened. "Well!" Cerúlia pulled in a lungful of air. "I think that's the worst. Sorry if I scared you. Now, you can stitch it up."

Stahlia threaded her needle, but hesitated before commencing.

"Go ahead, Teta; I'm sure you are the best person with a needle in the palace," Cerúlia encouraged her. "And I can handle it. I've learned a lot about pain."

"Where did you learn about pain?" murmured Stahlia, talking to distract herself as she planted the first neat stitch and pulled the ripped skin closed.

Cerúlia had seen several Raiders get stitches; now she didn't understand how they had kept from screaming and cursing. "Lots of places," she said, squeezing her eyes shut and biting her lips. "Leaving Wyndton for one. Matwyck's men had chased me down. Wilim warned me. That's why I left."

"Hmm," said Stahlia. "We'll talk about this another time. Hold still. Stop breathing. Your chest keeps moving."

"Kind of hard not to breathe," muttered Cerúlia. "And you were the one who wanted to know everything."

"Hold still, I said!" admonished Stahlia, biting her tongue in concentration.

Through the intense discomfort, Cerúlia realized that if Stahlia was sewing her wound and chastising her, her foster mother had not disowned her even though now she knew the reason behind Wilim's suicide.

Nana's voice floated into Cerúlia's dizzy consciousness. "You've got her, missus? Looks like the fire is getting worse. I've gotta go and see if I can help." As she was almost out the door she threw over her shoulder, "I'll send up some victuals. You'll both need fortifying, I'd wager."

Cerúlia took shallow little pants while the stitching proceeded. She grabbed Whaki's ruff for comfort.

In idle moments on *Misty Traveler* she had predicted that when she became queen she would feel transformed—grander, nobler, wiser—but she still felt disappointingly just like herself, only a version of herself jabbed in the arm. She tried to relive the moments when Whitsury anointed her and when she pulled out her very own token of Nargis Ice. She reached her free hand up to make sure she still had the necklace. The events of the morning had happened so fast that she'd hardly had time to absorb them.

"There!" said Stahlia, tying off and snipping the thread from the more jagged exit wound. "It's still bleeding, though."

"Yes, it will, for a few days. Let me see." Cerúlia scooted to the side of the bed. "Help me up?"

Stahlia put her arm under her shoulder. Cerúlia led the way to the large looking glass, but the shreds of her white shirt obstructed her view.

"Get this off of me?" she asked Stahlia.

"I need to cut it," she answered. "No loss. 'Tis ruined anyway."

"Here. Use my dagger," offered Cerúlia.

Stahlia pulled the dagger from its sheath. "Oh, the Waters! Look at this!" She marveled at the golden catamount heads. Then she cut the fabric from the neck down the shoulders so it fell away without Cerúlia needing to move her arms or torso.

Turning sideways and stretching to look over her shoulder, Cerúlia examined the wounds on both sides of her arm in the mirror. "Nice job, Teta," she said. "Cerf would be pleased." But in the glass she saw that Stahlia was not listening; her foster mother was distracted by the burn scars on her back.

"We'll talk about *that* some other time," Cerúlia announced firmly. "Right now you want to put a soft bandage on the stitches and find a cloth to wrap around my arm so it will stay."

Cerúlia sat down on a chair while Stahlia finished dressing the wound with fabric she tore from linens she found in the wardrobe.

From the lower floor of the palace the new queen heard screams, the sound of running feet, and growls. The smell of smoke also grew more pungent. Cerúlia yearned to be in the midst of the action, but she accepted that right now her shaky presence would only hamper others' efforts. She had to trust that the dogs and her supporters could deal with the remnants of Matwyck's forces and this unforeseen fire.

"Now," said Cerúlia. "Yonder is my moth—Queen Cressa's wardrobe. You've never fancied how I dressed. Find a gown for me to wear, the more regal the better."

Cerúlia sat, holding her throbbing arm, while Stahlia pulled out various possibilities. They decided on a loose, dark blue velvet sleeveless shift (which wouldn't bind her wound), and its matching robe with a trim of soft white feathers.

After Stahlia helped her dress, her foster mother turned to her hair, grabbing the loose locks from each side of Cerúlia's face, twisting them, braiding them together in the back, and tying off the braid.

Cerúlia stood and gazed at herself in the looking glass. The gown fell too short; everyone's eyes would immediately be drawn to the scuffed leather boots she still wore. But then she looked up from this defect.

Who is this woman in velvet, with cascading blue hair and a shimmering necklace of Nargis Ice?

I've played other roles so long: now I must play Queen. Or finally . . . is this not a role, but the real me?

A knock on the door woke her from her self-contemplation.

Cerúlia glanced at Whaki, who looked alert, but whose ruff lay smooth. She nodded at Stahlia, who called, "Enter."

A blue-caped shield held the door for a servant carrying a heavy tray.

"Who are you?" Cerúlia asked.

As the servant carefully set the tray down, the guard made a formal bow. "Your Majesty, I am Yanath of Riverine. I was a member of Queen Cressa's Shield. It is my honor to lead your Shield until such time as you choose your own captain."

"No. I don't want a new captain—you and your men performed admirably today. But I am afraid I don't remember you from my childhood. Whom *do* I recall? . . ." She rummaged in the storehouse of long-ago memories. "There was a sergeant who protected us that night—a Sergeant Bristle. And I was quite taken with Shields Pontole and Seena."

Captain Yanath gave a dim smile at the familiar names. "Your Majesty, most of those are no longer with us. From Queen Cressa's original troop, myself, Branwise, and Pontole are all who remain. Shield Pontole was injured in the Throne Room just now."

"Would you find out how he is doing? And after I have eaten, I wish to talk to you more."

She turned to the servant, whom she didn't recognize. The servant sank into a low curtsey. "Your Majesty, Nana asked me to bring you this tray."

"Good. You've brought enough for an army; I can feed my guards too. You are?"

"If it please you, I am one of the under-cooks. My name is Kiltti."

"Kiltti, I need you to find me a bottle of willow bark syrup and either oil of thyme or oil of tarragon to ward off miasmas in my wound. Those would be in the healers' cabinets. Can you do that?"

The under-cook nodded, smiled, and curtsied again. "Welcome home, Your Majesty. Most of us is overjoyed to see you. Anything we can do."

"Thank you," said Cerúlia, but neither Yanath nor Kiltti left the room.

The captain cleared his throat. "Forgive me, Your Majesty, but it is customary to say, 'You are dismissed,' when our presence is no longer required."

"Ah! Yanath and Kiltti, you will be my private tutors in royal protocol. For now, though, you are dismissed."

They departed. Stahlia made her sit, poured her tisane, and bade her eat. Cerúlia had lost her appetite in worry over what was happening throughout the building, but she forced herself to eat a few pieces of cold meat and fruit. Whaki sat on the floor beside her, resting his head on her knee, gazing up at her face with sighs of adoration.

Thou shouldst not have sent this dog away for these days, Your Majesty, he sent. *Thou canst get hurt without one to look after thee.*

I feel much safer having you by my side now, Cerúlia told her dog.

Wiping her mouth with a napkin, she glanced at Stahlia and straightened her shoulders. "Well. Here we are. I've claimed the throne, but this turns out not to be the end of struggle, just the beginning.

"Are you all right, Teta?" she asked. "You've just been through your first battle."

"And sewn up my first arrow wound and had my world turned upside down," said Stahlia. "But never you fret over any of that. I'm of sturdy stock."

And to Cerúlia she looked sturdy; her capable hands were as steady as ever around her cup.

"Then drink up your tisane, Teta; we've got to get to work."

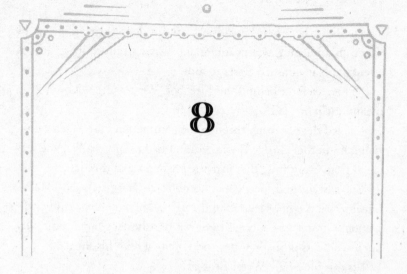

8

After Nana had delivered the message about a tray for the new queen, she followed the smell of burning, running outside the Kitchen Door, glancing about.

The darkest smoke wafted from the Administration Wing; the heart of the fire lay near the offices of the royal treasury.

Scores of men and women were already engaged in fighting the blaze. People filled buckets in Pearl Pond and passed them from hand to hand, and men swung axes to clear the burning debris. As Nana moved closer, the crackling noise grew louder and the heat became fierce. While she watched, the stranger with the braids ran into the accounting chamber, tearing down curtains to prevent the fire from spreading upward.

Yet for all the firefighters' efforts, the conflagration appeared to be winning out. Nana spotted sections of the floor above burning, with sparks reaching toward the roof—if the roof caught ablaze, nowhere in the palace would be safe.

With her senses enhanced by her status as Agent, she heard Pozhar's growl in the fire's noise. *So, Water Bearer, you think you have the Weir Witch back? What a price you will pay!*

"Gunnit," Nana shrieked. "Gunnit! I need yer help!"

He didn't hear her; he had just run inside to throw a bucket of water on a burning wall. Calling and waving frantically to get his attention, Nana dashed closer to him.

"There's a force behind this Fire, boy. We can't fight it by earthly means. Help me, lad."

She led the way back through the commotion to the Dedication Fountain in the Throne Room. Gunnit had to support her; she was taxed from everything that had already happened this day.

She cast around for a container to catch Nargis Water. Healers kneeling on the floor tended to the myriad of wounded. On her direction, Gunnit tore a bowl right out of a healer's hand, dumping out its contents of soapy water and wiping it with his shirt.

"Is this too small, Water Bearer?"

"'Tis not the size that matters, lad. Fill it from the Fountain. But we need something else; we need seawater too."

"No time to get to the harbor," said Gunnit.

"Right, right." Nana chewed her own fingers. "The harbor's too far, so rush to the kitchen, get a bucket of water, and pour in a handful of salt. I'll wait here."

Nana waited, oblivious to the moans around her, trying to still her heart so she could hear the voice of the Dedication Fountain.

Three Spirits. To conquer any One, you must have Three.

She had Nargis Water and a bucket that mimicked Lautan's Seawater. Nana couldn't think of anything Vertia or Saulė could do against Fire. Restaurà couldn't heal a Fire or put it to sleep. Ghibli could blow it out, but why would Ghibli help them? Her mind skittered. 'Chamen—earth, stone, rock, marble. You could smother a fire with sand, but how could she quickly lay her hands on a bucket of sand? Did any of the palace tradesmen use sand?

Gunnit came back, his arm stretched by a heavy bucket. Together they made their way through the corridors once again, slowly, guarding their precious containers. Now this wing was empty because everyone had fled from the heat and smoke that rose around them.

They exited through the Administration Door. Even more volunteers had joined the firefighters; despite their efforts the blaze had grown in strength and fury. The first-floor ceiling of this wing collapsed. The Fire crackled louder in triumph.

"Make way! Make way!" shouted Gunnit.

He got as close as he could to the flames and dashed in his bucket of salt water.

Lautan! Help us! Nana pleaded.

She then walked close with her bowl of Nargis Water, passing the magenta-haired stranger, whose clothes and face were covered in soot. He was doubled over at the waist, coughing. Moved by she knew not what, Nana offered him a sip of fresh water from the bowl. He drank sparingly for a moment; his breathing eased.

Nana trod as close to the Fire as she dared and splashed in her bowl of Nargis Water.

Nargis! Yer palace! The palace of yer queens! Don't let Pozhar burn it down!

The Fire drew back; it paused as if regrouping.

The sooty stranger had also given up on fighting the burning rooms by physical efforts. He knelt before the flames deep in prayer. Nana wondered which Spirit he venerated.

The stranger opened his cupped hands and blew on the air between them.

All of a sudden, a mighty gust of wind blew down upon them. One by one each burning plank, furnishing, roof tile, and ember shuddered . . . and winked out.

Ghibli, the Spirit of the Wind, has come to our aid. Why? Because of the stranger's prayer? Due to pure caprice?

Mysterious are the ways of the Spirits.

Exhausted, Water Bearer fell to her knees next to the stranger who worshipped the Wind and joined him in giving thanks.

9

Later that afternoon Cerúlia gathered all of her closest allies in the room called the Nymph Salon, a spacious chamber with an elaborate ceiling painting of water nymphs holding hands as they danced above a long conference table.

The new queen gingerly seated herself in a plush chair at the head and looked around at the people arrayed on either side of her. For family, she had Stahlia and Tilim. For trusted retainers, Nana, Hiccuth, and Brother Whitsury. For allies from her travels she had Gunnit and Ciellō. Captain Yanath and Seamaster Wilamara represented the Queen's Shield; the eighteen others who hadn't been injured or killed currently patrolled the Royal Wing. And Whaki, lying with his head on her foot to keep in physical contact with her, represented her Talent.

She started the meeting by going around the table with identifications and explanations, because at the present moment she needed the secret histories to be shared and the separate compartments of her life to be thrown open.

Stahlia and Tilim explained that Cerúlia had grown up with them, but had disappeared from Wyndton almost three years ago. Brother Whitsury and Nana spoke of their gathering together the

New Queen's Shield. Cerúlia was delighted to learn that Seamaster Wilamára, a trim woman considerably taller than herself, with leathery skin that peeled back from a raw, red nose, had known her parents from their days fighting the Pellish pirates. Gunnit offered Tilim back the metal soldier that he carried as a keepsake, though Tilim, bemused, politely refused his forgotten childhood toy. Nana merely raised her eyebrows at learning that the magenta-haired man was actually a Zellish bodyguard Cerúlia had hired during her stay in Salubriton. And if Ciellō was surprised to discover that "Damselle Phénix" was in reality the missing queen of Weirandale, infuriatingly he gave no indication whatsoever.

Whaki got up and wandered beneath the table, sniffing each person so that he would know their scent forever. Hiccuth and the boys were the most eager to get acquainted, but the dog wouldn't let Nana alone until she petted him, with many fake grumbles about how she never liked dogs.

Good pack, Whaki told Cerúlia, *brave, loyal.*

Cerúlia transitioned the meeting from introductions to current crises. "Does Matwyck still live?" she asked.

"The healers are with him now," Captain Yanath answered.

"How many prisoners did the dogs capture?"

"About fifty," Tilim said. "Chamberlain Vilkit has the complete list."

"How many people have been kilt today?"

"About thirty in the Throne Room," Captain Yanath said. "And the dogs took down several more. Maybe half a dozen."

"So many? So many people were so enmeshed in Matwyck's regime that they fought to the death or had to be captured by the dogs?" Cerúlia cursed herself for her lack of foresight; she should have expected that Matwyck would never have stayed in power this long without supporters who would fight to keep their wealth and status.

Aloud, she said, "I need to know the dead's names and stations. Nana, will you work with the New Shield to get me a complete list?"

"If it please Your Majesty. But as to who's who, Chamberlain Vilkit would know better than me, since he knows both the visiting gentry and the regular folk."

"That's the second time Vilkit has come up. Should we ask him to join us?"

"I dunno if'n we can trust him, Your Majesty," Hiccuth said. "Matwyck had a spiked bit in his mouth." The stableman mimed a horse's bit by sticking his own thick finger between his wide-open jaws.

"Hmm. Send for him and we'll find out."

Nana rose to speak to a guard stationed outside the door.

"If it please Your Majesty, there are other knowledgeable people I'm certain we can trust," said Brother Whitsury, "such as Sewel, the royal chronicler."

"Send for him too." Cerúlia looked around the table. "How do our injured fare?"

"Four of my Shield are with the healers now," Yanath said.

"Who is the palace's head healer?"

Nana replied, "A man named Finzle—and yes, I'll send for him."

"Tell me about the fire," Cerúlia asked, shifting a bit in the chair, trying to rest her arm comfortably since she had refused to wear a sling. She elicited from several sources theories about who might have started the fire and why, learned that it had been deliberately set, and that it had started in the accounting chamber. Exactly how it had been quenched was more of a mystery.

"How many rooms were destroyed or damaged?" When no one immediately answered, Cerúlia sighed and said, "I'll ask Vilkit."

Sewel, however, arrived at the Nymph Salon first, covered in soot stains and nursing burns on his forearms and ear.

"Chronicler, you are welcome to our conclave," Cerúlia said, inwardly wincing at the sight of his burns. She could well imagine how much they would hurt, blister, and scar.

"Your Majesty, might I—might I approach?"

When she nodded assent, he came up to her chair and bowed to the ground.

"Your Majesty, you must recall I failed you when you were young. Every moment under the Usurper, I have prayed for your safe return. This is the day I have pinned all my hopes on."

"Please rise, Chronicler Sewel, and take a seat at our table. You have a wealth of information about royal customs that may help our deliberations. With your experience, what do you think my first steps should include?"

Seating himself near the end of the table and mastering his emotions, the chronicler offered, "Your Majesty, might I suggest that you quickly form a Circle Council of respected leaders to support you?"

"Councilors betrayed my mother," said the new queen, looking down and toying with the feather fringe on her robe. What she didn't say aloud was that having finally achieved her position, she was loath to have anybody boss her around.

"Yes, because she left the selection of them to Lord Matwyck. You must choose for yourself and choose more wisely. If well-known and respected leaders or gentry would rally to your side, their standing in the realm would solidify yours. And their advice would be valuable. No one can rule alone."

Stahlia spoke up. "I can think of two such leaders right now: Duke Naven and Lordling Marcot."

"Yes, I'd say those are an excellent beginning," Sewel said, nodding. "Of course, we'll also need to hold an election for a new steward."

"Ma'am," Hiccuth broke in, "excuse me. Why is the steward only elected by the big landowners? Why can't the people vote for someone to sit on your right side?"

The queen considered. "One of the ways that Weirandale went awry is that the gentry, with the steward egging them on, accrued too much power. I will need to balance the interests of all the people, so I think that's an excellent idea, Hiccuth.

"Sewel, how do I make that happen?"

"You issue a proclamation, Your Majesty."

"Really? As simple as that? I wonder why no queen has done it before."

"No one before would have thought the folk were wise enough to have a say in their government," Sewel answered. "They may have thought that their votes could be purchased by the highest bidder."

"Hm-mmm. We will have to change this situation, in several ways. As for councilors, Seamaster Wilamara, I would like a representative of the military—a person of your bravery and experience who, like you, knew my parents. Would you be willing to serve on my council too?"

"I—I—I would be honored, Your Majesty," Wilamara sputtered. "But, you should know, I'm used to speaking my mind straight out. I'm not a courtier."

"All the better," said Cerúlia. "Then I will speak my mind straight back. There. Now the council begins to take shape. We will wait a bit to fill in the last two seats. What else do you suggest, Chronicler?"

"I would suggest that you share the news of your return to the city dwellers and the entire country, that you get the people on your side."

Brother Whitsury said, "Indeed, I've been wondering what the Cascadians are thinking right now. Surely they heard the bells and saw the smoke, so rumors must be running rampant and people may be anxious. Have the gates been locked all day?"

"The gates!" replied Cerúlia. "I never gave them a single thought! Captain Yanath, do you know?"

"Your Majesty, I ordered them locked shortly after the battle in the Throne Room. I didn't want any of Matwyck's allies escaping, nor any reinforcements coming in. But I don't have the manpower to keep policing the gates with only the New Shield. We need to determine double-quick who amongst the palace guard we can trust. I wish there was a way to find out who is telling the truth."

Cerúlia toyed with the pommel of her dagger, pondering. *Who is telling the truth. A way to know who is telling the truth.*

"Aha!" cried the queen. "There is. Lady Tenny once told me she had an object called a Truth Stone. Does anyone know where it is?"

Everyone looked blank. Nana said slowly, "I once heard tell of such a Stone. It was stolen from Rortherrod, and the Rorthers want it back."

"Well, we must search for it. Until we find it, we will have to use dogs to tell us who is deceptive. But Sewel's key point—that we must spread the news to Cascada and beyond—must be acted upon at once. I am open to suggestions."

Ciellō, standing watchfully behind her chair, offered, "In Zellia, we use town callers."

"We don't use those," Brother Whitsury explained. "Tidings are usually disseminated by broadsheet. The major broadsheet in the city is the *Cascada News*. We must issue an official proclamation and get it to the *News,* which will print it and spread it far and wide. The *News* will make a windfall today; all and sundry will want a copy."

"Very well," said the queen. "Sewel, you will write it, and Whitsury, you will take it into the city. Hiccuth, you will find the horses more tractable now; be sure Whitsury has a good mount. And Whitsury, I give you leave to bring back to the palace a large handful of trusted Sorrowers. The injured will need comfort, as will any bereaved."

"Your Majesty," said Chronicler Sewel. "There is another way of informing at least the city that the queen has returned. When the footman found me I was on my way to unpack the Queen's Flag and have it hoisted from the highest pole."

At the mention of the flag, many of her allies around the table broke into smiles, and Nana issued a small cry of delight. As a foreigner, however, Gunnit was bewildered. "What? What are you all talking about?"

Sewel responded, "There is a long-standing tradition that when a princella is Defined (that is, when we recognize the Talent that Nargis granted her), we fly a special flag from the top of the palace. It has an emblem of the Fountain stitched in silver on a blue background. If we fly it today—at long last!—everyone looking at the palace will know that the queen has returned. After all, I Defined her a few hours ago, and we all saw a demonstration of her Talent."

Nana turned to Gunnit with tears in her eyes. "You can't know, lad, how much her mother yearned to see that flag fluttering on high."

"Chronicler Sewel," Cerúlia smiled, "you have my permission to return to your duties. But please get your burns tended right after you see to the flag."

As Sewel departed, the palace healer, Finzle, entered. He reported that Matwyck was in critical condition, with a broken pelvis and internal bleeding. The four injured shields, whose hurts he described in great detail, would most likely survive (including Pontole), but three servants and two of the gentry being tended were so grievously wounded their hours were surely numbered. His team of healers had not yet examined the more minor hurts of the prisoners held in the stable, but they planned to do so before nightfall.

Cerúlia didn't suspect Finzle of disloyalty, just of painful longwindedness. She made a mental note to herself that she needed to replace him with someone smarter as soon as possible. She realized she also needed a scribe to keep reminders for her.

The third knock on the salon's door foretold a guard's announcement: "Chamberlain Vilkit."

"Your Majesty." Vilkit entered, bowing low and gracefully. "How may I be of service to your gracious self?"

"There are several matters I would speak to you about, Vilkit. Stahlia and Ciellō, I wish you to remain beside me.

"Tilim and Gunnit, here's a new task for you two: go examine the palace dogs. Decide on those that are the smartest and most responsive to people. I'd like to meet your selections first thing tomorrow.

"The rest of you, I believe you know your immediate duties, so you are dismissed for now. I ask you all to come with updates to this salon before supper."

Everybody bowed their way out, except for Ciellō, who stayed beside her coiled with watchfulness, and Stahlia, who moved her seat to sit closer to Cerúlia at the head of the conference table.

"Approach, Chamberlain," Cerúlia ordered. "From what I hear you hold many strings of power and most of the information in the palace."

"This is true, Your Majesty," Vilkit said, "and I place my skills and knowledge totally at your service. I was slightly delayed in coming here because I was completing the lists you asked for." He held out a sheaf of papers in his hands.

Cerúlia ignored the papers for now.

"Totally, Vilkit? Less than a day ago you were Matwyck's right-hand man."

"Lord Matwyck was my superior and I respected his intelligence. I also feared his wrath; but as you see, my eyes hold no tears for him.

"Now *you* are the ruler of the realm. I am in awe of how brilliantly you carried off your rustic disguise. If I offended you yesterday in even the slightest way, I most humbly pray for your sweet forgiveness." He bowed again, even lower.

"You feared Matwyck. Do you fear me, Chamberlain?" asked the young queen.

"I fear your dog and the Talent you hold over animals. What a magnificent demonstration!"

"But not my wrath."

"Your Majesty," parried Vilkit. "I have observed that rulers govern more effectively by making people love them, rather than fear them. Matwyck's cruelties might have won him allies, but no friends."

"Matwyck. Who pushed Matwyck over the balcony?" the queen asked.

"I saw: 'twas Duke Inrick. He did it for revenge against Matwyck's insult, not, I would hazard, out of loyalty to you. He is in the stable prison at the moment. I would suggest you tread very carefully with that one."

"Who shot me?"

"I'm afraid I did not see."

Cerúlia made a gesture of impatience with her hand. "What would you suggest—what steps should I take to make myself a ruler who is loved, rather than feared?"

"I would suggest that you address the palace tonight and the city as soon as possible. You've been missing a long time; the people felt . . . abandoned. You must show you trust the people, you are eager to be among them, and you are overjoyed to have returned to Cascada. The townsfolk must have an opportunity to see you and appreciate your loveliness."

"Go on," Cerúlia prompted.

"I would suggest that you go lightly in punishing the prisoners in the stables. Some may need to be exiled." Vilkit shook his head and made *tsk*ing sounds. "But hangings or beheadings would not show mercy befitting a young, beautiful, and gracious queen."

Cerúlia had grown irritated by all this flattery and Vilkit's stress on her femininity but heard the practical wisdom in his advice. "Pray, continue."

"I would suggest"—here he paused as if trying to find the smoothest way of imparting bad news—"that you allow me to provide you with a wardrobe and maids appropriate for your station. You are a dazzling queen: many people have longed for your appearance, pinning their hopes and future on you. Let us show you off to full advantage so that the people will fall in love with you. Your garb at the Dedication was not . . . regal. If you had been dressed as you are now, mayhap you would have received more respect. Possibly, there might have been less bloodshed."

This topic surprised Cerúlia, who had learned many things during her travels but not the power and influence of rich clothing.

"I could not have climbed down ropes or wormed my way through the catamount tunnel dressed like this," she said, defending her choices.

He stayed quiet, merely bowing lower.

Should she trust this palace functionary? She looked at Ciellō, who read the question in her eyes.

"He speaks too sweet," her bodyguard murmured.

"Yes," said the chamberlain. "How very perceptive you are, foreign sir. I know I am officious and ambitious. Ofttimes a flatterer—especially to those above me. But inquire of the palace workers if I have treated them fairly."

Whaki, is this man to be trusted?

He will always find a tricky way to the food bowl and eat the best scraps first. Then he will roll over and show his belly.

Cerúlia made her decision. "Vilkit, you are on probation. I will see how well you serve me, and I will indeed ask the staff about your past performance. Give your paperwork to Mistress Stahlia for me to peruse later.

"Now." She cast her mind back on what she had learned from Commander Thalen as to how a leader behaves. "I need to show myself around the palace as hale and in control. I will visit the wounded and tour the fire damage. Ciellō, you and Whaki will be my only escorts. That will indicate I fear no one."

She took a closer look at her bodyguard, whose clothes showed singe marks. "Oh, Vilkit, Ciellō needs a new manservant costume."

"It will be done, immediately," Vilkit boasted.

"And Chamberlain, you must find me a dressmaker capable of

making me a gown for my crucial address to the city. I badly need new footwear, so also fetch the best cobbler to my rooms with his wares within an hour."

"Of course, Your Majesty," murmured Vilkit.

"I would like to speak to all the staff at a supper tonight in the Banquet Hall. The food doesn't need to be fancy; we can eat what is left over from the gentry's feasts but still wholesome. But every servant from the lowest chimney sweep to you, Chamberlain, is invited to sup with me to welcome me home."

"Such wise decisions, Your Majesty," said Vilkit, bowing low again. "All will be in readiness."

Cerúlia decided to ignore his unctuous compliments while she judged whether he could produce what he promised. She stood up, noticing that her arm throbbed quite nastily now.

"Oh, Vilkit! Another thing. Make sure that every gown fashioned for me accommodates my dagger. I may look like just a slight young woman. But you badly underestimate me if you hold *no* fear of me. 'Twas *I* who cut Duchette Lolethia's throat."

She was pleased to see the look of shock on both Vilkit's and Ciellō's faces.

She walked out of the room, Whaki on one side and Ciellō on the other, pretending she had been queen for more than a few hours.

10

EXCERPTS FROM THE CHRONICLE
OF QUEEN CERÚLIA

Kept by Chronicler Sewel
Queen Cerúlia's Reign began in Blood and Fire [. . .]

In the late afternoon, the Queen's Flag, showing the world that the princella had been Defined and Nargis's grace continued unbroken, flew again over the palace.

By evening all outright hostilities had ceased. Palace staff, gentry visiting for the wedding, the New Queen's Shield, and the sovereign broke bread together in the Banquet Hall.

The atmosphere of the room was subdued rather than joyous. Most workers and visitors were anxious about the immense upheaval—and some wondered if now the newcomer would institute a purge of those who worked for Matwyck the Usurper.

Many, no doubt, examined their actions over the past

fourteen summers and worried as to whether their associates had information or cause to inform on them.

This chronicler sat at the head table with Queen Cerúlia's trusted associates, which included both Duke Naven and a stableman. Our new queen appeared weary and in pain from the assault on her person in the Throne Room. Her Zellish bodyguard stood behind her the entire time, his eyes raking the room.

After supping, the queen rose to speak.

She announced a tally of forty-two people killed during the day, nineteen wounded, and fifty-three being held in the stable paddocks. Sixteen of the dead were recruits of the New Queen's Shield, drawn primarily from the ranks of our navy. Seventeen were members of the palace guard, five were gentry, and four servants or staff. This chronicler noticed outbreaks of grief over the losses.

The fire in the Administration Wing destroyed five rooms, and another four suffered much damage.

The queen spoke further about her years of hiding in Wyndton, as the foster sister of Lady Percia, and how growing up amongst the people has given her a unique perspective on Weirandale life.

Finally, the queen solved the murder of Duchette Lolethia by confessing to the deed. Duchette Lolethia had paid her a visit in her bedchamber. When the duchette discovered Her Majesty's blue locks, instead of bowing and pledging fealty as a proper Weir should have done, the duchette screamed for guards. The queen deemed she had no choice but to kill her. To forestall suspicion she had the body moved to Lord Burgn's chamber.

This makes Cerúlia the Gryphling the only known monarch to have killed a Weir citizen by hand before her rule had even begun. Because Duchette Lolethia was an agent of Lord Matwyck the Usurper, this chronicler will consult with judiciaries as to whether this act should be considered "self-defense" or "defense of the realm," and append their decision when available. [. . .]

11

Exhausted from stress and her wound, Cerúlia slept past daybreak. When she woke she was loath to rise—this bed and its linens felt so soft, and the morning light that filtered through the covered window made the water feature in the room, a small waterfall down rock to an enameled basin, shimmer and shine.

A knock, however, brought Nana with a tray, on which stood more willow bark tea for the pain that afflicted her arm. And Nana insisted on spreading more herbal oils on the wound—which looked swollen and bruised but not infected—before she rebandaged it. Cerúlia decided that she would wear a sling today to take the weight of the arm off her damaged muscles.

"What's the situation?" Cerúlia asked as her head cleared of sleepiness and pain and she sat herself at the table with the fastbreak.

"Quiet, but kind of tense-like," said Nana as she poured the tisane and took the cover off the ham. "Even though Shields march the corridor, that brother of yourn, that Tilim, he stood with his sword by the doorway in your old bedroom half the night; and your man, Ciellō, slept in front of that door." Nana pointed to the door that separated the Queen's Bedchamber from the Queen's Reception Room.

Her followers sensed that her hold on power was still tenuous; she had so few dedicated supporters that a strong counterstrike could retake the seat of government. Cerúlia realized that she needed to enlist a larger contingent of loyalists without delay.

"Nana, help me put on that blue dress and robe."

"Finish eating first, Your Majesty. You've only taken three bites. Look what I've got—that cinnamon bread of Borta's you used to favor when you was young." Nana unwrapped the bread and slathered it with butter.

The bread, still warm from the oven, was redolent of cinnamon, cloves, and currants, and the butter was cold and creamy. Cerúlia sat back in her chair and closed her eyes, savoring every bite, and then, like a child, licked her fingers and picked the crumbs off her napkin. Whaki looked reproachful that Cerúlia didn't offer him the crust, but Nana's eyes twinkled as she poured more tisane.

"*Now* will you let me wash and dress and pin up my hair?" the queen entreated her nursemaid.

When she emerged from her room, she found that Gunnit and Tilim waited in the corridor with five dogs from the kennels for her approval.

"Bring them in the Reception Room and let's take a look at them."

The first was a short-haired, reddish-brown hound; he reminded her of Didi, her Alpetar companion, though he was more than a hand bigger and more heavily muscled. When she plumbed his mind she found him to be mature and loyal, with a keen sense of smell.

Would you like to work for me? she asked.

My honor, he replied.

I name you Vaki, she told him, her fingers scratching the softest spot behind his ears. Whaki yipped jealously, but she raised a displeased eyebrow at him, so thereafter he approached his new companions with get-acquainted sniffs and elaborate play bows.

Three sleek, white-with-patches deerhounds waited their turn: two sisters and a male from another litter. They offered their agility, their fearlessness, and their experience working as a team. Delighted to be released from the kennels, they stretched in front of the fireplace, relishing the warmth, immediately making themselves at home. After discussion with the boys, Cerúlia named them "Mimi," "Nini," and "Haki."

"We weren't sure whether to bring this one," said Tilim, "because she's so small. We couldn't figure out whether she'd actually be useful."

"But really she wouldn't let us leave without her," added Gunnit. "She insisted."

Cerúlia laughed at the wire-haired terrier that had lurked in a shadow and now, understanding that this was her moment, self-importantly bustled around their feet.

"That's because she's so dominant," the queen remarked. "Her heart is bigger than her chest. She bossed you around, and she'll boss the bigger dogs around too."

Cerúlia knelt, supporting her aching arm. "Come here, *Cici,*" she said, "I'll wager you'll end up the leader of this pack. Just don't stick that little chest out at *me.*" Cici wagged her stumpy tail furiously and bounced about, trying to lick the queen's chin.

Captain Yanath interrupted their time getting acquainted with the dogs to announce that he had all the palace guards gathered and separated into groups outside the Salon of Queen Cinda.

The queen needed just a moment to brief the dogs.

Dogs, you six now comprise the Queen's Canine Corps. You will often be stationed near me, providing extra security. However, your first duty this morning is to smell human nervousness, deceit, or ill will. I know you can do that if you concentrate.

Naturally we can do that, Young Majesty, Cici replied. *Humankines never understand how much they smell. Big clouds of stink. Verily, pack?*

As shields brought the guards into the room, thirty at a time, the queen asked the men to pledge their loyalty and let the dogs roam and sniff as the soldiers bent a knee. The dogs bayed or growled at those who should be relieved of their posts. A few soldiers protested at this "trial by scent," saying that they had done nothing wrong and how could she trust the judgment of a dog; the queen replied that they weren't being arrested, merely no longer trusted with sensitive postings.

When the fourth set of soldiers was ushered into the room, Cici didn't yip or growl—she immediately launched herself through the air and sank her teeth into a man's lip. Before the man could even react, Ciellō had his knife at his throat. Cerúlia called the dogs off while shields searched the suspect inch by inch, finding a stiletto secreted in the seam of his boot.

"You were going to use this needle sharp?" Ciellō asked, cutting a layer of skin with his dagger at the neck.

"If I got a good opportunity," the man admitted as blood coursed down his chest.

"Who do you work for?" asked Wilamara, standing in front of the suspect, her gray eyes pinning him in an intense glare. The man stayed silent until Ciellō twisted his arm behind his back.

"General Yurgn!" the would-be killer shouted.

"Are there others in the general's payroll?" Wilamara asked.

"I think so," the man answered with a snarl.

"Who are they?"

Ciellō had to twist his arm again.

"The general kept us separate," he said. "I don't know who they are."

Wilamara had the would-be killer taken away, and they continued surveying the guards, now even more attentive to watch the dogs' reactions because Cici had proven their superior ability to judge people.

Over the rest of the morning the dogs winnowed seventeen men and one woman out of the ranks of the palace soldiers. The rest were either genuinely delighted to welcome the Nargis Queen home, or content enough to work with a will for whomever paid their salary. Branwise took their vetted troops off to get the men and women organized.

Returning to the Queen's Closet, followed by Ciellō and encircled by canines, Cerúlia discovered a narrow-chested young man in clean but threadbare clothes waiting at her door. He bowed low, revealing a premature bald spot on his head. Vaki took advantage of the man's posture to sniff him deeply, relaying no suspicion to the queen.

"You may rise," Cerúlia said. "Who are you, and what is your business?"

"Your Majesty, my name is Darzner of Vittorine. I worked in the chronicler's office for over ten years as a clerk, until the Lord Regent dismissed me. Chronicler Sewel sent word to my lodgings to come to the palace this morning; he thought I might be of use to you as a secretary. During my years I picked up a fair amount of knowledge about how things tend to work here."

"I see," she responded. "Well, let's make a trial of how we get on together."

As soon as they entered the room she began to rattle off issues that needed attention, from calling Percia and Marcot back from their honey trip, to finding out the locations of Matwyck's secret prisons, to requesting updates about the condition of the wounded. Darzner's quill moved rapidly across a page of paper, and his questions evinced a knowledge of palace process and an astute weighing of priority.

He was leaving her to put her requests in motion when Captain Yanath, in evident distress, almost collided with him.

"Your Majesty, Regent Matwyck has vanished from his chambers!" cried the captain of her Shield.

"What!? Was he not guarded?"

"Indeed, I left two of my best outside his door. We found them unconscious in the hallway. They seem to have been poisoned."

"Poisoned? Dead?"

"No, a sleeping draught."

"Thank the Waters. Did anyone see anything?"

"We were so shorthanded, I had two mariners at the Kitchen Gate. They were ambushed. The sailors put up a fight; one of *them* is dead and the other badly wounded."

"Drought and damnation!" The queen kicked her table leg in anger. "Do we know when this happened? In the night?"

"No, I checked on this prisoner right before dawn. It might have been just an hour ago, while we were judging the loyalty of the guards."

"Aha! I see," said Cerúlia. "Yes, our winnowing of the soldiers might have provided a perfect opportunity. And it was hardly a secret—everyone in the palace knew our plans, and so villains took advantage. We should have foreseen . . ."

"As much as I rue this," Captain Yanath remarked, "I don't believe that Matwyck can mount a threat to us wherever he goes. Healer Finzle said his injuries are grievous."

Ciellō had stood silent during this colloquy. Now he spoke. "The stable jail is full; this morn we discover more guards with black hearts. But still more traitors stole your enemy away. Who? Where are they now?"

"You're right," Yanath agreed, his growing estimation of the Zellishman showing on his face. "There must be more blackguards among the servants or staff. We must be alert and protect the queen at all times."

"Gentlemen, I think your fears are overblown," said Cerúlia. "Besides, now I have a canine corp."

Chamberlain Vilkit joined the three men standing in her closet. The small room had become quite packed.

"Your Majesty has heard the news, I take it," Vilkit said after his bow.

"Yes, we were just discussing security."

"I have come to tell you that the dressmaker awaits your pleasure in the Royal Bedchamber."

"Maybe we should reschedule for another day . . . I have so many other things to attend to." She addressed the other men. "Yanath, you need to talk to the shields, find out what they can tell us about the escape. Cielló, do you think you should take a look at the room and the escape route?"

"With the greatest respect," Vilkit interrupted, "my dear Majesty, I believe that your wardrobe is a crucial element of security."

Cerúlia wanted to argue, but she bit her tongue. She saw the wisdom of Vilkit's contention; if they couldn't uproot every person in league with the previous order, they badly needed to win more people over to her side, and perchance the proper wardrobe would help.

"Very well," she assented. "Mistress Stahlia . . . ?"

"—awaits you in your bedchamber," Vilkit informed her.

Yestereve's cobbler had been a gentle, stooped, elderly man. Tears had coursed down his face while he was fitting her, and when she asked him why, he said that he was so happy she had returned, and felt so privileged to serve her in his humble way. He had his team of cobblers craft her three pairs of appropriate shoes overnight, with more to come.

By contrast, accompanied by an army of assistants and a mountain of packages, Mistress Editha of Editha's Exceptional Garments for People of Quality stormed the Royal Bedchamber like an invasion force. She was a small person, with piercing black eyes, wearing glittering tailor's tools in a custom-designed belt around her waist. Obviously, she was accustomed to commanding her squad of underlings.

Cici, the terrier, barked at Mistress Editha, one dominant dog to another, warning that these rooms were *her* territory. Wisely, Editha chose to overlook the challenge, though she glanced around at the other five large dogs draped around the floor, shedding, with a look that spoke of unyielding, fervent disapproval.

After her curtsey, her first words showed that Editha intended to take no prisoners.

"Your Majesty, with your coloring, dark blue is a mistake. And that neckline is all wrong for your Nargis Ice pendant. From now on, you will wear lighter, brighter colors, and the necklines *must* follow the contour of your pendant."

"What you say about the neckline makes sense, but I am not used to wearing bright colors," Cerúlia replied.

"Aye," Stahlia agreed. "You always wore quiet colors."

"I was trying not to attract attention."

"*But Your Majesty,*" protested Editha, "*You-Are-the-Queen.*" She held a gold-handled scissors in one hand and tapped it into her open palm at every word. "All eyes must be on you, all the time." Editha snapped her fingers, and one of her assistants pulled out of paper wrappings a half-finished silk gown of a pinkish-orange, the color of a sunset.

"That's beautiful material, but don't you think it's a little gaudy?" asked Cerúlia.

"If I thought it was gaudy, I would not have kept the girls up half the night sewing in these pleats! Besides, you haven't seen my plan for the robe. Allow us to fit it to you. Let's get rid of this blue monstrosity."

Cerúlia was not comfortable having her mother's clothing labeled monstrous, nor at undressing before a crowd. Even though she was wearing an undershift, several of her scars would be visible. But evidently she had no choice.

Stahlia moved forward to help her pull the gown off and to shield her from prying eyes.

Mistress Editha, however, made no concessions to either modesty or privacy.

"I see," she said, squinting at the bandage from yesterday's wound, the scars from her burns, and her shoulder injury. "We are going to need to make adjustments. Let me measure too the difference between your left and your right shoulders. . . ." The seamstress's hands flew across Cerúlia with a measuring string edged in silver, but her touch felt like feather tickles. "Not to worry, not to worry—we can cheat the left shoulder so that this discrepancy never shows."

The new gown flew on over Cerúlia's head.

"Kindly step up on this footstool, so that we can pin the length. As nothing is sewn yet—every piece is just pinned—keep your arms straight out."

Mistress Editha stood on a chair to adjust the left shoulder personally through meticulous fussing and repinning, while her aides worked on the hem of the gown. Standing bored, like a mannequin, Cerúlia took a little pleasure in discovering that, as she had stipulated, the dress included a reinforced loop for her catamount dagger to hang accessible to her right hand.

"Now, girls, the robe. Come on, now, step lively!"

Out of another parcel came an open robe of the softest light gray, which flared in the back with set-in panels of the sunset color.

"Oh, how lovely!" Stahlia cried.

"Can I see it? Can we move in front of the looking glass?" asked Cerúlia.

"No, we cannot take the time," said Editha. "We have so much work to do to finish. Stand still, Your Majesty, as we unpin. . . . Girls, make haste to the sewing room! Now, you two, the green one."

A dress of sea green with white flew over Cerúlia's head, then a robe of white with a green leaf embroidery. Quickly, this too was pinned to her figure, and just as speedily snatched away.

With arms overflowing with fabric, more assistants scurried out.

Cerúlia was left standing, chilled, in her shift. Stahlia brought her a night-robe and assisted her off the footstool.

"Now, Your Majesty. Your hair." Mistress Editha surveyed the way Cerúlia had pinned it this morning with a look of distaste. "I foretold that you have not had time to find a hair maid, so I have brought with me an experienced girl. She knows how a queen should look; she used to dress Queen Cressa's hair."

Editha quick-stepped to the Reception Room, calling, "Geesilla, I am ready for you."

This Geesilla was hardly a girl, but rather a mature woman of about thirty-five summers; she entered the room and curtsied low.

"You worked for my mother?" asked Cerúlia with eager surprise.

"I had that honor, Your Majesty."

Editha cut off any further exchange of pleasantries. "Girl. I want the hair up, in a regal style. This gray cloak will cover that unfortunate burn on your neck, Your Majesty, but I should have been told about that. In the future, all your gowns will include winged side collars that fall to the collarbone in the front. You will be glad to know this won't cause a design problem but will further emphasize the pendant.

"Girl," Editha spoke while turning back to Geesilla, "Hair jewels would be a nice touch, as sparkle would show off its color. And the hair needs to be ready an hour before departure. Not one tick later."

Editha curtsied perfunctorily. "I must be off to supervise the sewing. A second shift of seamstresses will work all night so that you have more changes ready. Now that I have your measurements, fittings will proceed with more dispatch. But you must be sure to notify me if you lose or gain any weight." She turned to leave.

"Mistress Editha," Cerúlia called out. "I don't believe I have dismissed you."

Editha paused, turned around, and curtsied again, this time lower.

"I recognize, mistress," Cerúlia proceeded, speaking slowly and clearly, "that you know your business. You have been practicing your craft for years and have reached a level of expertise. I, on the other hand, have inhabited my position for only one day. Nevertheless, you will at all times respect the throne if not the woman."

Mistress Editha lowered her head. "Beg pardon, Your Majesty. Please chalk my manner up to the haste with which we must work, and my desire to have Your Highness look radiant in your first public appearance."

"I suspect that your manner is much the same, no matter the circumstance. Tyrants sometimes rule realms and sometimes smaller fiefdoms."

Cerúlia let her words sink in for a few moments. "One day I will talk to your assistants as to how well they are paid and treated. I noticed that one of them had welts on her forearms; I would not like to think that *my* clothing provided the excuse for a beating.

"In the meantime, you are now dismissed."

"Thank you, Your Majesty," murmured the dressmaker, and she curtsied her way out.

Stahlia erupted in laughter. "Where did you learn to do that, Birdie? Did Queen Cressa teach you that?"

Cerúlia gave her foster mother a wry look. "No, my mother was too mild. Actually, I was modeling my tone on you, Teta. Do you remember the time Tilim brought a frog to church and you scolded him? I was striving for exactly that tone of reprimand." Cerúlia mimicked her foster mother: "You will at all times respect the Church of the Waters. I'd hate to think that my allowing you to visit the pond was the cause of such tomfoolery."

The forgotten hair maid cleared her throat.

"Ah yes, my hair," said Cerúlia.

"Your Majesty, if you would care to sit in front of the looking glass, I could show you half a dozen styles, and you could choose those you prefer."

Cerúlia sighed with relief at Geesilla's more deferential manner.

She sat in front of the mirror while the hair maid gently twisted or puffed her hair into different configurations. Together Cerúlia, Stahlia, and the maid decided on a style for today and a dressier one for the event tomorrow, with the sides twisted into small curls and pulled up on top of her head, while the back flowed loose in larger curls.

The next morning passed in piecing together what they could about Matwyck's flight and confederates, which added up to precious little.

Afterward, Cerúlia met with the rich or aristocratic guests who had come for a wedding and ended up trapped in the middle of a restoration. She tried to allay their fears and win them over to supporting her reign, but she was uncertain how well she succeeded. Although outwardly all were polite, even unctuous, her dogs told her most were dissembling to greater or lesser degrees. The canines gave their full seal of approval only to the elderly couple from Maritima. The visitors asked for leave to return to their homes; except for Duke Favian and Duchess Gahoa, the queen bid them enjoy her hospitality for a few more days (until she'd had more chance to judge the conspiracies against her).

After midmeal Cerúlia had to turn herself over to maids to be bathed, then sit still for hours while her hair was fixed, and then stand still while the last pieces of the gown were stitched in place with her inside.

In the late afternoon, Tilim and Gunnit, smartly attired themselves, knocked on her door to tell her that her entourage was ready for her.

When Tilim saw her dressed in her full regalia, his mouth fell open. "By the Waters, Wren—I mean—Your Majesty, is that you?"

"I think so, Tilim, but I'm not sure myself."

The fancy gown made her hold her body rigid and her chin

up. She not only looked completely different, she felt like another person.

"This train trails—I need train bearers, and I wanted you boys."

"We'd be honored," said Gunnit.

"Good. Well, here we go!"

Cerúlia swept out of her chambers with the boys holding up the long back of her robe. The Queen's Shield flanked her. She discovered that she had to walk with precise, uniform steps so that the trainbearers and the shields could match her pace.

At the palace's front entrance a surprise awaited her. Hiccuth held the heads of two black horses hitched up to a large and ornate open carriage.

Your Majesty, Your Majesty, the horses called in her mind. They would have reared if Hiccuth hadn't been holding them so tightly and pulling down with all his considerable weight.

Smoke! Nightmist! Oh, the Waters! You are alive and you are here!

The horses echoed her excitement, *Thou art alive and thou art here!*

Realizing that she couldn't get horsehair or slobber on her gown, Cerúlia held herself back from running to stroke them.

Hiccuth bowed. "I'm not sure these two have ever been hitched to a carriage afore, Your Majesty, but I don't expect they'll give *you* any trouble."

"Have you been looking after them all these years, Hiccuth?"

"Indeed, Your Majesty. Your mother sent them home."

"Oh, there's so much I still need to know. . . ."

Ciellō, wearing a new blue-and-black manservant's costume due to Vilkit's magical talents, handed her into the carriage, and Editha arranged the fall of her gown and her robe for maximum effect. A coachman prepared to climb in front.

"Thank you, but no," ordered Cerúlia. "As proof of my Talent I will drive them with my mind. Just tie the reins off. Ciellō may stand behind me for protection."

The Queen's Shield gathered around the carriage. At a sign from Captain Yanath the procession set off down the straight Arrival Avenue and through the open Arrival Gate. The six dogs trotted around the carriage in a loose formation.

Duke Naven and Seamaster Wilamara had been allotted pride of place in a small open carriage behind the queen; then came the rest of her allies and her visitors. Scores of palace staff followed on foot, eager to be part of this historic event.

Cerúlia was shocked to see the number of people packing the sides of the avenue as soon as they left the grounds. Men, women, and children—some watchful, some curious, and some joyous—crowded the streets. They called out at her, but she could only hear snatches.

Horses, easy now. I know you've never worn those collars or pulled those traces, but they won't hurt you. Slow and stately—it is an honor to pull the queen's carriage. Pick up your feet in a prancing step and match your legs together. Watch out for small children on the sides of the street. No matter how people move about, don't startle.

People smell of fear. A few of anger, Cici reported.

Cerúlia half turned to speak over her shoulder to Ciellō.

"Not everyone is pleased to see me," she told him.

"I see their eyes, damselle," he answered. "I watch."

An arm threw a small item at her, and automatically she cringed. But it was merely a bouquet of white lilies of the valley.

Soon enough they reached the Courtyard of the Star. Guards had to make the crowds part to make room for the carriages. Cerúlia instructed the horses to drive right up to the Nargis Fountain, which she would use as her backdrop. The Queen's Shield herded the crowd back to make a semicircle of free space in front of her. Cerúlia dismounted from the carriage, finding that a speaking stand had been hastily erected and covered with a carpet; it stood three paces high, well over the height of the tallest man. Ciellō mounted the platform and then reached down to assist her. After she stepped up,

Ciellō stepped down; she felt the boys adjust the drape of her robe behind her. The six dogs roamed the crowd, sniffing for anyone with hatred in his heart.

With the Fountain murmuring behind her, Cerúlia stood on high alone. More than two thousand of her citizens looked up at her.

What do they see? Do they see me, or the blue hair and accoutrements of a queen? Can they see both? Have they been waiting for me, or dreading my return? How can I rule a country? My sole experience of leadership lies in taking charge of the Sweetmeadow refugees.

Ripples moved through the crowd as groups of citizens lowered into bows. Here and there some people stood defiantly with their knees locked straight, but none dared stand thus within range of the guards. Cerúlia picked out a sullen man in a yellow weskit standing upright with his arms crossed as an example of a person she needed to win over. She wondered if the woman who had sold her apple fritters was in the press.

Cerúlia waited a few more moments as people in the back bowed; she had to finish sending her instructions to a flock of wild white geese.

"Please rise," she called out in her loudest voice. "It is *my* honor to finally be among *you*." Here she dipped into a half curtsey. "I am Cerúlia the Gryphling, and after many years of exile, battle, and travel, I have returned to take up the Nargis Throne!"

On these words hundreds of wild geese flew over the Courtyard, straight to the Fountain. Then they broke up into five separate flocks and shot out up the five avenues of the Star.

The crowd shouted and applauded at this display of her Talent.

When the noise quieted, Cerúlia spoke slowly and loudly, with pauses between phrases so that her words could be repeated to those far back in the crowd.

"Fellow citizens! In the years since a queen has occupied the Nargis Throne, many things have gone awry. Powerful councilors have colluded with our enemies, gentry have enriched themselves to the detriment of the people, and innocent folk have been rounded up for the 'crime' of hoping for the queen's return.

"I will not pursue a vendetta, nor will I rush to judgment. But with the help of judiciaries, we must uncover the facts and bring guilty parties to justice. There is no lasting peace nor reconciliation without acknowledgment of crimes and atonement."

Here, to Cerúlia's shock, an old woman near the front of the crowd interrupted her.

"My Jeren was thrown in one of Yurgn's jails. Oh, please, Your High Majesty," she cried, "can't you release him?"

"Indeed," nodded Cerúlia. "One of my top priorities will be to examine the rolls of the prisons and uncover secret jails."

"And will you give us back land that was stolen from us?" shouted a man.

Cerúlia knew that she had to maintain control over this event. This was not the time for individual pleas.

"If you have a missing loved one or any other grievance, you may bring a written petition to the palace gates. But you will need to be patient. It will take time for my administration to take control and function well."

She returned to her memorized script. "I have made a beginning by appointing Duke Naven of Androvale and Seamaster Wilamara as my councilors." (A group of sailors standing to her right applauded loudly.)

"Which brings me to this: *I* am going to need *your* help. Together we must untangle a conspiracy that many in Cascada found profitable, so profitable that even now my life may be in danger. I need not only your petitions, but also your protection; not only your loyalty, but also information about those whose loyalty we must probe. For instance, Lord Matwyck himself has disappeared, and many of his Marauders have faded from sight.

"Only with your help will justice flow down like a river through a parched landscape."

Cerúlia noticed that the people standing next to the man in the yellow weskit were now giving him sidelong glances. He softened his belligerent posture.

"And once the immediate danger has passed, I need your help in improving Weirandale. During my exile I lived in a small Weir farming village. I saw how too many of our citizens suffer in a famine, and I know well the inadequacy of a poor rural school. We must work together to stockpile food for bad years, alleviate hardship, and spread the realm's riches more equitably.

"Finally, we need to rededicate ourselves to a proper appreciation of the gift we have been given. Nargis blesses us with sweet Water. We forget how precious this gift truly is. We must never waste this bounty, never pollute it, and never take it for granted. From its generosity we quench our thirst and water our crops. Should the Spirit ever withdraw this gift, our lives would be wretched and short. Nargis Water is the Water of Life.

"'Twas the Talent Nargis gave my mother that allowed her to hide me in safety in Androvale. 'Twas the Talent Nargis gave me that allowed me to survive the perils I have faced. The realm rests upon Nargis Water and Nargis's favor."

Cerúlia called down, "Does anyone have a cup?" Sewel produced a golden goblet that looked vaguely familiar and filled it from the Fountain with Nargis Water. He handed it to Tilim, who climbed the platform and offered it to the queen on bended knee.

She drank half of the Water, savoring it after her nervousness and public speaking. Then she dipped her fingers in the cup, and as water dripped off each finger she recited the five traditional prayers for Home, Health, Safety, Comradeship, and the Future of the Realm. As she did, more and more of the crowd chanted the words aloud with her. By the time she got to Safety, the whole crowd (including the man in the yellow weskit) had joined in; by Comradeship, people started linking arms with friends and strangers standing near them. By the prayer for the Future of the Realm, the entire ocean of people prayed in unison.

When the prayer ended, she ordered the flock of geese to fly back from the five points of the star and unite again over the Fountain, which the birds circled in a widening gyre as the crowd tossed their hats and cheered.

A woman in the crowd started shouting something that Cerúlia couldn't make out. Gradually other voices joined in, swelling the sound, so that as the chant continued it became more audible. By the time the citizens got to the second quatrain, the queen recognized that they were reciting "The Dusty Throne."

Someday the drought shall be broken,
And the wondrous Waters course clean,
One dawn the words shall be spoken,
As the long-lost heir becomes queen.

Cerúlia looked for and found Ciellõ's hand waiting to assist her down. Once resettled on the carriage seat, she invited Whaki and Cici up to keep her company, and she commanded the Queen's Shield and her horses to proceed.

On the route back, the people lining the streets bowed low as her carriage passed by. The sun sank behind a bank of evening clouds.

12

Nana had precious little time left to find this Rorther Truth Stone. A few days after Cerúlia took the throne, the queen sent a messenger to Lord Marcot and Lady Percia on their honey trip in Maritima, informing them of events. They would be returning any day, and explaining to them why she, Nana, was pawing through Matwyck's rooms and belongings would be awkward.

Though a Nargis Queen was more likely than others to sense her connection to the Spirit, Nana had not admitted to Cerúlia that she served as Nargis's Agent. She had not told Hiccuth either. She had not told anyone. She would never tell anyone . . . and nor would any of the other Agents. Such things just could not be spoken, and few would believe an Agent if she did. To have Gunnit, Saulě's Chosen Apprentice, close by her side these moons—to have someone who *knew* her—had been a treasure.

Obviously, this Stone would be well hidden away; Matwyck wouldn't have wanted that strumpet Lolethia or one of his oily functionaries finding it. Nana searched every out-of-the-way corner of his business chamber without success. In his bedroom, she looked under the bed, inside his wardrobe, and in the drawers of his jewel chest.

Out of breath, she perched on a bench at the foot of the bed.

Use yer head not yer eyes, she chided herself. *A Stone possessing Earth Magic would call out. Stop yer huffing and listen.*

The Agent sat, unmoving, until she could hear the room's quiet. Finally, she felt a pulse through the air.

She stood up, keeping her eyes shut, and moved one tiny step at a time in the direction of the pulse, which got stronger and stronger as she approached the window. When she put her hand on the sill, she could feel the wood vibrating. Opening her eyes, studying the sill, Nana realized it wasn't nailed in. She pulled the saddle up: underneath lay a chamois bag, and inside of that a palm-sized, flat stone, smooth and cool to the touch.

"Ooh-ho, Master Matwyck," she said aloud. "You must have been in very bad shape to leave this behind. I hope yer suffering, you shitwit. I hope you fester. I hope you bloat and crack with all the evil stuffed inside you. Well, I do!"

Chuckling, Nana tucked the stone into her apron; there was a particular someone she was dying to interrogate.

It took her an hour to corner Geesilla, the queen's hair maid, in the servants' common room, with its scuffed long tables and raw wooden benches, where the maid sat sipping a cup of tisane. No one else was about, at least for the nonce.

"Geesilla," said Nana, pouring herself a cup and sliding next to her on the bench, "Strange that tides have dropped you back at the palace. You didn't reckon I'd forgotten you, did you?"

Geesilla bit her lip. "Nana, you never forget anything, do you?"

"Not when it comes to my own darling. Tell me now, how much did you know about the plot against Queen Cressa?"

Geesilla's eyes fixated on her cup. "I reported to Lord Retzel about her activities and meetings. I knew the councilors were watching her, but I chose not to think about why. When they tried to kill her, I was terrified and ashamed."

"Where have you been since Cressa was forced to flee?" Nana

pressed. "Why have you suddenly appeared again, right at the side of her child?"

"Retzel followed through on his promise to set my man up as overseer on one of his estates in Lakevale. We got married. I was bored away from the city, but thought I'd be content once kiddies came."

Geesilla sighed and softly knocked her fist on her forehead, as if knocking sense into herself. "Then I found out that my husband chased anything in skirts—the scullery maids, the dairymaids, the village girls, teachers, even noble visitors—so I left him, by fortune's grace before he could get me with child. About ten years ago I drifted back to Cascada, wanting to ply my trade, working first for one lady, then another. Until this spring I worked mostly for Duchess Latlie and her daughters. That's how Mistress Editha knew my skill, because she dressed that family."

"And now? Why is it that dogs haven't sniffed out yer treachery?"

"Because I *am* loyal." She looked up and met Nana's suspicious glance. "Don't you believe in second chances, Nana? I was young, greedy, love-blind, and stupid when I served Queen Cressa. Life has paid me back some hard knocks. Now, all I want is to serve Queen Cerúlia faithfully."

"Huh," said Nana. "If you be so regretful, you won't mind being put to a test?"

"What kind of test?"

"I am going to lay yer hand on a stone and ask a few questions."

"A stone? I don't see how this—"

"Just do as I say, or I will call the Queen's Shield and have you arrested," snapped Nana. She pulled the Truth Stone out of its bag and laid it on the table between them.

"Put yer hand here and keep it there."

Geesilla complied.

"Did you spy for Lord Retzel?"

"Aye," admitted Geesilla.

"Did you do anything else for those Usurpers? Did you help the assassins?"

Geesilla tried to take her hand away from the Stone. Under Nana's glare she placed it back. "I did nothing for the assassins. . . . But twice, I pleasured Councilor Prigent. With my mouth. I didn't want to, Nana, but he cornered me and threatened me!"

Nana's face softened for the first time. "I don't care about that, Geesilla. You should have reported him to Chamberlaine Teonora."

"I was afraid to. He was a councilor, Lord Matwyck's friend, and I—I am just a hair maid."

"Yeah, well. You were a foolish, pretty young thing, and Prigent's a pig-fuckin' worm. That doesn't count as treachery. What do you intend in regards to our new queen?"

"To serve her faithfully, to make her hair look beautiful, to be a comfort to her if she ever needs me in any way."

"What would it take to turn you into a spy or make you disloyal once more?"

"Oh, no! I wouldn't; I couldn't. I'd sooner die. This is a chance to earn back my own respect. And I'm good with her hair, Nana, you must agree. She's pleased, isn't she? Not everyone knows how to handle a queen's hair. And often, I know how to soothe or distract her."

Nana repocketed the Stone. "I'm going to keep my sharp eye on you, Geesilla. But for now, I'll not bring up bygones."

Geesilla burst into tears and tried to kiss Nana's hands in gratitude.

"Now, none of that. Drink yer tisane and buck up. I must be off."

Nana left the servants' quarters in search of the queen. She found her in her closet in conference with Duke Naven and Seamaster Wilamara.

Their discussion continued a long time; weary from these stressful days, Nana dozed in her chair until Kiltti, who had been reassigned upstairs, gently shook her shoulder. "The queen will see you now."

When she entered the small chamber, Cerúlia greeted her. "Good day, Nana. You wanted to see me? Are you all right? Is anything amiss?"

"Yer Majesty," curtsied Nana. The main dog, that Whaki with the curious line of fur, leaned against her leg affectionately, half knocking her off-balance, so she steadied herself with a hand on his head.

"Why does he pester me so?" Nana asked. "Doesn't he know I don't like dogs?"

"He has good taste," Cerúlia smiled. The water feature in the room sounded *Plink!*

The queen continued, "Nana, people are expecting me outside to survey the fire-damaged wing. What can I do for you?"

"Yer Majesty, I've found something important." Nana placed the Stone out on the table.

Cerúlia recognized its shape. "The Truth Stone! Where did you find it?"

"In Matwyck's quarters."

"Does this one work? The one Lady Tenny used on me did nothing."

"Aye, Yer Majesty. I tested it." *Plink!*

"Ah! Wouldn't I like to question our stable guests!"

"Yer Majesty, this is Magic; it belongs to the Spirit 'Chamen. The Rorthers want it back. Think how angry we would be if the Rorthers stole Nargis Water. You can't keep it hidden from them, because we need all the Spirits' favor."

"I understand," she responded. "I won't keep it hidden; I'll contact the Rorther envoy immediately." She raised her voice to call, "Darzner!

"And thank you, Nana. This is a boon indeed."

Nana spoke to the dog. "Not a bad morning's work for an old lady, eh?" Whaki nuzzled her hand, and she gave him a grudging pat.

* * *

Perchance because Nana had found the Truth Stone, the queen made a point of inviting her to observe the hastily arranged proceeding that took place the next day.

A crowd of people had gathered on the chairs and settees set up in random rows in the Salon of Cinda. Nana recognized Duke Naven, Seamaster Wilamara, Chronicler Sewel, and Captain Yanath. She guessed that the jowly gentleman seated near the front was Duke Burdis and the elderly lady by his side, Duchess Pattengale. She looked for the Duke and Duchess of Maritima, but they were absent; then she recalled hearing that they had departed to return to their duchy.

The men and women with long, blue, fringed scarves hanging around their necks had to be judiciaries summoned from Cascada; they conferred animatedly with one another. And a table had been set up for several scribes, complete with vellum and paper, penknives, quills, and a line of ink pots.

Chamberlain Vilkit gestured that Nana should take the chair beside him—this was above her station, but Vilkit, who to give him his due had always been respectful, was now unctuously solicitous of the queen's intimate companion. This afternoon the chamberlain rubbed his hands together as if expecting a very fine show and winked at Nana, which was such a departure from his normal demeanor that Nana had trouble keeping a straight face. He pointed to a well-dressed, intense man sitting a few rows away who had paper on a portable writing desk, several quills at hand, and others stuck behind his ears.

"The best writer for the *Cascada News,*" he mouthed.

"Why does he have so many quills?" she whispered.

"So he doesn't have to stop to sharpen them."

In the front row of the room, in an upholstered chair, sat a woman who must be the envoy from Rortherrod. Her hair shone bright red, and she wore a black, ministerial robe.

The queen entered, accompanied by two dogs, two shields, and the Zellishman who always shadowed her. The assembly stood as she paused by the envoy for a few whispered words and then seated herself in her chair in the front.

"You may be seated," Queen Cerúlia called out in ringing tones. Nana noted, with a bit of a pang, that her little girl gained confidence and presence by the hour.

"We are gathered here today for an important and unexpected development," she said.

"Among Lord Matwyck's many crimes lies the theft of a priceless treasure from our ally, the kingdom of Rortherrod. We have recently located this treasure in his quarters.

"We are returning it forthwith to its rightful owners, as represented by Envoy Rakihah of Feldspar."

Sergeant Athelbern approached, carrying a golden tray, on top of which sat the Stone on a bed of velvet. He brought it to the envoy and took a knee with stately solemnity.

Envoy Rakihah stood and spoke. "Thank you, Your Majesty. This is one of the Three Stones of my country blessed by 'Chamen. It had been lodged in our royal treasury. I am most curious as to how it came to be here in Cascada; perchance this is one of the mysteries we can unravel. I have sent a letter to King Kentros the Third, telling him of its recovery, and His Majesty will no doubt dispatch a ship to retrieve it.

"However, in celebration of Your Highness's safe return, and in gratitude for your prompt recovery of our sacred treasure, I have agreed to allow a demonstration of its Power. We—the Rorthers— are most pleased to showcase 'Chamen's most Sacred and Enduring Strength."

Cerúlia inclined her head to Envoy Rakihah. "And Weirandale will be forever grateful for Rortherrod's generosity. Be it thus and ever so." She nodded to a judiciary to begin the proceedings.

The judiciary called, "Bring in the first prisoner."

Soldiers brought in Councilor Prigent. After days in the stables, bits of straw stuck to his hair and clothing. His skin and hair had taken on a layer of grimy sweat.

One of the judiciaries, a woman of about thirty summers, with a sharp chin and smart eyes, opened the ritual.

"As it pleases Your Majesty." She bowed to the queen and then turned to the prisoner.

"Councilor Prigent, this proceeding is a questioning, a gathering of evidence that will later be used to determine the charges and which will feature in your trial. We often hold such procedures to examine the contours of major crimes. Today, however, because of the Rorther Stone, we will have the rare surety that those questioned will speak truthfully.

"Sergeant, place the Stone on top of the table in front of the councilor. Hold his hand on top of the Stone, gently but firmly."

She waited while her commands were followed.

"First, Councilor, while in the captivity of Queen Cerúlia, has anyone inflicted bodily harm to your person?"

"No," he answered.

"You have not been tortured in any way?"

He shook his head.

"Please describe to this assembly the conditions of your captivity."

"We are lodged in stables—men and women separated from one another. They brought in clean straw the second day. We've been fed water, bread, dried apples, and raw carrots. Porridge is served for fastbreak. There are horseflies, though, and these plague us."

"Has anyone offered you a bribe or inducement to testify one way or another or pressured you in any way?"

"No."

The lead judiciary turned to the assembled onlookers. "Each of my colleagues will concentrate on a particular period or crime. We will start furthest back in time, with the circumstances that caused Queen Cressa the Enchanter to flee the realm. Sir, you may begin."

An old man wearing judicial robes stood up. He had so many years, he could have known her darling Cressa. Nana's mind wandered a bit, wondering whether this man grieved for the former queen.

"Councilor, who was responsible for the attempt on Queen Cressa's life?" The man's voice was weak and reedy with his age.

Prigent sputtered, but words came out. "Lord Matwyck."

A general gasp came from the audience at hearing the statement, long suspected, actually spoken out loud.

"Not the Oromondians?"

"No."

"Why did the Lord Steward turn to high treason?"

"Because his term on the Circle Council was drawing to an end and he knew he was better at governing the country than Queen Cressa."

"Whom did Lord Matwyck conscript in his plan?"

"General Yurgn, Lord Retzel, Lady Tenny, Duchess Latlie, and me." More gasps and an audible buzz of conversation.

Cerúlia broke in, "Lady Tenny was a full conspirator?"

"Well, she was and she wasn't. She said no at first, but after Matwyck had a private talk with her, she agreed. But afterward she immediately regretted her involvement and we mistrusted her."

The judiciary continued, "What was your role in the conspiracy?"

"I was the paymaster, so I negotiated deals and paid the mercenaries we hired. I paid the member of the Queen's Shield who spied for us. I tricked the queen into signing a document appointing Matwyck as Lord Regent."

"What did the others do?"

"General Yurgn hired the mercenaries, and he made sure the palace guard would not interfere. Lord Retzel bribed many of the servants. Lady Tenny talked with Envoy Thum from Oromondo;

I'm fairly sure she manipulated him into sending the letter. Latlie kept a close eye on the gentry, reporting on any royalists."

Vilkit made a loud "ahem" noise. Nana wanted to hide when all eyes turned in their direction.

Cerúlia said, "Chamberlain, do you have something to add?"

"Your Majesty, I beg pardon for this interruption. Duchess Latlie did not reside in the palace during the wedding because her city mansion is so nearby. If I may be so bold as to suggest . . ."

Captain Yanath took his meaning and nodded at a Queen's Shield at the door.

"What was the involvement of the Oromondians in the treason?" continued the judiciary.

"Well, because of their plagues, certainly they would have liked Cressa dead. But they didn't set up that assassination attack. And they wouldn't have wanted the princella to assume the throne with Lord Matwyck as regent. They hoped to wipe out the line of Nargis Queens forever and"—he tried to take his hand away, but Athelbern would have none of it—"take our Waters."

The room fell dead silent, contemplating this prospect. Nana silently blessed her fortune that she had not been Nargis's Agent during such a perilous moment. She wondered, not for the first time, who had preceded her.

"So Queen Cressa was wise to flee—there would have been more attacks on her royal person and the princella if she had stayed?"

"Undoubtedly."

The man nodded. "I concentrate on the coup. My colleague will take over now." He sat, and another judiciary claimed the front of the room.

"Councilor, what actions did the council take once Queen Cressa fled the realm?" she asked.

Prigent was led through the bounty the council had placed on the heads of Lord Ambrice and Queen Cressa, and through their various attempts to track down the princella with magicked bats, searches, and bounties.

Nana noticed that Missus Stahlia looked very peaked during this part of the hearing; she hoped that Duke Naven was spry enough to catch her if she swooned. She looked around the room for someone to send for smelling salts, finally spying Gunnit in a corner. She beckoned the lad close to her.

"Gunnit," she whispered. "There's a bottle of smelling salts in my room. Run and fetch them."

Vilkit had overheard, and he grabbed the boy's sleeve. "Best bring a flask of brandy too," he whispered, and he winked at Nana again, "just in case."

When Nana turned her attention back to the front of the room, the judiciary was asking, "What do you know about the theft of this Truth Stone?"

"Only that I discovered a large bag of jewels missing, and when I asked Matwyck about it he said to shut up—that with General Yurgn's help he had purchased something that would help us find the princella. Now, I put two and two together."

Cerúlia interrupted by asking, "What do you know about the death of Lady Tenny?"

"Nothing direct. But I suspect Matwyck had her killed because she didn't capture the princella when she had a chance to do so in Gulltown."

Cerúlia snapped, "Don't bandy words with me. Who would know the full details about her death?"

"Captain Murgn took care of such . . . details. And General Yurgn would have been kept informed. Perchance Matwyck's secretary, Heathclaw."

Captain Yanath stood, drawing everyone's attention. "Do you have a comment to add, Captain?" asked the lead judiciary.

"Milady, I just wanted to remind everyone that Heathclaw was among the Throne Room casualties."

The judiciary nodded. "Pity. So noted."

A younger judiciary took over questions about the council's governing practices. Prigent didn't know the location of the secret prisons, even though he had allocated funds for them. How did the council decide who received lucrative royal contracts? What kind of kickback schemes occurred? How much public funds had Prigent himself embezzled? How had he spent these monies?

Everyone laughed at revelations of how much he had lavished on his mistress.

A fourth judiciary, a man with webbed fingers on his left hand, which he tried to keep hidden in his robe but kept bringing out when he got excited, took over on the subject of this week's Battle of the Throne Room. Prigent had not been present and thus knew nothing about what transpired there except for the comments he had overheard in the stable. Instead of rushing in the direction of the commotion like everyone else, he had hurried to his office to burn his most incriminating ledgers.

"I burned the ledgers in the fireplace. Paper—it burned well and quickly. I have no idea how the big fire started. I did nothing but burn the ledgers, in the hearth. . . . I started the fire with a big clump of these and threw in more once it got going."

The last questions had to do with Matwyck's escape from his sickroom. But on that matter, Prigent, being already confined to the stable, had no firsthand information. He did agree, however, that having an escape plan would be typical of Matwyck's character.

When the judiciaries had finished, Cerúlia herself addressed Prigent. "I have a most urgent question that has not been covered. Councilor, *why* did you act in the ways that you have described for us here?"

"I felt no loyalty to Queen Cressa," Prigent answered. "She'd never shown me any favor. Like the rest of the gentry, she looked down her royal nose at me, because I was just an administrator, and common-born. Why should I stick my neck out to protect her?

And Lord Matwyck, as everyone in this room knows, is much too strong a personality to oppose. If I'd even thought of warning the queen or upsetting the plans, he would have had me killed.

"And then the money . . ." He smiled in remembrance. "Matwyck sent me with Vanilina to this tropical island to do paperwork. Every night we dined sumptuously and drank the best wines. I bought her jewels I'd never have been able to afford. When it was hot we hired servants to fan us all night long. I'd never have been able to do this on my paltry salary."

"And so," Cerúlia pressed, "for those things you betrayed your queen and pilfered from your countrymen?"

"Anyone in my position would have done the same—haven't all of you sitting in this room profited from some fiddle, large or small? Life is short. Why shouldn't I live as well as anyone? I was able to make my brothers look up to me; little people pulled their fetlocks to me. The money bought me comfort, prestige, and respect."

Then he looked up at the queen. "Besides, fiddling with funds isn't such a big deal. Unlike others I could mention, *I've* never stabbed anybody."

During his speech, the queen had gazed at him in rapt contemplation; now her eyelashes batted together in an angry gesture that Nana recalled too well. Cerúlia motioned to the little terrier, who stalked over to the prisoner, raised her hind leg, and pissed on his legs.

Grabbing her long skirts, the Rorther envoy rose to move away from the trickle, trying to restrain herself from laughing. "Your Majesty, this has been such an illuminating event. I would hate to be the one to cut such a flow of valuable information short. And we would dearly like to know more about the theft of our Stone. Perchance you would like to arrange for a few more such sessions while we wait for the escort ship?"

"Envoy Rakihah, I was hoping you might come to this conclusion," replied the queen. "Might you be free to discuss this matter further with me over dinner?

"Chief Judiciary"—Cerúlia turned to the functionary—"I know you must digest the information that we have received today and make decisions about how best to proceed. But we must not presume upon the Rorthers' generosity. The most important thing we must concentrate on tomorrow is the location of the secret prisons."

13

By changing horses at every hostelry along their route, Marcot and Percia's carriage arrived at the palace in the dead of night, five days after the wedding, four days into the reign of Queen Cerúlia. The newlyweds' anxiety and distress pummeled them so they couldn't wait until dawn; when they found out that Stahlia had forestalled her move to West Cottage and still stayed in the guest suite she'd occupied before the wedding, Percia charged in to wake her up.

Marcot paced the corridor and ordered a sleepy footman to fetch them all coffee and whatever was handy in the kitchens to eat.

When the women invited Marcot inside to join them, Stahlia had thrown Percia's traveling cloak on over her nightshift, while Percia had made herself more comfortable by shedding her boots and taking down her hair, which she twisted in her hands as they talked. The three pulled up chairs and drank the coffee while Stahlia—thank the Waters he had such a steely mother-in-marriage!—managed to narrate the events they had missed in a coherent fashion.

By daybreak, Percia, incensed about all those years of secrecy and duplicity, announced that she simply could not hold back any longer from seeing her sister.

Marcot tried to dissuade her. "She's probably still sleeping. You can't go barging in on a queen without a by-your-leave."

"I don't care if she's queen," Percia snapped at her husband. "She's also my Birdie, and she's played me false!"

Marcot tried to restrain his bride from running shoeless through the corridors, but Stahlia said, "Let her go. The girls will need to work this out between themselves."

Dazed from this rush of information, Marcot took leave of his mother-in-marriage. Stahlia offered him a sheaf of special broadsheets rush-printed by the *Cascada News* (and chockablock with spelling and printing errors); these he carried back to his own quarters and read three times to try to absorb all the startling information.

Then he sat a while with his eyes closed and his head in his hands. For the first time, Marcot was glad that his mother was dead. He knew how much she would have suffered from these revelations of his father's misdeeds—he knew because of how much he writhed.

Oh, he'd been fully aware that not everything his father did was ethical. He knew his father was an ambitious plotter and that money flowed through his hands much too easily for it all to be fully legal. But treason? Multiple murders? Marcot wanted to deny such serious charges, but he realized that over the years he had avoided facing clues and inconsistencies because he couldn't bear to face the truth.

Guilt settled like a stone in his gut.

He would have to spend the rest of his life atoning for his father's actions.

After a few hours of fitful sleep, Marcot made an appointment to see the queen. A strange man with braided hair made him relinquish his dagger in the hallway outside her closet, and then an unfamiliar figure serving as secretary announced him.

Entering the room, Marcot was taken aback, because the face between the blue hair and the necklace of Nargis Ice surely belonged to the sister he had met a week ago, and yet the queen who sat at a table before him was a different person in dress, bearing, and voice.

"Your Majesty." He bowed. She rose and crossed to him, holding his hands for a moment. "Marcot, my brother, how are you bearing up? A difficult business, I know." She reseated herself, holding her right arm in pain, and motioned for him to sit, but he preferred to stand.

"'Difficult' indeed. During the wedding festivities I behaved like such a fool; I thought I was noble and high-minded for defending you and your family. Now I discover that the Weir gentry and I are about as noble as the dirt beneath your feet."

"Marcot, no one blames *you* for your father's crimes."

"*I* blame myself. I should have stopped them; I should have denounced him; I should have done something, though I know not what."

The queen shrugged as if he were just being obstinate, but Marcot knew the hard truth of his responsibility.

"Are there any tidings regarding my father's whereabouts?" Marcot forced himself to ask.

"No. We suspect that General Yurgn's people took him in, but whether to protect him or to snuff out what spark remains, we don't know. You've heard he was grievously injured in the Battle of the Throne Room?"

"Yes. I heard that."

The queen allowed a long pause, and in the silence Marcot heard the *plink* of water drops from the room's water feature.

"I regret that I had to interrupt your honey trip. But Marcot, I need to ask you for a service. I am a stranger to the court, and I know little about its factions or its customs. You have partially grown up here, and the people must know and trust you. Would you be willing to serve on my Circle Council?"

"I am yours to command, but I don't know how you can trust the son of a traitor."

"Was your mother a traitor?"

"Never!" said Marcot with a flash of heat. "In fact, I now believe she died to get away from my father."

"I can trust Lady Tirinella's son," said the queen. "And, I can trust Percia's husband. But you are more than the sum of your connections: you are your own person, and I can trust *you*."

A dog that had been sniffing him licked his hand, but Marcot was in too much turmoil to pay attention to an animal. *Plink!*

"As you wish." Marcot bowed again. "Your Majesty, if I am to serve, could I be given jurisdiction over making amends to those my father wronged?"

"Interesting proposition," said the queen, rubbing her upper right arm again. "Yes, I think that would restore balance. This afternoon we are holding another questioning session. Our first accused is Captain Murgn, whom we believe to have been in charge of the disappearances. We need to know where folk are being held and who ordered the arrests. I am most eager to find our Wyndton friend, Lemle.

"As long as you are here . . . Chronicler Sewel urges me to complete my Circle Council. Naven is a duke and you are now a lord; Seamaster Wilamara can represent the military; the citizens will elect a steward. What should I do with the last two seats? Who would give me good counsel?"

"I believe that a person who represents the merchants or the guilds could help us think about how decisions affect trade and business. Suppose I invite five or six notables to a midmeal"—*Plink!*—"and we see if anyone emerges as a strong and wise voice?"

"Fine. For the sixth councilor we need someone to fill the role Lady Tenny once held as a councilor for diplomacy. Someone who has traveled the world and can advise us on foreign affairs."

"No one immediately comes to mind, but I will ponder these qualifications."

"Very well." The queen changed the subject. "You've been through a great trauma; I'm glad you have Percia to support you. By the same token, Percia has been through a shock; she will need your love more than ever."

For the first time, Marcot felt a hint of a grin move his lips. "If it is not presumptuous, how are *you*, Your Majesty? When Percia and I parted this morning, she was so distraught I feared for your safety."

Plink! Queen Cerúlia cleared her throat. "Aye. My sister and I—we had a difficult confrontation this morning. My most sensitive dog started yowling in the middle of it." She leaned forward to stroke the animal by her side. "I had fretted about Stahlia; but I had thought Percia's and my bond superseded any barrier.

"Secrets are corrosive," she said. "For years I knew the toll that keeping so many secrets took on me. But I didn't stop to consider fully how much their revelation would crush other people. As much as secrets hurt the one who keeps them, they also hurt the ones who have been deceived."

With a sense of betraying his wife, Marcot commented, "But as I understand the situation, you didn't have a choice."

"No," said the young queen. "I had no choice whatsoever. But it is always a mistake not to take the measure of the pain of others. Even if one is helpless to alleviate their suffering, one must give it the respect it deserves."

That afternoon Marcot witnessed a questioning for himself. The room was overflowing with people—people who might be whispering about his years of blindness to his father's crimes. Marcot avoided their glances, choosing to seat himself on the side of the room on a two-person couch next to Duke Naven, who greeted him with a hearty clap on the shoulders. Stahlia and Percia did not appear in the salon; Marcot hoped that they were lying down.

The judiciaries called Captain Murgn first. Murgn struggled against the guards escorting him with his whole body while he shouted out curses and threats. The shields had a difficult time controlling him and looked apprehensive about cutting loose one of his hands to place it on the Truth Stone.

The man whom Naven identified as the queen's Zellish bodyguard left his post behind her chair and approached the prisoner on light feet. He used his left hand to grab Murgn's private parts and produced a gleaming knife in his right. With an impassive face he whispered a few words. Murgn froze. The Zellishman nodded to the Queen's Shield, and they cut loose Murgn's right hand. Sergeant Athelbern brought forth a tray and placed the prisoner's hand on the Truth Stone. Then the bodyguard squatted on his heels so he was no longer so visible, though he kept his hands as they were throughout Murgn's testimony. If his position strained his muscles or his patience, the man gave no sign.

After preliminaries, the lead judiciary asked, "You are the captain of Matwyck's Marauders, are you not?"

"Aye. Stupid question, bitch. You know who I am."

"And what were your duties?"

"I reported to the Lord Regent himself. Only the Lord Regent. Not to you."

"What did Lord Matwyck order you to do?"

"Various things."

"You are trying my patience. Tell us what you and Matwyck's Marauders did."

"We guarded the palace and the Lord Regent's interests."

"Against whom did you guard the palace?"

"Against any threat and—and against any woman who might be trying to sneak in."

The judiciary paced the front of the room. "So against the rightful queen, returning to claim her throne. Your orders were to . . . ?"

"Apprehend her or kill her. Either way." Marcot felt the room stir and audience members stifle expressions of shock.

"So you guarded the palace. Did you have anything to do with Lady Tenny's death?"

"Who's that?"

"She was a councilor, an elderly woman. Reports circulated more than two years ago that she committed suicide off SeaWidow Cliff."

"Oh, the dried-up cunt with the turban? I carted her up to the cliff, but I didn't push her off. She jumped on her own."

"If she had balked, what were your orders?"

"Oh, she was going over—one way or another."

"Aside from guarding the palace from its legitimate queen and making sure elderly ladies jumped to their deaths, what else did the Marauders do?" The judiciary tugged on both sides of her blue scarf.

"We arrested people who was disturbing the peace."

"Disturbing the peace in what way?"

"Plotting to overthrow the government." Murgn snorted and threw his head high.

"How were they plotting to overthrow the government?"

"Mostly by advocating for the blue-haired one to return." His eyes briefly flicked over the queen sitting before him.

"Were these people threatening anyone? Harming anyone?"

"They were agitators. Talkers. Plotters."

"When you arrested them, what did you do with them?"

"Various things."

"Did you kill them?"

"Some."

Irritated, the judiciary tugged harder on her blue scarf and phrased her question very precisely. "How many people suspected of being 'talkers' did you and your men kill in the last two years?"

"Several hundred."

"That's a vague number. More than three hundred?"

"Aye."

"More than five hundred?"

"Probably not, but I didn't keep count."

"Are there any records of the names of the people you went after?"

"No. We aren't stupid."

"That's a matter of opinion," sighed the judiciary. "The people you didn't kill, did you beat them?"

"Sure."

"Punch them in the stomach, break their arms, break their legs? Smash their heads?"

"That's what beating means." Murgn smiled at the woman's ignorance.

"Did you molest them?"

"Only if the gal was really a looker." Murgn glanced around as if expecting a laugh, but the faces in the room gave him no comfort. Marcot recognized many of the guests his father had invited to the wedding; they seemed to be shrinking away from this bald revelation of his father's ruthlessness.

· The judiciary took a step closer to the witness. "How many women—or men—did you and your men rape?"

"Lots. I didn't keep count. Taking a little pleasure is good for my lads' morale. Also, nothing else strikes fear into the populace like knowing what will happen to their mothers or daughters. Good, effective tactic."

"How many did you, personally, rape?"

He counted on the fingers of his left hand. "Fourteen? If you count the lads, which I usually don't." He smirked.

"What did you do with the prisoners after you beat or raped them?"

"We took them to jail."

"Which jails?"

Murgn listed eight scattered locations in four duchies. These were not official duchy prisons, but secret sites set up by Matwyck and Yurgn to hide their captives. Marcot rushed to borrow implements from a scribe and wrote down their locations with shaking hands.

"Did Lord Matwyck know what you were doing?"

"Of course."

"He knew about the killings, the beatings, the rapes, the jailing?"

"I never spoke to him about the fuckin', but I'm sure he knew."

"Who else knew about your activities?"

"General Yurgn, for sure. Tips on those we should arrest mostly came from him or his people."

"Which of his people?"

Murgn rattled off the names of army officers and enlisted men. The judiciary made him repeat and spell the names. Marcot didn't try to keep his own record of this information; he assumed the judiciaries planned to issue warrants and follow up.

"Where is General Yurgn now?" the lead judiciary asked.

"He didn't come to the wedding, so he must be at his manse. I've been entertained there several times."

"What about the other councilors?"

"Did they go to the Riverine manse?"

"No, did they know about or order the arrests of hundreds of 'talkers'?"

"I never spoke to them. Lord Matwyck said they were fools and lickspittles."

"What about Lord Marcot?"

"Lord Matwyck told us to make sure he didn't find out. A weakling, that one."

Marcot had stopped breathing at the mention of his own name. He realized that the judiciary had just (purposely?) cleared his reputation.

"The night before the wedding there was an altercation at supper in this salon."

"Heard about it."

"Who told you, and what did you hear?"

"One of my men told me that Inrick and Burgn had a spat with Lord Matwyck."

"And later, when Duchette Lolethia's body was found, what instructions did Lord Matwyck give you?"

"To send fifty of my men to apprehend Burgn."

"Did they do so?"

"I sent them off, but I've been in the stable, as you well know, stupid bitch."

Another judiciary got up and took over the questioning.

"Describe where you were and what you did the morning the queen claimed the throne."

"I was asleep in my quarters, up to no mischief. I heard the bells and the shouting, and one of my men shook me. I pulled on my boots and grabbed my sword. I took on several of the blue-caped bastards. Killed at least one; injured quite a few."

"Were you on the ground floor or one of the balconies?"

"On the ground floor."

"Did you see who was shooting from the balcony?"

"Lord Matwyck's personal guards. Four of my best. They did a damn good job."

"Did you see who pushed Lord Matwyck?"

"No."

"Did you see who shot the queen?"

"No."

"How were you captured?"

"By a pack of savage dogs."

"Isn't it true that all of the captives surrendered to the dogs? Did you throw down your sword and surrender to the dogs?"

"I had no choice."

The judiciary turned to the queen and looked around the room. "Does anyone else have any questions?"

"I do," said the queen to the judiciaries. "You've heard this brute damn himself with his own words—murders, rapes, assaults. What kind of punishment will fall upon him?"

"We haven't heard the whole case yet, Your Majesty. It is vaguely possible there might be exculpatory . . ." The woman's voice trailed away at the impossibility of further information substantially mitigating the man's crimes.

The queen stared at Murgn. "You strike me as a man who takes pleasure in other people's anguish. I can see why Matwyck found you a useful tool. By the Grace of the Waters, your days of power are over."

As Murgn was escorted out of the room, many people in the audience spit on him. He walked without bravado; he had lost his cocky demeanor.

The next person brought forward was Duke Inrick. His comportment provided quite a contrast in that he strolled in with cool contempt. Recalling how the duke had insulted Percia, Marcot felt his own cheeks burning.

The blue-scarfed man who had asked questions about the events in the Throne Room continued with the examination.

"Duke Inrick, you reside in Crenovale, do you not?"

"Yes, you are correct. I rarely come to Cascada; it is a long trip and the capital does not amuse me."

"Did you attend the supper before the wedding of Lord Marcot and Percia of Wyndton?"

"Yes."

"Describe the altercation you were involved in during this supper."

"I made a comment. Duke Naven and Lordling Marcot chose to take offense." Inrick shot daggers toward Marcot's settee. "Lordling Marcot made a childish fuss and threw water in my face."

"And then what happened?"

"Lord Regent Matwyck sided with his son and publicly dismissed me from the room."

"This made you angry?"

"Indeed."

"Very angry?"

"Naturally. I am a gentleman."

"Describe your actions the next morning," said the judiciary, who paced in front of the duke.

"I was asleep in one of the guest bedrooms; the bed was quite comfortable. I awoke because of the bells and the noise. I rushed out on the balcony. 'Twas quite a chaotic scene."

"Yes, and then?"

"One of the queen's mercenaries shot Lord Matwyck in the thigh."

"Yes, and then?"

"Then . . . I pushed him over the balcony."

"Why?"

The prisoner tried to avoid the question. "Wasn't that my patriotic duty? Doesn't the queen sit yonder due to my action?"

The judiciary asked again, "In the moment when you pushed Lord Matwyck over the balcony, were you thinking about your patriotic duty?"

"No."

"What were you thinking about?"

"Revenge. He'd humiliated me. He deserved to die."

The judiciary turned to the queen. "In the law, intentions matter, Your Majesty. And due to the Stone we have a rare opportunity to ascertain the truth." He turned back to the prisoner. "One more question. You were on the balcony. Did you see who shot the arrow that did strike Queen Cerúlia?"

"Oh, that? Yes. The would-be assassin was Duchette Lolethia's mother, Duchess Felethia of Prairyvale."

The room dissolved into hubbub as witnesses discussed this news.

The questioning recessed for a short time while guards were

sent to the stables to bring the duchess. During this break Marcot conferred with the queen's secretary about mustering a force to free the prisoners in the secret jails. Darzner suggested that they consult the captain of the Queen's Shield, who would be available as soon as these proceedings concluded.

Duchess Felethia bore a faint resemblance to her daughter in stature, jaw, and forehead; she might have been a beauty in her youth. Now her face looked haggard under the mourning circlet someone had provided her. She must have been wounded during the dog chase, because her hands and one of her ankles wore bandages. As she entered the room she limped on the arm of her escort, but she stood erect when they brought her to the table in front. Craning his head, Marcot looked around the salon, recognizing Lolethia's younger sister and brother sitting side by side in the audience, also sporting mourning circlets.

"Aren't there more children?" he whispered to Naven.

"Two little boys still in the nursery in Prairyvale," Naven answered.

The same judiciary continued the questioning. "Duchess, when did you learn of your daughter's death?"

"The night she died. The Lord Regent came to my suite to inform me. In this, he followed correct procedure. I was her mother."

"That night, did you believe that Captain Burgn had killed your daughter?"

"Indeed, that is what the Lord Regent told me. And she was found in this Burgn's chambers."

"When did you find out that Queen Cerúlia was the person who actually killed your daughter?"

Marcot looked at Duke Naven in shock; his neighbor nodded his head.

"I'm not sure. Men in the stable were talking in loud voices. I can hardly credit their gossip. Was *she* in Burgn's chambers?" Her voice quavered. "Why would she kill my daughter?"

"Please describe your actions the morning of the Dedication."

"I had not been able to sleep after the news. As it started to get light, that healer—an odious little man, I've forgotten his name—gave me a sleeping draught and I managed to drift off. I awoke to all this commotion, and I followed the crowds of people to the balcony. I almost thought I was sleepwalking; my youngest boy ofttimes wanders in his sleep. I was dressed only in my nightshift, but no one seemed to notice or care. I saw her" (she pointed at the queen) "standing up on the dais, all proud and bold. Young, and about to seize all the riches and power of the realm.

"Lolethia—my eldest, my most beautiful, the one in whom I had such hopes—had been chosen to marry Lord Matwyck. Those riches, that power, should have been hers. *Should have been* my daughter's—and mine. I could have paid off all my husband's debts and provided for my younger children.

"There was a bow lying on the balcony floor. No one was paying any attention to me; I'd been an important figure in court before, but now they think me just an old widow woman. Long ago, my husband taught me to shoot. . . . We used to go hunting together. . . . One day I brought down a doe, all by myself. He was so proud of me; he often repeated the story at our dinner parties."

"Go on," prompted the judiciary.

"I picked up the bow." She said nothing more.

"Did you intend to kill the queen?"

The duchess faltered; she pulled her hand off the Stone and used both hands to sweep her hair back from her face and straighten her circlet. The sergeant next to her reinstated her contact with her right hand.

"Duchess Felethia, I must repeat, did you intend to kill the queen?"

"*Kill?* . . . I wanted the woman standing on the dais, the woman who was stealing everything from my family, to vanish, to go back to whatever hole she'd sprung from."

"Do you understand, Duchess, that Queen Cerúlia is the rightful heir to the Nargis Throne, and Lord Matwyck was a traitor and a usurper?"

"So they tell me," she answered in crisp tones, but then her voice faltered. "I am finding all of this somewhat hard to credit."

Marcot had heartily despised Lolethia. He had met her mother on numerous occasions, discerning in her no redeeming qualities. Still, he felt a pang of pity for her losses and confusion.

"Judiciary, what is the normal penalty for assaulting the Throne?" asked the queen.

"Your Majesty, the penalty is death. This is the most grievous of all crimes."

The room held its breath.

"No," the queen replied slowly. "Unless you discover that this lady was in other ways involved with the traitors, that doesn't fit her crime. She was half-drugged and out of her senses with grief. You've just taught us that intent matters."

"Your Majesty, the monarch always has the power to show mercy," commented the judiciary.

"Oh, please!" came a cry from the middle of the room. All heads turned in the direction of Lolethia's younger siblings. Marcot couldn't tell which one had shouted out, the girl or boy.

The queen nodded. "I would not orphan more of my subjects. And perhaps, because of my own responsibility for their misfortunes, I owe extra consideration to this family. I will discuss other possibilities with you, Judiciaries, at a later date."

This ended the official proceedings for the afternoon. The queen formally thanked Envoy Rakihah for the use of the Stone and the judiciaries for their careful gathering of the facts. She dismissed the onlookers; as the judiciaries packed up their papers and books she turned for a word first with her bodyguard and then with the Rorther ambassador.

Marcot lingered in hopes of speaking with her about his plans for freeing the political prisoners.

He was not the only person lingering for the opportunity of a private word. An intense young man holding a writing folio, with quills behind his ears (and a trickle of ink running down his neck), jumped from his seat and bowed very low.

"Your Majesty, a moment, I pray," said the inky man.

"You are?" asked the queen.

"My name is Alix of Cascada. I work for the *Cascada News*."

"What do you ask of me?"

"Actually, I wish to beg the envoy if I might place my hand on that Truth Stone."

The queen looked at Envoy Rakihah, who replied, "I am intrigued. We can allow this."

The sergeant carried the Truth Stone over to the young man. He glanced at his hand, vigorously wiped the ink on his shirt, and then placed his hand upon it.

"As I said, I am Alix of Cascada. I have heard rumors that all the people, not just the gentry, will choose the new steward. I intend to stand for this election. But given Weirandale's recent experience with stewards, I want all to know that I would serve the crown and the country most faithfully.

"I should probably tell you straightaway that I have been involved with the Parity Party and I would work for equal treatment under the law for all classes. I do not believe that the rich should profit from the labor of the poor." He spoke very quickly, as if the queen might object or the Truth Stone might be taken away from him at any moment.

The queen merely smiled at his eagerness. "Do you think you have a chance of winning the election? Do you know who else has declared his or her candidacy?"

"I believe I will be the first person to bid for the position. I intend to canvass everywhere."

"Well. I'm glad you had the opportunity to show us your heart. I wish you luck in the election, Master Alix. Whether you win or no, sometime after the current emergency, I'd like to hear of the Parity Party's concerns and the redresses you propose."

Then, appearing pressed for time, accompanied by her body-guard and her dogs, she swished out of the room before Marcot had a chance to consult with her.

Taking the responsibility on himself, that night—in consultation with Darzner, Captain Yanath, and Chamberlain Vilkit—Marcot organized several expeditions of soldiers, healers, and supplies. At dawn, he sent four of these convoys to the secret holding cells that lay in duchies removed from the capital.

The largest caravan he personally led to the location closest to the palace.

Perhaps originally a warehouse, the shabby building sat hidden in a dark alleyway. It was deserted. From what he and Captain Ya-nath could tell, the jailers had abandoned their posts when the queen seized power, and the prisoners had managed to break down the cell doors and had scattered into hiding. Marcot had soldiers search for any record books they could find in the noisome and grimy location. Then, his expedition moved on to the next-closest location Murgn had revealed.

Here too the jailers had fled, but the bars of the cells holding the prisoners had been too firmly set in concrete to fall to their desperate efforts. The prisoners had not been fed or watered in Waters knew how long. A third of their number had died from this deprivation, and the others were in terrible straits.

Marcot moved amongst the living, helping the healers give them water. But seeing how these unfortunates barely clung to life, he felt a desperate urgency to get to the other jails.

Leaving a contingent of healers, he split his followers into two teams. Captain Yanath guided one half to the prison in the western suburbs, while Marcot escorted his team to an address south of Cascada.

No one accosted his men as they broke down the locked street door. Inside the dark, cavernous building, which had once been a factory, Marcot lit a torch. His light revealed a few tables and chairs, debris and playing cards littering the floor.

"We're here! Help us!" came faint cries from the basement.

Hastily, the soldiers located the stairs that led to the cells. On that end of the building closest to the stairs, a horrible sight met their eyes: a room filled with a dozen dead women, each with her throat cut.

"What . . . ?" Marcot choked out.

One of his guards spit to the side. "Probably silencing them. They would have been used, you know, and the jailers wouldn't want them able to accuse or identify."

"Used?" asked Marcot, his mind moving slowly.

"Raped, sir," said the guard.

"Down here, help us!" came a cry, louder now.

"Prisoners are alive down here," said Marcot, tearing himself away from the ghastly sight and running down the stone corridor.

At the end of the sloping hall, they found a large cage holding on the order of forty male prisoners. Although a few could hardly hold up their heads, many stood on their feet, their thin arms straining toward their rescuers through the bars.

Marcot ran to the door, but of course it was locked and wouldn't move to his grasp.

"They left the keys hanging, over there," cried a chorus of prisoners, pointing. A guard threw them to Marcot, and he unlocked the cell door.

Soldiers and healers helped the men out of their cell. The floor was disgusting with urine, but Marcot soon figured out why these prisoners had survived: before absconding their posts, these jailers had rolled into the room a large barrel of water. Even with this precious gift, three bodies lay stretched out near the back of the cell.

Two men—one very old and one very young—sat together on a bench near the bodies instead of rushing toward freedom. The younger one looked familiar.

Marcot knelt down even with their faces. "Can I help you?" he asked.

"Lordling Marcot?" the young man asked.

"Yes?"

"I am Lemle, from Wyndton."

"Lemle! I feared something like this had happened to you! Oh, won't Percia be overjoyed I've found you! Here, let me help you stand up."

"Lordling, see to my friend first, would you?" the gaunt young man pleaded.

Marcot turned to the old man, whose thin hair stretched down his back. He didn't talk or react, but he still had a pulse in his neck and wrists.

"What happened to him?" Marcot asked Lemle.

"He was all right—he was himself—just a few minutes ago. But when we heard you calling out, he just went blank."

"He might have had a heart attack or a stroke," said Marcot. "I'll see that he's brought to the palace healers. Come now, Lemle, let me get *you* taken care of," said Marcot, putting his arm around the scrawny back and draping the boy's arm around his neck. "Let me take you away from this place!"

Marcot dispatched Lemle and his elderly cellmate to Finzle's care in the palace infirmary and then returned to Yanath's office. He heard from Yanath that at the western address keepers had still held their posts, so his Shield had the satisfaction of rescuing living captives, killing jailers, and taking prisoners. Two messengers from farther-away locations returned at nightfall, with the glad news that in one case, the local populace, once the news of the queen's return had reached them, stormed the jail, killed the captors, and rescued the incarcerated. In the other case the keepers had fled, but tossed the keys inside the cell. The prisons in the central duchies were too far away for any news to reach the palace for several days.

With nothing more he could do this evening, Marcot turned to personal matters. He sent a note to the queen and escorted Stahlia, Percia, and Tilim to the infirmary, where Finzle, who had finished inspecting and treating his patients, came out into the corridor to speak to them.

Finzle was discoursing at tedious length about all the effects of malnourishment on a human body when Mistress Stahlia literally pushed him to the side and stormed the door.

Lemle had been sleeping in a narrow cot, but he woke when the Wyndton family ambushed him.

"Hey," he said, half rising on his elbow. "Did I miss the wedding?"

"Hey, yourself," said Tilim. "That you did! And a bit of other excitement!"

"Oh, Lemle! To think of feasting ourselves while you were starving!" said Percia, bursting into tears.

Stahlia's response was more helpful: she spoon-fed the patient more of the gruel that sat by his bed while Percia held his hand and stroked his hair and cried over him. Tilim stood at the foot of the bed, patting Lemle's feet.

Knowing that Lemle was only one of the newly freed prisoners and that similar scenes might be taking place throughout Cascada, Marcot found the scene too painful to witness. He slipped out of the room and headed back in the direction of his own quarters, contemplating all the suffering his father had inflicted. As he turned a corner, Queen Cerúlia, voluminous silk skirts gathered up in both hands, ran into him—the collision sent him sprawling on the floor.

"Beg pardon," she shouted over her shoulder as she sprinted onward, dogs bounding around her. "Which door? For Water's sake! *Marcot!*"

"On your left—past the staircase—three more down!" he called to her.

The strange bodyguard helped him regain his feet. "Lord," he said with a slight incline of his head, "you have done her a service. You have gladdened her heart."

As Marcot continued on his way, he saw the old nursemaid, Nana, hustling down the corridor in the queen's wake; she cradled water in a golden bowl.

PART
TWO

Reign of Queen Cerúlia

SUMMER

14

Jutterdam

After the last petitioner left, Destra exhaled and rested her forehead on the bottom of her palms. Not for the first time she wished she had a magic wand to erase the crimes of the Oros and to ease the suffering and grievances of the Free Staters. Although the Jutters had named her "first minister," she rued the limits of her powers and resources.

"Let's get out of this stuffy room and go for a walk," suggested Quinith, who was serving as temporary treasurer, and who had sat by her side through the long afternoon in the Assembly Hall of Jutterdam, a dark wooden chamber.

The late-afternoon sea breeze made their hair and clothes ruffle. Destra breathed in the air, thankful that it no longer smelled of charred flesh. They ambled around the center of town with no particular destination. Summer Solstice Fest approached, and wreaths hung on many doorways.

"Much better than the decor here when we first entered the city," Quinith remarked, nodding his head at a particular cheerful array of dried flowers and greenery.

"Indeed," said Destra, thinking back on the burned bodies that the Oros had hung on every street corner.

It had taken only four days for the occupiers to board the Green Isles ships she had arranged and retreat from the city, but it was taking moons to bring the city back to life from its traumas. Commander Thalen had organized burial crews to remove those grisly sights while teams of searchers broke down every door, locating the wounded, malnourished, and terrified citizens hiding away. Destra had been arranging for the succor of Mìngyùn's people ever since.

The Spirit of Fate communicated with its Agent much less frequently these days. Destra assumed that this silence connoted satisfaction with her efforts to shape the peace.

As Quinith walked beside her at a steady pace, Destra realized that she could see small yet tangible signs of recovery in every direction. Shops had their doors open for evening custom, and the open-air market boasted more stalls and more customers than just a few weeks previously. Now that cold weather and spring rains had passed, reconstruction projects had begun; the two strollers constantly needed to detour around piles of bricks and lumber. Some roofers were working through the last moments of light, their hammers beating a loud but cheerful tattoo.

When they turned a corner and stumbled upon a group of children playing a game with a ball, they paused to watch the scene for a few moments.

"Did you know we would see this?" she asked Quinith.

"Not this precisely, but I saw other children playing during Planting Fest while you were busy entertaining the Jutter luminaries and listening to their complaints."

"They have a right to their sorrows and grievances," Destra answered mildly. "Jutterdam suffered. To the extent I listen to and acknowledge their claims, I can lessen their pain."

"I understand," said Quinith, "though I don't know how you manage it—*you* didn't cause the Occupation."

"No, but like every Iga citizen who refused to accept that the threat loomed and take active steps, I bear a portion of responsibility."

"These very Jutter merchants and gentry bear more. They, at least, were living here in the years before the Oros invaded and they didn't take the proper steps to protect themselves. *You* weren't even in the country."

"That's true, but I wasn't here to help my people because I was preoccupied with licking my personal wounds in the Green Isles." She lightly touched his shoulder and met Quinith's gaze. "Oh, reason not the apportionment of guilt, Quinith. Now that we have picked up the reins of government, the redress of suffering lies in our hands."

Half the children they watched broke into cheers. "What's happened?" Destra asked.

"The ball hit that gutter; I take it they are using that as a way of winning a point."

"I'm hungry," said Destra. "There's a tavern down by the wharf that doesn't overcook their fish. Shall we head in that direction?"

They walked on to the eatery, pointing out to one another more encouraging signs of progress, such as the number of ships berthed in the harbor that Jutters had so laboriously cleared of sunken boats.

Apparently others had also discovered the cookery skill of this establishment, because all the seats of Hulia's Tavern were filled and many other would-be diners gathered by the doorway.

"They are going to set up tables out here in the street," Quinith relayed to Destra after he pushed his way back through the press. "Is that all right with you?"

"Of course."

After a short wait, the proprietor fixed them up with a trestle table and stools, and—when she realized her guests included Minister Destra, the savior of the city—a carafe of their best wine.

They clinked glasses in the glow of a glass lantern. "May your Spirit bless you," said Quinith.

"As Fate disposes," Destra responded.

Destra had broken bread with Quinith many times before, but always in the company of Commander Thalen and others, such as the healers Cerf and Dwinny, or Bellishia of Yosta, who had assumed direct responsibility for the city's security and formed a city watch. But Thalen and the rest of the Raiders had departed yesterday for Sutterdam.

"We'll miss Commander Thalen," she said to Quinith. "*I'll* miss our chats." Many a time, Thalen had accepted her invitation for a cup of Green Isles tisane and they had stayed up late, debating the books that Tutor Granilton had assigned to each of them. This escape into theories and ideas had provided both a needed respite and practical guidance for their day-to-day decisions.

"It was time for him to go," Quinith commented. "He was restless here because he wasn't as needed anymore."

Destra took another sip of her wine and pulled on the long plait that fell over her right shoulder. "I would have gladly shrugged more of the responsibility for administration on his shoulders."

"He hasn't your patience or your knack with empathy or diplomacy," said Quinith. "He would just order folks to do things his way. And if they asked why, he would reel off a passage from a book."

"Perhaps so. I'm very grateful you agreed to remain, Quinith. I'll be leaning on you quite shamelessly." She looked at the young man across the table from her, conscious of actually studying him for the first time. His gray eyes had tiny flecks of a warmer, hazel color. His lined face made it hard to tell his age, which she guessed at ten to fifteen years younger than herself, but he had an easy way with people and a pronounced aptitude for organization and management.

"I have nowhere else to go," Quinith said, with a self-deprecating smile and an openhanded gesture. "Besides, being needed, feeling competent at one's work, is a great joy. I was never a soldier, but these tasks I can handle."

"Building a peace is just as hard and in many ways more admirable than fighting. It takes patience and tact. But weren't you tempted to follow your fellow Raiders?"

"A little, but I don't really belong with that group."

"Even though you've known Commander Thalen the longest, I heard?" Destra took another sip of wine.

"Aye, I knew him at the Scoláiríum."

"Was he Commander Thalen then? Did he carry the same aura of command and authority?"

"No." Quinith smiled and shook his head at the memory. "When he first came he was gawky and shy. Somewhat coltish. He didn't become 'the Commander' until the war started. He changed after the Rout, and after his year in Oromondo I hardly recognized him."

The server plunked steaming trenchers of crab poached in wine in front of them.

"To be strictly honest"—Quinith waved his hand over his food, letting it cool—"that's another reason why I didn't travel on with the Raiders. I haven't told this to another soul, but when you're with Thalen, it's rather like the light of every room pools around him. Originally, I planned on being a singer; I've always enjoyed the warmth of a crowd's attention. But with the commander in a group, even when he's silent and shirking attention, everyone waits to hear him speak."

"You're so right," Destra agreed. "Whether he wants it or not, the Spirits have set him apart. It's a burden for him, and in some ways for everyone around him."

They addressed their food with appetite. Destra concentrated on savoring both the flavors and the waves of conversation and laughter swirling around their table, finding the sound of happy voices a welcome balm. As the sky darkened, Hulia set up outdoor lanterns on poles. The evening air grew crisper and the wind off the harbor carried a bite even now in midsummer. Destra shivered because her ministerial "uniform"—a dark skirt and a fitted white jacket with a bit of gold braid on the sleeves and yoke—was not particularly warm. Quinith took off his olive-colored coat and draped it about her shoulders.

"Warmer?"

"Thank you." She was glad of Quinith's coat, which, she realized, carried an odor of maleness. Quinith poured her another glass of wine.

"I heard a tale, Quinith, about you losing your fiancée," Destra remarked with deliberate offhandedness. "I believe we have that in common. Would you care to talk about it? Of course, if the subject is too painful . . . I don't mean to cause you any distress."

"I haven't spoken about it to anyone in depth. But it doesn't feel as raw anymore." Quinith told Destra the whole story of his relationship with Gustie and her death. Sipping her wine, Destra listened intently, and then, to repay his openness, she told him about Graville's murder and her years of mourning.

At the end of these confidences, Quinith asked, "Does one heal from such experiences? How does one go on to have a full life?"

"If by a full life you mean love, marriage, or children, I'm the wrong person to ask," said Destra. "I squandered my youth *nursing* and *savoring* my grief and fury. Only now, as an old woman, have I found the strength and reasons to move on."

"'Old woman'—I wouldn't say that! I would say you've merely reached your full bloom."

"What gallantry!" Destra laughed, wondering if her young companion was just being courteous or whether flirtation lay under his words.

Glancing around, Destra realized that the noise and crowd had thinned; most of the other patrons had left, and the tavern staff were bringing inside the tables they had set up out-of-doors.

"We must go back to our lodgings," Destra said. "The tavern people tire and long for their beds. We have a full day of meetings tomorrow, including the discussion of tariffs and tithing we've been putting off with the merchant guild."

"Oh, joy," Quinith remarked sardonically, making Destra grin.

As they started to stroll back to their inn, Quinith said, "The streets are so dark now; won't you take my arm?"

"I'd be happy to," said Destra, as she threaded her arm through his, and they walked back through the recovering city, chatting about how to convince the guild tomorrow—almost as if they were a cozy couple.

15

Riverine

Despite himself, Matwyck listened for General Yurgn's boots clicking down the hallway every morning. Yurgn came to visit his guest once a day like clockwork. The rest of the time the former Lord Regent had to make do with only the intermittent attendance of a manservant named Cosmas, an evil-eyed scamp who took advantage of his patient's powerlessness, often running off for hours, leaving him abandoned and prey to varied discomforts.

Thus, Matwyck planned conversational gambits to make the general tarry. Usually they deliberated about what they would do once one of their schemes to eliminate the inexperienced queen succeeded. Discussing how they would gather their forces, whom they would discipline, whom they would forgive (if they showed the right contrition) held great appeal. But as the weeks progressed, these plots had been thoroughly chewed over and had lost most of their savor.

So in recent visits Matwyck had tried to steer his host to more personal issues, such as confidences about his family. Yurgn fumed about his nephew Murgn's capture and almost busted a blood vessel when tidings arrived about the captain spilling his guts at the questioning. He assured Matwyck that Yurgenia, Clovadorska, and Burgn had held steadfast. But he didn't warm to the topic of discussing his children or grandchildren like many people did.

Actually, this indifference did not surprise Matwyck, because as the years had trickled by he had recognized that the only things the general truly cared about were money and a long life. Inside of his coconspirator was an insatiable hole that could never be filled. Yurgn was a miser, hoarding his gold as he hoarded his days.

"How are you feeling today?" asked Yurgn, as he always did, a question that set Matwyck's teeth on edge. *How do you think I feel,* he wanted to shout, *with a shattered pelvis, a gouge straight through my right thigh, pissing blood, and anchored to this bed in your lesser guest wing?*

Instead, Matwyck answered with a forced smile. "I'll dance on your grave yet, you old bastard, if not by Solstice Fest, at least by Harvest Fest."

The general grinned as he settled into the sole chair in the underused room where spiderwebs gathered in the ceiling corners. "Not much chance of that. You forget I've seen injuries in my day. Even if your bones knit, that leg will never be strong enough for a jig."

"You're probably right." Matwyck knew that arguing would hasten his visitor's departure. "Is there any news?"

"Dispatches came from my people in Cascada." The general grunted. "Word is that they sent that Stone back to Rortherrod."

"Well, that's good. It will keep them from untangling the rest of your network."

Yurgn nodded assent. "And I got a foolish letter from Latlie."

"What does that ancient cow want?" said Matwyck, trying to shift his body so he sat up a little straighter.

"Ancient?" Yurgn replied, with a hint of surprise. "She's ten years younger than I am."

"But she doesn't wear her years anywhere near as well."

"No," agreed Yurgn. "I've sat beside her at meals; she eats too much custard. So much cream puts a strain on the body."

"While you've stayed as trim as any military man," Matwyck commented, "which is why you'll dance on *her* grave."

The general proudly patted his muscular belly, enjoying the hollow sound the slap made enough to do it again.

The erstwhile Lord Regent had to prod him back on the subject. "What did she say in the letter?"

"Oh. She wants a loan. Claims that her own funds are out of reach for the nonce and she needs money to escape with all her family and retainers to the Free States or the Green Isles."

"And you will respond . . . ?"

"I shan't respond at all! I don't have time for idle correspondence. Let Latlie see to her own. I've already paid out a fortune these last moons, what with my agents angling for double prices, and what with healer's fees and paying off the crew who brought you. . . ."

Matwyck caught the general's gaze. "I know you shelter me here out of military virtue—leave no comrade behind on the field and so on—but you have my word of honor that you will be repaid three-fold."

Actually the night the cart brought me, he took me in with bad grace, and then only because he feared that if I were captured and talked, the full extent of his involvement would be revealed.

Yurgn had heard this promise before, so he just grunted. He started to clutch the chair arms, in preparation for rising.

Matwyck rushed to say, "What do you think her next move will be?"

The general understood they were no longer talking about Latlie. "She will consolidate her hold on the city and the harbor, which do offer certain strategic advantages."

"Such as popular support." Matwyck tapped his fingers together as if deeply considering the general's military acumen.

"The little people can be such a pain in the arse! Properly

whipped up, you can make a mob," his confederate added, as if this was a rare pearl of wisdom. "But I purposely chose this manse because it lies between the Catamount Cavalry barracks and the Ice Pikemen stockade. The officers are bought and paid for. I have fed those troops, led those troops, and personally trained them. They know who butters their bread.

"What's that little queen going to do—challenge five hundred cavalry and one thousand pikemen and archers with the palace guards, a crowd of rabble, and flocks of geese? Ba!" He swatted away the notion.

Matwyck rubbed his beard stubble, annoyed that Cosmas never shaved him properly. "She wants us both, Yurgn. Does she know I'm here?"

"How do I know what she knows?" his visitor said.

Matwyck tapped his fingers together thoughtfully.

"If I were you, I'd make sure of your neighboring officers."

"Offer *more*?" Yurgn gripped the chair's arms.

"Attention or flattery often works as well as funds," answered Matwyck. "You know that. Why don't you have them over for dinner? You used to host such lavish feasts, storied parties."

"That was before the price of beef went up fourfold!" said Yurgn.

"Come, come," said Matwyck. "Doesn't red meat nourish the blood? Wouldn't it be good for your health?"

"Well, that's not really a bad notion," the general admitted. "Men can be frail. Sometimes junior officers need a bit of fortifying, a sense that their superior is watching them."

"Just so."

"Well"—he levered himself off the chair with an effortlessness that Matwyck now envied—"I must be off; if I'm going to host a party like that, I'll want to talk to my daughter about preparations." The general looked around the sickroom vaguely, adding his routine farewell, "You have everything you need, I take it."

"Yes, yes, I do, thanks to your generosity."

As the general left, Matwyck leaned back against his bolster. He found it hard to judge whether he was healing or weakening. The sadistic prick of a military healer had cauterized the arrow wound all the way through and it hadn't festered, but bed confinement did nothing to reknit the mangled muscles. Yet he couldn't move about because of his fractures; he was forbidden even to stand up lest he disrupt the bones. And if his innards hadn't totally ruptured, they still leaked blood. Some days he thought the bleeding had stopped, and the next day the white chamber pot would again fill with red.

And the pain. Each day Matwyck resolved to wait until after his early supper to ask Cosmas for milk of the poppy. That meant he still had tiresome hours to get through.

He took out the cache of broadsheets he kept hidden under his pillow. Yurgn forbade these on his grounds probably because he didn't want his family or retainers to know what had been revealed as the new administration started poking around, going through the ledgers, picking up rocks that were better left undisturbed. Matwyck had had to bribe the illiterate laundress with his pinky ring to fetch them, and he had to bribe Cosmas into silence about his forbidden trove by giving the man his own daily portion of wine. Yet no matter how many times Matwyck reread the *Cascada News,* the crumpled and smudged sheets never fully answered his questions.

That country girl! He'd have had her, if he hadn't been distracted by Lolethia's murder. Not the murder itself so much, but the placement of the body in Burgn's chamber had provided just the right diversion. Sly little fox. Cressa, so naive, would never have had those wiles.

If only I'd carried through with arresting her the night of the wedding. My instinct was right. If only. If only.

He shoved the broadsheets back and picked at lint on his coverlet. He rubbed again at the patch of stubble on his jawbone, eager to upbraid the careless servant, suddenly desperate to be rid of the aggravating scruff.

He closed his eyes and tried to think—if he could have anyone's

THE CERULEAN QUEEN   141

company in his sickroom to make the time go faster, whom would he want? Not Marcot; he had soured on the boy. Not Lolethia; she would just flirt and pout. Not Tirinella. Not the mother he barely remembered.

Eyevie. He recalled that whenever one of his siblings was poorly, his older sister would sit by the bed and read to them. She would act out the voices of the characters in such a creative way that they'd be distracted from their illness. He'd always meant to find her and favor her with his acknowledgment and riches. It would be such a balm to have a loving family member with him now.

I wonder if I could get Yurgn to smuggle her in here. I wonder if she'd cry a little, seeing how I suffer. Her hands would be soft as she shaved me perfectly, and she would move all the pillows around without my having to cajole. She would anticipate all my needs and add little touches to show her concern and devotion.

Leaving the guest wing, which lay in the oldest section of the stone edifice, the general consulted with Yurgenia, the daughter who ran his household since his wife's death, about a fancy dinner. He'd decided to follow Matwyck's suggestion. Matwyck was always a clever shopkeeper—very clever—even if he was common to his balls.

As he marched an inspection circuit around his bailey, Yurgn relished his security here; he'd chosen to restore this ancient keep, which long ago had been a ducal seat, because of its high and thick stone walls and its single gateway. Comfort and grandeur might be sorely lacking, but it had been designed for defense. Over many years he had strengthened this fortress until it was nearly impregnable.

The manse's well was deep, and his storerooms bulged with food enough to survive a long siege. His treasure room, where he passed many a pleasant hour rearranging and polishing, held coin, jewels, and rarities such as expensive swords and bolts of silk brocade. If truly necessary, more bribes could be paid.

And if the physical defenses should show signs of weakening, he had a trump card. Yurgn planned to offer the new queen a trade: he would deliver her the Lord Regent, to do with as she would, if she would leave his manse in peace.

"Catreena died; Cressa died; Cerúlia will die. Sooner, rather than later," he said to the sky. "I outlived them all. *I* will dance on *her* grave."

16

Travels in the Free States

When their grim work in Jutterdam was complete, Thalen asked his followers—Kambey (the weapons master), Cerf (the healer), Fedak (the cavalryman), Kran (the swordsman), Wareth (the scout), Jothile (the traumatized), Dalogun (the young archer), and Tristo (his adjutant)—if they wanted to disband and return to their families or hometowns. To a man the Raiders protested that they either had no family left or carried no attachment to their life *before*; they preferred to stay together, and they wished to follow him, wherever he chose to settle.

Thalen smiled at his mental image of himself as a mother duck, followed by a string of grim and scarred ducklings. But relief washed away his irony, because he knew he would be just as unmoored without his friends nearby as they would feel without him. Like the smaller moon, he was held in place by the bigger moon; without the Raiders, he would just wobble off into the depths of black space. A few of the Raiders were easier company than others, but even Kran's hot temper or Jothile's clinginess helped Thalen cart around the burden of so many deaths.

When they left Jutterdam, he led the Raiders on a meandering route. First, they paid a condolence call on Gustie's family in Weaverton. Thalen couldn't determine if her relatives were naturally cold, ashamed of Gustie, or frightened of the Raiders, but the visit was uncomfortable and they did not linger. They rode on instead to the twins' home in Jígat, where they were more warmly received and Dalogun grieved fully and with honor. Afterward, the Raiders detoured to the gristmill Jothile's sister ran, wondering if reconnecting with family would help Jothile with his nervous disorder, but they found that, if anything, their comrade's shakes and startles became worse.

Ultimately, Thalen recognized he could no longer delay his visit to Sutterdam, so they turned their horses in the direction of Lantern Lane. They didn't hurry, making this leg of their journey last more than a week.

"At long last!" Norling scolded him when she met him at the doorway.

"Where are Hake and Pater?" he asked when he broke from his aunt's hug.

"They're not here. They're at the factory!"

She turned to the men waiting politely in the street. "You're friends of Thalen's, I assume? I met some of you before? Come in, come in and make yourselves at home."

Norling poured them all glasses of buttermilk and relayed that Hake had reopened Sutterdam Pottery, to the delight of the former workers who wanted their positions back and the satisfaction of customers who needed containers to replace everything that had been smashed by the Oros.

"You should have seen your father when we first put him at his wheel! It was like he'd needed his old occupation. Immediately he starts kicking and humming, and a fellow puts a hunk of clay in the center, and damned if he can't use his bad hand to shape it. He even paints the oddments he makes. I'll show you."

Norling fetched a set of four goblets to show the Raiders. They were not perfectly symmetrical, and each one had been painted in a different jagged pattern, though they all shared the same color scheme.

The Raiders politely passed them around. "I like them more than normal goblets," Cerf commented. "They have a kind of fierceness to them." Thalen felt a surge of gratitude toward the healer, who often did not show much sensitivity.

"And how are you, Teta?" Thalen asked.

"Well, the nights are long—nobody sleeps well in this house."

Thalen noted the lines of deep weariness in his aunt's face. Carefully arranging the odd goblets in a row, he wondered whether solitary and interminable care for two disabled patients was more heroic than anything Raiders had ever done on the battlefield.

"We won't add to your burdens, Teta Norling. We're too many to fit here; we'll take rooms at the Three Coins."

"You haven't come home to stay, then?" she asked, her face already mastering her disappointment.

"No. But a longer visit, this time."

Thalen managed to linger in Sutterdam for a week. While he spent time with his family, the Raiders alternated between nights carousing at taverns and daytimes taking care of neglected maintenance at Lantern Lane. They brushed out the chimney and repointed its masonry; they reattached broken shutters and then built ramps for Hake's chair. When Norling chided them about all the extra dirt they spread about the house, Thalen hired a strong fourteen-summers girl, Fordana, to help with the cleaning. She turned out to be an eager young woman who needed the wages and showed no pique at Norling's exacting instructions. To Thalen's great relief, Norling started musing aloud about having her sleep in, to help her with Hake and Hartling at night.

Spending time with his father, aunt, and brother brought Thalen little joy because they all were so altered from the people he had known before the war. Hake had thrown himself into the business with a manic energy that had much to do with restoring the family's finances but also, transparently, with restoring his own feelings of competence. Try as he might, Thalen could not work up any genuine interest in kiln temperatures or the number of commissions from Yosta and Jutterdam.

He was happy to perform a small commission for his brother: Hake asked Thalen to check on the candle shop that once belonged to Pallia, the girl he had kept company with before the war. Thalen had to report that it had been burned and none of the neighbors had any news about the family.

And despite—or maybe because of—the closeness he had shared with Norling when he was a boy, Thalen could not lay on his aunt's slumped shoulders any of his war experiences or his sorrows.

The only moment of comfort that week came, unexpectedly, from his father, one morning as Thalen assisted in pulling on Hartling's boots. His father rested his good hand on his son's upper arm and said with one of his unpredictable moments of clarity, "You've grown so strong, Middle. Your mother would be so proud."

Sutterdam could no longer be his home. He saw Mater in Lantern Lane and at the Pottery; he heard Harthen's laughter in the pub room of the Three Coins. When he traversed the city he ran into faded phantoms of himself as a carefree and callow boy on every bridge.

So soon enough he set off, followed by his remaining Raiders, as he had long dreamed of doing, for the Scoláiríum in Latham.

While they followed the High Road the riders saw signs of the recent Occupation, such as fields untilled because their owners had died or fled and farmhouses overflowing with children collected from several disrupted families. They passed empty barns, ransacked houses, and bridges with broken spans.

When they reached Trout's Landing, they found that the old ferryboat was a casualty of war. Only charred timbers broke the surface of the lake like a giant's rotted teeth. To get to Latham they would have to detour far around Clear Lake on woodland paths.

Once riding the thin forest trail, they put the signs of war behind them. Sunlight and birdsong filtered through the greenery of summer trees, so they rode single file, joshing and chatting, without looking over their shoulders or fearing attack—at least most of the time.

Thalen fell into a muse. He wondered if the Scoláiríum would also be filled with ghosts—if he would see Gustie or Granilton around every corner. But he anticipated it would also be filled with books; more than anything he wanted to read, because only in a book could he escape from his own dark thoughts. He'd read anything, but he was especially keen to get his hands on all the books about Alpetar.

Would the Scoláiríum rue his bringing in so many mouths to feed? But eight (fairly) hale men, which were now so rare in the Free States, could help with physical work. Thalen also had a vague idea that someday Kambey might teach weaponry at the Scoláiríum. (Never again should students neglect this side of their education.) And perhaps Cerf could open a clinic for the readers and townsfolk who lived nearby, or offer classes in healing.

Around midday Wareth scouted ahead for a likely place to halt. He came back with news of a small opening to the right of the path, edging Clear Lake.

They dismounted. It still felt so strange to drink straight from a lake without worrying about it being polluted and to allow their horses to take their fill. Tristo and Kran started a contest of skipping rocks over the water's surface. Wareth challenged Kran and bested his throw. The champion of them all, however, turned out to be Fedak, whose rock touched down six times before sinking.

Though the water was cold, most of the Raiders ended up bathing, splashing and dunking one another like children, their bodies crisscrossed with white, red, and black scars against their varied shades of brown. Only Thalen and Cerf declined, sitting like grumpy old-timers, warming their aged bones in the sun.

Refreshed, the Raiders dressed again and mounted up. A league onward they came to a larger sandy beach alongside the lake.

"I should have scouted farther," said Wareth. "Look how pretty this is."

"This is quite a spot. Almost as if people cleared it and dressed it. See those stones there? Don't they look like benches?" said Kambey.

Wareth and Thalen caught one another's eyes and simultaneously turned to face in the opposite direction. Silently, Wareth's index finger traced the path: although the woods had reclaimed its territory, the contours of a broad roadway remained visible, climbing the rise through gentle switchbacks.

"Let's investigate," Thalen said, clucking his horse onto the roadway, and the others followed, the horses' hooves striking against ancient, moss-covered cobblestones. Overhanging branches created the effect of passing through a green tunnel out of the present day and into some ancient past. Thalen fancied he could almost picture carriages carrying laughing bathers with midmeal baskets down to the lake.

In less than an hour of gentle climbing they came out on the crest of a hill in a large clearing. A magnificent structure, demolished and then further destroyed by countless years of weathering, lay in heaps of gigantic stones, scattered as if someone had broken a shelf of pottery.

"What is this?" asked Dalogun.

"This," said Thalen, gesturing all around, "is all that remains of the Castle of the Kings. Iga's Castle. Sacked and burned in the Bloody Revolution, three centuries ago."

Kran whistled. "Huge. Think of the work to build it! How did they get these marble blocks up here? Hundreds, thousands of workers?"

"The kings of Iga could command such a workforce. But they also had the power of Transformation, remember?" Thalen said.

"For all we know, they built a toy castle out of clay, mumbled magic words, and turned it into a real castle."

Kran said, "Then think of the work the rebels had to tear it down! *They* had no Powers."

"Just the power of hatred and anger," said Cerf. "Which we've learned is pretty fuckin' strong."

Wareth had been poking around. "This would be a good place to spend the night, 'Mander, if you like it. There's shelter. And a magnificent view." He gestured back over Clear Lake, whose whole expanse rippled in the glow of the afternoon.

Thalen agreed, and they set up camp in a circular hollow, now covered with soft moss, which might once have been the bottom of a turret.

While the Raiders tended to the horses and started a cook fire, Thalen neglected his share of the chores and went to wander among the tumbled rocks, trying to determine the outline of the original castle. The marble endured, but wind, rain, and vegetation had left it pockmarked and dull. Sunset found him wondering how many people had died in taking this objective, and thinking about Cerf's insight into the power of fury and the transience of men's ambition.

He meandered on. On the far side of the castle, down a path that led away from the main building, he came across an awesome sight: nine giant rectangular stones set in a circle. These were untouched by the rebels and barely marked by the passage of time. They stood tall—silent and judging.

From his evening discussions with Destra, Thalen realized that he had stumbled upon an ancient Circle of Mìngyùn. There was a more modest Circle in Jutterdam—the Oros had hung bodies from the tallest stones and built a fire in the middle, so now everyone walked blocks out of their way to avoid the sight. Thalen had read that others had been placed in diverse regions of the Free States, but this must be the biggest and best preserved. He almost called the rest of the Raiders to share his discovery, but then he decided to spare them. The stones radiated an unnerving sense of appraisal. A person who submitted himself to a Circle of Mìngyùn opened his thoughts, intentions, actions and inactions, and their consequences to the Spirit for weighing.

With steady steps he walked into the middle of the Circle, took his hat in his hands, and knelt. He lost track of time as he laid bare his soul. Master and Apprentice Moon shone on the timeless stones and his human shoulders.

The next day, high scattered clouds kept interrupting the sunshine, so they rode from brightness into shade every few paces. After many hours, Latham appeared in the distance. Thalen pulled his hair back into his leather and brushed the woodland spider threads and leaf litter off his sleeves. As the Raiders traversed the town they could see that this fairly remote area had been spared obvious sacking; most of the buildings and farms remained intact. People hoeing their vegetables in their kitchen gardens looked up at the troop of mounted men with surprise and not a little trepidation.

The front gates of the Scoláiríum stood open and unmanned. Thalen led his squad right through up to Scholars' House. At the sound of their hoofbeats, Rector Meakey came dashing out the front doors. She wore a gown of yellow-and-red stripes, and a bright yellow kerchief on which she'd affixed several seashells held back her dark ringlets. She shaded her eyes to try to see the men's faces; then her hands flew over her mouth.

Thalen reined in.

"Rector," he said, "you are a cheering sight. I can't remember when I've seen anyone look so—so bright and colorful."

Rector Meakey replied, "Part of my job is to keep spirits up. Thalen, how are you?"

"That's a complicated question," he answered as he dismounted.

"The short answer would be hale in body and troubled in mind. How have the tutors fared?"

"You've heard about Granilton?" she asked. When Thalen nodded, a tightness in her face relaxed. "The rest of us are well enough. Two tutors who had left have even returned to us in recent weeks. I've hired a new tutor for Literary Arts, and I've had six letters about students returning or coming to take entrance exams! We might start up again before the end of summer."

"Rector, I do not ride alone," Thalen said. "May I introduce my companions?"

"They look fierce enough to be Thalen's Raiders," she said, with wide eyes and a touch of girlish flirtation.

"Indeed. It was these and others who did all the daring deeds." Thalen introduced his followers, who tipped their hats. Meakey welcomed them warmly for themselves and as Thalen's colleagues.

The daylight began waning. Thalen pointed the way to the stables, the dormitory, and the kitchens, and the men scattered to get settled.

Meakey said, "Come into my chambers, Thalen. I will send Hyllidore for tisane—or hard liquor if you prefer, now that you're a grown fighting man—and we will have a good long chat. I have *sooo* many questions."

Just then Tutor Irinia, the master with whom he had originally studied Earth and Water, with her pinned-up hair askew (as always) but much more gaunt, came flying around the corner of Scholars' House and skidded to a stop.

"It's true," she said, at the sight of Thalen.

"Yes, Tutor," said Thalen. "Here I am."

"Welcome home, my dear, dear boy," said Irinia as she stepped forward to embrace him. "Welcome home."

And in her bony hug, Thalen knew a sense of homecoming that had eluded him since they had landed in the Free States.

17

Cascada

A moon after Cerúlia's Dedication, the cautious healer declared that her arrow wound had knit well enough for her to go riding. But by then the early summer rains had arrived, so the outing was further delayed.

As she strode to the stables this morning, accompanied only by Ciellō and the dogs, she realized how much she needed this break from the pressures of her new life. She spent her days either conferring with others or making decisions on her own. But her decisions were, at best, stabs in a fog at invisible targets.

Money was the prerequisite for every action, but no one could offer a tally of how much funds remained in the treasury, because Matwyck had solidified his power with a web of bewilderingly intricate, financial cross-obligations that were now completely opaque due to Prigent's destroying the most important ledgers. Naven set a team of Cascada's best calculators to work on untangling the realm's finances.

As for the chief plotters, Lord Matwyck and General Yurgn, responding to her plea for assistance in the Courtyard of the Star, villagers had sent the palace news that these two were barricaded within Yurgn's estate, out of reach of her justice. Although Cerúlia chafed at the admonitions, all who counseled her insisted that she prove herself adept at governing before she challenged them directly.

And twenty times a day, someone—usually Darzner, Marcot, a judiciary, or Vilkit—needed to consult with her about a problem or get her permission before he or she took a certain action. In many ways, shaking off the fake timidity she had been forced to assume for so many years came as a relief, but she found that always being constantly deferred to brought its own burdens of responsibility.

When the new queen wasn't dealing with matters of state, she was besieged by emotional tumult. Percia nursed her sense of betrayal that her sister had never confided in her. Meanwhile, to set her own heart at rest, Stahlia needed to piece together, in exacting detail, the chronology that had led to Wilim's suicide. And Lemle and Master Ryton deserved all the time and comfort Cerúlia could spare as they haltingly recovered from captivity.

(One rainy afternoon, she had felt so besieged that she'd run away to the stables and hid in Smoke's stall for hours. They didn't talk; she had patted him and crooned to him and he had smelled her all over, lipped at the edges of her sleeves and collar, and huffed into her neck. She returned to her duties refreshed and defiant about the state of her gown.)

On the way to the stables now Cerúlia and Cielló passed Gunnit and Tilim, who were absorbed in a game involving horseshoes. After their initial wariness, the boys had become fast friends. Usually, they served as her personal pages, streaking through the palace shouting, "Make way for the queen's messenger!" just to cause a ruckus, but she had sent them away this morning for their own holiday. They grinned at her as she approached, but with the insouciance of children and old friends, neither bothered to bow.

"Gunnit, you didn't change your mind overnight?" she paused to ask.

"No, Your Majesty," the boy said. "It's not my druthers 'cause I'm happy here, but my job is done. I'm needed elsewhere now. Gardener once told me that it'll be my lot constantly to roam about, kind of like the Sun."

"I can't argue with Gardener's wisdom," Cerúlia sighed. "Well, your passage has been bought on a ship that sails tomorrow morning. Nana is arranging a little farewell fete, so I'll see you later." What gift could she possibly give the Alpetar boy that would reward him for the shouts that had saved her life?

"Boys," she called over her shoulder, "make Cici stay with you. She can't keep up with horses."

"Have a great ride," Tilim called.

Hiccuth had Smoke saddled for her and Nightmist ready for Ciellō.

Cerúlia rushed to their heads and stroked their glossy black skin; they stretched their long necks down to her level and lipped her riding hat.

You remember me; do you remember my mother, Queen Cressa?

One remembers her, answered Nightmist.

What do you recall?

The aging mare sent her a jumble of sensory impressions about how lightly Cressa had perched on her back; the way she smelled; the sound of her voice when she said, "Good girl"; and a confused image about a fight on a sandy beach.

The queen rubbed the broad bone up from the horses' noses. *I must make more time to talk to Nana and Yanath, and I must visit with Sewel. If I am to know who I am, I need to know more about my parents as people and rulers. And if I am going to succeed as queen, I need to know why she failed.*

Ciellō interrupted her thoughts. "Damselle, may I assist you into a saddle?"

She nodded. Ciellō knitted his hands and gave her calf enough of a boost that she could grab the saddle pommel and throw her other leg over. The movement did not reawaken the pain in her arm, so she exhaled with relief.

On top of Smoke she breathed more easily and felt more comfortable than she had in moons. This was *her* horse—even if from years ago—not Pillow. Hiccuth had warned her that the gelding had returned from the Green Isles with a bitter temperament, but he showed none of this to Cerúlia. His gait moved through her like a half-forgotten tune, and he anticipated the direction she wished to go before she even put any pressure on him, as if he were aching to please. She led the way, exploring the grounds, wondering at groupings of trees or shrubs that whispered of long-ago playtimes, even if the greenery now stretched higher. Her scent hounds and deerhounds ricocheted around the two horses, sniffing and peeing everywhere, and their happiness at their freedom was contagious.

She spent too much time indoors, in meetings and reading reports. She needed to get outside more: this sparkling summer morning welcomed and quieted her.

One of Ciellō's most excellent qualities was that he knew when to be silent. He merely scanned the surroundings with watchful eyes.

She laughed at his protective posture. "Ciellō, if assassins lurked in the honeysuckle, the dogs would have sniffed them out. I think you've also earned a few moments of relaxation."

"Habits, damselle, keep one alive," he replied, but he grinned back.

She led the horses around a stand of trees. "Ciellō, why do *you* stay with me? I am as safe now as I probably ever will be."

"I will not leave your watch."

"Why?"

"I do many things in my life, damselle." Ciellō sighed. "At the time, I feel they were right. Now, many I regret. Some of the men I have killed perchance they be better men than me. With my regrets, I stew and drink. Sad music I play. Then a young woman walks into a tavern shabby. She is smart; she is strong-willed; she is beautiful.

Peril hangs over her like—like a parasol. And I realize: if I can keep this body alive I will make up for all those deaths. Ghibli may look on me again with favor."

Cerúlia rode next to him in silence as they climbed a low hill. The dogs joyously chased squirrels; the rodents ran up trees and scolded, *Your Majesty! How canst thou allow this? Control thy canines!*

Her bodyguard spoke again. "Also, I think, damselle is the most solitary person I have ever met. If I leave her, her cup would overspill with loneliness."

Cerúlia glanced up at him in surprise. "True, I had only a few friends in Salubriton, and on the ship I had only you and Whaki, but now I am surrounded."

"You are surrounded by people who love you, but you no talk to them."

"What? I spend hours talking, trying to explain why I did what I did, said what I said."

Ciellō snorted. "I do not try to overhear, but I stand very close to you. Never do you tell them what is in your heart. You do not give confidences."

"That's not fair, Ciellō! Just because I couldn't tell anyone my true identity . . . Drought damn it, I can't handle another person angry at me for the disguises that kept me alive!"

"Oh, I am no angry about 'Damselle Phénix.' From the moment I see her eyes, her dagger, *I* am no fooled by her. Not I, to need the blue hair or shiny necklace. But now the Big Secret be out, and you still keep secrets. You talk only to animals."

Cerúlia's protest didn't make it past her lips. In all her years of exile, Ciellō was one of the only people who had seen through her disguise. Gardener and Healer had wielded Magic, but Ciellō had recognized her without it. He understood her better than others, so she'd be wise to respect his insights.

Has my life of secrecy cut me off from everyone? Has my Talent really cut me off from people?

"Habits, Ciellō. Habits keep one alive," she quipped, but he didn't smile back at her.

Their path took them around a stand of weeping willows, each with a curtain of leaves that trembled in the bit of a breeze. Had she played a hiding game with her real father here?

Thou art tense, Your Majesty, but no scents linger that should nay be here, sent Vaki, the hound. *All is well.*

"Well, what would you have me confide?" she asked Ciellō.

Ciellō paused, as if to make the most of this opportunity. When he spoke, his voice was solemn. "Your thoughts. Your feelings. How you feel to be queen?"

"Terrified. I am so afraid of making mistakes."

"You will make mistakes. Then you will fix them," he said. "Unless you kill people. *That* cannot be fixed."

"But I will embarrass myself. Everyone will say, 'She doesn't know the right way to address an architect or promote an officer.'"

"Who will say such things?" he asked. "The court people who allowed a usurper his rump to set on your throne?" Ciellō spit to the side in contempt. "Foolishness!"

"Matwyck didn't actually sit on the throne, but I take your meaning—that these are hardly people whose judgment should concern me."

"Also," he added, "if the thing is important, you will learn. It has only been weeks that you wear the pretty necklace. Being queen is like learning the dagger. One practices and then one practices more."

Cerúlia felt a lightness bubble in her chest. They crossed a small stream and paused to let the horses and dogs drink. Whaki and Vaki strode into the water, drinking by biting at the hurrying liquid, but Mimi, the deerhound, didn't like getting her feet wet; she found the place where the bank was driest, and then she leapt to the opposite bank.

Now that Cerúlia had begun disclosing her worries, she didn't want to stop. "Ciellō, how will I know whether people truly care for me, or whether they are drawn to the power of the throne? Vilkit flatters shamelessly, but he's only one end of the spectrum. *Everyone* flatters me, if only by bowing and scraping." She paused, aware of the contradiction: "Yet, if they don't, I wonder if they disrespect me."

"Damselle," Ciellō spoke through gritted teeth.

Cerúlia looked him in the eye and yanked back on Smoke's reins. "And if you get angry with me, I will never confide in you again—only in Whaki."

Ciellō held his hands out cupped in front of his chest, the gesture he used when praying to Ghibli. He must be either praying for patience or swearing on the name of his Spirit.

"Damselle, I understand now. It is important to know if people say the truth." He took up Nightmist's reins again. "You can trust people who were your friends before you had position. Then you must learn (as all people must learn) to watch eyes; to hear the words not said; to smell the lies. You rely too much on your dogs. You must learn to smell people's hearts."

The queen tried sniffing in the air and smiled at the image. They rode on for a time while Nightmist swished away flies, the queen recalling that Sergeant Rooks, in Wyndton, had also tried to teach her to school her senses.

When they came out of a wooded thicket, they saw the swell of the foothills ahead.

"Race you to the top of that rise!" challenged Cerúlia, removing her hat and urging Smoke to a gallop.

With the head start she gave herself and a faster mount, she instantly pulled ahead of Ciellō. Smoke's gait was smooth and effortless, and she gave him his head to choose his path and he flew up the incline. The deerhounds caught up to Smoke in a moment; as Cerúlia waited for the others, a flat rock outcropping that promised a view called to her. So she dismounted and ventured out for a look on the shelf that stretched twice the size of her closet chamber. Below, she spied the white palace towers and tiny people going about their daily routines. Stable lads were exercising the horses and turning some into paddocks. Carts were delivering goods through the Kitchen Gate. Beyond the grounds rose the jumble of rooftops of the city of Cascada with the abbey steeples and the Church of the Headwaters providing landmarks but the Fountain obscured from this angle and far in the distance the glint of the Bay of Cinda and Cascada Harbor.

She sat cross-legged to study the view and didn't turn around when she heard Nightmist's hooves clatter on the rock. Whaki, panting heavily, came padding out on the escarpment, nosing her arm for a caress, and flopped beside her, his chest rising and falling. Ciellō made no noise, but she knew that he too had come to lounge a few paces behind her.

"The palace and the city look pretty from here," she mused. "You can't see the ugliness, the sewers, the garbage, the slums, all the roads I must find a way to fix. When I was a child in Wyndton, I pictured Cascada as all that was comfortable, well-ordered, and beautiful. I didn't know . . ."

"What?" he prodded.

"I didn't know how much ugliness lingered here. How many people were happy to cooperate with Matwyck for their own selfish reasons. How many were greedy, sadistic, or cowardly or just didn't care about injustice so long as their own bellies were full."

"Weirs are no different than other people," Ciellō said.

"I guess not," replied the queen. "But I thought—I *imagined* they were better. Perchance because I wanted them to be."

She lay back on the warmed rock a moment, closing her eyes against the direct sun, which made her sight fill with the red glow of her inner eyelids. "The sun feels so good." She wasn't sleepy, but the warmth rising from the rock softened the focus of her thoughts, and her mind drifted a little under Saulė's gift.

A shadow in front of her face prompted her to open her eyes. Ciellō leaned over her; he had removed his doublet and folded it up.

"Lift your head, damselle," he said, so she angled her neck up, and he slid the garment under her head like a pillow. For a half tick longer than necessary Ciellō stayed so close that she could smell his sweat.

She guessed that his chief purpose was to make her more comfortable, but the gesture sent a current of sexual desire through her. She wouldn't put it past Ciellō to know exactly the effect he would create. She lay still another few moments, listening to Whaki lap rainwater left over in a depression in the rock. As soon as seemed polite, she sat up, opened her eyes, and stretched. Ciellō sat a few paces away, surveying her with alert eyes.

"Let's mount up again," said Cerúlia, moving to gather her feet underneath herself. Ciellō, faster than she, was on his feet and offered her his hand to assist her rising. She shook her head that she did not need it and purposely addressed the dogs. "Had enough time to catch your breath, you lazybones?" she asked.

As they started to ride the ridgeline, the day grew warmer. Cerúlia made a note of the birds' nests that hung in the trees and inhaled the scents of horse and crushed grass. Then despite her wishes, her thoughts turned to all the meetings and tasks awaiting her inside. Answering her unspoken wish, Smoke turned onto a deer path that headed back down.

Cerúlia cleared her throat. "Ciellō—"

"Do you wish me to leave Cascada?"

"*What*? No! That's not what I was going to say; I have so few real friends I could not bear to lose both you and Gunnit." She cleared her throat again. "I think, however, if we are careful to keep more distance between us" (she had practiced this sentence in her mind and was pleased with the choice of wording) "we can better control the—the spark that arises."

"Yes, Your Majesty, I will be more mindful."

"Ciellō!" she rebuked him, and Smoke broke off his stride at her tone. "You always call me 'damselle' when we are alone."

"No," he said, staring down at the path, "'Your Majesty,' I think, is better."

Cerúlia had been through too much emotional drama the last few moons to put up with these enigmatic pronouncements.

"I. Have. Had. Enough!" she snapped. "First you say you'll never desert me; then you offer to leave. You tell me to confide in people, and then you get sullen. You treat me informally, and then you pull away and act the courtier. You bed me, and then you say this is dishonorable!"

She had gotten angrier and angrier as she went through the list; the dogs gazed up uneasily, and the horses halted without instruction, their ears moving in all directions to find the source of such strife.

"Ciellō of Zerplain, I *command* you to tell me why it was dishonorable! Was it because I was your employer?"

Ciellō made a dismissive shrug. "Damselle Phénix had no power over my body."

Her cheeks had grown hot from anger and embarrassment, but Cerúlia would not back down now. "Then what?"

"In your country village," he began, in the patronizing tone of voice that irritated her so, "what did they teach you about men and women?"

"You mean, about *sex*?" she said, wanting to shock him with her directness. "Very little. They are loath to discuss it."

"Foolishness! In Zellia, we say 'Both partners must dance the same dance.'"

"I don't understand."

"I know that now," he said, "but on *Misty Traveler,* I was bodyguard and manservant and weapon instructor, not grandfather."

He clucked Nightmist to walk on down from the hill; in a few moments the path broadened sufficiently so that she could urge Smoke to catch up and ride alongside.

"Ciellō—"

"Damselle." He sighed with exaggerated patience. "In Zellia when a boy or girl comes of age, the grandfathers and grandmothers pull them aside. They explain that there are many dances between adults: a dance for when wine stirs the loins; a dance for tonight only; a dance until the next moon or season for sailing; a dance for a begetting of children; a dance for forever. Many different dances. All are sweet. But in Zellia it is not honorable for one person to sway to one and the partner to dance to another."

"And we were not dancing the same dance?"

"Correct." He rolled the *r*'s with exaggeration.

Cerúlia sat back in her saddle and cast her mind back on their night together, which, given all that had happened since, seemed like ages ago. She had never considered what kind of commitment—if any—she was offering when she invited her bodyguard into her bed.

"But what if you don't know how you feel? What if dancing is accidental or spontaneous? What if you don't want to talk about it or don't know how?"

"The dance is never truly accidental. That is a pretty lie dishonorable people tell themselves, ofttimes with drink. You must not invite a partner until you are clear in your own heart and mind because people can get hurt."

"That night, were you clear in your own mind . . . ?" she asked.

"Of course."

"And I hurt you with my muddle and confusion?"

"Ah."

"People can get hurt when they are mysteriously shoved away too!" she said with clenched teeth as she pretended she needed to free tufts of Smoke's mane from the back of his bridle.

A long silence was punctuated only by the ripping and chewing noise of Nightmist naughtily taking advantage of their slowed progress to grab mouthfuls of fresh forage.

"This is true," Cielló said. "I pray you forgive me, damselle."

A group of blue jays jabbered for the queen's attention, but she closed herself off to them. More angry words formed in her mind, but she shunted them away too.

"I pray you forgive me, Ciellō," she said after a pause.

"Oh, I forgave you the next day," he said with irritating cheerfulness. "Holding anger makes the jaw and neck tense—like you, now." He grinned at her.

"Besides, I cannot hold anger at you," he continued. "No grandparents to teach you. Why are the Weirs so foolish about desire and so casual about honor? Such a bad upbringing you had."

Cerúlia was yawning to stretch her jaw and rotating her neck in a circle to work out the tension, but his insouciant comment made her laugh. "Oh, don't tell Stahlia that!"

"Mistress Stahlia raised you? She is a woman of much backbone and honor. Often I think you were raised by curs."

"Did you hear that, Whaki?" Cerúlia said, leaning to the side on Smoke to address the dog and to hide the slight spring of tears that moistened her eyes. "Ciellō thinks you're a cur."

Whaki wagged his tail. *Thy heart be lighter now?*

Smoke and Nightmist moved forward again, matching their strides. Cerúlia stretched her arm, pleased that it didn't hurt and realizing that her back and left shoulder did not ache from riding as they had in Salubriton.

To change the subject away from their night of lovemaking, Ciellō began describing an animal native only to Zellia. It had a long striped tail and fingers that were almost humanlike. Cerúlia was intrigued, but after a while her mind ran on a different course.

Cerúlia interrupted, "Ciellō, in Zellia, do people actually dance? I mean *dance,* to music?"

"Not as Lady Percia dances. We dance to the mandolin. The Zellish, we are the best dancers of all peoples in Ennea Món."

"I thought we were going on this ride so I could get a break,"

Cerúlia said, with laughter that was only slightly forced, "but you are so full of ego and lessons, I'm not going to ride with you anymore; I'm going to race you back to the stable!"

And she urged Smoke forward, delighting in his speed, and—for those brief moments—outrunning her complicated worries.

18

Cascada

"Your Majesty wished to see me," said Vilkit, bowing low to the queen as she sat in her Reception Room, her feet propped up on a footstool, reviewing sheaves of papers.

"Ah, Vilkit, yes. I sent for you because I'd like to make changes in palace routines."

"Of course, Your Majesty."

"It is my understanding that the servants dine in the servants' common room and the gentry and administrators eat either in the Banquet Hall or order food to their rooms?"

"Indeed, that is the practice."

"Well, I think this creates unnecessary divisions. Why can't we all eat together in the Banquet Hall as we did my first night back?"

"Your Majesty, that was a special occasion. For every day, many administrators would object to dining alongside of a dirty stable lad or a scullery maid. And I don't believe that the staff would enjoy its mealtime either. This way, the servants relax and joke around; they don't have to worry about their manners or coarse talk. Before you assume that the servants would appreciate your gracious invitation, you might inquire as to their wishes. Besides, there would be the question of the price of the food; the kitchens use one set of provisions for the gentry and another set for the servants' meals."

"Ah, Vilkit, *that*'s just what displeases me most. I believe that if the chimney sweep dines on turnips, then I should dine on turnips. I've dined on turnips and worse in my day. If I sup on quail, then Nana should sup on quail. But couldn't we all meet in the middle with chicken?"

Vilkit was so flummoxed by the parade of poultry that he stared at his liege in astonishment.

"What about the wine?" he asked faintly.

"Aye." The queen nodded as if he had made a solid point, but Vilkit had a suspicion she might be mocking him. "Wine. Well, I believe we should do away with wine at midmeal for the gentry and administrators. It makes everyone sleepy, and I don't get as much work out of anyone in the afternoons. At dinner we should all be able to drink wine, or ale, or mead, each to her own preference."

"Your Majesty, as always, your ideas are bold and exciting. But perchance this mealtime plan might be a wee bit too foreign? Folk like the customs they are familiar with."

"Humor me, Vilkit," said the queen, without a smile, and the chamberlain realized that this was not a discussion.

"Of course, Your Majesty. When would you like this experiment to begin?"

"Tomorrow. And I intend to set an example of getting to know workers who are new to me by moving around and sitting at various tables. I would like you to follow my example."

"Your Majesty, I know all the employees."

"Really, Vilkit? Then wouldn't you care to know them better? Know them as people?"

"Whatever you command, Your Majesty." Vilkit bowed. "Though I believe that breaking down barriers can lead to lax discipline."

He arranged for midmeal to be served in the Banquet Hall for everyone the next day. The stable lads and chimney sweeps surprised him by washing up very carefully; though their clothes were none too clean, their hands and faces shone, and they had wiped their feet with great care.

The queen entered, escorted by Nana and her foreign bodyguard, who watched over her like a hawk. While everyone stood, she looked around the room with unhurried consideration and chose to join a group of gardeners. In a short time Vilkit heard a lot of laughter arising from that table.

Lord Marcot and Lady Percia rather self-consciously sat themselves at a table of chambermaids. Marcot ate his food quietly, but Vilkit overhead Lady Percia talking with the girls about dancing.

Vilkit was so occupied making sure that the platters came out of the kitchen hot and in good time he did not have a chance to seat himself.

Dinner went off about the same. The queen and Nana sat with plasterers and painters while the Zellishman watchfully stood by. This time, Lord Marcot steered his lady toward the stable staff and found a common interest in talking about horses.

Vilkit's own habit was to take his meals privately in his office accompanied only by the head cook, but tonight, tired and hungry, he approached a table of the Queen's Shield. Captain Yanath energetically waved him to a seat at his side.

"Hey, Chamberlain, I need your advice."

"*My* advice, sir?" said Vilkit, genuinely surprised.

Yanath launched into a story about a farm and a family outside Cascada. He didn't want to give up the farm, he didn't want to leave his family alone in the countryside, and he missed them. Vilkit suggested that he move his family into South Park (right close to the palace) and lease the farm for a time. Yanath acted very grateful for the suggestion.

The next day, as Vilkit was checking that the Queen's Closet had been tidied to his standards, he noticed a nosegay of daisies and lavender. He asked the maid about it; she said the head gardener had himself brought them up this morning. Of course, if Vilkit had known that the queen desired flowers in her rooms, he could have easily ordered them, but for the gardener to send them spontaneously as a present . . .

He needed to stop underestimating this young queen. Her upbringing in rural Wyndton had given her a touch with the common people, and who knew how her travels in foreign lands might manifest.

19

Tidewater Keep, Lortherrod

Mikil was scrubbing the salt crust off the wall of the keep's Dwelling of Lautan (all of Lautan's churches being built over coastal abysses, so that the ocean ebbed, flowed, and splashed within their walls), when a page dashed through the door.

The lad gasped, "The king—" but he did not have the ability to continue.

"You've found me," Mikil encouraged. "Catch your breath now. Whatever the message, it is probably not worth panting over. My brother always says to pages, 'Race away' over trifles; once it was merely to ask whether wild boar at High Table would suit my wife." Mikil dropped his scrub brush and wiped his hands on a towel.

This brought a lopsided grin to the face of the winded boy. He started again, "The king requests that you join him (*gasp*) in the Map Room (*gasp*) immediately."

"Im-me-di-ate-ly, eh? Then I don't want to hear any guff about my work robe. Do you know what this is about?"

The boy could talk now. "All I know is that there was a ship and a letter for the king on it."

"Interesting. Well, I'm off." Mikil pointed to a stone shelf carved in a nook of the wall. "There's a jug of water over there, lad, and meat and biscuits. I'll probably end up dining at the keep and that's no reason for good food to go to waste."

Mikil set off on the cobblestone path for the center of the castle at a quick but not frantic pace. The Dwelling sat at the edge; most of the royal buildings were tucked farther away from the ocean. The interior paths and courtyards were gray and austere, as befitted a keep constructed for defense rather than comfort or show. His heart had leapt at the news of a letter, but it was prudent not to get his hopes up. In the moons since he had sent Cerúlia to Wyeland, he'd heard nothing about her, and Lautan wouldn't allow him to ask questions.

His father, who was mostly confined to his sickbed, had managed to precede him into the Map Room, a solar on the second floor of the stone castle, suitable for small conferences. Nithanil sat by the fireplace, which had probably been fed to chase away the damp chill; a roaring fire made the crossed walrus tusks on the mantel gleam. Nithanil, as usual, was compulsively tying knots in a ragged piece of rope. Rikil, the king, who was generally of imperturbable disposition, today sat jittering his crossed foot, holding a sheaf of papers. Several ministers clustered around the family group, looking grave.

"Your Majesty," said Mikil, with a small bow. "What's the news? Is it truly urgent?"

"It is urgent that I share it with you, for it is of great moment. I have here a letter from our envoy, Bakilai, stationed in Cascada. It was written a moon ago." Rikil paused, and then added with a dramatic flourish, "Cressa's daughter, Cerúlia, has returned to claim the Nargis Throne!"

Mikil cried out, "Lautan the Munificent!"

"Shh," said Rikil, raising his palm, wanting to get out the whole story. "Bakilai writes he heard news of fighting in the palace. Lord

Matwyck is in hiding, and many of his followers imprisoned! He attended—"

"Is 'he' Bakilai or that Matwyck?" interrupted his father.

"*Bakilai* attended an event in the middle of Cascada at which Cressa's daughter presented herself to the people. Her Talent involves communicating with animals; she demonstrated this by commanding the birds of the sky to fly in flamboyant patterns. He, *Bakilai,* waxes quite poetic about this address.

"Here, read this part." The king shoved a page at Mikil, who read aloud:

In the Courtyard rainbows shimmered around her. A pendant of Nargis Ice lit up her face—one sees a marked resemblance to the late queen. Her hair shone with that particular shade of blue-green. The dress of pinkish, the robe of gray—as if a nymph of sunset decided to pay a visit to Weirandale. No one there ever will forget the sight or her speech. She entranced the city.

A smile broke through Nithanil's stern face. "My grand-girl! Alive!"

"Yes, Sire," said Rikil. "Such great news. And I am so relieved to be rid of that regent. He was impossible to treat with."

"Well, at least she was alive and triumphant a month ago," continued the king. "Sounds as if powerful forces are arrayed against her. Let's hope she overcomes them."

"Sail to her aid," urged his father.

"Now, Sire. That's not practical. It would take more than three weeks just to muster the fleet, and more than a moon to sail there. By then she will either have defeated her enemies or succumbed to them. We are just too far away to provide timely assistance."

"She is beloved of the Spirits," Mikil broke in, grinning. "She will win out. What we can and should do is offer a libation and thank Lautan. I will prepare a High Tide Mass for tonight."

Nithanil was stubborn. "We should sail to Cascada."

"Sire, we should wait for an invitation," rejoined Rikil. "Once Cerúlia has established control, naturally she will reach out. We have never met her, but we are her only kin."

"I met her! Sailed there for the Naming. Held her when she was a babe in arms. Little wispy blue hair, like Cressa's," said the king-that-was, as he mimicked rocking a babe. "Not the whole blasted fleet, not your armies. *My* ship. I still have my own ship. I will sail to Cascada. Cressa's daughter may need me."

"Sire," said Rikil, in a tone of patient reasonableness his father would find doubly aggravating, "you are too weak for such a voyage. You are just this day out of your bed after such another bout of pneumonia. You wouldn't help Cerúlia by arriving there for her to nurse or arriving there dead."

This angered their father, who always railed against his increasing infirmities. "I'm not dead yet," he snapped at Rikil. "And by Lautan's Beard, I will see Cressa's child before I dive." He thundered out of the room, his dignity somewhat compromised by a fit of heavy coughing that forced him to accept the arm of a nearby footman.

Rikil addressed his ministers. "Please withdraw. I would have a few words with my brother," he said, and the men and women took themselves away, with polite murmurs about what a glorious day this was for Lortherrod.

The king shrugged at his younger brother. "I don't think I handled that skillfully. But Bakilai is one of our brightest envoys. He will know how eager we are to hear news—why, more letters may at this very moment be heading this direction. Let's not impetuously jump on ships without more information. If Bakilai even thought that we should make preparations, he would have suggested the same. He must have thought that our 'sunset nymph' had the situation well in hand. If I didn't know Bakilai to prefer men in his bed, I'd say he was smitten with her."

Seeing Mikil hungrily eying the letter, Rikil passed it to him. "Here, read the whole thing."

Mikil devoured every detail. "Though I too am eager to greet Shrimpella, I agree with your interpretation. I'll suggest to Sire that he make her a present. Mayhap he can channel his impatience in that direction."

"That's a grand idea," Rikil said. "Don't think that I too am not stirred by this development. And a renewed, strong alliance with Weirandale will remake Ennea Món for the better. I'm sure realms will immediately start scheming about marriage alliances. But you know our father has other grandchildren nearby, grandsons he takes for granted."

Nithanil's emotional remove from Rikil's sons was a sore point in the family; Mikil tried to think of how to soothe that wound. "Oh, you know how he doted on Cressa, in a way he never favored either of us. He also pays no attention to Gilboy."

Rikil's brow stayed furrowed. "It's not that he likes women more than men, for he generally takes no interest in our wives either."

"I see that every day." Mikil nodded. "Such a shame. I wonder if Sire cares only for certain *Weir* women—Catreena, Cressa, and now, Cerúlia. They hold a particular appeal for him. I wonder why. . . ." As Lautan's Agent, Mikil had insight into the particular pull of Magic. "Perchance he responds to their Talents. . . ."

Rikil returned to his polished wooden desk. "How is your wife? She doesn't often join us at High Table. You know she is more than welcome."

"Arlettie is having a little trouble adjusting: her new position, and the fact that my duties keep me so busy. A little more time . . ."

"Of course. No pressure."

Mikil swiftly added, "Your boys have been very kind to Gilboy, very kind indeed, to include him in all their activities."

"I would whip them if they weren't, but they genuinely like and admire their new cousin. Ingenious and good-humored, they tell me."

Being of such opposite personalities and both vying for the scraps of affection from their father, Rikil and Mikil had never been close. Since Mikil's miraculous return they had tried their best to remedy their past—settling into a scrupulous, if a little forced, cordiality.

Mikil said, "I would like to run and tell Arlettie and Gilboy about Shrimpella. They will be so happy. Your family will join us at High Tide Mass tonight?"

"Of course, Mikil." Rikil smiled with genuine warmth. "The Sea keeps giving us back treasures. First a brother and now a niece. We know where gratitude is due."

Mikil stopped by his father's suite on his way, discovering that his father had independently struck on the idea of a present. He was sitting up at his worktable with a thick woman's shawl wrapped around his shoulders, and he had his jewelry tools out. He was grumbling at Iluka, the simple fisherwoman he had invited to be his bed wife after the failure of his marriage to Queen Catreena.

"What's the problem?" Mikil asked the room.

Iluka had her hands on her hips. "The old walrus wants diamond chips, and there ain't any in the jewel chest. So he says I'm a blind old biddy."

Mikil peered into the wall cabinet where his father stored the gems he worked with, patiently opening drawers and opening wrappers.

His father had made Arlettie a ring studded with emeralds as a wedding present. She had never received such a costly gift, and she marveled at it. The ring, however, was about the only thing in Lortherrod that pleased her; ofttimes Mikil regretted dragging her so far away from the Green Isles. And his new love, his total devotion to the Spirit of the Sea, cast his former passion for Arlettie into shadow.

Mikil finished poking around in the drawers. "Iluka's right, Sire.

No diamonds. But I see several blue sapphires. Were you saving them? Maybe *this* is the time to use them."

"Bring them to me," ordered his father.

Mikil sorted through the stones and carried them to his father, who picked them up and studied them in the light coming through the window.

"They'll do," he grunted grudgingly. "Old Biddy, find me some silver wire."

"Good. Crisis averted, then. Don't sit up too long, Sire."

His father waved him away without looking at him, and Iluka saw him to the door with a grateful wink.

Softhearted Arlettie cried a bit with joy at the good news. Although Mikil had never told her the identity of the castaway they had rescued, she still remembered Queen Cressa fondly, and she had been worried about the fate of her daughter.

At High Tide Mass, Mikil led the court in prayers of gratitude to Lautan and poured bottle after bottle into the churning surf. His own heart felt nigh to bursting, to learn that Cressa's daughter had survived and had won back her throne.

20

The Scoláiríum

Thalen was disappointed to discover that he could not immediately immerse himself in the Scoláiríum's books because the books were still housed in the limestone caves where the students had hidden them from the Oros.

So the first and most crucial task the Raiders took on was emptying the caves and bringing the volumes back to the library. Thalen had absorbed enough about pulleys from the tutor of Engineering to be able to set these up again. The nine men didn't have scores of students to help, but the strong and disciplined Raiders worked with less chatter and less wasted motion, ferrying cartload after cartload.

Once the books had been unloaded from the wagons, tutors set about reorganizing them on the shelves. Occasionally Thalen had to prod them back to their task; often he would find Tutor Andreata, Gustie's former teacher, sitting on the floor, dreamily lost in reviewing a treatise she'd feared mislaid forever. Tutor Helina, a newcomer hired to teach Poetry, worked with the most discipline and will; during breaks she and Thalen would discuss the merits and drawbacks of alternative categorization schemas.

With Granilton gone, Thalen assumed responsibility for organizing the History collection. He found the job satisfying, as if by creating orderliness in one corner of the library he could restore a sense of order in the world at large.

During these weeks each of the Raiders settled in and chose interests to keep him busy. Tristo found his way to the kitchens, offering himself as the cranky cook's assistant, and to balance out his boss's sourness he took on the role of master of revels amongst the village children. Between bouts of rigorous sword practice Kambey slept in the sunshine for long hours, rebuilding the muscle strength he'd lost to the woros. Kran and Fedak, with Jothile helping as much as he was able, started making long-needed repairs to the Scoláiríum buildings. Cerf tended to the ailments of the school's and village's people.

In the absence of a midwife, Cerf even helped birth a babe, an event that provided an occasion for joy all round.

The rector came to find Thalen in the library one morning as he moved a shelf of monographs. Concern clouded her jovial face.

"Three students are arriving this week and another four next week. You will serve as our History tutor, I assume?"

"I would be a fraud as a tutor."

"Ha!" barked Meakey. "Just as you were a fraud as a commander?"

Thalen held his hands up, surrendering without even suiting up for battle.

"Your adequacy doesn't perturb me," continued Meakey, tapping her foot. "I just don't know how the students will get here, what with the ferry down and coach service disrupted."

"Let's send Wareth to rendezvous and guide them here," suggested Thalen, who had been worried about the scout's lack of finding satisfying occupation.

This plan proved agreeable to both Wareth and the rector. And once students chattered in the refectory and left broken quills scattered about in the library, the Scoláiríum slowly came back to life, regaining its rhythm and habits.

After much searching, Thalen laid his hands on the library's slim holdings on Alpetar. He read the four tracts cover to cover. Then he searched through the Religion section for everything on the sun Spirit, Saulė. But he put the books down in frustration, not finding anything that answered the questions he obsessed over.

"Commander Thalen." Tutor Helina's little shoes clicked on the floor one afternoon, when he had laid aside another tome on religion without finding anything useful. "Could you help me reach a top stack? I could hunt around for a chair or step stool, but I'm just too lazy in this heat."

"I'm delighted to be useful." He accompanied her to the bookshelf. "Which one?"

"The one with the gold binding. It's a volume of Kentros I's sonnets."

He grabbed the book she desired. Afterward they walked together to the refectory, deep in discussion of Rorther sonnets and how much they did or did not capture the true history of that kingdom. Helina, he couldn't help but notice, had a comely face and Rorther red streaks in her hair. Her voice, low and husky for a woman, held a special allure.

At the dining hall, Wareth, recently back from an excursion to a larger town, passed around a broadsheet that relayed the news of the sudden appearance of the Weir queen.

"*Now* she appears," Thalen said bitterly, glancing sideways at the broadsheet as he poured Helina a tankard of ale. "After all the fighting is over."

"No," said Wareth. "She's had her own fight seizing power."

Cerf had grabbed the sheet and read aloud about a skirmish and a fire in the Weir palace. But the bottom of the paper, which seemed about to launch into more details about the queen herself, got splotched with gravy when Jothile grabbed the platter on the other side of Cerf.

21

Cascada

The day Cerúlia finally assembled her complete roster of councilors in the Circle Chamber, the air smelled of summer. They opened the room's windows, and occasionally a warm gust blew through, disarranging their papers.

Master Alix, who—to her surprise—had been overwhelmingly elected steward, beating an influential lordling from Patenroux, sat on the queen's right. Thus far, his energy and intelligence impressed her, and she found that his desire to improve the lot of the people matched her own. Master Fornquit (a middle-yeared and thoughtful cheese wholesaler from the duchy of Lakevale) and Mistress Nishtari (younger and bolder in temperament), whom Cerúlia had decided to appoint as her councilor for diplomacy, completed the Circle. Nishtari hailed from a family of shipbuilders in Maritima; she had already traveled Ennea Món seeking commissions for the company's ships.

However, just as her Circle closed, Naven sought Cerúlia out to tell her that he had come down homesick for his family in Androvale; he was willing to serve her for a year, but asked that afterward she replace him. Since she had chosen him more for his loyalty and common sense than for his reputation in the realm or superior intellect, a year's duration suited her fine.

Overall, she was pleased at how balanced the council had turned out: men and women, young and older, gentry and commoners, and representatives from several different duchies. Most importantly, she trusted them all.

"The first and most pressing item of business, Your Majesty," Steward Alix began, "is the problem of what to do about General Yurgn. Duchess Latlie has fled; reports indicate that she bribed a shipmaster and bolted. Other than confiscating her properties and ill-gotten gains, we need do nothing more about the duchess. Lady Fanyah will serve a three-year term in prison and all her goods have been confiscated. But General Yurgn was not only one of the original traitors, he has been the instigator of most of the worst treatment of the populace in recent years. And we believe him to be sheltering Matwyck—though we cannot be certain. At any rate, we have found no other trail that leads to the Lord Regent."

"Marcot?" Cerúlia asked. "Can you tell us anything about where your father would hide?"

"If he still lives—and I hope he doesn't—I agree he would slink to Yurgn's manse."

"Moreover," argued Wilamara, "the longer the general remains free, the longer he serves as a flag of defiance to Your Majesty's authority. This raises questions about the loyalty of the army."

"Even without the Stone," said Marcot, "we have been making progress getting our stable guests to inform on one another. I've learned that the worst offenders in terms of fingering innocent people as 'agitators' were army officers. They need to be brought to justice."

"Ah, but the problem lies in *how* to bring these renegades to heel," Fornquit removed his unlit pipe to say. "The queen does not command a force equal to the numbers in the barracks under Yurgn's direct influence."

"But do we know that all those troops are loyal to him?" asked Wilamara. "I would wager that many of those lads and gals would prefer to get themselves straight with Nargis and bend a knee to the queen."

"Well," Fornquit commented, "we can hardly just march up the valley to South Fork and take our chances on an insurrection."

"We're in dry cask, there's no denying," said Steward Alix.

"There must be a solution," Cerúlia said, rising but motioning for her councilors to stay seated. She stared out the open window as if the answer lay in the bright blue sky or the birds pecking on the grass.

"I suggest," said Nishtari in a meditative manner, "that we write to both General Yurgn and the officers of the cavalry and pikemen, assuring them that if they were to turn themselves in to face questioning they would find justice."

"And why would they do that," said Marcot, "when their just deserts would be harsh? Yurgn, at the very least, would be hung. Though we could offer to spare his family—well, not Burgn, but the rest of them. I wonder if clemency for his family would sway him."

Cerúlia interrupted their discussion. "Would you all agree that Yurgn deserves to die?"

"Oh, if you had seen what I saw in the jails!" Marcot's voice shook, and when she looked around, the rest of her council nodded agreement.

Wilamara again spoke up for the enlisted men. "Amongst the soldiers, though, we don't have as much certainty about who is guilty or to what degree."

Cerúlia made her decision. "As Nishtari proposes, we will write to General Yurgn and the supervising officers at the army headquarters, offering them a chance to surrender. Nishtari and Alix, you will bring drafts of these letters to me for approval. As a sign of my seriousness, I would like to send a high-ranking deputation to deliver the letters, though I'd wager . . ."

Alix finished her thought. "Those scoundrels might not be above arresting or killing the messengers!"

"I will go," said Wilamara, without hesitation. "I expect the uniform and the rank will stir a modicum of respect."

"And I will escort you, Seamaster," said Naven with surprising alacrity and a little bow. "I am a duke with royal blood. I will shake out my fanciest velvets, and together we will make an imposing pair."

"I have been wrong about so many things, but I do not believe that Yurgn would kill me," Marcot began, but Cerúlia shook her head at him.

"No, Marcot. I think older envoys, with the weight of their years of loyalty to the realm, will make the best statement.

"So," she summed up, still standing by the window, "Wilamara and Naven will hand-deliver stern ultimatums, offering safe passage and fair trials to all who surrender. And generosity to their dependents. If they refuse this opportunity, they will have to face the consequences."

"But surely you don't mean to march on South Fork, Your Majesty!" said Fornquit, removing his pipe and waving it in his hand. "That could be a bloodbath. Think of the wounded and injured, and the loss of face for a queen to war with her own troops."

Cerúlia returned to her seat. "We will not march on South Fork. But I cannot allow this mutinous holdout to continue. I must eliminate traitors and murderers. How I intend to accomplish this, I will not divulge at the moment."

Fornquit tapped his empty pipe against the table—a nervous gesture—while the other nonplussed councilors looked at one another and found nothing to say.

Rays of sunlight struck the water feature in the middle of the room, making the small, swirling pool glint and sparkle.

"By the Grace of the Waters," murmured Steward Alix, and they all bowed their heads.

After a moment Wilamara broke the silence. "Vilkit—that insufferable toady—keeps speaking of how a ruler must be feared and loved. Concentrating on the *love* part, it has been nearly three moons since your Dedication and we've held no public celebration, no festival. We have been working so hard to restore order and bring justice, but all sailors need shore leave. Could we plan a Midsummer's Fest in honor of your safe return, Your Majesty?"

"What a splendid idea!" said Naven. "Fests tie people together."

Fornquit said, "I'm a-thinking that the people were recently taxed to pay for a court wedding (no offense, my esteemed lord), and that they might not take too kindly to being taxed for another lavish gala."

Cerúlia nodded. "I am also concerned about expense, though I've been thinking along a parallel path. Has there ever been proper acknowledgment of the bravery and heroism of the Weir sailors who fought beside Queen Cressa and Lord Ambrice? Or of the loyalty of the Queen's Shield who helped my mother escape? I don't yearn for a feast to honor myself; I had in mind commending the loyalists and celebrating the return of those released from Matwyck's jails."

"Ah," said Alix. "Wouldn't that be grand! Healing-like. A great morale booster. We could have one celebration for everything."

"Honoring our own citizens would be proper and overdue, but shouldn't we think too about the Lorthers and Rorthers who fought as part of the Allied Fleet?" added Nishtari, mindful of her duties as international ambassador.

"Well, if we're going to tack on allies," said Alix, "I've read reports from Jutterdam broadsheets about a group of commandos from the Free States who penetrated Oromondo and burned down Femturan and killed the Magi. Don't we owe them acknowledgment too?"

Cerúlia's pulse jumped. Of all the events of her previous lives, her time with the Raiders in Oromondo was the only chapter she had never disclosed. But she yearned to have the power and means to celebrate their heroism!

Wilamara's eyes got a faraway look, thinking back more than a dozen years earlier. "Magistrar Destra was key to the fight against the Pellish!"

"She's no longer in the Green Isles," Nishtari informed Wilamara. "The Isles envoy told me that she's returned to the Free States and a merchant, Olet of Pilagos, has been elected to her place."

"I totally agree with the advisability of the type of festival you propose," said Fornquit, "but, again, where will the money come from? We can't spend money we don't have. Well, we could, but that way lies trouble."

"I *know* where the money lies," said Duke Naven. "In General Yurgn's treasure chests."

Alix laughed. "We've talked ourselves around in a circle. I always heard of meetings doing that, but never witnessed it before!"

"Nor are we in a circle now, Lord Steward," said Cerúlia, "for I have a plan to deal with Yurgn."

She continued, "Duke Naven and Master Fornquit, see if you can get a clear answer out of our calculators about the state of our finances after this recent spate of forfeitures and fines. Lord Marcot and Seamaster Wilamara, I'd like you to have a chat with the chamberlain about the food and lodgings and with Lady Percia about the dancing and entertainment, so we would have an estimate of how much such festivities would cost the realm. And draw up a tentative list of the honorees and invitees. Midsummer, I believe, would be too soon—let's look at Harvest Fest.

"Now, what else did you have on your agenda, Steward?" she asked.

They talked for another hour about administrative issues. Fornquit wanted permission to take a census so that the tax rolls could be carefully restructured. Alix was also working on a series of laws and proclamations to provide the common folk redress against illtreatment by employers. Naven was eager to get work crews started on various building projects, both because the projects badly needed doing and because the unemployed needed productive work to keep them out of mischief. Marcot wanted to talk about the condition of Cascada's under schools; Cerúlia suggested that the Sorrowers be conscripted as masters until proper teachers could be located or hired. Nishtari reported on a series of meetings she had had with envoys from other lands and stressed that the Lorthers were eager to reestablish relations.

Cerúlia was pleased to note that the councilors worked as a team, supporting one another's priorities with fresh perspective and sound advice.

"Councilors, all, it has been a pleasure. I thank you for your frank guidance," said Cerúlia as she rose and ended her first official council meeting.

Ciellō stood on guard outside the door of the Circle Council.

"I would have a word with you," said Cerúlia in a low voice. "Follow me."

Once they were alone in her closet, Cerúlia said, "We are sending letters to General Yurgn and other military leaders, inviting them to come forward to face justice."

"I think, damselle, that these people, they will not agree."

The Weeping Swan, the water feature in this room, dropped one tear of water into a bowl. *Plink!*

Cerúlia walked over and stared at the brass sculpture: a swan's neck and head curved above a quivering bowl that sat in a nook in the wall. "Do you see this little fountain, Ciellō? The water droplet grows and grows so slowly until it gets so heavy it drops in the pool. Every day it suggests something different to me: 'time is passing' or 'patience is everything.' Yesterday, staring at it, I saw how just one drop makes the bottom pool wash over the sides. One drop."

She watched it for a moment, waiting. *Plink!*

She turned back to her bodyguard. "Remember when we went riding and you spoke about how you regret killing people?"

"Of course," answered Ciellō.

"I am considering assassinating General Yurgn. I think only *one* person needs to die for the pool to overflow."

Ciellō nodded without any other reaction.

"How do I know this is wise, as opposed to one of those mistakes that darken one's soul?"

"Motives matter, damselle," said Ciellō quietly. "Some people I killed for pride. Or to show off my skill." *Plink!*

"Ah. Displaying my anger at his defiance would just be prideful. Showing that my Talent is fearsome and my daring high would constitute another kind of pride.

"These motives influence my decision, I cannot deny, but the crux of the matter is this: Yurgn is responsible for hundreds of murders and imprisonments. His guilt is second only to Matwyck's. He needs to be brought to justice. I can't say to the men and women in my jails, 'You will be held accountable because you were close at hand, whereas the man who gave the orders I will spare because he is barricaded in his fortress.'"

She paused, waiting for the sound of the droplet striking. *Plink!* "Nor can I say to the palace soldiers, 'Come die so that I can yank Yurgn out of his manse.' I will not sacrifice one more life for the likes of Yurgn or even Matwyck.

"I will offer a safe surrender and a fair trial. But if that offer is refused, I must bring justice without more innocent bloodshed."

"How can I aid you, damselle?"

"I will use my Talent. I take full responsibility. In fact, I *want* these acts to be traced back to me." *Plink!*

"First, I need a quantity of an appropriate poison. Then sharp hooks for the claws of the gray owls that nest in the foothills behind the palace."

Ciellō smiled a thin smile. "How fortunate that the evenings are warm and men often take the air." He rubbed his hands. "I am not a chemist, but I can obtain an appropriate potion. The hooks—ah! the metal needs be soft"—*Plink!*—"so to shape exactly to the claws, no?"

"Yes, that would help." She walked back to stare at the water feature.

"What is the timetable, damselle?"

"If the letters are written today, and the messengers leave tomorrow . . ." *Plink!* "Three nights from now."

"And the owls will know the right target how?"

"I've already planned for this. I have sent hawks to the South Fork manse to scout and carry instructions. They have conferred with both the flock of crows and with a screech owl who know the lord of the manor by sight."

Ciellō grinned his shark smile and rubbed his hands together again.

"You are pleased, excited?" she asked. *Plink!*

"Yes. A man like me does not kill so many people and survive if he is unskilled. And there is always a joy in using one's skill."

"But will killing again, or in this way, stir your regrets?"

"Not this man."

"Nor for me. I killed my first foe when I was a child of twelve and never looked back. I wonder if my name should actually be 'the Ruthless.' Animals, you know, kill to survive without compunction.

"I will make certain that the ultimatums convey a very clear warning: turn yourselves in or face death."

"That will salve your honor. But the general, an old man, is used to military weapons," Ciellō said. "He will not believe the threat. He will think: a pretty young damselle, beloved of dogs and geese."

"I fear so, Ciellō. But later in my rule, my enemies will believe me." She stuck her finger under the swan's beak to interrupt the droplet's fall. Then she solemnly licked the water on her skin.

My mother never fought back against her councilors. They neither loved nor respected her. She never used her Talent against her internal enemies. She found her courage against the Pellish, but by then it was too late.

That evening, the queen walked around Pearl Pond and then strolled in the garden; her shields and the dogs left her alone with her ruminations. Her thoughts mostly circled around how the slanting light of a clear summer evening made every leaf look charmed, and how few of such evenings any person could count on enjoying.

At dawn the next morning, Cerúlia saw Wilamara, Naven, and their honor guard, commanded by Captain Yanath, on their way. A long day's ride would take them to the headquarters of the Catamount Cavalry, to General Yurgn's manse, and then to the Ice Pikemen's base.

After delivering her ultimatums her ambassadors had instructions to return to the High Road crossing in the middle of the destinations, set up camp, and wait for further instructions from the palace.

22

Sutterdam

As money started flowing into Sutterdam Pottery, Hake decided he could spend a little on himself. He had a new wheeled chair constructed out of lighter materials, with bigger wheels that helped him get around more easily. Also, he relocated the pottery's former business office downstairs and had ramps constructed so that he could wheel himself everywhere around the factory floor and yard.

Free Staters clamored for quantities of jugs, pitchers, plates, cups, and all manner of vessels. The pottery hummed every day of the week, which pleased Hake, because whenever he took a rest, he felt forlorn. He became acutely conscious that he was crippled for life, with only his ruined father and his overworked aunt for company, and though Norling and he tried their best to put on cheerful faces, every day brought a reminder of what they had lost.

Hake was checking off a supply list when one of the workers knocked on his office door.

"A lady wants to see ya," said the man.

Thinking it was someone with a commission or an applicant seeking work, Hake absently replied, "All right. Show her in."

When he looked up, Pallia, his sweetheart before the war, was standing before him in a faded and worn dress decorated with a new pink ribbon.

"Pallia, you're *alive!*" said Hake, stupid with surprise.

"So are you," she said.

"Are you—are you all right?" asked Hake.

"We've all been through rough times," she said, looking away.

"Your people?" he asked.

"I lost my father and my brother in the Rout. My mother is doing rather well, considering. She and my father fought all the time; though it's a sorry thing to say, ofttimes I think she's happier with him gone. And my little sister escaped any real harm—though she's been running wild and I'm having a time reining her in and making her go back to school."

"Where are you living?" asked Hake.

"With a great-uncle far on the other side of town. Hard by Pot Menders Bridge."

Pot Menders Bridge, Hake knew, lay in one of the poorest sections of Sutterdam.

Pallia continued, "I heard about your family, Hake. I'm real sorry about . . . everything."

"Thank you." Hake cleared his throat. "Well. On the plus side, now we have a national hero in the family. Thalen shone like a meteor." He gestured around himself at the business that he had thrown all his energy into. "And the pottery's still here. Obviously. Actually, we're as busy as we were before the war."

Pallia smiled and returned to the subject of the Raiders. "From what I heard, Thalen had help, invaluable help, from his clever older brother."

Hake hadn't the slightest idea what to say to that compliment, although it pleased him mightily.

"Um—do you need anything? Maybe candleholders? How is

your candle shop?" Hake didn't want to reveal that he knew that the candle shop had burned down.

"No candleholders," said Pallia. "But I do need something." She chewed her lip and twisted her apron.

"Go on, tell me," said Hake. "Pallia, I'm overjoyed to see you. You know I'd do anything for you if I can."

Pallia scrunched her eyes closed. She almost whispered. "That's the problem: I don't know if you *can*."

Hake waited, bewildered and anxious.

Pallia kept her eyes closed as she continued. "I heard the pottery had reopened, so I thought I'd take this chance. What I need is: I need a husband and . . . children. Could you give me children, Hake?" She rushed the next sentences. "I couldn't be happy without them, don't you see? Of course I'm not assuming that you'd even still like me anymore. Or you might have found a beautiful woman in the Isles. Can you forgive me for coming, for asking? But otherwise it wouldn't be fair to you or me. . . . And before I tried to care for anyone else, I thought I should know. . . ." She ran out of courage and stood silent, twisting her apron.

Various emotions warred in Hake. Horrific embarrassment. Amazement at Pallia's bravery. And joy.

The pause grew even more awkward. Hake cleared his throat again. "Pallia, I can't walk. I can't stand. But I am physically capable of begetting children."

"Do you—do you want children?" she asked. "With *me*? After . . . everything?"

If he could walk, Hake would have rushed to her and swept her into his arms. The moment called for such action; her courage and her embarrassment stung his heart, and she looked unsteady on her feet. He grabbed his useless thighs in each hand.

"Actually, I hadn't ever thought about children. For all this time, in the Green Isles and back in Sutterdam, I have thought of *you,* not any other woman. I want *you,* no matter what 'everything' might be. And if you want children, then I want to have them with you."

She opened her eyes and walked a few steps closer to him. "I no longer own the shop. I come to you empty-handed. And I'm not young and pretty or carefree like I once was," she said.

"Neither am I," Hake answered.

A wisp of a smile. "Oh, I don't know about that," she said. "Your blue eyes still shine, and your arms look so strong. I can imagine that they'd feel comforting around a body."

Hake patted his lap. "Would you care to try?"

That made Pallia laugh her familiar laugh. "Not today, if that's all right with you. It took all my courage to come here and ask. But another day?"

"I'm going to hold you to that. Now." He cleared his throat again and settled his shoulders while she wiped the corners of her eyes with her fingertips. "Let's plan our courtship. It has resumed somewhat peculiarly. Would you like to come for dinner tonight at Lantern Lane? Or would you prefer me to come to you? Speak to your mother?"

"How about tomorrow night? I'll come to Lantern Lane."

"That's grand, because I can give Teta Norling a warning and she will set out a feast. Promise you'll come. You won't change your mind and disappear again?"

"No," said Pallia. "You are going to be stuck with me, like—like melted wax in a holder. But right now I'm going to leave to give us time to recover. I feel like such a brazen hussy."

Hake said, "I don't think I'll ever recover." He meant that as an expression of his happiness, and since she grinned she must have caught the meaning of his maladroit comment. "Let me escort you to the street." He wanted to demonstrate his adeptness in the pottery, to show that he was not as helpless and useless as he might look. He wheeled beside her to the front yard. At the gateway, she briefly gave him her dry hand and then walked off up the street, her back held very straight.

Long ago Mater had made a disparaging comment about Pallia. "Very pretty, but I don't think she's got any grit." Either Mater was wrong then, or the war had given Pallia grit.

Hake wished his mother were here to take back her words. And grand-babes! How Mater would have fussed over them! Hake tried to imagine holding a babe in his arms, or rolling around with a toddler on his lap.

23

Riverine

A day and a half after Naven and that seamaster delivered their risible ultimatum, General Yurgn, fully dressed in his uniform, as usual, came down to fastbreak with a spring in his step. The delegation had gotten a good look at his wall, gate, and well-trained forces, and it had departed after a brief conversation that had gone entirely to the general's satisfaction. The queen's deadline had come and gone, and of course he still ruled his household—his own private kingdom—unmolested.

The five grandchildren waiting for him to start their meal greeted him with smiles and little bows, as was fitting. He ruffled the hair of the two youngest and nodded to the footman to begin serving, even though the middle generation had yet to make an appearance, which was unusual, since his sons and daughters liked their food. Especially Clovadorska, who had eaten at his table all these years.

The general had just tucked in to his egg tart and cold meats when his daughter, Yurgenia, swept in with a curdled expression.

"What ails you, Daughter?" he asked, surprised that she brought such a face into his presence.

She threw a packet of papers beside him on the table. Yurgn used his knife to lift the first few pages of the sheaves, realizing that she'd gotten her hands on a stockpile of broadsheets. She must have read all the slanted, hysterical accounts coming out of Cascada about his "treachery," "venality," and "butchery."

"How did you get these?" he asked. "I've forbidden anyone to bring such calumnies on the grounds!"

When she didn't answer, he stabbed his dagger through the pile and into the tabletop. The knife swayed back and forth.

Yurgenia was not the biggest ninny in his household, but the sound of the knife striking wood prompted a tiny shriek to escape from her lips.

"Is this true? How much of it is true?" she dared to ask her father.

"Of course this isn't true. Everything I did, I did for good reason. For Weirandale. To keep the people safe. To keep order. To stop malcontents from spreading restlessness."

"But, Father! What have you done? You've ruined us!"

The children gaped at the argument, their open mouths full of victuals he had provided.

Yurgn stood up with dignity. "Ruined? Ruined? When was the last time you looked in the storeroom? We are rich, rich for years to come!"

Yurgenia made no reply, but she moved to drape her arms around the shoulders of her two boys.

This protective attitude enraged her father.

"I don't have to justify my actions to you lackwits! Who has kept you fed all these years? Who paid for your healers, your necklaces? Your feasts? Who paid for the well, the new wing, and the new roof? Would you rather the roof dripped on you as you slept?

"I do not explain my actions to *anyone*. Certainly not a slack-dugged woman who cannot keep her husband from dallying with the maids."

He looked around the table at the children, who were struck dumb by the confrontation and were staring at him with startled eyes. "Leave the table! All of you!"

Lurgn's youngest son, a youth of fifteen summers, whined, "But Grandfather, I haven't finished."

The general lunged over and cuffed the boy on his ear. He had never struck any of them before. *That* got them moving—Yurgenia hustled the children out of the room as if she were shooing chickens away from a fox. One of the maids dropped her brew pot and ran out too, but the footmen remained at their posts, even if they trembled a little.

If the servants haven't read the broadsheets already, they will soon. How dare they deign to judge me? Who's paid their wages all these years?

Reclaiming his seat, Yurgn tried to finish eating as if nothing had transpired. But the tisane tasted bitter, and the bread had turned stale and dry.

He threw his napkin at the table, deliberately knocking over several flagons, and stamped out.

Shortly after this aborted meal, the general paid a visit to his old ally. Preoccupied with events and giving orders to his soldiers, he had forgone the visit yesterday, but resuming his habit (reminding himself of his routine and duty) had a steadying effect after the unpleasantness.

Sweat ran down Matwyck's forehead, either from the heat or from a fever—the healer last week had spoken about an infection of the kidneys—and the room smelled more than usual, while the bedding looked none too clean.

"Ah. Matwyck, how are you feeling today?" Yurgn settled in the chair, not pausing for a response. "She sent me a threat, that uppity bitch." He waved the parchment at the invalid.

"Has she indeed? She must be feeling her oats. Tell me."

So Yurgn recounted the visit that had transpired, regaining his good temper as he described how Naven and the *woman* seamaster had come with a tiny escort of twelve, and how one of his own guards had ruffled their feathers by shooting an arrow just close enough to their horses to make the animals shy.

The general read from the parchment: "'If you do not take advantage of this offer within one day, your life will be the forfeiture.' Ha! It's been more than that since I sent them away. There's no march of boots down the road, no dust in the distance. Whimpering little queen with water in her veins instead of courage, just like her mother.

"She can't touch me in here; she daren't even try."

"And if she did," said Matwyck with a glint in his eye, "you'd offer me up as a bargaining chip."

"So you've figured that out?" Instead of feeling ashamed, Yurgn was pleased by his colleague's acumen. "Well, Matwyck, you must admit it is the most logical solution."

Matwyck did not remonstrate against him, which spared the general an argument. He'd already had enough scenes for one day; Matwyck (like himself) understood the ways of the world and would not give in to hysteria.

"At this point," Matwyck said dryly, "I would almost welcome arrest, because I would delight in a change of scene. These walls are driving me mad."

Yurgn looked around the small room, but he didn't see anything wrong with the grayish walls, though the room was indeed very hot.

"Why are children so ungrateful?" Yurgn mused aloud. "Your son, and now my daughter. Don't they know how much we have sacrificed for their benefit?"

"I've had a lot of time to puzzle on that," answered Matwyck, "and not come to any satisfactory conclusion."

"Well." Yurgn slapped his knees. "You have everything you need, I take it."

"Yurgn, I'd like more wine."

"*More* wine?" the general repeated, wondering how much his generosity was going to end up costing him. "Oh, very well," he assented with poor grace.

General Yurgn took midmeal and dinner in his chambers, rather than with his family. He'd decided to deprive them of his company until they mended their ways. After eating he grew restless and elected to take a turn before bed. It was hot and stuffy inside his bedchamber; the air outside was fresher.

He stopped at the iron front gate. "All quiet?" he asked the guards.

"Yes, sir!" His guards saluted.

"Very well," he said. Then he added words of praise and warning: "You're all good men. Keep alert now."

Slowly he climbed the stone steps that led up to the fortified wall around his manse. He touched the stone balcony, reassured by its thickness, marveling at how it retained its heat even as the sun began to sink.

Bringing his midmeal tray his daughter had shouted at him, "You don't care what happens to us! All you care about is your money."

Do I like riches? Of course I do. Everybody does. Show me a man who says he scorns gold, and I'll show you a liar and a fool.

In the dark the general reached the walls. The breeze was brisker up here, cooling the sweat under his neck. His uniform was hot, but of course he wouldn't unbutton or discard any layers. He could breathe more easily out here. He looked north in the direction of Cascada but could see nothing in the gloom, certainly no torches heralding an approaching force. He gazed east toward the pikemen's camp, but even in daylight the lay of the land hid their barracks. All he could see by moonlight and starlight were a few lanterns twinkling in cottages clustered near the manse's walls.

He had tripled the guard tonight. His men walked the walls

assiduously—very assiduously now when he had come out to monitor them.

The guard on that section of wall kept marching back and forth. The general liked his company, though he wouldn't say so. The rhythmic slap of his feet soothed his disquiet after the disagreeable events of the hot day.

General Yurgn was startled from his reverie by a gust of air from the flap of a bird's wing. An owl swooped down from the dark and perched on his shoulder for a moment. Yurgn felt its sharp talons rip through his clothing and cut into his flesh. It sailed off before he could react, other than to cry out.

"General! General!" called the guard. "General, are you all right?" he asked from far away.

Spasms of pain built to a wave of agony that crashed and shattered within him.

24

Riverine

Of all slights or insults, Matwyck couldn't abide being ignored. Everything about his situation was intolerable, but when Yurgn had failed to visit him yesterday—had failed to show him the least scrap of courtesy nor even sent his regrets—Matwyck had stewed in anger.

He'd had his revenge, of course; he'd sent Cosmas to distribute the broadsheets throughout the manse. He might be flat on his back, poorly tended, and losing strength every day, but he still had his wits, and he was able to strike back against those who treated him badly. The servant had insisted on recompense for this trifle of a commission (the man's greed knew no bounds), but Matwyck had been able to persuade him with promises of more wine.

Even though the Lord Regent himself thirsted mightily for wine's balm, he handed over the flask off his dinner tray. Cosmas in return passed him his nighttime milk of poppy, so Matwyck drifted off into sleep idly listing all the wines, sherries, clarets, and ports he had ever sampled. He'd taken them for granted in his past life; when he recovered and left this horrid sickroom, he vowed he would savor every swallow.

He didn't sleep as deeply as usual after his tonic. Movements disturbed the courtyard below his tiny window—people screaming? Shouting? Toward morning, as the drug wore thinner, he heard more distinct noises of a gathering of many people, the clop of horses, the wheels of carriages. The floors vibrated with the sound of running footsteps; women wept; and the flicker of torches danced on his spotted ceiling. At first Matwyck grew anxious, thinking the manse had been stormed, but he didn't hear any clash of swords. After a while, the house and grounds grew still, and Matwyck slept again.

The next day broke hot and humid and no one brought Matwyck his fastbreak. Cosmas didn't show up to help him with the chamber pot or help him wash. Matwyck marinated in fury for hours, trying to think of what revenge he could take on the neglectful attendant.

As the morning grew hotter, Matwyck began to shout out for attention. He shouted until his throat felt raw and his thirst redoubled. Only when no one appeared to his summons did it begin to occur to him that the nighttime noises had not been a poppy dream: he had been abandoned.

Abandoned! And helpless. After all I've done for Yurgn.

He swung his legs to the side of the bed and sat up. The room swayed with his dizziness. Very tentatively, he bent down to reach under the bed for his chamber pot. He hitched up his nightshift, held it between his legs, and pissed, feeling the relief of pressure as a blessing, but dismayed by how dark the liquid looked. He set the bowl back on the floor, disgusted by the fact that his arms were unsteady and he sloshed a little on the floor.

He collapsed back on the bed for a while, gathering his strength. He must have water. There was no pitcher or basin in his room, but water had to be available close by in the house, because Cosmas always fetched it.

He inched his feet back onto the floor. Gingerly he put some weight on his left leg. The son of a bitch of a healer wanted him to stay in bed for three moons while his pelvic bones healed, but Matwyck didn't have a choice.

Aha! This doesn't hurt much. I will walk out of here; I will tend to myself. My vengeance will be epic.

His right leg, the one with the wound and mangled muscles, screamed when he tried to stand, and Matwyck staggered, barely managing to stay on his feet.

Crossing to the door took all of his strength and willpower. He stood on his left leg and rested his forehead against the door, taking shuddering breaths, sweat pouring down his face. When he opened the door, the air in the hallway had a sheltered coolness he found refreshing. His room, he discovered, was at the end of a disused wing. The floor showed the dirty footprints of his servant and the general, while discoloration from roof leaks intermittently painted the walls.

Laboriously, Matwyck made his way down the hallway, trying each door. Most were locked; others opened onto rooms that were barren or in which the furniture sat clumped under dustcloths. No signs of fresh water anywhere.

Matwyck's dizziness worsened, and drops of fresh blood leaked down his leg. Ahead he saw a steep flight of stairs; undoubtedly these led down to the more populated parts of the house. And water.

He managed the first two steps. On the third he put too much weight on his right leg, which buckled beneath him, and he fell, scraping his skin in innumerable places. Dazed and smarting, terrified that he had jarred his pelvic bones out of place, he lay still on the staircase, waiting for his pulse to quiet, and took inventory.

The pain of his injuries was nothing compared to his thirst. He was tormented by his chalky throat, his pounding head, his longing for water. At least the staircase was cooler than his bedroom. He crawled a rung downward. He crawled another, and he was craning his dizzy head to see how many more he needed to manage when a faint overtook him.

25

Riverine

In late afternoon on a long summer's day, Cerúlia rode up to the inhospitable gate of General Yurgn's keep. The massive, high stone walls looked down on the entourage she had led out of Cascada after she had assassinated the general.

A little more than an hour before, the queen had paused at the campsite on the High Road to confirm that the cavalry and pikemen had surrendered their headquarters and taken the knee once news reached them of the general's assassination. As she had expected, the general's death was the only drop of water they needed before their resolve broke.

She invited Captain Yanath, Seamaster Wilamara, and Duke Naven to accompany her for the last leagues, but she had ridden from Cascada because she intended to take the defiant traitor's lair herself.

From a few paces behind Smoke, Ciellō scanned the walls warily, not quite trusting the crows' reports she had conveyed to him. No helmets showed over the crenellations, and no arrows pointed outward.

Captain Yanath urged his horse to the protective front doors. He called out in a loud voice, "Open in the name of the queen!"

No one answered.

"Whoever is within," Yanath shouted again. "Open the gate!"

Again, no response came back.

Yanath walked his horse forward and pushed at the massive oaken door leaves, finding them unbarred and the iron portcullis raised.

"Your Majesty, please wait while we take a look inside," he called over his shoulder, then he and a squad of shields disappeared inside the walls.

Cerúlia patted Smoke's neck, knowing that her guard would not encounter any soldiers or armed resistance, but allowing the men to discover this for themselves. Her canine corps took advantage of the pause to flop down in the grass, tired from the long, hot journey. She reached around to the pannier behind her saddle and grabbed little Cici; then she leaned to the side of her horse so the terrier would not have too far to leap to the ground. The dog relieved herself, then sniffed the noses of her pack, taking stock.

A recently hired shield, Gatana (one of Yanath's recruits), offered Cerúlia a drink from her waterskin. After several long swallows the queen doused a kerchief and wet her hot and dusty neck. Excess drops trickled down the military-style riding habit Editha had designed for her, with a split skirt and a formal doublet. Cerúlia wished she had insisted on a more utilitarian hat; the stylish little thing she'd worn today had not shaded her eyes well enough.

Swishing his tail, Smoke tried to discourage the flies that wanted to settle as soon as they stopped moving.

The party waited under the hot sky without chatter until Captain Yanath reappeared after a short time. "Your Majesty, on first glance, the place appears deserted." His men pushed the front doors open wide for the queen and her followers.

"Very well," said Cerúlia. "Walk on, Smoke."

The horses scattered a flock of loose chickens and geese. The

stone manor house sat lifeless. However, after a moment of vigorously sniffing the air, Cerúlia's hounds raced across the expansive
courtyard, heading straight to the right rear of the manor house,
where a well-kept whitewashed barn stood closed up, keeping its
secrets. Whaki and Vaki scratched at the door and started howling.

Humankine! Humankine, stink of fear.

Alarmed, the shields drew their arrows or pulled their swords.

"Please, Your Majesty, stay back," Yanath called. "You there, in
the barn. We know you hide within. Throw down any arms you
have and come out."

A pause ensued, broken only by the dogs' racket.

That's enough noise, now, Cerúlia ordered her dogs.

In the abrupt silence the door creaked open. Slowly, more than a
dozen people emerged, single file, their arms above their heads, their
hands visibly trembling. Men, women, and children, all roughly
dressed, with their garments and hair speckled with hay.

Cerúlia clucked Smoke forward. "Where is your master? Where
are his soldiers? Where is his family?" she asked.

"Mercy! We yield! Mercy, please! Why, it's the queen herself.
Your Majesty!" came cries from various throats as the servants
threw themselves on their knees.

The Shield patted these captives down for weapons, confiscating a few work knives. The dogs watched, slant-eyed, but neither
growled nor attacked.

No danger from this herd, sent Cici.

"Calm down and answer my questions," Cerúlia ordered.
"Where is your master; where are his soldiers; where is the family?"

"Gone," said an old woman in a white cap. "They hitched up the
wagons, took all the horses, and hightailed away. You kin see the
wagon tracks if you don't believe me."

"When was this?"

"Before dawn, a few hours after the general died."

"Did everybody flee?"

"Well, not exactly," a whiskered man piped in. "The lady of the house, that is Yurgn's daughter Yurgenia, she and her boys, they didn't want to go."

"And where are they?"

The servants looked at one another. Finally, a lad spoke up. "They're hiding in the millhouse."

"Point out the millhouse to me!" Duke Naven ordered. This smaller structure stood down a path a long walk away. Naven rode over, flanked by a couple of soldiers, to roust the hideaways.

Cerúlia dismounted, stretching after a long day in the saddle, and spoke to her dogs.

Are there any other people hiding in any of these buildings or the grounds? I want you all to spread out and search every corner.

Soon enough, Duke Naven escorted out—not over-gently—a strained-looking middle-aged woman in a mussed silk dress with a white collar and two young boys. He pushed them in front of the queen.

"You will bow," Seamaster Wilamara hissed. The mother and children instantly made obeisance.

"Mistress Yurgenia, I believe," said Cerúlia.

"Yes, Your Majesty." She was afraid to look up from her deep curt-sey. The smaller child started crying, the tears tracing tracks through a light flour dusting on his face. He wiped his nose on his sleeve.

"You are General Yurgn's daughter?"

"I am, Your Majesty."

"Who fled?"

"My brother, my cousin, and his family. Lurgn's widow, Clova-dorska, and their children. My husband, Karlot. Our chamberlain. All of our guards. Our chief cook and our head stableman."

"But not these here, the lower servants."

"No, they didn't have room for them."

"Is this everybody who didn't join the escape? Are any soldiers hiding away to ambush us?"

The woman glanced at the nearby people on their knees, taking a rough count. "I don't see all of the field hands, or the apprentices, or the under-cooks here. I would guess that several servants ran away to hide with relatives in the village."

"The soldiers?"

"They took all our guards for protection."

"Why did you stay behind? Did they refuse to take you?"

"No, Clovadorska entreated me to join them." Although her legs faltered in her deep curtsey, she maintained the pose. "I didn't want to flee. I don't fancy being hunted. And I thought that, mayhap if I stayed, mayhap I could plead for my sons."

She sank on her knees on the ground, looking up with her palms pressed together. "Please, Your Majesty. I beg you, *please* do not harm my boys."

"Do you really think that I would harm your children?" Cerúlia wondered whether, by killing the general, she had already turned herself into a monster in her people's eyes.

Yurgenia replied, "If half the things I read in the broadsheets are true, I can imagine wanting revenge. But, Your Majesty"—now she looked up—"these little boys are completely innocent of my father's deeds, however awful those may be."

"Set your mind at rest about your sons, mistress. Though I will have you questioned by the judiciaries, your children will not be arrested or mistreated in any way. I suggest you select one of these family servants to look after them during your stay in Cascada."

Cerúlia turned to the people who had hidden in the horse barn. "This is a large estate, and it would go to ruin if deserted or untended, and that would be a waste. If you wish, you might remain here, water the stock, and watch over the children while we debate what to do with General Yurgn's holdings."

"As it please Your Majesty," said the white-capped woman. "That is, most of us, we have no other homes to go to and—"

Cici interrupted the conversation by rushing down a flight of stairs that led out from the main house, yipping an alert. Cerúlia turned back to Yurgenia with narrowed eyes.

"Who is still in the house, mistress?"

Yurgenia mumbled something with her head down.

"Speak up," Yanath barked.

"I wasn't lying! I hoped they took him with them. I didn't want to harbor him, but my father insisted! I haven't talked to him, nor seen him, not once! Believe me, it wasn't my choice nor my doing!"

"Aha! *Matwyck* still lives," Cerúlia said. "Ciellō, I brought a healer and Chronicler Sewel with us just for this possibility. Fetch them."

Despite the day's heat, her body broke out in a cold sweat.

"*This* is a meeting I have long anticipated." She turned to the rest of her entourage, ordering, "The rest of you, wait here."

Cici led Cerúlia into the manor through a side door into an old wing, though Ciellō, drawing his sword, rushed to precede her.

From a staircase, Ciellō called out, "Here is the man you seek. He is unconscious."

The healer and Ciellō picked up Matwyck between them. Sewel ran ahead, opening doors, looking for a place to set him down. They carried him into the first room that boasted a made-up bed, which appeared to be the room in which he had been hiding away these moons. This small chamber had a bed, a bedside table, a chair, and pegs on the wall that held a few bits of clothing and some cloths. It had but one window, and the air was very close.

The healer listened to Matwyck's heart, pulled back his eyes, and chafed his hands, while Ciellō fetched a pitcher of water from the kitchen pump downstairs and then stationed himself on the opposite side of the bed. Sewel readied his portable writing desk.

Cerúlia stood by the narrow bedside while these ministrations were underway, studying the patient's face. She had known him as a child; she had seen him at the wedding; and his likeness had loomed at her from everywhere in Cascada until she had had the portraits and statues removed. Lying here unconscious, he was just another man, past his mid-years, but still trim and rather good-looking. Except his face showed recent scraping and bruising; his complexion had a grayish tinge, and his nightshift was badly stained. All in all he looked like a marionette whose animating strings had been cut. She wondered at her years of fear of him.

The healer spoke to everyone in an undertone, "He rages with fever. Some infection—probably of the kidneys. See how yellow his eyes are and this blood?" Again he passed the smelling salts under the patient's nose and gently swatted at his cheeks and the backs of his hands.

Matwyck opened his eyes. With effort, Cerúlia mastered her instinctive jolt of fear, though Cici began to growl. At first his eyes refused to focus; then clearly he recognized her.

"Water," he said through chapped lips, looking away from her face. The healer sat in the chair beside him and held the heavy pitcher to his mouth. After he drank several swallows Matwyck remarked over the rim, "Dressed up, you look like your mother. I should have seen the resemblance instantly." He choked a bit. "More!"

After he'd drunk more swallows, Matwyck continued, "Your disguise as a rural wench didn't fool me. I was just hours away from arresting you."

"I look like my mother, the queen you betrayed."

Matwyck cleared his throat. "Cressa was pretty, not actually dumb, and, I suppose, well-meaning. But naive. Frightened. Weak." He grabbed at the healer's hand holding the pitcher and drank more, dribbling a stream down his chin and neck. The healer yanked the pitcher away to keep him from drinking too much at once.

"I doubt you describe her fairly," said Cerúlia. "But if this were true, your duty was to teach and support her, not supplant her."

"I'm so hot," said Matwyck to the healer, closing his eyes. "Bathe my brow."

The man moistened a cloth and swabbed Matwyck's face and neck; then he put the wet cloth behind the back of his neck. This seemed to provide the patient partial relief. The healer opened the window wider. Matwyck lifted his lids again and noticed Chronicler Sewel.

"Oh, you're here too, imp? Scratching away with that damn quill again?"

Cerúlia asked the healer, "Can he be moved? Brought back to Cascada for trial?"

"No, Your Majesty," he answered. "He would not survive the trip. His pulse is very rapid; he fevers; he's dehydrated; I don't know exactly—"

She waved her hand to forestall any further medical details, then folded her fingers and brought her thumbs to her chest in a formal gesture.

"Well then, Lord Matwyck, now is the time to face your reckoning.

"I, Queen Cerúlia the Gryphling, do charge you with plotting treason and assassination against your liege, my mother, Queen Cressa the Enchanter. I charge you with the death of Lady Tenny. I charge you with attempting to kill my sister, Lady Percia, in her Wyndton home. I charge you with misuse of the public treasury. I charge you with innumerable illegal arrests, persecutions, and deaths of citizens."

Sewel's quill scratched against the paper, writing down her words. Matwyck waved his hand in front of his face as if these accusations were but midges; his dismissive attitude made her nostrils flare.

"What say you to these charges?"

His lips twisted into what might have been a mocking smile. "You don't know the half. You don't know about Retzel, I'm sure."

Cerúlia looked at Sewel for clarification. He responded, "Lord Retzel died on his Lakevale estate many years ago. We heard—we thought—of natural causes."

"Retzel was always a fool, and as he got older he couldn't keep his fat lips shut," said Matwyck.

"So you killed him?" Sewel guessed.

"No." Ciellō broke in, shaking his head. "This man, his own hands, never killed a chicken."

"Ah," Sewel replied. "You *had* Retzel killed. But it was never a scandal. How did you do it—poison?"

Matwyck grabbed his bolster with his hand and winked, indicating that he had ordered Retzel smothered. Sewel started and moved farther away from the bedside.

Seeing him sidle away, Matwyck hissed, "You've been a thorn in my side from the beginning, Sewel. Should have dealt with you much earlier."

"Lord Matwyck," said Cerúlia, "you will attend *me,* not the chronicler. I am waiting for your answer to the charges and for you to confess to any and all further crimes you have committed." She nodded toward Sewel's writing desk. "Be sure to add the murder of Lord Retzel."

"I want my sister, Eyevie," Matwyck said fretfully, avoiding her face. "She lives on a farm not far from the city. Heathclaw knows where. I want her; fetch her to me; let her nurse me in a bigger, cooler room." He coughed. The healer offered him more water, which he gulped eagerly. "If you bring her I will answer your questions.

"However, I will want your word of honor that I will be buried next to my wife at her manor house. My goods, my fortune, will underwrite the local under school she favored. The children will look upon me as their patron, their benefactor. They will offer songs of praise to my generosity at the beginning of each term. Write all this down, Sewel, every detail."

Cerúlia had a hard time mastering her rage to keep her voice level. "You mistake the situation, Matwyck. Heathclaw is dead, and Sewel is not *your* secretary. You are not in any position to bargain here, nor would the throne permit such an outrage. As for your fortune, it was stolen from the people of Weirandale, and it will be forfeited with your death. Tirinella's personal wealth will pass on to Marcot. No one will say prayers for you; no one will honor your name unless Marcot finds a smidge of charity in his heart. But since he freed the prisoners in your secret jails and was horrified by what had been done to them, that is unlikely."

"Marcot," Matwyck echoed, turning his head restlessly from side to side.

Cerúlia thought of her brother-in-marriage and mastered her fury. "As you lie dying, is there a message you'd like us to pass on to your son?"

Matwyck's fingers now clawed at the bedclothes. "Serves him right—marrying against my wishes. He did it on purpose. Let *him* be widowed; see how he likes it."

Ciellō curled his lip and explained to the queen. "He still has plans to kill Lady Percia."

A jolt of fury seized Cerúlia. She wanted to dispatch Matwyck this instant, with her own hands, which she had instinctively balled into fists. She drew a deep breath and looked around the room.

"Leave us," she ordered the healer. "Out! Go! He gets no poppy oil, no bathing, no fanning, no hand-holding, no comfort, nothing whatsoever!"

The healer made a slight noise of protest, then placed the water pitcher on the table and packed up his satchel. Ciellō took the man's elbow and hustled him out of the room, firmly closing the door behind him. Sewel backed a little farther into the corner, as if to hide from being dismissed too.

Cerúlia's hand clutched her dagger handle tightly. The patient had frozen in position, with his eyes closed.

"Matwyck of Cascada, I know you can hear me. Here is the throne's judgment. We do not need your testimony or confession. By the preponderance of evidence, you are found guilty on all counts listed." She turned to Sewel to make sure he had written this down. "The sentence for such crimes is death. Actually, it could be death many times over. It could be a particularly gruesome and painful death."

Keeping his eyes closed, Matwyck replied, "Bravo. A very adequate performance, if somewhat overwrought. You'll forgive me if I do not clap."

Cici growled low in her throat and the three people standing in the room gasped at his audacity, but Matwyck wasn't finished.

"I wonder, will you get your own hands bloody for me, little *wren*?" Matwyck kept his eyes closed and succeeded in making his tone lazy. "Will you stab me, as you stabbed poor, defenseless Lolethia? Or will you play the highborn royal and assign this job to your foreign henchman?"

Defeat filled Cerúlia's mouth with a taste like ash. She finally faced her foe, but she could wring no contrition from him. In fact, he insisted on goading her. Why would he do that, when clearly she held all the power?

She paced by the bedside down to his feet and then back to his head until insight struck her. Pulling out her golden-headed dagger, she slid its point across his neck lightly; Matwyck opened his eyes at its touch; he strained his neck toward it, but the blade merely creased the skin without drawing a drop of blood. The queen flipped the dagger and caught it out of the air just for show, then resheathed the weapon in the scabbard that hung around her waist.

"Now, why would you rush toward death . . ." she mused, "unless you dread to linger?"

Refolding her hands in front of her chest in a formal gesture, she spoke in ringing tones. "Here is your punishment, Matwyck of Cascada: you will die here, alone, and—I devoutly pray—in agony. By your actions, you have forfeited any right to comfort or companionship, whether of sister or healer. When you are dead, your corpse will be dragged into the woods like the rubbish you are, for carrion eaters to feast upon."

Matwyck lay still and closed his eyes, still depriving her of any reaction or satisfaction.

Her eyes fell on the pitcher of water on the bedside table. The water he had gulped so eagerly.

Cerúlia picked up the heavy, nearly full pitcher and began, drop by drop, to pour the liquid out onto the floor.

At the sound of the splash, Matwyck's eyes flew open and his hands stretched out as if to stop her. "No!" he cried. "No! Leave me the water!"

She poured more. Terror now distorted his features. Matwyck's mouth became a snarl, his peeling lips flecked with foam, his cheek muscles taut; his gray pupils glinted, while the whites of his eyes looked yellow. Cords stood out in his neck. He attempted to rise, but Ciellō pushed his shoulders back into the bedclothes.

The pitcher was half-empty. Cerúlia paused, savoring the moment. "Matwyck, your crimes are so heinous and so many that you have forfeited all claim to the Waters of Life."

"You dog-fuckin' cunt!" he howled as she resumed spilling the contents away.

Although she shook with rage, Cerúlia had time to think about her action, to reconsider, to show compassion to an injured and dying man. She kept pouring away the water.

The pitcher was nearly empty when Matwyck began to plead, "Please! I beg you. Leave me some—leave me a little. Just a few swallows!"

Perchance her mother or father, who by all accounts were very decent people, would have shown leniency. Certainly softhearted Wilim or Percia would have been unable to resist such a piteous plea. Just moments earlier, she had worried her people would judge her a monster. Were these actions not monstrous? Wise in the paths of pain and the trials of thirst, Cerúlia could well reckon the amount of suffering the lack of water would cause her captive. But her character had been forged by her losses—losses this man had set in motion.

Wilim was not here to plead for mercy, because he was dead. If Matwyck had had his way, Percia would be dead too.

She measured not only her own sorrows, but the agonies of all of Matwyck's victims—the murdered, the tortured, the wounded, the raped, and the bereaved—against the liquid left in the vessel, and wished she had more to pour away.

When it was completely empty, she threw the pitcher against the wall, where it shattered into a dozen shards, and Cici yelped in fear. Matwyck startled at the crash and then crumpled back on the bedding.

Cerúlia looked from Ciellō to Sewel with her eyebrows raised, asking if either of them wished to speak for clemency. Neither of them uttered a sound. Would she have relented if they had? No.

"Come," she said. "We are finished here."

And they left the room.

Cerúlia turned to Ciellō. "He had enough energy to mock us; I believe, despite what the healer predicted, that he is far from his last breaths. I saw with Sezirō at the Bread and Balm how long it can take a strong will to leave even a very weak body. Have the door barred shut and station guards at the head of the stairs to ensure that no one goes to his aid."

26

Sutterdam

"Norling, you just don't understand," said Hake. "It's not that I don't want Thalen at my wedding. Of course I'd like my brother to stand beside me. It's just—I don't want *Commander Thalen* at my wedding."

"Hake, you're talking in riddles!"

"No, listen! If Thalen comes, the wedding will be about *him*: 'Look, isn't it sweet that the hero's crippled brother has found a woman to marry him.' I don't want Thalen's long shadow at my wedding. Can't I have that day just for Pallia and me?"

"I do understand, Hake, but I still think you're making a mistake. Thalen has to carry that shadow around with him all the time, the way you have to carry that chair. It's a burden. Such a burden that his own brother doesn't want him at his wedding. How would you feel if Thalen didn't want you at his wedding because of your chair?"

"This is different."

"Is it?"

"Yes, because being a glory-dappled, national hero is a position most people would envy, whereas being a cripple is not something anyone wants."

"I'm not sure I see the difference, Hake. Both of you went to war. Both of you came back changed by happenstance, not by choice. I'm not sure that Thalen wouldn't be happier in your chair, reading his books, and you happier in his position, garnering acclaim. Everyone has been affected by the war, Hake. Look at your father. Look at me. The question is, will our family crumble because of these changes, or pull together? Thalen's holing up in Latham worries me so.

"But I'll say no more about it. I want you to be joyful at your wedding, not fretting that everyone is looking at your brother. Or fretting over whether your *bride* is looking at your brother."

Hake thought that Norling's last thrust was unfair. Of course he worried about Pallia and undamaged men, but he didn't think she would yearn after his brother. At any rate, it was going to be a very small, quiet affair. Just family, a handful of neighbors, a few of the most senior workers from the pottery. Less than twenty people. Hardly worth Thalen or Quinith traveling all the way to Sutterdam.

Yet a week before the wedding, with Norling's chastisement eating at him, Hake sent for Thalen. He compromised by inviting just his brother and not his armed and adoring followers.

Pallia thought it strange that Hake wanted to be married in a Courtyard of Vertia. On occasion she joked that she should go to Pozhar's Worship Citadel so that her candles would burn properly (she was back to making candles in a corner of the pottery), but religion didn't figure strongly in her family. But when Hake told her that his friend Olet had prayed for this union and blessed it before Vertia, she grew comfortable with a Courtyard ceremony.

About a moon after Pallia found him, everyone—including Quinith, who rode all the way in from Jutterdam, and Thalen, who arrived the night before—gathered in Vertia's one Courtyard in Sutterdam. Pallia's little sister gravely carried a basket of fruit for the Spirit. The resident gardener spoke about Pallia and Hake nurturing one another and growing together like two entwined trees. She bound their hands together with a green vine. She closed by saying, "And let the love of Pallia and Hake create a garden of abundance, a haven to all in this troubled world," to which the assembled small crowd murmured the correct response, "May ye grow strong and grow fruitful."

Hake and Pallia needed their blessings. He wasn't confident about his feelings for his bride. He had wanted to marry her for so long that the goal had outstripped the original infatuation. He no longer knew if he loved this woman, almost a stranger, bravely holding on to a smile in her new pink dress.

Pallia ruffled his hair and leaned down to speak softly to him. "Hake, don't look so anxious. I will make you happy."

The wedding party took carriages back to Lantern Lane for the party. Norling had prepared a cold midmeal in advance, and as per usual, all the dishes were delicious. Hartling was much taken with Pallia and her little sister; their presence brought life back into the house and a bit of a light into his father's eyes. Pallia's great-uncle brought several bottles of sparkling wine; after a while Hake found it hard to tell if the room's gaiety was forced or genuine. Thalen stayed in the background, speaking only when spoken to by a guest, jumping to help Norling with heavy platters.

Hake wheeled over to converse with his brother. "Thank you for traveling all this way. Not a grand ceremony."

"It was lovely, Hake. I would have been devastated to miss it. I'm jealous that you've found someone."

"Yes, I guess in this I am fortunate," said Hake.

Thalen was following his own train of thought. "I keep thinking of Mater. Wouldn't she have been happy to see this day! To have a daughter in the house at last! And Harthen would be teasing you unmercifully. You'd find garter snakes in your marriage bed."

When the wedding guests finally left, Pallia insisted on helping Norling with the cleanup. Hake realized that it had been years since Norling had anyone to talk to or help in the kitchen. Thalen, Hake, and Pater sat outside in the small backyard in the early evening light. Hartling had his pipe.

"I remember my wedding night," his father abruptly broke out, lucid as can be. "Jerinda looked so beautiful, Eldest, that I felt I would never be good enough for her. I was so nervous about proving myself. Just be gentle and patient, lad, and give it time. All will be well."

Hake and Thalen shared a glance over his head. His brother's face echoed Hake's own sentiments: astonished pleasure that Hartling had surfaced from his fog to give fatherly advice, mixed with anger that he didn't acknowledge that Hake's wedding night would inevitably be much different from his own. Thalen closed his eyes and rubbed his forehead a moment in frustration.

For their honey "trip," Hake had rented a small, one-story house across the lane and down the way for him and his bride, so they would have privacy, if not travel. After the dishes were washed, Pallia came to the back courtyard to fetch him. She kissed Hartling on the forehead in farewell, making his father glow. Then she wheeled Hake across the bumpy cobblestones and up the ramp into the little house. One of their friends had festooned the house with daisies, but the flowers were already starting to wilt.

Now, after all these years, I am alone with her, yet I can't take her in my arms. What if she finds my limp, withered legs repulsive?

They talked a few minutes, delaying. Hake told her how much her presence had meant to Hartling and Norling, which pleased her. She told him that while she would miss her sister, she was glad to be parted from her mother, a cold and grasping woman.

"Do you know what she said when we arrived at Vertia's Courtyard? She hissed at me: 'You should have bought the cheaper dress and given me the extra money!'"

"You look lovely in that gown," said Hake, dutifully and almost truthfully.

Pallia's smile was sad, as if she knew she had lost her youthful sparkle, but appreciated Hake's pretense.

"Do you know what I'd like to do now, Husband?" she asked.

"Tell me."

"I'd like to go to bed with you."

"Look, Pallia—if during the Occupation, anything happened to you . . ." Hake couldn't bear the idea of lying with her if she would shudder at his touch. "I mean, there's no hurry. . . ."

Pallia shook her head vigorously, but Hake didn't know whether she was denying she had been raped or refusing to revisit the past. "Husband, I would like to go to bed with you," she repeated.

"I think that can be arranged," he answered, in a tone that came out sounding more hesitant than he wished.

Hake wheeled himself into the bedroom, scratching the doorway only a little. He was skilled and strong enough to lever himself from the chair onto the side of the bed. Pallia knelt to take off his boots and then left him to wrestle with his own clothes.

Though light still streamed through the unglazed bedroom windows facing this house's back courtyard, Pallia lit several sandalwood candles on a side table. Hake liked the scent. Very slowly and deliberately, she let down her hair from the top of her head. She unfastened her pink dress and stepped out of it. Knowing his eyes were on her, she slowly took off her shoes and unrolled her stockings. Then she slid out of her underclothes, standing before him totally nude, trembling a little.

In a husky voice, Hake said, "Come here."

She came and sat next to him on the bed. He lifted her hair and kissed the nape of her neck. She smelled like lilac soap and the wine they had been drinking. He moved around to her throat.

"Everything's going to be all right," she whispered fiercely. "We lived. We're damaged, but we'll start life over. We will make it all right."

"To me, you're not damaged," said Hake. "You've just been, well, tempered into someone stronger."

"Ah, Hake." She kissed him on the mouth. "And can't you see that this is true of you as well?"

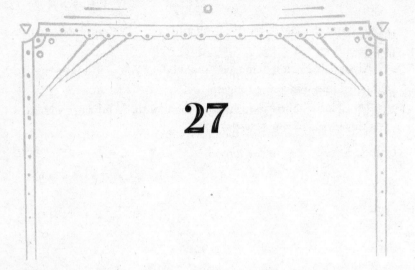

27

Cascada

Tilim missed Gunnit after he sailed away, but he was not homesick for Wyndton. He enjoyed the knowledge that instead of living in a backwater village, he was witness to important events.

As soon as Lemle recovered a modicum of strength, Mama insisted that Tilim, Lemle, and she move into the house in West Park that Marcot had leased for them. She wanted to establish a private home away from palace people (whom she distrusted), and she hankered to get back on a loom.

When the carriage with their meager belongings pulled up to the house—modest compared to the houses nearby, but still imposing by Tilim's standards, since it was constructed of brick with three chimneys and glass in every window—a brown-haired, middle-aged woman in a servant's apron came rushing out.

She curtsied. "I'm Tovalie," she said. "Lord Marcot hired me. I come with the house to take care of your needs."

Tilim and Mama exchanged a glance; they had never lived with a servant before and they weren't at all sure they wanted to. But Tovalie had already grabbed parcels and cases and led the way up the stairs. Mama put her arm around Lemle's waist while Tilim heaped the rest of their packages in his arms in a high pile.

"This is the main bedchamber," Tovalie said, showing them to a nice room on the second floor and gently setting down Mama's cases on a bench. "The young men are just across the hall."

"There are *two* extra bedrooms!" Tilim discovered. This would be the first time that he had a room to himself.

"Tilim, you choose," said Lemle. "I'm only going to stay until Lord Marcot finds me another apprenticeship, so I don't care."

Tilim chose the room facing the street, from which he had a view of the palace. He bounced on the bed a few times and explored the rest of the room's features.

"Lem—you all right?" he shouted down the hall.

Getting no answer, he dashed in to check on Lem. Tired from their short journey, Lemle sat resting in a chair pulled up by a window, smiling at the view of the sunshine and tiny back garden.

"Do you need anything before I go exploring?" Tilim asked.

A small knock on the door announced Tovalie. "Begging your pardon, I brought the young man tisane and sweet cakes—something a little fortifying after all this shifting around. And I'll unpack your parcels."

"Thanks, Missus Tovalie. Do you know where my mother is?"

"I saw her head toward the workroom in the back of the first floor."

Tilim found Mama crouched down, studying the mechanism of the loom that was set up in a room with newly set-in large windows that let in heaps of light.

"Mama, is it all right?"

"Well, it's not mine own. The weight feels all wrong in my hands, and it's a little stiff. But in time, I think it'll suit fine." And she smiled one of the first full smiles Tilim had seen in a long time.

"Let's go find the kitchen!" he urged, running through the house.

"Oh, gracious!" said Mama, when they found the basement room, as she surveyed the gleaming pots and stocked shelves and ran her fingers over cutting boards and a panoply of knives.

"Bet you could cook anything here!" said Tilim.

"Ma'am?" said Missus Tovalie, entering. "Can I help you?"

"Now let's get one thing straight," said Mama, crossing her arms and preparing for battle. "I do the cooking for my family."

"Of course. As you wish, ma'am," said Missus Tovalie. "Is it all right if I do the washing up?" A smile lurked in her eyes.

Mama saw it and grinned back. "Yes, that would be all right. Wonderful, in fact."

"And mayhap, just now and again, a fastbreak or a tidbit for the young gentlemen?" Missus Tovalie suggested. "Just so, ma'am, you aren't disturbed at your loom, or when you are consulting with Her Highness?"

"Missus Tovalie"—Mama's tone grew warmer—"they aren't gentlemen, and you can't call me 'ma'am.' We've never had a maid before."

"That don't matter. I want the job. It's a small house, easy to maintain, and a small family that don't put on airs. We're going to do just fine," said Tovalie, "so long as you tell me whenever you find me in the way or overstepping."

"Thank you. And you'll tell us if we're wrong-footed by Cascada customs?" Mama held out her hand, and the two women shook on it.

Mama unpacked for herself, and then she came outside with Tilim to explore the green space in the back.

"Not big enough, or sunny enough, for a garden," Mama sniffed. "I guess we'll have to buy all our vegetables. I wonder if they'll be crisp. And our eggs and our dairy. Will they be fresh?"

"Mama, it'll be great not to fuss over the chickens!" said Tilim.

"I guess," she agreed, in a dubious tone, "but chickens always were the sound of home to me."

The next day, Percia and Marcot arrived in a carriage, bringing a basket of wine, bread, and salt as a housewarming present.

After they had admired every room and every cupboard, the family gathered around the wooden dining table over tisane.

"I also bring news," said Marcot. "Lemle, Steward Alix knows a fine engraving company on the outskirts of town, High Road Engraving. He's explained that you are a little older than most apprentices, and that right now you need gentle tasks. The master—her name is Kinorya of Riverine—is willing to take you on as a trial. Next week, if you're ready."

"Did you have to bribe her?" Lemle asked suspiciously.

"I would have, if I needed to," Marcot admitted. "I would do anything to make up to you what my father has done. But Kinorya lost her nephew to Matwyck's Marauders. She is truly eager to take you on."

Lem looked around the room for everyone's opinion. "Say yes," Percie urged.

Mama spoke to the tisane leaves in the bottom of her cup, "Getting back to work is how one recovers."

"I don't want you to go so soon!" said Tilim. "But I suppose you could still visit. We could keep your room ready for you, for whenever you have a free day."

"Ah," said Marcot. "The queen has a plan for you too, Tilim. She says she knows that the under school in Wyndton was very weak, and she wants you to grow up well-educated. She proposes that you study each morning with Tutor Ryton, who will teach you things like mathematics and geography."

"I don't wanna go to more school or have a tutor! I want to be a soldier."

"But soldiers need to know all these things," said Percia. "If you are going to be a strong soldier, a clever soldier, and a help to Cerúlia, you need to study."

Lem joined in, "He's just the sweetest old man. And I'll wager that the queen believes that he too will recover more quickly if he has a young mind to instruct. Tilim, you can't refuse—he was imprisoned for fourteen years! You must at least give this a trial, like I'm going to try at High Road Engraving."

Tilim knew when he was trapped. He tried to give in with good grace. "All right, I guess."

"Good," said Percia. "Here's the thing. The queen wants to spare Ryton any travel, and she has a sentimental attachment to her old schoolroom, so she'd like you to work with the tutor there."

"That's fine," said Tilim, realizing that in the palace he'd be close again to the Queen's Shield.

"Ah, but the trek there every morning would eat up a lot of your day. So come outside a moment, would you?" Marcot invited.

Wonderingly, Tilim followed Marcot; the rest of the family, curious, stepped out behind them. The groom who had driven the young couple over now held the reins of a young gelding, so glossy black that he looked almost blue.

"What's this?" said Tilim, drawing in a deep breath.

"This," said Marcot, going over and throwing his arm around the horse's neck, "is Indigo. He is one of Nightmist's offspring. The queen, Hiccuth, and I thought that the queen's brother should own a horse."

"You mean, he's for me? He's mine?"

"That's right."

Tilim walked up to the horse slowly, allowing the gelding to sniff him all over. Then he pressed his face into the animal's neck. Indigo nodded his head vigorously several times.

Dimly, Tilim heard Tovalie say, "Ma'am, I'm not real used to— I'm not real comfortable around—"

"Not to worry, Tovalie," his mother replied crisply. "The boy knows the drill; he will take care of the horse himself. If he can't do that, he can't have a horse."

"Indigo," Tilim whispered. "Indigo."

"He looks awful fast," his mother said.

"Not to worry, Mama," said Percie. "The queen talked to the

horses before she chose this one. Indigo knows all about boys and how to keep them safe."

Thereafter Tilim's day started with an exhilarating ride to the palace. He turned Indigo over to the stable lads for the morning, while he rushed up to his lessons. Ryton spent the first week testing Tilim to find out his strengths and weaknesses, then decided on a lesson plan that actually was rather interesting, especially since it only lasted until midmeal.

Midmeal he ate in the barracks with the Shield. He tried not to make a pest of himself, but these were the men and women he admired; these were the men he wanted to be. He hung out in the guardroom, watching them play cards. He studied them, copying the way they wore their capes, the way they bowed to the queen, the way they spoke. If a shield was free, he or she would spar with Tilim or give him an archery lesson. Whenever they practiced drills on horseback, Indigo and Tilim joined their ranks.

The other reason to hang out at the palace all afternoon and evening was the dogs. Since Tilim had helped pick them out, he felt responsible for them. The dogs, like the guards, rotated being on duty. When they were off, Tilim would take them romping out-of-doors, letting them have fun just being free.

When the timing worked out, he brought one home with him for the night to the brick house they named "West Cottage." In many ways, this was best, because he suspected Mama was lonely. If he stayed too late at the palace, he would feel a twinge of worry about her.

Lemle reproved him one night when they were alone after supper. "I know, Tilim, that to you the queen's soldiers and their doings are fascinating. Could be, they fill the emptiness left by your father. But you have to think of your mother, all alone in this new house, in this new city.

"She's lost Wilim; Percia got married; and the queen is always busy. That leaves you and me, boy. I come by as much as I am able, but you know I can't set my own hours. 'Twas your mother, Tilim, who kept you fed and safe all those hard years in Wyndton. Don't you go deserting her now for new amusements."

Tilim didn't mean to desert his mama. He saw that she didn't really know anyone here, or at least not like the way she'd known everyone in Wyndton all her life. He saw how she worried about Cerúlia "running herself into the ground," and how she perked up whenever the queen or Percie came to visit. But he would be hanging around with Branwise, who was teaching him how to care for his sword, and time would just fly, and it would be late before he got home, and he would find his mother sitting alone in the dark, rubbing her sore neck.

Eventually he took this problem to Captain Yanath.

Yanath listened to the whole situation as if this was the most serious problem he had to consider today. He thought for a while before he answered.

"Tilim, one thing a soldier must have is discipline. He must be able to control his own desires to follow his duty. You have a duty to your mother—and from what I have seen, a fine mother she is. I suggest that you set up a schedule, kind of like I put shields on duty-schedules."

"A schedule for my mother?"

"No, no! A schedule for yourself. So. Say you decide that the first and third day of the week, instead of staying here after lessons, you will go straight home. Soon your mother will get used to this, and the two of you will go to the market those days, and you'll cheerfully carry her basket and tell her all about what you've learned. Say that on Waterday you decide that you will go to church with her, have a nice midmeal, and go out for a stroll to the Fountain. That way you will be around more, and most importantly, she will know when to expect you, so she isn't waiting and wondering.

"The discipline comes in sticking to this schedule, no matter what. You can't say, 'Oh, just this time, I want to stay at the palace because—'"

Tilim finished his sentence. "There is no 'because' for a shield on duty. When you're on duty, you show up and do your drought damn best."

"Right! So although you've been learning many skills that will hold you in good stead later in life, this is actually one of the most important. And you can practice it with your own mother. I'd rather have a shield who faithfully kept to his duty than one who was a perfect swordsman."

"Aye, Captain. I understand," said Tilim.

"I'm sure you get the gist, because you're a bright lad. But what you may not realize is how many of the soldiers here would give anything to have their mother or father back. While you might look at this schedule as your duty, I hope you also realize how lucky you are."

Thereafter, Tilim kept to a routine. Occasionally, he missed an exciting happening in the training yard. But his mother looked quite a bit happier; when he went to market with her he could choose his favorites; and chatting with her as she wrapped skeins of yarn around his hands was not actually a hardship. He put Mimi, Nini, and Haki on a schedule too, taking one of them home to West Cottage at a time. Soon the proper deerhound would be waiting outside the lesson chamber, eager for his or her day following Indigo to the cottage for a chance to live as a pampered pet. The dogs' expectancy helped remind Tilim what day it was.

Both Lemle and Captain Yanath commented that they were proud of him.

28

Cascada

Like a lady-in-waiting, Percia assisted the queen at the end of her day. Night was the only time when Percia could reliably catch Cerúlia alone, and Cerúlia often said that—no matter how fatigued by her duties—she looked forward to these moments with her sister. The ritual carried a whiff of their whispers and giggles as children put to sleep in the same bed.

Tonight the queen had dined late with all the foreign ambassadors.

Percia sat with a piece of needlepoint in the Reception Room. Cerúlia's personal maid, Kiltti, had already turned down the bed and lit the lanterns. It was too warm to need a fire this summer night.

Cerúlia swept in, her fancy gown itself making a stir, but she was also accompanied by her shields, her bodyguard, and her cloud of canines. She wore yellow lace, made over from a garment in Queen Cressa's wardrobe. Her hair was mostly down—the better to show off its color to the ambassadors—and fixed in ringlets. Percie knew how much Cerúlia hated to sit for hours while Geesilla curled her hair.

"Percie." Cerúlia smiled. "Kind of you to stay so late for me." The women left the men in the antechamber.

"How was your event?" Percie asked as she closed the door.

"Interesting. The Lorther envoy hinted that my family would want to visit. Odd to recall that I do have blood relations. I thought of seeking their protection once. But I never truly needed them as family, because I had you all in Wyndton."

Percia unhooked her trailing train.

"Never mind affairs of state, Percie, how are you? Don't you have a new husband waiting for you in bed?"

"Oh, he can wait for me tonight. 'Twill do him good. Married three moons, and he is already taking me for granted! This morn he left without stopping for a kiss."

Cerúlia sat down at the dressing table, kicked off her shoes, laid her dagger aside, and began removing pieces of jewelry. Percia took the pins down from the front of her hair, rubbed her head a moment, and started on the back of the gown. When she got it all unfastened, Cerúlia stepped out of it with a sigh of relief. Percia laid the gown on a bench and fetched a night-robe.

Unexpectedly, Cerúlia pulled up her undershift.

"Percie," she asked softly, "would you mind—would you take a look at my scars?"

Percia was surprised. "Mama says you won't talk about them or anything."

"I've been wondering," said Cerúlia, "how bad they look these days. When I saw them in Wyeland, they had just started to heal. Are they red, puffy, blistered, and disgusting?"

"Not at all. Some are faint; mostly the skin is hard and ridged." Percia described each scar to Cerúlia as she traced them with her finger. The longest scars were the thinnest and lightest—almost unnoticeable white lines down her side and from her underarm to her elbow. The biggest lay right on top of her shoulder blade, extending a hand's width in all directions, a puckered area of dark, discolored, and thick tissue. Smaller, scattered but raised scars laced the rest of the left side of her back. As she could see herself, the burned area of her neck had a reptilian texture and a reddish color.

"How did this happen, Birdie?" Percie asked as she held out a night-robe, hoping that her sister would stop hoarding her secrets and confide in her.

In a few dry sentences, Cerúlia told her a hair-raising story about fighting the Oros, being imprisoned, and being hit in the back by a fireball thrown by a Magi.

Percia could not imagine surviving such peril. She wanted more details about this misadventure, but her sister cut her questions and exclamations short.

"That's over now, Percie. Can I tell you what's on my mind? I want to know—I need to know—Would you tell me?—You are the only person who could tell me—"

"*What?*"

"You're a married woman now, so you would know," mumbled Cerúlia. Then she blurted out, "Would any man ever find me appealing? I mean, would any man ever want me, or would he just pity me?"

Hearing Percia's pause, Cerúlia demanded, "You have to tell me the Water's truth."

"Your scars are not your most attractive feature," admitted Percie. "When I first saw them I was a little shocked, but I've gotten over that. They're not repulsive, but they tell a story of pain that might distract a lover."

"Thank you for speaking aboveboard with me," Cerúlia said with a nod. "That's what I thought."

Percia shook her head. "No, no, no, no. I don't think you understand. If you loved a man and he had these scars on his back, would you love him less? If Marcot had these scars, I'd still want him in my bed! I didn't fall in love with him because the skin on his back was perfectly smooth!"

"Didn't Marcot fall in love with you because you're so pretty?" Cerúlia threw back at her.

"Mayhap. Yes. So you think these scars destroy your beauty? Perchance in Wyndton for all those years you hid as a plain brown wren, and no one saw you and you didn't see yourself. But by the blessed Waters, haven't you looked in the mirror these weeks?" She twirled Cerúlia around so she faced the looking glass at her dressing table again. "Now. Even without your gown or your hair fixed, just look at yourself in the mirror, and tell me, honestly, that you are not beyond fetching."

Percia leaned her head next to Cerúlia's so they both stared in the mirror at their reflections. Percia knew herself to be fair of face, with regular features. But her sister! Her hair's color provided a dramatic frame, and the Nargis Ice necklace gave her a kind of glow.

The young women regarded themselves in the mirror for a long moment, and then Cerúlia stuck out her tongue. This sent them both into hysterical giggles.

Cerúlia rose and poured them both glasses of lilac wine.

A flash of intuition struck Percia. "Are we talking about some unknown future husband, or are we talking about an actual person? Birdie?"

Cerúlia threw herself on the bed and sipped her wine for a few moments. Percia curled her legs up on the couch and held her breath. Already tonight her sister had confided in her with more openness than ever before. Had she pushed too hard? Would the distancing gates come crashing down again, shutting her out?

"I'm going to tell you something I've never, ever spoken about. I'd like to tell you . . . about what happened before I was burned. I'm going to tell you about my time with the Raiders and Commander Thalen. So many times, I've longed to unburden myself to you."

Out gushed a story of separation and love unspoken. As Cerúlia narrated and Percia asked questions, the bottle of wine emptied.

"My goodness, Birdie!" cried Percia when she reached the end.

"This is so sad. This story: 'tis almost like one of the ballads you sang to the Raiders."

Cerúlia threw a pillow at her. "You're not to tell a soul, Per-ci-a. Do you hear me! That's a royal command."

Her sister flopped back on the bed melodramatically. "What am I going to do? What am I going to do? There is no man in the world for me but Thalen, and he thinks I'm an Alpetar shepherdess."

"And drowned," said Percia. This matter-of-fact statement brought forth such a shriek of giggles that a dog woke up and looked at them reproachfully.

"And burned to cinders," said Cerúlia, topping her, and the black humor elicited more laughter.

"Besides," said Percia, sobered by a sad thought, "do you even know that he's alive? Or where he is?"

"I know he's alive, though I was terribly wrong about Wilim, wasn't I?" Doubt had crept into her voice, but she continued firmly. "Thalen, Tristo, Eli-anna—what a formidable team. If they could penetrate to the heart of Femturan to rescue me, I'd bet my golden dagger they still live.

"Oh, Percie, what am I going to do? What if he never cared for me? What if we never find one another again? What if he's found someone else? What if he can't adjust to my being who I am, or if he's angry about my disguise and lies?"

Percia stood up, a tad wobbly from all the liquor. "You are going to go to bed, because it is getting very late and you have a full day tomorrow. Give me a little time to think about this."

"Fine," mumbled Cerúlia as she crawled to the head of the bed. "I'll take care of the country, and you can take care of me."

"I plan to, Birdie, if you'll just let me."

Percie blew out the lanterns and was almost to the door when Cerúlia's voice floated to her through the dark.

"Percia, you don't recall the day we met, do you?"

"Of course I do," said Percia. "We played with kindling dolls in the workshop."

"No," said Cerúlia. "My mother Enchanted you to make you forget. I mean the *first* time. It was here, in Cascada. Here on the palace grounds. We met one day by chance in a play park. My mother tried to separate us and we both screamed. That's how she knew about your family; that's why she brought me to Wyndton. She trusted Stahlia and Wilim, but you and I, we chose one another first."

"Huh! Which just goes to show," said Percie, "that we should never be separated. We're better than blood sisters, because actually I found you, and you found me."

29

The Scoláiríum

In conversation with a student from Jutterdam, Thalen learned about the new queen of Weirandale's Talent of communicating with animals. After a day of mulling over the information, he sat in his (actually, Granilton's) study at Scholars' House, his thoughts askew.

White mounds, a frightful waste of expensive paper, accented the wood floor.

This is the most impossible thing I have ever attempted. Much harder than attacking Femturan.

Dear Queen, of course you don't know me, but could you possibly be the quiet, sore-footed woman who rode with the Raiders in Oromondo? I played the fife and you sang? I fell for you but was too much of a coward to admit it? By the way, I saw you die from the Magi's fireball so how did you get to Cascada and on the throne?

Naturally, he couldn't write something so ridiculous to the Weir queen. Her secretaries would never even pass such blithering idiocy forward. They would think he was a madman. He probably was a madman to even consider the idea, based solely on the ability to converse with animals, which, for all he knew, might not be that uncommon a skill. . . .

Though in all his studies, he had never come across any mention of such an ability.

Maybe Skylark was the queen's long-lost twin?

This thought made him snort.

A knock on his door interrupted his useless ruminations.

"Enter," Thalen called.

Wrillier the tavernkeep bent to avoid knocking his head on the low doorway. He held his cap in his hands.

"Begging your pardon, Commander, but you know that Latham has no law these days, so we thought to come to you."

"What's the problem?"

"Well, there's been a string of thefts, and we hoped the Raiders would look into it."

"Thefts? What's gone missing?" Thalen lay down his quill.

"A lot of things. Little things. A blanket on a line, a couple of chickens, and yesterday, a pie."

Thalen was not impressed by this inventory. "Oh, Wrillier, really? A pie? Probably kids took it. Or an animal."

"No, Commander. No village child would steal from Mam Setty; she lost her whole family in the Occupation. And an animal couldn't unlock a chicken coop and would have no need for a blanket. We're worried that there's a squatter living hidden hereabouts; could be someone unmoored by too much loss or war."

Obviously, Wrillier had put thought into this list of scattered objects. Thalen couldn't deny that a disturbed veteran might be a possibility; after all, Jothile had been unhinged by what he had undergone.

"Just when students are coming back, and things is getting back to normal, folks don't want to be anxious about some poor fool what's lost his senses," urged Wrillier.

Thalen sighed. "All right. I'll gather a couple of Raiders and look into the matter."

He found Kran stacking wood to dry for the winter and Wareth in the stable mending tack. Both were eager to leave these chores for a more interesting task.

Although they could easily walk to the village, they decided to take horses in case they needed to track the thief any distance. Wareth and Kran brought their weapons; Thalen reluctantly strapped on his knife but purposely left his rapier behind.

The first thing they noticed was that all three thefts had occurred at houses facing the woods on the western boundary of Latham. Wareth told Thalen and Kran to keep the horses and their own clumsy feet out of the way while he examined the moist weedy patch between the houses and the forest.

Thalen held the horses while Kran cajoled the village children, who always gathered at the sight of the Raiders, into staying out of Wareth's way.

Mam Setty, a woman of about forty summers but aging rapidly, came out to chat with Thalen. One of her eyes was completely clouded with a cataract, the other on its way. She wanted him to know that it was a *peach* pie that was stolen.

Thalen thought the filling of no consequence and listened with only half an ear to the woman's nattering.

"Aye, 'twas a peach pie. My baby's favorite. Every summer I'd bake him a special peach pie, and he always said it tasted like sunshine. My older girl—oh, she was so pretty and bright as a button (she, the one the Oros carted away to Sutterdam)—now she loved blueberry. When she found them she would also bring me a handful of raspberries to mix in, and we'd laugh about how the pie made our lips purple. My husband, now, autumn squash was his favorite.

"What kind of pie do you favor, Master Thalen?"

"I always liked berry myself," he answered, his mind on his own concerns, not really making an effort to be polite.

"Ah, I'm sorry, but the berries are all gone now; those we didn't gather got gobbled by the birds. Would another suit you?"

"There's no need for the bother. We're fed enough at the Scoláiríum."

"'Tis no bother." She held up her hands. "My hands are right skilled, you know; they can tell the flour and sugar by the weight and the texture." She turned half away from him, talking to herself. "I don't know why I baked the peach pie this year with no one here to eat it. Habit, I guess. Such a silly old fool am I."

Thalen realized that the pie had been her way of holding on to her son. He also realized that Wrillier was right: no local would steal from this heartsick widow.

Wareth whistled from the edge of the forest.

"We've got to be off now, mam," said Thalen, and he doffed his hat at her.

"You be right careful now, young master," she called after him.

Wareth had found footprints in the damp earth at the edge of the woodlands. He walked in front, watching the trail, Kran behind him, and Thalen came last, pulling the horses.

After a short distance the signs Wareth followed merged with an animal track. The men mounted up with Wareth in the lead, leaning over to watch the earth as the track climbed rather steeply. Thalen, as was his wont, fell into a half muse on horseback, comparing everything about this current mount (unfavorably) to Dishwater.

The path led them past the foot of a rock ridge that rose two paces over their heads. Thalen, though lost in his thoughts, still noticed Wareth suddenly shrink and duck. That warning was just enough for Thalen to tense his body, which served him well, because in the next half tick a man vaulted down from the boulder, knocking him off his mare.

Awkwardly grappling with one another, Thalen and his attacker rolled a ways down a wooded slope, banging into and scraping against tree trunks. Thalen struck the back of his head on a rock and for a moment saw only blackness, but as they continued to grapple together, he found himself the stronger. He knocked a knife from his assailant's hand. Then he perched himself astride the man's back, positioned his own dagger at the man's throat with one hand, and with the other grabbed a fistful of hair so he could crane the man's neck backward. His foe went limp in surrender.

The hair in Thalen's hands was white.

Breathing heavily, Thalen looked around. Because they had come to a stop below the slope, he couldn't see anything but tree trunks, downed limbs, bare earth, and greenery.

"Kran? Wareth?" he shouted.

"Aye. Up here. You all right?" called Wareth.

"I've got an Oro captive. Bring a rope, will you?"

Wareth, looking unhurt, brought a rope. Thalen kept sitting on the Oro's back while he bound the man's hands, then he hoisted his attacker to his feet. The three of them climbed back up to the horses, slipping on steep, slick patches.

Kran leaned against the rock face, bleeding profusely from a stab wound in his right shoulder. Thalen tore off his own shirt and used his knife to make a bandage, which he tied on tightly.

"Put pressure on this with your other hand," he told Kran.

"When he jumped me I landed on a rock," Kran said through gritted teeth. "My hip hurts more than the shoulder."

Thalen gently prodded the hip. "Can you stand?"

"If I have to," said Kran, putting a bit of weight on the leg. "I got the bastard back, though."

Thalen turned to examine the second Oro, who slumped in shock on the ground, a jagged bone poking out the skin of his forearm in a grisly fashion.

"Wareth," Thalen ordered, "find something we can use as a splint."

Using his sword to cut off small protrusions, Wareth shaped branches to serve. Then Thalen and he held the Oro captive's arm tight, pulled the bone straight, and wrapped the bleeding forearm tightly with the captive's own shirtsleeves. The young man sagged in his knees and broke out in a sweat but still said nothing. With a length of rope, they fabricated a crude sling.

"Right," said Thalen, standing up from a squat. "We've found our pie thieves. We need to know that these two are the only ones. Wareth, did you see them before they jumped us?"

"I felt the change in the light as they stood up," he said.

"I'm glad at least one of us was awake. Can you scout ahead while Kran and I keep an eye on these two? Don't be long, though."

"I'll be quick," Wareth said. Kran leaned his back against the rock to rest his leg. Thalen, knife in his hand, used the time to scrutinize the captives, noticing that their clothes had been worn to rags, and they were so thin their facial bones and ribs stuck out.

"Deserters, I'll wager. When the orders came through to rendezvous in Jutterdam, these two took to the hills. Hey, did you chaps know that the Occupation ended with all the Oros leaving the Free States and sailing for home? The war is over, and you've been left behind here."

The Oros looked at each other.

"What are your names?" Thalen asked.

They maintained their stubborn silence.

"What will happen to them?" asked Kran.

"It depends what mischief they've been up to," Thalen said. "The stealing counts for naught. But have they harmed folk?"

"They just tried to kill *us*," Kran pointed out. He spit the bloody dirt caught in his mouth to the side.

Thalen got the water bag off his horse and offered it to Kran. Then he rinsed his own mouth, discovering it was full of tiny bits of leaf litter. He didn't know whether the blood all over him came from the patients or from scrapes, so he rinsed off his forearms and hands. Then he offered the bag to the Oros. They refused.

Just as Thalen was starting to worry about time and Kran's blood loss, Wareth gave a whistle to indicate he was riding back.

"Their cave is just around the hillside. A bunch of empty sacks and bones of small game. Broken spears and swords. I saw two beds of leaves and blankets. It's just the two of them."

Thalen nodded and handed Wareth the water bag. Wareth took a long drink and tossed it back. Only a little remained, so Thalen poured the last liquid down the front of his face to rinse off the dirt and blood spatters.

Wareth burst out laughing.

"Something funny?" asked Thalen.

"Oh, 'Mander. When Death comes for you, you'll first stop to cool off that overheated brain of yours and then figure a way out of the jam."

Thalen managed a weak smile. "Okay, here's the situation," he said. "We need to get Kran and Broken Arm back to Cerf posthaste. Wareth, you'll take my Oro on your horse, because you're in the best shape. Broken Arm will ride with me; Kran in the middle."

"Commander, we could tie the Oros here and come back for them later—or never," said Kran.

"We could, but we're not going to," said Thalen, checking his mare's cinch.

Kran said, "We could drag them behind the horses—at least the one that's hale."

Thalen just looked at him. Wareth imitated Thalen's rebuke, "We could, but we're not going to."

Kran gave Wareth a sour look.

Trying to be gentle with their injured, they got everyone onto the horses. Thalen called to Wareth, "Can you head straight to the Scoláiríum and Cerf?"

"Hey! Don't insult my scouting. Just follow me."

Thalen's head ached with every lurching stride that the mare took, but the ride proved to be short and the Oros made no escape attempts. Soon enough, they rode through the gate.

Within moments Cerf had Kran on his table, first sewing up

the knife wound and then putting his femur in a corset-type brace he laced up. "I'll wager it's just bruised, but it could swell up like a son of a bitch. I'm marking the laces; if it puffs so much we have to loosen them, I'll use my new leeches to bring down the swelling." Cerf sounded quite excited at a use for his equipment and ignored Kran's grouchy expression.

After he had done all he could for Kran, Cerf moved on to the Oro with the shattered arm. He stitched the wound up, splinted the bone more carefully, and gave the Oro milk of the poppy.

"Your turn," Cerf said to Thalen. "You're such a mess, I can't tell where you're hurt. Strip." Cerf examined him all over, forgoing stitches on the gashes under his knees but spending a long time on the longer one on the back of his scalp, washing the bits of debris out of his torn hands, and soothing his multiple scrapes and bruises with unguents.

Rector Meakey wanted to talk to Thalen as soon as he was decently reclothed.

"Commander! What are we to do with these captives? The Scolárium is not set up as a prison!"

"Rector, the town asked me to find out who was behind these crimes. I've brought in the culprits. The injured one will stay in the infirmary, tied to a bedpost. The other one mostly needs food, a wash, and clothes. Tomorrow will be soon enough to question them."

"But where should I put him? Is he dangerous? Does he need to be guarded?"

Thalen's injuries ached quite a bit, and Meakey's questions were too stupid for a smart woman. He gave the rector an exasperated look.

"Never mind, never mind, I'm sure we'll manage," she said, beating a hasty exit.

The day had already been so eventful; Thalen was surprised to discover it was only midafternoon. He asked Kambey to lock and guard the front gate, just in case angry townspeople showed up. Tristo had set up a leather sling chair in a sunny spot near the library; he appeared with tall flagons of mead and bread smeared with olive paste for Thalen and Wareth.

Tutor Helina came bustling outside, carrying pillows of varied sizes. "Thalen, are you hurt?" she asked.

Thalen was touched by the worried look on her face. "Not seriously; a little banged up and a headache. No need for concern."

She handed him pillows to soften the chair. "Is there anything else I can do for you? Anything at all?"

"No, I think I'll just sit here and relax a bit."

Helina returned to her student; Thalen gingerly lowered himself down and drank down half the mead in long swallows. Tristo had brought his kitchen work—a big basket of peas to shell—outside. Thalen idly watched how deft the lad had become; he was able to split the peapods and drop the peas into a bowl one-handed.

Thalen thought about how they could easily have been killed. Danger could lurk anywhere, even so close to home.

The sun feels so warm. It's good to be alive.

Thalen dozed off in the chair, with his head and back cushioned by Helina's pillows. When he woke, a little groggy and quite stiff, he saw that Tristo slept next to him, lying on his back with his one hand pillowing his head. Glancing around in a wide arc, Thalen realized that Wareth had brought the tack he needed to repair out into the better light in front of the stable. Fedak stood a distance behind Thalen, remeasuring the library windows that needed new glass, giving Jothile directions about holding the string for him.

Thalen smiled at the sight of all these Raiders clustered around him. Thinking about the day's events, he realized an opportunity had opened before him. In Oromondo he had never talked to any Oros. All he did was kill them.

Thalen found moving painful, but he'd known much worse days.

"Hey Raiders," he called, gently nudging Tristo awake with his boot.

Wareth, Kambey, Fedak, and Jothile gathered around his chair.

Thalen opened his mouth, but Wareth forestalled him. "Wait a tick for Cerf—here he comes now." Indeed, Cerf strode across the green toward them.

"We was all watching to make sure you didn't die in your sleep from your wee concussion. People do, you know," Cerf explained.

"So you're still with us, Commander," said Fedak. "What's up?"

Thalen said, "I was thinking: undoubtedly we will face pressure to hang our Oro captives. However, we are going to keep them alive and protect them against any danger."

"Whatever you say, Commander," replied Kambey.

"What's on your mind?" asked Cerf, raising his eyebrows.

"Answers," said Thalen. "I read books all the time looking for answers. Now two people who possess essential knowledge have fallen right into my lap. This knowledge is valuable. We've killed enough Oros."

Thalen sent a message to Helina, asking her to fetch a book he'd once seen, *Prisoners: Methods of Interrogation,* from the library. He dispatched Wareth to find out where the rector had stashed the un-injured Oro (in a locked cellar, with Hyllidore pacing in front with a scythe).

Thalen retired to his own quarters. Although he had assumed possession of Granilton's office and books, he blanched at living in his former tutor's suite. Meakey had offered him a smaller set of rooms in the building set aside for male tutors. Thus far, Thalen had done nothing to make the place more comfortable or personal, other than hanging his mother's flowered hat on the wall.

By the time Tristo arrived with a light supper, Thalen had skimmed most of the library book.

"Just the person I was thinking about. Tristo, *Methods of Interrogation* says that you can extract information with pain and threats, but it's liable to be worthless. The better way is through building trust.

"You know how to get around anyone. Tomorrow I need you to win their confidence and get them talking; get them to tell us their names, their homes, why they deserted, anything at all. Once you make them relax, I'll be able to probe for more information about Oro ideology and cultural mores."

"I kin do that," said Tristo. "But—"

"But what?"

"I'm trying to square things in my head. When we were over there, we killed them all. When we was in Jutterdam, you, sir, well, you went kinda rabid, wanting revenge for your friend. These two prisoners might have had a hand in killing people around hereabouts. And now, you want to keep them alive and make friends with them?"

Thalen laid the book down and rubbed the bump on his head. "I know it sounds like a contradiction. Maybe it's as simple as different situations call for different responses."

"What if they had killed you or Kran?" Tristo asked.

"I don't know. I really don't. I'm just glad they didn't."

The next morning Tristo and Thalen visited the infirmary. Kran had been released back to his lodgings to recover in quiet. Broken Arm, however, had red-and-black streaks running down his brown arm to his hand and up toward his shoulder. Fever set his teeth to chattering.

"He's too weak to fight off miasmas," Cerf commented. "We either take the arm, or he'll die. Good chance he'll die even if we do amputate the arm."

Tristo pulled up a chair to the Oro's healthy side. "My name's Tristo," he said. "Look, see, I've lost an arm too. You get used to living with only one. Two is just extra." He grinned at the Oro and got half a grin back.

"They let you eat with only one arm?" asked the Oro, surprised into speech.

"Sure, why not?"

"In my country, if you are not intact you are worthless—just a mouth that can't contribute."

"Oh, you'd be surprised what you can do with just one arm," Tristo said in his confiding way. "For instance, I'm a very good cook."

"Yes, I've seen men cook here. In the Land, only women cook."

"Really? Are they good cooks?"

"They would be, but food is short."

"Hey, did anyone feed you last night? Do you want anything special this morning? How about I make you beef soup? What's your name?"

"Alnum."

"Fine. One bowl of soup for Master Alnum." Tristo scooted off toward the kitchen.

Cerf said, "Young man, what about your arm? Unlike our friend Tristo, you'll have a stump of your upper arm; that's useful and will give you even more mobility. We could take the forearm today or wait till tomorrow, try to build your strength up with more food. Your choice."

"Tomorrow," said Alnum.

When Tristo came back with the soup, Thalen took a seat a distance behind him with writing implements. Tristo chatted as he fed the patient. Alnum's biggest concern was for his friend; he wanted to know if his comrade was being treated well. Tristo promised to check on him soon, and in the meantime he casually steered the conversation to topics that interested Thalen.

Alnum thought he was nineteen summers old. He had grown up on a cattle ranch in the heart of the Iron Valley of Oromondo, but the blights had killed off all the cattle. Alnum's two brothers and his sister had died from tumors brought on by the Weir witch. His mother had turned to midwifery to support the family; the fifth time she delivered a stillborn babe, Protectors had slaughtered her, claiming that she herself was in league with the witch, a charge

Alnum couldn't quite believe, though he had no other explanation for the stillbirths. His father, the only person remaining in the family, had sent him off at age fourteen to enlist with the Protectors, believing that this was the only way to ensure he would eat.

Alnum had been too young to be involved in the first invasion of Alpetar. He had crossed Melladrin under the leadership of General Sumroth. All the troops feared Sumroth; he would whip a man as soon as look at him—take the skin right off his back with a barbed whip. Though he was so hungry many times he thought he couldn't move another step, he had tramped across all of the steppe. His best chum in his squad was killed by a Mellie arrow that had hit him out of nowhere in the middle of the night. Alnum was frightened of and despised the Mellies, who would never fight man-to-man in the daylight.

Tristo gave Alnum swallows of whiskey; he was rewarded with the story of the harrowing crossing of the Causeway of Stones and the Oros' delight at finding the causeway unguarded.

They learned that Alnum had not participated in the Rout; he'd been stationed behind the lines tending aurochs. In the aftermath, desperate for food, he had done his share of pillaging of houses around Sutterdam. His fifth-flamer was ordered to move his company inland; they had arrived in Latham about a year and a half ago. Latham was his best posting, because for the most part the men were well fed and enjoyed comfortable lodgings. He hadn't been involved in killing Granilton, though he had enjoyed burning a pile of books in the library lobby—they made such a nice blaze, and burning blasphemous books was payback for his siblings' deaths.

When the order came to pull out and meet up in Jutterdam, he and his comrade had been reluctant to leave the area that had provided them the most food they had ever enjoyed in their lives. They had deserted six moons ago, but having exhausted the supplies they stole, the demon of hunger crept back, causing their stealing, which attracted attention.

By afternoon, despite the draughts Cerf gave him, the young man raved with fever. Thalen could directly ask him any question he wished, because the boy was too sick to be guarded about his answers. Thalen learned that Pozhar was the mightiest of all the Spirits because he gave them Fire that fought off the cold of the high mountains. People who didn't worship the Magi had no souls; they would never join the Eternal Flames, so one could treat them like animals or worse. Raping a Free States woman mattered less than killing a goat: both had been created only for the Protectors' needs and pleasure.

Every time a Magi died, Pozhar would find a replacement. Alnum had never been to school nor learned to read, but before the blights nearly everyone learned to read so that they could study the sacred texts. Only strength, obedience, and piety counted as virtues. When Thalen offered other qualities, such as studiousness or empathy, Alnum dismissed these concepts as signs of weakness. Because he had broken the commandment of obedience by deserting, and because he had lost his strength by neglecting his practice drills, he might be exiled from the Eternal Flames, but the way he was burning up with fever now, perchance Pozhar was already coming for him.

By afternoon he lapsed into unconsciousness. Cerf decided delay was too risky; he took advantage of Alnum's coma to saw off the arm a little above the elbow.

"Will he live?" asked Thalen.

"I don't know," answered Cerf. "And to tell you the truth, after spending so much sweat slaving to save Free Staters harmed by those bastards, I'm not sure I care."

Thalen then repaired to see what progress Tristo had made with the other captive, whose name turned out to be "Unvelder." It had taken Tristo no time at all to break down Unvelder's reserve, because he was so extremely worried about Alnum. He would tell them anything they wished if they would let him visit the infirmary.

Thalen got the distinct impression that his friendship with Alnum was the most significant relationship in his life.

Unvelder had been born in Femturan. His mother had a position as a servant to Magi Four, so he grew up in a collective child asylum, a loveless and abusive place. Because of his proximity to powerful people, as a boy he ate somewhat better than many Oros, especially those in remote mining villages.

He had met his mother's Magi twice. On the first occasion Four tried to get him to swallow dried lava, but he spit it out when he left her quarters. On the second the Magi had asked Unvelder if he was possessed by the soul of a goat. From these close interactions, and from what his mother told him on her infrequent visits, Unvelder became convinced that the rulers of Oromondo were dangerous lunatics. He had joined the Protectors (not that he really had any choice) to get as far away from the Magi as he possibly could. He had been elated when they marched through the Mouth of the Mountains and left his country behind.

Unvelder had served as a pikeman in the Rout (during which he had been terrified of the Free Staters and just tried not to get killed), and then he had been assigned to a scavenger team, putting down wounded enemies, countrymen, or animals. He disliked that assignment but knew that if he didn't obey he would be killed. He put on a tough swagger like the other members of his team and kept his eye peeled for items of value. He'd found a jeweled dagger and several rings, all of which he traded for extra food.

Stationed in Latham, he was struck by the countryside's plenty and peacefulness. He had fallen in love with Alnum (those were not the words he used), and worried that if they reported to Jutterdam as ordered they would be separated. So he had instigated the plan to desert.

Unvelder had never heard anyone speculate that the water in Oromondo was poisoned, though they did notice that certain streams tasted bad. Mining jewels and ores was the key source of the Land's riches, and these riches brought it power against enemy countries; his people would never stop digging.

At the news that Alnum might die, Unvelder broke into shuddering sobs. Thalen took him out of his lockup to his comrade's bedside and let him hold his friend's good hand for a while.

As he sat in the infirmary, watching Unvelder weep over Alnum's peril, Thalen reflected on all he had learned that day.

Blighted boys. These fearsome soldiers were really just blighted boys. Warped by hunger, surrounded by religious fanaticism, and subjected to a cruel military regime. Their lives had been stunted through little fault of their own; the pressures were too strong to resist, and the regime locked them in a worldview that allowed them no alternatives.

The face of the wounded Oro that Thalen had executed in the Raiders' first skirmish in Oromondo reappeared in his mind. With a sinking heart he realized that boy had been no more guilty than Alnum or Unvelder. Even less culpable, because he was merely minding his own business in his own country. Thalen knew that the Raiders could not have kept prisoners, but now he writhed to recall that he had killed the boy with only a fleeting moment of pity and regret. Maybe the murder was unavoidable, but he'd had no right to commit it so damn casually.

Thalen didn't ask Unvelder if he had participated in Granilton's death, because he didn't want to know. Even if Unvelder had, he hardly would have had a choice, nor did he possess the moral compass to understand that the act was wrong.

Can people like this be reeducated? At least the boy is capable of love and loyalty. That's a start.

A student arrived, sent by Kambey to find Thalen. With the fall of darkness, about twenty-five townspeople had worked themselves up to gather at the gate armed with torches, pitchforks, and clubs, demanding that the captives be turned over to them. As he walked to the gate, Thalen reflected that Free Staters could be just as bloodthirsty as Oros.

Thalen nodded to Kambey and Fedak to open the fence of iron posts enough for him to slip out to talk to the crowd. His head throbbed as he contemplated the complications of this situation. Other than the Raiders (and even they would support Thalen only out of loyalty, not out of conviction), he couldn't be assured of the Scoláiríum community's backing. He must not betray Meakey or the standing of the institution by alienating the populace of Latham. And yet, at all costs he couldn't allow passions to lead to more strife and bloodshed. He wished he had Destra's touch with negotiating.

"Good evening, Wrillier. Good evening, all," Thalen said.

"Evening, Master Thalen," Wrillier answered. "We hear you found our thieves, that they be Oro deserters, and that you're sheltering them here."

"You heard correctly, Wrillier. You asked me to get involved in this matter, and I have proceeded as I saw fit."

"Thankee for capturing the Oros. We'll take them off your hands now."

"I'm sorry, but no," said Thalen, careful not to raise his voice. "These two are under my protection." He made sure his tone conveyed unshakable conviction.

Wrillier tried to reason with him. "Meaning no disrespect, sir, you weren't living here this past year. You didn't see the Oros kill us, beat us, steal everything in sight, and subject all of us to a hundred insults."

Other villagers' voices broke out, so inflamed that Thalen suspected they had already done a great deal of drinking, to bolster their courage. "My sons died in the Rout!" called a man in the back.

"My sister died while she was hiding in the forest. She should never have suffered that cold and wet!"

"They slaughtered my milk cow and laughed at me when I complained."

"THEY TOOK MY GIRL." A woman broke out in loud wails.

The litany of grievances kept pouring forth, and with each one, the crowd got angrier.

"They must pay for what they done to us! Why should they have life? Even if these two didn't do it, they have to pay!"

Thalen let the mob voice all its losses, then raised his hands for quiet. Kambey had to bang his sword on the metal gate to get attention.

"Your sufferings have been horrendous," Thalen said. "Unfair. Unbearable. We all agree. I know this in my own bones, because I too have been directly affected by the Occupation. My mother was stabbed to death by would-be rapists. One brother was killed at the Rout, another crippled. My father was tortured when he was en-slaved. I completely understand your desire for vengeance. I'm no different from you: at one point I was so consumed by this hunger I licked Oro blood off my sword."

The crowd had grown quiet to listen. He wasn't scolding or shaming them for their bloodlust; he had heard their anguish. He knew what they felt.

"Then don't talk to us about forgiveness!" shouted a villager.

"No, I won't," said Thalen, for how could he describe to them the tiny seedling of fellow feeling for the Oro captives he'd only just discovered in himself? "But I will talk to you about all the other vil-lages, all the other families in the Free States that have suffered just as you have suffered. You have heard enough tidings to know that if anything, Latham escaped rather lightly. I could tell you tales about Jutterdam that would keep you quaking at night for months."

"All the more reason," said Wrillier, "for you to hand over those two. We'll enact justice for all our countrymen."

"I only point out the losses of other towns so you will understand that Latham's sorrows are not unique. And to point out to you that in Jutterdam, the people decided that restoring the peace was more important than enacting vengeance."

The crowd listened, but stirred restlessly, not wanting to be swayed from their purpose. Tristo had slipped through the opening in the gate and now stood beside him.

Thalen licked his dry lips, knowing that his argument rested on concepts of time, history, and planning for the future that would be unfamiliar to those who lived for today, tomorrow, or at most next season's harvest. He pitched his voice louder. "What I want you to consider is this: we have two Oro soldiers under our control. I have already talked to them enough to know that they possess valuable information about why the Oros invaded, their strategies, their military command. I have a chance to cross-examine them, to extract knowledge that might keep future generations safe.

"You are thinking only about what you have already endured. But what if the Oros attack again in twenty years? And what if from the data I glean, we could forestall that future misery, the misery that your children would bear?"

The villagers began talking all at once. Thalen caught only snatches: "Let the future take care of itself"; "We owe a debt to those who died"; and "Don't Oro pigs lie?"

Mam Setty pushed herself to the front of the crowd and turned to face her fellow villagers.

"I'm just a blind old woman," she said. "I have no kin left; you all know. I'm not clever. I never had no education." The crowd had to quiet down to hear her; "shhh" broke out on many sides.

"But I've counted," continued Mam Setty, holding up the gnarled fingers she had counted upon. "Thirty-two younglings live hereabouts, from the new babe to near-grown gals. I would do anything to keep them safe. Commander Thalen defeated the Oros in Oromondo and at the siege of Jutterdam. He found these deserters while you sat on your arses. If he says he needs them alive, then—well, for me, that's that." She brushed her hands as if dusting off flour.

Wrillier wasn't so easily dissuaded. "How long will it take you to question them? A week? Will you turn them over to us then?"

Thalen said, "I think they possess enough information that I would want to write a book about what I learn, to save this information for posterity. I would need to keep them handy throughout this process."

Kambey cut in as if a new thought had just occurred to him. "This is the Scoláirium, you know. Think how many students and scholars might be drawn by the chance to question our captured Oros. Myself, I'd like to ask them about their armor. Of course, that's on top of the students who are going to want to come here to study with Master Thalen, of the world-famous Thalen's Raiders."

Thalen marveled at Kambey's cleverness; he had just subtly touched on Latham's economic self-interest, a string Thalen himself had not thought to pull. And his sword master's words conveyed just a touch of threat: *Do you really want to defy or drive away the Raiders?*

"How will you insure that these wretches don't escape or murder us all in our sleep?" shouted a man.

Wareth spoke from a few paces behind Thalen, chuckling. "Do you really think that *Thalen's Raiders* can't handle two Oro pikemen—one of them on death's door? Hey, folks, I'm a little insulted by that."

This brought answering chuckles from the crowd. The townspeople began, almost unconsciously, to step back a few paces from the gate.

Thalen spoke up loud enough for all to hear. "Wareth, Kambey, Tristo, I'm tired tonight, and I still have that headache. Could I ask you to stand these good folks a round at the Humility Tavern?" He tossed Tristo a gold coin.

"Our pleasure, Commander," said Tristo. Wareth pushed the gate wide open, sauntered out, and draped his arms around two shoulders. "Hey, what did you name that new babe? It was a boy, wasn't it? Isn't 'Wareth' a grand name? Much better than 'Cerf' or 'Kambey.'"

Rubbing his aching head, Thalen turned back in the direction of his cheerless room; he had spoken truly about his fatigue.

All day, while questioning the Oros, a thought had chilled him.

As long as those blights persisted, as long as the Oros starved, they could not prosper, and they posed a peril to other realms.

He wondered if Irinia would help him set up more experiments, looking for elements that would bind with cadmium and lead suspended in water. Could they turn these toxic metals into inert compounds?

30

Cascada

Sewel had been pressing Cerúlia to visit the royal library. She was eager to do so—after all those years of hunting down bits of information about her lineage and history, she finally had, ready at hand, a trove of wisdom. But establishing security and dealing with emergency financial issues pressed more urgently.

The days had been hot, and Cerúlia had slept fitfully the previous night. She was weary of meetings, talking, tabulating figures, and performing under public scrutiny. More than anything she wanted to sit alone with a book. At fastbreak she decided to clear her schedule, and she sent Darzner to tell Sewel to expect her.

He was watching for her outside the room where the chroniclers worked, holding the keys in his hand. He frowned at Whaki and Vaki accompanying her, but did not voice a protest. Ciellō took up a post outside the door.

Cerúlia gasped when she entered the library. It was cool and airy. The water feature—water streaming inside two panes of glass—provided a soothing, continual play of shadows from the hot sun. From floor to ceiling she saw heavy volumes, each embossed with the name of a queen. She walked slowly through the space, her first finger sliding over the books' spines in wonderment.

A chest-high podium and stool sat in the middle of the room, and a slim new volume had been set out on the small flat surface. It had her name on it. Cerúlia turned the pages idly. Here was the Royal Announcement of her birth. Next came a description of the Water Ceremony of her Naming. Sewel had penned a description of the day he had failed to Define her Talent. Then many pages had been left blank; but the book resumed on the day of her Dedication, and the pages thereafter were filled with her recent decisions and proclamations.

Sewel, standing quietly beside her, interrupted her quick scan of her own life. "Your Majesty, one of my most urgent duties is to fill in the pages of your exile. Will you give me permission to interview Lady Stahlia, Lady Percia, Duke Naven, and others who knew you before your return? And of course, yourself? It is most important to keep good records, especially of your Talent, to guide future queens."

"Of course," she answered absently. "Though it may be hard to find the time."

"Here"—Sewel produced a very aged-looking volume and laid it gently down on a small table—"is the *Chronicle of Queen Carlina,* the only other Gryphling in our history. I trust you will find reading it very revealing. And it will convince you of the crucial role of our record keeping."

Cerúlia gasped at the notion that she was actually not the first queen with this Talent.

"And here," Sewel said, pulling down a newer-looking volume from a nearby shelf, "is the *Chronicle of Queen Cressa.* You will want to read this, I'm sure."

"Oh, yes," said Cerúlia, grabbing her mother's volume to her chest. "Oh, yes, I'd like to know more about my mother."

"I will leave you in privacy, then," said Sewel, bowing. "Should you desire a repast, the table in this corner is situated at a bit of a distance to keep food away from the books. Just tell your man when you are hungry. And I will be in my office next door, should I be able to be of any further service."

Cerúlia sat down in an upholstered chair near the water window. The dogs stretched out on the floor beside her with dramatic exhalations. She read about her mother's birth and childhood, her Definition as an Enchanter, her trips to Lortherrod, and her engagement to Seamaster Ambrice. She read on about her mother's sudden assumption of the throne. Hereafter the entries grew more numerous and detailed, chronicling her governing decisions, which Cerúlia would have to study in more detail later. And every twenty pages or so, first Rowatag and then Sewel had transcribed her mother's thoughts.

The transcriptions of her mother's voice particularly gripped her. Cerúlia read her mother's words of pride over her healthy daughter; her growing suspicions of Matwyck; and her feelings of isolation and loneliness, except for the company of Nana and the loyalty of one councilor, Belcazar.

Cerúlia found the flood of information overwhelming. She ordered midmeal and took a break, thoughtfully drinking her tisane and conversing a little with the dogs.

These papers tell me about my mother, she told them.

Didst thou have a mother? asked Whaki.

Yes. I loved her. She loved me, she told the dogs.

Vaki sent, *We love thee too, Your Majesty.* His tail began to wag vigorously. *Dost thou nay wish to leave here? This room reeks of animal skin and dust. Come smell the grass outside with us? Sunshine on thy back feels good.*

Not just yet, Vaki. If you are bored, I can send you outside.

Vaki took crumbs from her fingers. Whaki approached, looking expectant. She gave them both the rest of her meat, then the dogs settled down to sleep again. Vaki snored.

Cerúlia turned back to her mother's chronicle. She read:

This morning I received a very troubling missive from Oromondo claiming that a shipment of rice we traded was poisoned. The letter was full of threats. My councilors are dismissive of the danger, except for Belcazar. Belcazar feels that we must prepare for war.

Prepare for war! I am no warrior queen. My Talent for Enchantment is so undeveloped. Tonight I have perused the chronicles of other Enchanters, and I have hope that my Talents may grow as the need arises, though I hardly see how I can defeat our enemies from without or even my enemies within the palace. How I wish Ambrice were in port!

Whatever happens, I must protect Cerúlia.

The Waters of Life flow, and each of us rides along the current for but a little while. Yet we take comfort in knowing that the Waters will forever flow on. In Ambrice's and my case—in Weirandale's case— Cerúlia is our contribution to continuity. Every step I take in the next perilous days must take as its compass point the need to protect and shelter her.

At the worst, this may mean that I must separate from her, drawing danger away from my cub. To do this would shatter my heart. Ofttimes for the good of the country we must sacrifice our heart's desires.

The last pages of the *Chronicle of Queen Cressa* were filled with Sewel's account of the attempted assassination, her flight, broadsheet reports of her mustering of the Allied Fleet and her battle against the Pellish pirates. Sewel closed the volume with two documents: first, his own eyewitness account of the day the Dedication Fountain temporarily ceased to flow, signaling Queen Cressa's death; second, a copy of "The Lay of Queen Cressa" that Matwyck had commissioned upon her death.

One of the things I'd most like to do, Cerúlia said to the dogs, *is get the real story of my mother's last five years and her defeat by the Pellish. My uncle Mikil would be the best source for that information. Then I will order this lay rewritten—deleting all the tired clichés. My mother's life was heroic enough without embellishment.*

Whaki lifted his head and stared at her, indicating that he was paying attention even though he couldn't follow the import of her words.

Though her bravest act transpired in a little cottage in Wyndton one rainy night, an act for which she will never get the credit she deserves because it was a private loss, not a public battle.

The dogs got up and paced around, ostentatiously sniffing at nothing, and suddenly Cerúlia too wanted to leave this room, so crowded with history and ghosts—this room that one day would hold her own life, trapped within vellum. But just out of curiosity, she opened the volume about Queen Carlina.

This slim book was different. Carlina's chronicler was not so assiduous—fewer pages were in his or her handwriting. Also, it was filled with Carlina's own drawings, which were all of animals. A rabbit nibbling in a vegetable garden. A raccoon scratching its back. A cat sleeping in the sun. Each animal was named, and Carlina had written a phrase about its personality. Interspersed among the pages she saw many pictures of a small pig, white with black splotches, with shining eyes and an upturned nose. Captions, in a childish hand, said, "Muffin likes peas," "Muffin is my best friend," and later, accompanying a sketch of a Cici-sized pig, "Muffin rooted up the herb garden today, and Mummy was very mad."

Midway through, when the queen had grown older, she had drawn pictures of people, but she had drawn them to resemble animals. A councilor looked rather like a mule. A suitor resembled a crafty fox. She gave her consort the features of a bull.

Cerúlia laughed out loud, but she was also disturbed. Carlina's Talent had blurred the line between humans and animals.

Was she happy with a bull for a husband? And she draws her daughter as a piglet. A darling piglet, but a piglet just the same.

"Ciellō is right," she said out loud to the dogs, startling them awake. They looked at her with their ears pricked up. "You are dogs—all right, yes, lovely dogs, my wonderful dogs—but dogs just the same. In many ways it is easier to get along with you than to sort out messy relationships with people.

"But since I am condemned to be human, I must try harder."

31

The Honor of Your Presence Is Requested

At a Harvest Day Fest

At Which the Realm Will Acclaim Weirs
and Treasured Allies

Who Joined Queen Cressa the Enchanter

In Battles against Pexlia and Oromondo,

And at Which the Realm Will Celebrate

The Safe Return Of Those Unjustly Confined

And

The Restoration of the Nargis Queen

(Fashioned by Lemle of Wyndton)

32

Alpetar

Sent by Saulė's Mirror, Peddler stood on the end of the dock in Tar's Basin, waiting for Gunnit's ship to tie up at the rickety wharf. His spirits rose at the sight of the boy's snub nose and wide grin; he missed him more than he had realized.

The general store, Everything You Desire, doubled as a tavern, though the space was small and crowded. Gunnit sat on a cask, and strings of peppers and herbs hung from the ceiling. Over their meal of mutton stew, Gunnit told Peddler about his adventures with the Nargis heir and Water Bearer, while in turn Peddler conveyed that Gunnit's family and friends in Cloverfield prospered. He had re-assured them that Gunnit was hale and coming home soon, and though Dame Saggeta looked daggers at him, his mother's face had lit up. Addigale was walking now, and Limpett seemed more confi-dent with Kiki at his side.

After the meal, Peddler suggested they enjoy the bathhouse. Fortunately, the sailors had already moved on, so they had the place to themselves and could continue their confidential conversations.

The wooden building smelled of soap and the cedar shavings used to feed the coals that heated the water. As they undressed, the older man noticed a chain now hung around Gunnit's neck.

"What's that?" he asked.

Gunnit pulled it forward and squinted down his nose so he could see it too. "This was a leave-taking present from the queen and Water Bearer. Underneath this little gold token—it's a cat face, see? I think it's supposed to be a catamount—there's a glass vial, see? And inside the vial is one swallow of Nargis Water. Nana said that if I or someone I love is sick unto death, I should crack the glass and give them the water and it will revive them!"

"Whoa!" said Peddler. "That's a gift worthy of a king. Keep it safe, lad."

"I will," said Gunnit, carefully laying it with his clothes so as not to take it in the bathwater. "It's funny that for a shepherd boy with nothing to my name, I now have *two* pieces of gold jewelry!"

As they washed and soaked, Peddler explained the state of the Sun Spirit's chosen realm.

The Oro refugees from Femturan, spread across a series of five camps established down the length of the Trade Corridor, had now occupied Alpetar for a year and a half. Peddler had done everything he could to ameliorate the harm the Oros wreaked. Their presence, always an affront and intrusion, had become intolerable when the bored soldiers began ranging afield, raiding more hamlets. They pillaged, raped, and took slaves, causing suffering in Saulė's chosen land. Peddler desperately wanted to push the invaders back into their home country.

Alpetar had no army, and many of the men who might have been able to resist had died in Oro slave camps. So Peddler didn't have any ideas of how to force this retreat, but he hoped that now that he had been reunited with his apprentice, together they would come up with a plan.

After the bath, Peddler said his goodbyes to the folk of Tar's Basin, hitched Aurora up to his wagon, and the two of them jingled their way along the High Road.

When the strategy came to them, it arrived—as most blessings did—from Saulė.

One evening two days later, Peddler was consulting Saulė's Mirror (which steadfastly refused to show him anything but his own reflection), when a yellow jacket landed on the glass surface. Peddler impatiently swept the insect away, but it stung him in the forearm.

"Ouch!" he shouted.

"What happened?" asked Gunnit.

Peddler showed him the sting, already starting to puff, and Gunnit commented, "During our travels on the High Road, wasps almost killed Sheleen when she stepped on a nest. They may be small, but they pack a wallop. An army of yellow jackets could drive the Oros away."

"That's harebrained, boy. We don't have an army of yellow jackets, nor any way of mustering one," Peddler said.

In the morning the sting area had grown red and hot, and it had swollen as large as an apple. It bothered Peddler constantly; he kept rubbing it and watching its progress.

"I do have a friend who is a beekeeper," he conceded. "Culpepper's sister, Dame Dewpepper, lives about ten days south of here. Let's go pay her a visit and see if she can help us.

"Aurora! Get along!" He snapped the reins at the mule. "Pick up your feet, old gal."

Dame Dewpepper and her family welcomed them warmly in their cottage. When Peddler settled Aurora in the small, fenced paddock, he noticed a new mare—a small gray horse with such an expressive face she looked as if she wanted to talk to him.

"That's Cinders," the Dame told him as she laid food for them at her big table. "We got her over a year ago; Culpepper found her for me. She's just the sweetest thing. All of us dote on her, and we argue over who gets to take the honey to market.

"But back to your project. My bees won't help you, Peddler. Honeybees almost never sting. Yellow jackets are different—very aggressive, especially now in the late summer. If you could get yellow jacket colonies to converge on an Oro camp, they might raise a ruckus."

"But why would getting stung by yellow jackets send the Oros back north?" Gunnit pondered. "Why wouldn't they just scatter every whichaway from a swarm?"

"There's a gambit in Oblongs and Squares where you block all the directions your opponent can move except one," said Peddler.

Dame Dewpepper and Gunnit didn't understand what he was talking about, but that wasn't an immediate concern. After they'd eaten their honey sandwiches and tisane, on Peddler's insistence Dewpepper accompanied them out in the summer dusk to demonstrate where yellow jackets like to nest, either in the ground or in the shadowed recesses of evergreen shrubs. Dewpepper was stunned by what they found in just a few minutes.

Gently pulling back a branch of a juniper, she exclaimed, "Peddler, look at these nests! They're as big as soup kettles! And so many! I never seen so many afore! Mayhap something about conditions this summer has led to bumper colonies."

One of Dewpepper's older sons had tagged along behind them. "Ma," he called in a careful voice.

"What is it?" she replied, still staring with wide eyes at the size of the hives under a bush.

"Ma!"

Everyone looked at the boy. Twenty yellow jackets swarmed on the toe of his boot.

"Stand very still," she said in that fake calm voice one uses when trying not to panic.

Gunnit slowly took off his weskit and wadded it up in his hand as a potential weapon. Peddler noticed that the insects ignored everyone else and landed nowhere else on the boy.

"What's on your boot?" he asked.

"I might have dripped honey on it," said the lad, watching the insects with wide eyes.

Dewpepper said, "I wouldn't be surprised if they're attracted to honey. Like bees, they might love sweet tastes. We're all just going to stand still while they lick the boot clean. No sudden movements."

It took longer than any of them wished, but eventually the wasps lost interest in the boot. The instant he was freed from immobility, the boy scampered back to his cottage. Dewpepper, Gunnit, and Peddler followed behind, conversing and calculating.

"How would I get the nests and the critters into my wagon without getting stung to pieces myself?" he asked her.

"I dunno. The only thing that comes to mind is when I wants to get into a honeybee hive I set a torch on fire—the smoke seems to calm bees down some."

After his experience with just one sting, which was *still* paining him, Peddler needed more surety. When Dame Dewpepper went back inside the cottage, he pulled out Saulė's Mirror again. The last ray of sunlight hit the surface, and Peddler saw a vision of the flatlands of Alpetar, of one of the fields of hemp grown for fiber and oil.

Saulė—are you telling me to smoke the nests by burning hemp?

It was worth a try. In the morning Peddler drove his wagon to one of those fields and traded a bolt of woven cashmere for a large bale of hemp. The next day it only took Gunnit and him a few tries of parting branches of evergreen bushes to spot a gray nest with yellow sentries.

"Let's do a little test," Peddler suggested. "Find out if this is even possible."

Gunnit and he put on all the clothes Peddler had in the wagon (cursing that he carried no gloves), grabbed a long knife, and twisted three strands of hemp together to make a rough torch as long as Gunnit's arm. Gunnit tried to set the strands themselves alight, but the hemp was too fresh and green to catch; so Peddler rooted around in his wagon until he found his kerosene, which he doused on the tip.

Sweating under his layers of clothing from the heat (and terror), Gunnit finally succeeded in setting the hemp alight. Peddler heard him coughing and choking. "Stand upwind from the nest, boy!" The insects' droning slowed, and they moved much more slowly.

Whispering "May Saulè light my road," Peddler reached over and cut the nest off the branch, keeping it on his knifepoint so it didn't smash through falling. He moved the nest about three paces, set it down gently under the same evergreen, and sprang away. A dozen wasps buzzed lazily around their home, but none showed interest in attacking.

"Well," Gunnit commented, pulling back the spit-soaked scarf that protected his lower face. "I guess it's possible to move a nest. Now what?"

"Now we have to make my wagon one big yellow jacket home."

Peddler drove his wagon to Dewpepper's near neighbors. In exchange for two new saucepans, the family was happy to let him store his trade goods in their dry barn for as long as needed.

Back at Dewpepper's they got into long arguments about caulking the wagon. Gunnit and Peddler wanted to close all the small gaps between the planks of the wooden wagon to make themselves safer from their yellow-and-black assailants. Dewpepper insisted that the wasps would need air and that, besides, no matter how well they attempted to fill up the old wagon's myriad holes, the agile creatures would be able to wiggle out. Much to the dismay of man and boy, the beekeeper's expertise won out.

So the next day, when the family safely took themselves off to a market town (with the sweet mare and a shopping list from Peddler), the duo spent frightening hours stupefying yellow jackets with burning hemp and stashing their hives in Peddler's wagon. One hive broke when Peddler detached it from a branch; he thought he was a goner, but Gunnit jumped forward to protect him with his hemp torch, stilling any revenge-seekers.

Peddler set the hives either on the floor of the wagon or on shelves and hooks; Gunnit kept feeding more hemp into a tiny fire he tended underneath the wagon, making more smoke to subdue the aggressive colonies. A few hundred insects flew away from crevices in the wagon's roof, but Peddler and Gunnit didn't care because they still had thousands. Finally, when dark came, the buzzing in the hives ceased altogether.

During their labors, wasps stung Peddler four times and Gunnit twice; now, however, Peddler was perversely delighted by how much the stings hurt, because they were proof of their weapon's potency. Or all the hemp smoke he had breathed in might have made Peddler a little giddy.

"Look at this one!" he crowed, showing Gunnit a nasty welt on his neck. "Who would want to stay where they were exposed to hurts like this?"

In the middle of the night they drove Aurora and the wagon close to the Oro settlement the invaders called "Camp Diamond." They had named all their encampments after jewels; this was the southernmost Oro settlement and also the site most responsible for pitiless raids.

In the morning they approached down the Trade Corridor with all of Aurora's bells loose and tinkling, the better to cover the buzzing in the wagon. The camp was as large as a small village, with two-family sleeping tents laid out in an orderly fashion, and larger structures for cooking, schooling, washing, and worship clustered in the middle.

The Oro soldiers minding the gate recognized Peddler and his distinctive yellow vehicle; to keep on top of their activities he had made sure he was a welcome guest.

The fifth-flamer in charge came out of his tent to greet them. "Hey, Peddler. I hope you've brought something worthwhile this time."

"Goatherds in the mountains need to root out poison vines, and they've no gloves," Peddler said. "I'm in the market for all the gloves you are willing to part with. In exchange, I have brought a special treat—lookee here, a bushel of fresh plums."

"Plums!" said the officer, smacking his lips. "We can give up a few pairs of gauntlets for plums! Fetch what you can," he told his orderlies. Gunnit passed out the fruit, handing as many as he could to soldiers and men rather than the women or children.

"You don't mind if I drive around the camp, do you?" Peddler asked after he received some gloves in return. "I'm on the prowl for rare items to trade, and I'll take a gander to see what folk may be missing."

With plum juice running down his chin and dripping onto his clothes, the officer casually waved Peddler on.

Dispensing kindly nods, Peddler drove around the camp in a U-shaped pattern, while Gunnit surreptitiously tipped out a constant drizzle of honey from jugs hidden under the wagon seat. They treated the western, southern, and eastern boundaries of the camp, leaving the northern roadway clear.

"Here, fellas!" Peddler tossed the last plums to the guards at the settlement's gate when he had completed his circuit. Then he waved farewell and drove out of Camp Diamond. They halted the wagon behind a stand of trees just out of sight. Fingers trembling, Peddler fumbled as he unhitched his old mule.

"Gunnit, you know the plan. You get yourself, and you pull this stubborn old girl all the way into the pond we spotted. I don't care if you're cold; I don't care if it's mucky or scummy—you wait in the water, safe from stings, until I come fetch you." He slapped his mule on the haunches. "Aurora, you mind Gunnit. I doubt that a wasp could penetrate your thick hide, but I ain't taking any chances with you."

When he returned to the wagon, Peddler dressed himself in two layers of clothes and one of his new pairs of gauntlets. Then he threw a cloak over his head and for good measure tied a blanket around his body, trying not to allow even the smallest gap.

When he had waited long enough that he calculated that Gunnit and Aurora were safe, Peddler lifted the latch on the back of the wagon with a long stick, then threw himself to the ground, covering his head and face.

From the noise, the angry yellow jackets swarmed out of the wagon in a dark cloud. Peddler lay facedown in the dirt in terror, for without a doubt he had unleashed enough venom to kill dozens of men. The insects hung around the wagon for several heart-stopping minutes; then a breeze must have carried them the scent of sweetness. They took off like a starving, avenging army, straight toward the Oro settlement.

The shouts and screams would have been pitiful, but Peddler had hardened his heart to the men who raped and kilt Alpetar girls. He peeked out of his blanket: in the distance he saw figures racing north. The first looked to be soldiers, but civilians ran hard on their heels.

Within half an hour, Camp Diamond lay quiet and deserted. When Peddler gathered enough courage to visit the abandoned site, he saw that wasps had started building new nests in abandoned structures and the holes around tent poles. He doubted that any Oro would want to resume living here.

Later that afternoon, Gunnit put cooling mud on the two new stings Peddler had received from wasps that had still gotten inside his blanket, while Peddler picked bits of drying algae off Aurora, who was in a foul mood.

Gunnit broke into Peddler's thoughts. "Did you just make up the idea of poison vines? 'Cause I'm a-thinking that for Camp Topaz, mayhap we could use smoke from poison ivy plants. My father always told me that that's wicked dangerous."

PART
THREE

Reign of Queen Cerúlia

AUTUMN

33

Tidewater Keep, Lortherrod

Again tonight, Arlettie had begged off from joining Mikil at High Table. As the guests waited for King Rikil to join them, Mikil pondered how the closeness they'd shared on the isle had given way to frozen silences. Tidewater Keep had accepted her with somewhat grudging politeness, but instead of trying to become more habituated, she brimmed over with complaints that courtiers left her out of conversations; everyone compared her unfavorably to Mikil's previous amours; it was too cold and the sun never shined. Mikil knew that the crux of her discontent lay in his neglect, and the time he devoted to his duties as Sailor.

So Mikil was especially relieved when the king distracted him from his worry and guilt by entering with an invitation from Queen Cerúlia on a silver tray, which he passed around amongst the family, with great satisfaction that he had been proven correct.

Everyone was overjoyed to receive it and remarked on the card's fine engraving.

"To arrive by Harvest Fest doesn't give us much time," said Rikil. "We probably need to travel the longest distance. I shan't go myself, as the Moot of the Nobles is regularly scheduled then. But Mikil, would you represent Lortherrod?"

The-king-that-was banged his hand down on the table. "I'll sail to Cascada. My ship. My sailors. I'll take the old biddy."

Rikil and Mikil looked at each other over their father's head.

"What do you think, Mikil?" asked his brother.

Mikil addressed his father. "Might I come with you?"

Nithanil glared at his younger son. "I'll be seamaster, and I'll brook no interference."

Mikil said, with an irony that only he understood, "I am content merely to be a sailor." Still, he wondered whether his father was up to such a voyage. True, he had recovered from his last illness, and he appeared fairly hale these days. As to sailing, his father could outsail any of them from the grave. And Nithanil's determination could not easily be gainsaid.

Buying for time, Mikil asked, "Sire, have you finished Cerúlia's present?"

His father smiled his rare smile. "Aye." He bobbed his head. "Send a page to fetch it from the old biddy."

In a few minutes the page returned with a velvet box. Inside lay a pin crafted out of blue sapphires. It was the shape of a dolphin, and his father had used a tiny fleck of aquamarine for the eye.

"'Tis a present worthy of a queen," said Mikil truthfully, handing the box around so others could exclaim over it.

His father banged the table with his fist once more. "Get the ship ready, Rikil. I'm sailing a week from today."

Rikil, the king, took being ordered about more graciously than Mikil would have predicted. "Aye, aye, Skipper," he said with a salute.

His father chuckled, and as he left the table (wrapping his own tart in a napkin to take it up to Iluka, crumbled and broken), he rubbed his eldest son's hair with an even rarer affectionate gesture.

Rikil turned to his brother. "Will you take Arlettie and Gilboy with you?"

"I'll have to consider," Mikil replied. He wanted to revel in Shrimpella's return without distraction. And Lautan might have duties for him to perform that he could not explain to his wife.

It was late when he returned to the room he shared with Arlettie. Sometimes, so as not to disturb her, he slept on the couch in their antechamber, but tonight he entered the bedroom. Although the chamber was dark, he could tell from her stirring that she wasn't asleep. He lit a lantern.

"How are you feeling?" he asked.

"A little better."

"Are you cold? Shall I build the fire back up?"

"No, the blankets were warmed."

"There was news at dinner tonight. Queen Cerúlia has invited us to a Harvest Fest celebration."

"Ah."

"Sire and I will be sailing to Weirandale as soon as arrangements are made. We'll be gone for some moons. You and Gilboy will have to keep each other company."

"As we always do," she said, her bitterness clear in her tone.

"If you're *that* unhappy here, Arlettie, you could return to the Green Isles. I would not keep you here against your will."

"Thank you for your gracious 'permission.' Don't think I haven't been considering this."

Now was the moment when Mikil was supposed to speak up about how much he loved her and how much it would break his heart to lose her. He temporized by pouring himself wine from the carafe on the table.

In the bottom of his flagon Mikil saw the truth he shied away from admitting: that Lautan had rescued Arlettie and Gilboy to use them in service of himself and Cerúlia. At this point, Arlettie and her unhappiness meant nothing to the Spirit. Another woman, with more education and resources, would have found interests and occupations in court—perchance even taken a lover out of need or revenge. But the courage, inventiveness, and softheartedness that had made Arlettie so valuable on the isle didn't stand her in good stead in a Lorther court. And to Mikil, their years of closeness had floated away, crowded out of his heart by the tide of his spiritual rapture. She had become mostly an encumbrance and an obligation.

So instead of saying the things she wanted to hear, he blew out the lantern and got into bed.

"Sleep well," he murmured. And then, because he wasn't actually a cruel person, though the words were a pitiful substitute, he added, "May you have pleasant dreams, my sweet."

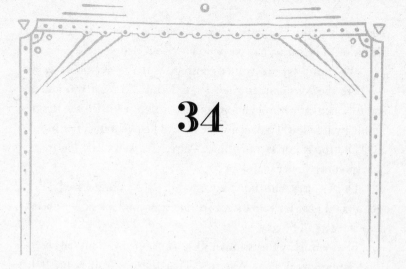

34

Latham

Wareth, Cerf, and Kambey sat at the bar in the Humility Tavern, nursing tankards of ale and discussing the upcoming trip to Weirandale for this highfalutin festival. An invitation for the Raiders had found its way to Minister Destra in Jutterdam, and her courier had brought it to the Scoláiríum two days before.

Wareth, who felt restless in this rural town, was the most eager to go. Cerf and Kambey thought it might be a lark, but they approached the prospect with less enthusiasm.

"You'd think," said Kambey, "that after all the sailing and trekking and fighting, the commander would be happy to just stay still. This is a likely place; as likely as any other. We don't need no honors from the Weirs for what we did. We didn't do it for them, anyways, but for the Free States."

"I know," said Cerf. "And I thought the commander was so dead set on getting here. Barely unpacked our saddlebags and now off we go again."

"Thalen didn't say you have to come," rejoined Wareth. "He *invited* you. You are free to stay here while me and Tristo go. You could stay and make eyes at Rector Meakey, Cerf, though I don't think she'd be such a lackwit as to have you."

"We didn't say we wasn't coming, Wareth," Kambey replied. "Where the commander goes, I go. Think I'd trust you and the lad to watch over him in a foreign land? Not fuckin' likely. Besides, Jothile will follow Thalen, and he'll need help looking after him."

"Did the rector say anything, Wareth," asked Cerf, "or are you just spouting your usual slop?"

"Don't worry. She didn't say anything." Wareth grinned. "But I got a good nose for romance. I see the way you look at her and the way she gets all fidgety."

"She's a mighty fine woman. Brightens up any room she enters."

Kambey winked at Wareth. "That she does, all right. If her clothes were any brighter we'd have to shade our eyes."

Cerf continued, "And smart. I don't care about sea life, but you can tell she knows her field backward and forward."

"You could spend your honey trip discussing the mating habits of seals," teased Wareth, laughing into his ale at his own jibe.

Cerf laughed too. "Actually, I don't know whether I am really attracted to the rector or whether I just feel an itch."

Kambey suggestively offered, "There's lots of ways to deal with that itch, Master Healer."

"No, I don't mean an itch to get bedded—well, that's part of it— but an itch to get *wedded*." Cerf turned around on the stool, idly looking out over the tavern room, leaning backward against the bar. "My Aprella and I—before—we had a home. We had a partner to share our supper, scratch our backs, sleep beside, and be there in the morning, talk about what the new day would bring. An itch to set up a life that's not about war or killing. Do you feel that way too?"

"I've always been a solitary cuss," said Kambey. "Spending time with you muckwits is about as much company as I can handle. But I think the commander feels that way. He's often with that red-haired woman."

"Tutor Helina?" said Wareth. "Aye, I've noticed that too. What do you think of her?"

"I barely know her. She seems nice enough," said Cerf, taking another swallow.

"I'm against the match," Wareth said decisively.

Kambey snorted in surprise. "Is it any of your business?"

"No," admitted Wareth. "But I'm still against it. 'Tis another reason why I think this trip is well-timed."

"What other reasons?" asked Cerf.

Wareth shook his head. "You guys aren't scouts, so you wouldn't know, but occasionally you get—you get like a hunch, like the hairs on the back of your neck stand up. Like you don't want to set up camp in this spot because there's a better one just over the hill."

"Oh, I get hunches like that, but it's more—'better take the limb today because tomorrow will be too late,'" said Cerf. "For instance, with that Oro. If we'd waited one more day, the miasmas would have spread such that he'd have met the grave."

"Our Oros!" said Kambey. "I didn't understand what the commander was doing with them. I'd just as lief have killed them and rid ourselves of the vermin. But now . . . the amputee is so pissin' grateful every time you hand him a plate, it kind of tugs at you."

Cerf nodded as he said, "Commander talks with them for hours a day. Pretty soon he'll know more about that country than they know themselves."

"I think that's the idea," said Wareth. "And you gotta admit—it's rather fuckin' brilliant."

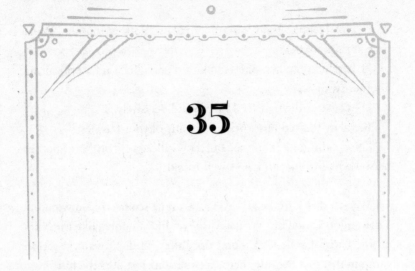

35

On Wave Racer

When his caravel, *Wave Racer,* finally pulled out of the harbor at Liddlecup, Nithanil, the king-that-was, sighed with relief. His son, Rikil, conscientious and organized, had kept adding presents for his half sister, and Mikil had kept pouring wine off *Wave Racer*'s bow to entreat Lautan's blessing on the voyage. Nithanil found all this ceremony tedious; he just wanted to clear the shoals before the light started to wane.

Striding the deck in the days that followed, Nithanil pulled in the tangy air with renewed contentment. It had been too long since he'd left Tidewater Keep behind his stern. Why had he allowed himself to become landlocked and decrepit? His legs felt stronger, his lungs easier, his mind clearer now that he found himself again amongst the gray billows. Almost all of the crew were similarly past their prime; these craggy-faced sailors who had lost tips of fingers in running lines had sailed with him for decades. They knew the ship in their bones, and they kept her sailing smartly with a minimum of gab. *Wave Racer* needed to make good time in order to arrive in Weirandale by Harvest Fest.

Nithanil recognized that he had not been a skilled ruler—he did not have the knack that Rikil had for listening to and calming the nobles or the people. Even conferring with his ministers had been challenging and often baffling. He would have been happier if he'd been born a craftsman; he loved the concentration of working with his hands and the predictability and malleability of inert materials. As a husband, he'd been equally inept; he had alienated his wives with his quirks, and on any given day he'd been mystified by why they had grown wroth with him. As a father he had made stabs at establishing connections, but he never knew what to say to his three children and rarely seemed to make the right gestures.

But he had always been a master at sailing. Anticipating the winds and currents, navigating by an unerring sense of direction and distance. And his confidence brought back his vitality.

Old Biddy grumbled and complained constantly about shipboard discomforts, but at night in the stern cabin built for a captain, she tittered like a young woman about the revival of his lusts. Afterward, he held her comfortable body against his and stroked her hair or shoulder until his unusual tenderness made her tears fall on his chest. Such a sentimental old thing, with her broad rear, hanging breasts, and saggy skin, but Nithanil knew himself more content with her than with either of his late noble wives. Nearly every day he tried to give her a gift—something sweet-tasting or cunningly crafted—to show the appreciation he could never articulate. He kept up this habit on deck, even if it meant just carving her dinner potato into the shape of a flower.

Several weeks out of Lortherrod, the sky to the south grew dark. Nithanil didn't need any squirt to tell him that a storm threatened. The crew silently made their preparations, bringing down the sails, keeping eyes on the horizon. The clouds turned black, with an ominous tint. The wind started to pick up, and the waves grew choppy rather than flowing in organized rolls.

Nithanil went to his cabin to put on his rain cloak. Iluka pestered him about catching cold, nagging he ignored.

But as he was about to exit he turned to her. "When we get into it, you tie yourself in the bunk, like this—see? Blankets and clothes, all tucked round. And don't you get up, even if you vomit."

"Don't you lecture me about sailing, you old walrus!" she snapped back at him. "I've been in boats since I was a wee thing."

"You've been in *fishing* boats, close to the shore. Never a real gale out at sea. You mind me, now." He gave her a little swat on her bottom.

Outside, the crew eyed the clouds with dread, marveling as they grew still darker and thickened into the consistency of syrup. Overplump raindrops fell; then the wind, which had already been strong, began tugging at everything not nailed down. Nithanil tied a rope around his cloak to keep it from fluttering so.

Quickly, the storm grew in intensity. Lightning bolts fissured the skies; thunder followed as if Lautan had decided to crash the heavens together right on top of their heads. The air became so heavy with pelting rain from all directions that Nithanil figured they couldn't be wetter if the ship had turned upside down. A cask broke out of its lashings and rolled wildly around the deck, a dangerous missile capable of crushing a man who got in its way. Nithanil was relieved when it finally bounced over the port side. Shuddering, *Wave Racer* crested each wave and creaked in the troughs. The seamaster's hand-selected mate at the wheel performed with skill, but finally Nithanil replaced him himself; he did not have the man's strength, but he was graced with Anticipation, able to read the waves a tick before they hit and adjust the rudder.

In his long years at sea he had never encountered a tempest like the one that overtook them now. Nithanil felt little fear for his own life—if Lautan had decided to take him down to the depths, so be it. But he would not give up the lives of his crew, his son, or Old Biddy without putting up a fierce battle. He tied himself to the wheel.

A mighty wave crest lifted his ship and then dropped it down with a horrendous crash such that seawater poured over the sides. Nithanil compensated with perfect timing, righting the craft.

"Is that the worst you can do, old Lautan?" Nithanil muttered, though he couldn't hear himself for the wind in his ears. "Bring it on, you stinking blowhole!"

Waves splashed water in his eyes, blinding him. Lightning struck not fifty paces off the starboard. The thunder that instantly followed deafened him.

"Eh! I don't hear so well anyway, Lautan. But my hands feel the ship, feel the current, and feel the waves. Fuck you, you greedy bastard! You ain't going to get this craft!"

Waves crashed over the sides—first from port and then from starboard. Nithanil knew that the crew would be frantically bailing and pumping below. The bigger problem was that his hands were getting too numb with the cold to hold the spokes of the helm.

He tried to call to Mikil, who had lashed himself to the mainmast, amidships, standing by, but the wind tore the words out of his mouth. Mikil saw his gestures; he cut his ropes and crawled on his hands and knees to his father. At that moment, a wave tipped the ship perilously.

"Damn you, Lautan. You saved that boy once. Don't tell me you want him now? What kind of a greedy bastard are you?"

The air was full of foam; it was hard to breathe. Nithanil had no idea what direction they were headed, since it was impossible to see the sun or the stars. Was it still daytime? Nighttime?

Mikil took the wheel. Nithanil slumped onto the deck, too exhausted to move himself far. He crawled under a tarp, out of the direct squall, though the ship's deck was awash with seawater and stranded fish flopped in his lap. He tied his belt to a turnbuckle and fell into a semiconscious doze sitting up.

When he awoke—who knows how much time had passed?—they were still in the storm. But from the sound of the wind and the pitch of the sea, it had lessened to a more normal squall, rather than an Almighty Temper Tantrum. Prodded by the discomfort of his clammy and heavy clothes, the former king pulled himself up and crawled out of the tarp.

The first mate now stood at the wheel. His sailors had added a sail; the sooner they escaped this weather the better. Nithanil stumbled forward and muttered a "Well done" to the men he passed. Then he staggered into his cabin. Everything looked a shambles and smelled of dead sea creatures, vomit, and spilled coffee. Nithanil hardly cared. He waded through the ankle-deep water. Iluka lay in wait for him, with towels and a hundred scolds, which escalated in octave when he made no response to her. She stripped off his sodden upper apparel. Getting his boots off took all of her strength, and when they finally popped free she went flying across the cabin, a quantity of water pouring out of each boot top. She toweled his wet and cold body and gave him a drink of stale coffee topped with a generous portion of rum. He lowered himself into the pitching bunk and patted the area beside him.

"Your hair is still dripping! You'll make the bed linens all moldy. Why would I get in bed with a stinky old squid like you, who doesn't even ask how I fared and doesn't know enough to get out of the storm?"

He patted the bed once more, and when she kept railing at him, turned his back to her. He felt her crawl into bed beside him, so he moved his icy feet in between her warm legs and fell asleep.

When he woke, Iluka was missing and daylight made its way through the porthole. It was only drizzling now, and the swells were unremarkable. He threw on whatever clothes he could find and went out on deck, scanning conditions and checking for damage. Sailors came up to him, all excited about the adventure now that it was over, and full of admiration for his seamanship in getting them through it with no hands lost. Mikil fretted about his health, inquiring again and again how he fared. A cabin boy came running to hand him a mug and a biscuit.

Nithanil ate the biscuit hungrily. He stared at the overcast sky and the immensity of gray ripples around them, realizing that he had no idea where they were. He didn't answer anybody's praise or concern.

He took a sip of equally bad coffee and spit it out over the side. Finally, he decided to speak. He cleared his throat, and everyone gathered near waited expectantly.

"We're going to miss the Harvest Fest ceremony," Nithanil said.

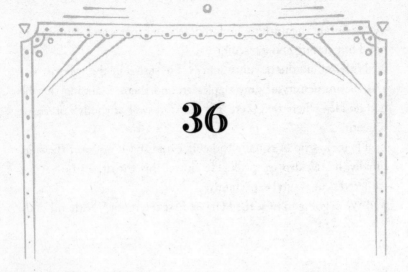

36

Cascada

Stahlia and Tilim had made the brick house in West Park cozy, or as cozy as any house that was twice as big as they needed could be.

Cerúlia made a practice of visiting West Cottage once a week for a meal. Her schedule was unpredictable—thus sometimes a messenger would ride over to say that the queen would be following in a few minutes, which put Stahlia into a panic about what to serve her. But Stahlia soon realized that her foster daughter came to her home to get away from fancy food and fuss. If she caught Stahlia with only potatoes in her larder, the queen was happier dining on those roasted in the coals than on whatever the royal kitchens would serve.

When Darzner could send Stahlia decent notice, Stahlia would invite Percie, Marcot, and Lemle to join them. She would fix some familiar recipe from the Wyndton years. The six of them would forget that a squad of guards and that scary Zellishman surrounded the house and laugh like the old days. Lemle would tell them all about his apprenticeship and, shyly, about a grocer he'd been spending time with. Cerúlia would bring along a few of her dogs, and Tilim would play with them. Stahlia herself developed quite a crush on the white deerhounds, who were so silky and had delicate feet. When no one was watching she would slip them scraps.

Presently, all of Cascada was frantically preparing for the upcoming festivities. Fortunately most of the necessary cleaning and painting had already been done before Percie's wedding. But palace carpenters and masons had to make the burned wing less of an eyesore; Vilkit had to prepare to feed and lodge all the guests; the councilors needed to map out the schedule of events, and so much more.

Stahlia wanted to be involved. Of course if she could have finished "Cerúlia and the Catamounts," that would have been best, but such a complicated tapestry would take her years. Especially since she'd decided to change the picture in her mind by dressing the queen in her Sunset Gown, the color and folds of which would be so challenging.

Stahlia cast about for a contribution where she wouldn't be in the way, but which was a task only she could do.

Eventually, she lit upon the under-groomed East Garden. The palace gardeners had been ordered long ago to focus on Arrival Avenue and the landscaping in the formal front of the building. With her eye for composition, her knowledge of Weir history, and her willingness to get her hands dirty, Stahlia could make this East Garden a credit again, a place where guests could stroll and take the air under the benign gaze of the Queens' Statues.

Cerúlia embraced this idea enthusiastically and put funds at her disposal. The first thing Stahlia did was to transplant blue asters into the floral "riverbed" to make it flow again. But the garden was so big, so overgrown, and so weedy that soon she found herself laboring there from sunrise to sunset. She made Tilim help her after his lessons. When the engraving shop closed for the night, Lemle would join them too, the three of them often raking and weeding by lantern light.

And then the garden staff, seeing the queen's closest relations working so hard, started to drift by when their first shift was done.

Together the two crews trimmed bushes and brought down dead limbs or trees. Masons joined in by polishing the marble and repairing the walkways.

After a few weeks the garden glowed in the crisp autumn light with yellow goldenrod, silver dead nettle, purple sedums, yellow mums, and a river of blue and white asters. Red burning bushes blazed in a neat row, and maple leaves drifted in the wind. Once the rosebushes had been properly trimmed and fertilized—from Duchess Naven's detailed written instructions—the banks of white roses sprang forth a final burst of blooms.

Captain Yanath called a meeting to discuss security for the upcoming festival. The eight officers convened in their duty room, which doubled as their dining mess. The rectangular stone room had a fireplace, a dartboard, and a few knocked-about upholstered chairs and footstools; the wall space was decorated with charcoal drawings that soldiers had idled away time with; these were primarily drawings of swords and horses, but also included a few landscapes. The other two walls held detailed maps of the palace and the grounds. Ten small private sleeping quarters branched off from the room, and the Shield barracks could be accessed from the south door, but the larger palace guards' quarters were situated in a separate building.

Yanath and his second-in-command, Pontole, represented the Shield; Captain Athelbern and his four watch officers—two men from the previous regime and two younger women who added fresh perspectives and intelligence—spoke for the palace guard. Ciellō, the Zellish bodyguard, served as the queen's representative.

"So, let's begin," said Yanath, calling the table to order.

"First item." He ticked a list. "Let's consider all our citizens who will be streaming in, either to be feted or as onlookers. We'll set up tables at the gates and have people leave any weapons they might be carrying, but it would be helpful if folk left their gear at home."

"What are we worried about?" asked Jadwinga, one of the new palace guard officers.

"Matwyck's Marauders have never been fully accounted for," Yanath explained. "And General Yurgn had quite an extensive spy network. With all these visitors to the building, might an assassin try to sneak in?"

"We should keep an eye on all the deliverymen too, in the week before," offered Sergeant Tade.

"Good point," said Yanath.

"On the days of the fests I ask the queen for four dogs," said Ciellō, holding up his fingers. "Two for the Arrival Gate and two for the Kitchen Gate."

Yanath said, "That would be very helpful. They could sort of smell out evil intent. But would that leave the queen herself low in terms of her canine corps?"

"We will not let her leave her wing until you close the gates after the audience has arrived and release the dogs," Ciellō said.

For several minutes they discussed which days which squads should take gate duty and who would be in command.

"Moving on," said Yanath. "Item two. The visiting royalty. They'll be lodging in the Guest Wing. From Lortherrod, we will have the queen's kinsmen: her grandfather and her uncle. We don't know how many retainers and servants."

"Do we know how many of their own soldiers they'll bring?" asked Pontole.

"No. Anyone have a guess?" Yanath raised his eyebrows.

"Let's ask Nana," Athelbern suggested. "She's the only one I can think of still around who will remember their habit from long ago when the Lorthers used to visit. If she doesn't know we'll have to have a councilor ask the envoys."

"Right," said Yanath. "Athelbern, will you talk to her today? And we'll go with that number for the Rorthers too, who are sending King Kentros and Filio Kemeron."

"I hear that the prince is coming to court our queen," said Sergeant Tade with a grin.

The comment was not rude, but the man's tone and smile grated on Yanath. He'd been looking at his list; his face muscles stiffened in disapproval. Picking up his head he started to reprimand, "Such is not our concern—"

With a thud, Ciellō's dagger slammed into the wood of the table an inch from where the watch officer leaned on his elbow. Tade snapped his body back, while everyone else gaped in shock.

"Her personal life is not to be discussed," said Ciellō. "Ever."

"Of course," said the threatened man, staring at Ciellō as if he'd gone insane. "I overstepped."

"I'm glad we've all reached an understanding," Yanath commented drily. "Let's continue discussing how we will work with the guards of our distinguished guests."

As the meeting broke up, Yanath asked Ciellō to stay behind. Yanath sat on the table, regarding the bodyguard whom he had come to respect, if not understand, over the last seven moons. Ciellō was about his size, though more muscled, and only a few years younger. The bodyguard rarely spoke and made no effort to make friends. He slept, ate, did his odd exercises, braided his odd hair, and then returned to his post beside the queen or outside her door.

Yanath had never seen him relax on duty; his eyes always watched for threats; his body stayed taut for action. While he was polite and respectful to the circle of the queen's familiars, his manner never invited closer acquaintance.

"Ciellō," Yanath remarked, "I had started a reprimand. When you brought out the dagger, you undermined my authority."

"That—that was no my intent, Captain," Ciellō said. "I believe that the queen, she is fortunate to have your services. My apology."

"Accepted," said Yanath. "I share your sentiments that the Nargis Queen must never be spoken of with disrespect. But why did you feel it necessary to throw your dagger?"

"Perhaps," the bodyguard replied, though he would not meet Yanath's gaze, "all this talk of strangers in the palace and threats made me overreact."

"I've never seen anyone so fast with a throw," Yanath continued. "Long ago, I had a shieldmate, a woman named Seena—damn, she was fast!—but not like that. Can you teach us?"

"I can try. Only some people have the reflexes. That officer"—he motioned to the place where Jadwinga had been sitting—"she moved back the quickest."

Yanath said, "Good. We'll have a go. After all the festivities are safely behind us."

37

On an afternoon a few days before the fest Percia found Stahlia deadheading some spent blossoms.

"Mama, I knew I'd find you here. I need your help with Birdie," said Percie.

"Why, what's the matter?"

"She's more nervous about this celebration than I've ever seen her. I don't think she's sleeping at night, and she's certainly not eating. Right now she's throwing a fit about her wardrobe."

"That's so unlike her! She'd usually rather wear trousers," said Stahlia. "Do you think it's being on display to the Rorther prince?"

"Something of that sort. Can you come put your foot down about the gowns? Can you convince her to take a sleeping draught tonight?"

"Right now? I'm all covered in mud and sweat."

"We can stop by my suite to clean you up. Really, I think you should come."

Stahlia noted the anxiety in her daughter's creased face. "Let's go, then."

When they entered the Royal Bedchamber they found portions of gowns laid out on surfaces; shoes, petticoats, hair ornaments, and

packaging strewn about; and Cerúlia arguing in a wrangling manner with Editha, Geesilla, Nana, and Kiltti. The little terrier was
yapping at everyone, turning the room into total turmoil.

At a glance, Stahlia realized that—if anything—Percia had underestimated the situation.

Stahlia clapped her hands together once. "My land, Queen
Cerúlia! Didn't I teach you never to treat clothing this way! *What-is-
going-on-here?*"

The queen looked at her foster mother in shock for a moment
and then managed a half laugh.

"Teta, it is important that I look my best over the fest, and I'm
not content with these gowns, and I can't figure out what's wrong,
and everyone is patronizing me rather than listening, and all their
advice is contradictory!"

"Your Majesty, I can recall when you didn't have a stitch to call
your own!"

"So can I," said the queen. "But for better or worse, hundreds of
people are going to be looking at me, many having traveled leagues
and leagues to get here. And Editha keeps telling me that the changes
I request are impossible or too time-consuming." As she talked, the
strain and anger crept back into her voice, and she glared at the
dressmaker.

"Oh, dear," said Stahlia, picking up a petticoat. "Let me offer a
solution. I'm hungry from all my gardening work. Could Nana fetch
us tisane? After we sup, you can show Percie and me the gowns, and
we'll give you honest advice, no matter how much work it entails.

"And if Editha needs another seamstress for alterations, I'll lay
aside the garden and pick up a needle myself. You know there's no
one faster. I promise the gowns will be ready in time and without
compromise."

Cerúlia nodded with a look of relief and threw herself down in
a chair. Stahlia escorted Nana to the door, whispering about tidbits
she thought the queen might eat.

"Come here, dogs," she called. "Ciellō, I want them all to wait in the Reception Room. Not a one of them has any fashion sense." Stahlia was proud of herself for making a joke. Percia smiled, but Cerúlia didn't show that she'd heard.

"Geesilla, my dear," said Stahlia. "Before we think about the hair we must settle on the gowns. We'll send for you if we need you this afternoon."

While they waited for the tray, Stahlia insisted that order be brought to the room. Kiltti, Percia, Editha, and Stahlia started picking up all the garments—underskirts and corsets, sleeves and doublets, and hose—that had been strewn around in a whirlwind. After a few moments, glaring at them all balefully, Cerúlia began crawling around the floor, picking up the pins that had gone flying when she had whipped a garment off her body.

"I can do that, Your Majesty," said Kiltti, very low. "It isn't proper . . . the queen on the floor."

"No," said Cerúlia. "*I* scattered them so, and I wouldn't want anyone to step on one."

"Your Majesty," said Editha with a low curtsey, "there are a few things I'd like to fetch from the workroom before we continue the fittings. Might I be excused?"

Cerúlia waved her away and within a few minutes the tray arrived. Stahlia smiled broadly, hoping her cheerfulness would brighten the room. "Oh, I'm so hungry. Look at these scones and this custard! Girls, I'll pour, sit with me and have a nibble."

When Cerúlia had eaten a little and began tapping her foot with impatience, Kiltti cleared away the leftovers and handed the tray to a servant in the Reception Room. Through the open door Stahlia caught a glimpse of Mistress Editha, who had fetched two baskets and a package, waiting (with a tactfulness that surprised the weaver) until a calmer atmosphere took hold.

Stahlia invited her back into the chamber of combat. "I think we're ready now, mistress."

"Finally!" said Cerúlia. "Now then. There are four major events, Teta. First, the Celebration of Citizens—the Freed and Loyal Combatants. That night we are holding a feast and the Harvest Reel. The next day is the Welcoming of the Allies, and again a feast and the Fountain Ball. So I need four gowns."

"Will you dance?" asked Percia, hope creeping into her voice.

"Yes," said Cerúlia. "I learned the steps long ago, you know, though you could give me a refresher."

Percia clapped her hands.

"Fine," said Stahlia. "Four gowns. So what are our choices?"

Editha laid out the first dress. It was a stiff cream brocade with a full skirt made of complicated, pleated panels that were currently the height of court fashion. As Percia and Kiltti helped the queen into it, Stahlia saw the expensive workmanship and the fine fabric, but she noted, "That dress swallows you up, my dear. It does nothing for you."

The seamstress opened her mouth as if she were going to argue, but Stahlia shot her a warning and she desisted.

"Thank the Waters, Teta! I feel like a mattress in it. Can it be fixed? So much money and work!"

"I'd have to consider. But give it to Kiltti for now."

The second gown had a sleeker cut: it was made out of white silk with a silk-screened pattern of autumn leaves and had very long bell-shaped sleeves. Stahlia walked around Cerúlia, looking at her and the dress.

"It's lovely. But Editha, how about making the waistband broader?"

"Like so?" Editha's birdlike hands moved pins from the velvet pincushion at her waist.

"Yes! And the sleeves are just a smidge too long."

"That's easy to fix," said Editha. "Let me show you with just the left one. Look, Your Majesty; look at it now."

Cerúlia smiled at her reflection in the glass, her face showing a hint of relief. "I do like the way the back flows," she admitted (probably the first compliment she had given Editha today).

They all helped Cerúlia change into the third, which was dark golden-colored satin with a white collar and rivers of seed pearls sewn in waves around the hem.

"Oh, how lovely!" said Percia.

"What do you think, Teta?" Cerúlia asked, unsure. "Is it, well, flattering enough?"

"Oh, it's very flattering. The color is perfect for your skin and brown eyes. Confident. But . . ." Stahlia had an intuition of why her daughter might not be as taken with the garment as she should be. "Editha, let's lower the neckline a bit and make the bodice just a tad tighter at the ribs?"

"Here, Your Majesty," said Editha. "I fetched this silk ribbon. I thought that these russet slashes on the arms might set off the overall effect. . . ."

Stahlia clapped her hands. "Now it's not only confident and regal—it's very fetching."

The last dress was blue, a river of watered silk that ranged in tones from greenish to sky blue. When Cerúlia put it on, it shimmered in the light, almost casting rainbows.

"Oh, how lovely! Editha, you are a genius!" exclaimed Percia.

"Wait," said Editha. "I haven't shown you the train yet." And she pulled out of wrappings a train of moiré silk. She affixed the train to the gown's shoulders and unfurled it down the queen's back.

"Let down your hair, Your Majesty, if you please."

"What?" said Cerúlia, looking at everyone's faces. "Does it look all right?"

"It looks," said Percia reverently, "fantastic. Your hair shimmers with the same tones as the dress and the train. You look—like a Nargis Queen."

"We all forget sometimes, I *am* a Nargis Queen. You forget (and treat me like the child I was) and sometimes I forget and act like a child. A spoilt child."

"We all need to do better." Stahlia cleared her throat, which had clogged up at the queen's apology. "Let's take it off carefully. Don't you dare let your dogs anywhere near it."

"But what are we going to do about the fourth gown?" asked Cerúlia, with a note of panic creeping back into her voice.

"The gown that will always mean 'Cerúlia has returned to Cascada' is the Sunset Dress you wore at the Fountain," Percia offered. "Editha's first masterpiece. Can't you wear that?"

Editha searched through the wardrobe for the gown and looked at it appraisingly. "It was designed for spring, but the colors could also work for fall. I could add a piping of scarlet here, and maybe one of gold. Maybe a little scarlet-colored lace at the sleeves. Yes, I think— yes, reworking it into autumn could be done in the time we have."

"That's settled, Your Majesty," said Stahlia. "You will wear the Sunset Dress for the Harvest Fest. And the blue—let's call it the Waterfall Dress—for the Fountain Ball with the visiting royalty. Which of the others for which daytime celebration? They both need robes, Editha; she will be sitting on the throne, greeting guests, and she must look both beautiful and royal."

"I considered that, and I brought a robe for Her Majesty," said the seamstress, unwrapping an object and shaking it out. "Fur for autumn. And this is the most luscious mink." Drawn by the sheen, both Kiltti and Percia crossed the room to stroke the robe.

"But I *told* Editha already: I can't wear a heavy fur robe on my shoulders all day," said Cerúlia. "My left shoulder can't take it."

"Hmm," said Stahlia. "Both day dresses have white—the background of the leaves and the white pearls. Would a white robe be too light?"

Editha looked off into the distance, designing in her imagination. "White velvet, with trim of white ermine. Hip length. Not floor length. That would match both day gowns and be light enough for Her Majesty to be both warm and comfortable."

The queen clapped her hands with pleasure and offered Editha rare praise, "Oh, that would be lovely. Could you do everything in time, mistress?"

"Yes, Your Highness. Robes have less stitching and fitting than gowns. I also know of a craftsman who could work a fall of golden leaves down the front panels to make it more seasonal."

"How will you keep the robe from falling off her shoulders?" asked Percia.

"Queens wear 'robe clasps,'" said Stahlia. "I've seen them in portraits. Nana would know if in the Royal Jewels there's a gold clasp. Something of Queen Catreena's or Queen Cressa's might provide just the touch of history and continuity."

"Kiltti, would you find Nana and bring me options?" Cerúlia asked. Kiltti and Editha curtsied and left to set about their work.

"Now, Your Majesty," said Stahlia. "I'm certain your gowns will be flawless. But the strain of all the arrangements appears to be wearing on you. To look your best you need to eat and sleep well. Doesn't Vilkit have things well in hand? Couldn't you go out for a ride to clear your head?"

"I had asked Vilkit to go over the guests' rooming arrangements with me this evening, but I think you're right. I'd do better to go for a ride."

She walked to the door and spoke to Ciellō and a footman.

But by the time she turned back, she was worrying again. "But Teta, what about my hair?"

Stahlia almost rebuked her for this unbecoming vanity, which was so unlike the woman she thought she knew.

"Look here," said Stahlia. "I'll come over tomorrow and sit with you and Geesilla, deciding on which hair arrangement for which dress, and on the jewelry too, *if* you take a sleeping draught the next few nights and come over to West Cottage for a real meal tomorrow night."

"Oh, Teta, I don't have time this week. I have to write speeches and memorize names, and have so many things to check on, and I need to consult with Councilor Nishtari, and there's only three more days—"

"Cerúlia!" interrupted Stahlia in her most scolding tone, her resolution to address her with due deference breaking immediately. "Give everyone a rest from your anxiety and come spend a little time with your brother, who's been working like a mule in East Garden."

"As has your mother," added Percia, though her tone was more sympathetic.

The queen closed her eyes and sighed.

"All right," she said. "Do you think you could fix eggs with herbs and leeks and your bread and butter?"

"Heavens, Birdie, we can have anything you desire, but how did you come up with that menu?"

"That was what you cooked the morning after Lemle and I got into that fight with the ruffians. I was very jittery that morning, mayhap as jittery as I've been these days, and I've always remembered that delicious fastbreak."

38

"Apples!" Vilkit shouted. And the chamberlain never shouted—he was fiercely proud of always keeping his temper—but today he was shouting at his favorite provisionary. "Where are the apples? You promised the bakers Androvale apples by yestermorn, and you still don't have them today!"

"I told you, Vittorine apples is just as nice and bake up just as tasty. Sea deliveries are always chancy. But you insisted on bringing them across the bay. Chamberlain, t'ain't my fault if the ship ain't on time."

"Get out of my sight and go stand on the dock and watch for the ship," said Vilkit, regaining control over his voice. The bakers would use local apples if they had to, but Vilkit had his heart set on offering the queen apple tarts made from Androvale's crop.

And he recognized that he was going to such lengths not because he feared she would puncture his eardrum, but because he wanted her to say, "Oh, Vilkit, how thoughtful!" as he often heard her praise others.

Vilkit circled "apples" on the long list in front of him. He was always so on top of everything, but the press of events was making him anxious that he would forget an important task.

A man knocked on his door. "Chamberlain, we are ready for you to approve the Harvest Archway."

Vilkit kept making a few notations on his list while he spoke, "And I am ready to come see your handiwork, in half a moment. There. Let us go."

The archway stood in the middle of the Great Ballroom. It stood about three paces wide and over three paces tall: large enough for a couple to dance through. The decorators had made it out of slats of a silvery wood and festooned it with bunches of grapes and lacquered autumn leaves. Planters built in the bottom held vines, ablaze with flowers, that climbed the lattice.

"Very nice, very nice indeed," said Vilkit, admiring their handiwork. "What's that hook for, at the top?"

"Ah," said the decorator. "A little extra touch. What with Her Highness favoring the birds so much, we're going to hang a birdcage—but not until the fest night. Don't want to stress the nightingales, and don't want to spoil the surprise."

"A lovely idea. I won't breathe a word. Now this is anchored sturdily enough for the first night, but you can replace it the—"

At this moment Her Majesty and Lady Percia entered the ballroom. Vilkit and the decorator bowed.

"Were you coming to check on the Harvest Archway, Your Majesty? You needn't have; as you can see—all is in readiness."

"Oh, no, Vilkit. I'm leaving those arrangements to you," said the queen.

"Actually," said Lady Percia, "we came to do a little run-through of the Harvest Reel. And I need two men for partners. I would have called in two guards, but you gentlemen will oblige us, won't you?"

Vilkit quaked. "Naturally," he answered, trying not to stutter. "We would be honored."

Percia took the poor decorator's right hand in hers, so Vilkit offered his to Queen Cerúlia.

"We are all at your command, Percie," Her Majesty said, with an amused face that put Vilkit more at ease.

Lady Percia led them through the reel. The first time, she walked them through the steps slowly, clearly, and with lots of encouragement (as if she'd been teaching dance all her life), occasionally stopping to adjust the angle of someone's foot or arm.

On the third occasion she stopped to adjust the queen's left arm, the queen said, "Percie, give it up—my left arm won't go any straighter, and this hurts my shoulder."

"Oh, I'm so sorry," said Lady Percia. "Very well. From now on we will use only right arm twirls."

She ran them through the reel at half speed. Then she took them through it at a normal tempo, clapping out the beats, though still calling out the moves.

Vilkit had never had so much fun in his life. Had he danced as a child? He must have, but since he'd gone into service he'd only watched gentry dance, never participated himself.

At the end of the reel he bowed low to his flushed and laughing partner.

"Wonderful," enthused Lady Percia. "You were all wonderful."

"Your Majesty," said Vilkit slowly, "do you suppose that at the end of the evening, after the guests dance, the servants might have the pleasure?"

"Vilkit!" said his liege. "The staff is invited to partake throughout the evening! Well, the serving boys should put down their platters, and we wouldn't want all the cooks to desert the kitchen at once, but everyone must dance. I'm afraid that Lady Percia insists, and on matters of dancing, we are all at her command. I will leave it to you how to arrange rotations."

"Thank you, gentlemen, for obliging us," smiled Lady Percia, and the two women left the room.

"Yes. Well! Where were we?" Vilkit asked the decorator, slightly dazed.

"You was asking about the swap-out."

Vilkit must have looked puzzled, because the decorator continued. "When we have to change the decor. That'll be no problem. We will have this gone the next morning, so we can bring in the Fountain."

"Any birds with the Fountain?"

"No birds. But I do have another surprise up my sleeve."

"You know your business. I'll leave it to you," said Vilkit, clapping the man on the shoulder and walking back to his office a little dizzy.

39

The Royal Navy kept meticulous records. Wilamara would have been willing to wager a year's wages that no other national institution kept records so complete. She had the names of every sailor and officer who had sailed with Queen Cressa. She had lists of those who had perished in fights with the Pellish pirates in the Green Isles. She had the name of every soul lost when *Freshwater Pearl* went down off the coast of Pexlia. She had the names of the next of kin of all the departed.

Locating the sailors who had mustered out or the kinfolk of the departed had taken moons of ingenuity and persistence. Some mariners could not be found, and many of those who perished had no family left to invite.

Sitting in her cabin on the *Sea Wind,* which, to her sorrow, was now dry-docked due to rot, Wilamara looked over the list once more. It hurt her heart to read these names, but she felt great satisfaction that at last these loyal mariners would be recognized. She had seen to it that all who would participate in the ceremonies had perfectly fitted dress uniforms. She had stayed up late last night, putting an extra coat of polish on her own boots and buttons.

One of her personal contributions to the fete was, on her own initiative, to send out scouting and escort ships. Visiting dignitaries should be met politely and piloted around Breakneck Shoal to their proper berth in Cascada Harbor. And her scouts could give the palace forewarning of who had arrived or who was spotted. She thought this would please the queen.

She called in a cabin girl. "I am writing to Chamberlain Vilkit. I want you to deliver it to him personally."

"Aye, Seamaster."

Wilamara wrote:

Rorther ship spotted. Will arrive this afternoon. A Free States vessel by tomorrow morning. No sign of Lortherrod. Sending a scouting boat farther north, but we should have seen them by now. Plan on the Lorthers being late for the festivities. Probably uncertain seas in the north. Could the queen send one of her birds?

Duke Naven waited at the dock when the Rorther ship arrived. A high-ranking dignitary had to greet the king of Rortherrod; the council had selected Naven, as a duke and a councilor, to accompany Envoy Rakihah.

He smiled to himself about the Rorthers being a day early. Everyone had been pleased with the king's acceptance of Cerúlia's invitation and the tidings that he would bring with him his unmarried, eldest son, Filio Kemeron. Amongst themselves the councilors had discussed what a wonderful match Kemeron would make for their queen. And to combine the might of the Rorthers with the Weirs would be a mutually beneficial alliance.

The councilors dined with Envoy Rakihah several times to piece together whatever information they could find about the prince. He was of suitable age: just shy of thirty. He had a reputation as a steady man, soft-spoken and without bluster. Of course Queen Catreena's marriage to the Lorther king had not been successful, but that didn't rule out the possibility and advantages of an international match.

Naven was eager to judge whether the Rorther prince was more personable than King Nithanil had been.

When the duke boarded the vessel, he discovered King Kentros to be a bluff and friendly man a little less stout than Naven himself, with shrewd eyes and bright red hair. Filio Kemeron turned out to be broad-shouldered and well-built, though he came only up to Naven's chin. His hair was cut rather short, with two thin lines shaved to the skin shooting back from each temple almost like chevrons; he wore a neatly trimmed beard along his firm jawline. Naven knew that his own daughters would swoon over this prince, but he did not presume to judge the queen's reaction.

As was polite, the son let his father take the lead in the conversation after Rakihah had made the introductions.

"We had uncommonly favorable winds," said King Kentros. "Guests who come too early always send my lady-wife into fits. How about you pretend we're not here until the day after tomorrow? We would hate to disturb plans or add complications."

"Oh, no, Your Highness. We are delighted that you have arrived safely. The queen has explicitly invited you to attend the ceremonies tomorrow in honor of Weir citizens' trials and loyalty. If agreeable to you, I will bring the royal carriage to escort you to a private meeting with Queen Cerúlia in the morning."

"Very fine, very fine," said King Kentros.

"My liege, the envoy mansion is ready to receive you," said Rakihah.

"Do you need anything this evening? Is there anything we can do to make you more comfortable?" Naven pressed.

"This is really working out for the best," said the Rorther king agreeably. "I'd like to soak in a hot tub and stroll a bit to get back my land legs before appearing in public."

Filio Kemeron escorted Duke Naven to the gangplank.

"I understand that you are one of the queen's councilors, but how well do you know her personally?" he asked Naven.

"Fairly well," answered Naven, not admitting that he had known her as a child, because in truth, he had paid no attention to Wilim's quiet ward.

"My father and I had a disagreement about what gift to bring. My father said that all women like jewelry. I had read that she is fond of animals and so thought to make her a gift of a breeding pair of Rorther's highly prized spotted lynx. But then I remembered this." He pulled a small velvet box out of a purse and opened it. Inside, lying on white velvet, was a sliver of a broken rock.

Naven's face must have showed his puzzlement. The prince explained, "This is a shard from our Protection Stone. Although we don't know how much Power it still contains, it is one of our national treasures."

Naven shook his head in amazement. "My queen would welcome any gift with sincere appreciation. But Filio Kemeron, this is an honor beyond price. I know that my liege will be sensible of the homage you pay her."

The prince looked gratified by Naven's reaction.

40

When she woke on the morning of the first ceremony, Cerúlia found herself calmer, relieved that the day had finally arrived.

Once Geesilla finished with her hair, piling it high and decorating it with ornaments, Percia arrived to help her into the Leaf Gown and velvet-and-ermine robe. They fixed the robe with a golden clasp that repeated the catamount faces on her dagger. Percia beamed at her, but Cerúlia did not even glance in the mirror.

"Don't you want to see?" Percia asked.

"No," said Cerúlia. "I'm ashamed of those fits of vanity. Either I look like a Nargis Queen, or I don't. Everyone has done the best they can."

Ciellō knocked softly on the door. "Damselle, King Kentros has arrived."

"I will meet them in the Nymph Salon," she called.

Percia came toward her to whisper in her ear. "Just keep an open mind. You might like him."

Cerúlia nodded. In her Reception Room she turned to the two dogs who weren't on gate duty.

Cici, she sent, *you accompany me, and, Whaki, you stay outside the door.*

"Ciellō and Percia, pray escort me," she said aloud, holding her head high and walking down the hallway, enjoying the sensation of the fur against her skin and the flow of the gown on the floor behind.

A match with a Rorther prince would be a priceless boon for Weirandale. My mother wrote that sometimes one has to sacrifice what is dearest to one's heart. If I hate him, that's another story, but I shall try to keep an open mind.

She entered the salon. Duke Naven and Envoy Rakihah made the introductions. King Kentros offered a practiced but nonetheless kind comment about once meeting Queen Cressa and knowing how proud her mother would be at seeing her daughter on the throne.

"King Kentros, you honor us by your presence at our festivals, as your fleet honored my mother by joining the Allies. I must again tell you how grateful we are for the use of your Truth Stone, which helped me bring justice to my people."

Cerúlia turned to Filio Kemeron. His dark brown outfit set off his red hair, and his shoulders looked broad. She found him handsome.

He made a graceful bow and kissed her hand. But when he rose and looked her in the eye, he stammered.

"Forgive me, Your Majesty. I had a pretty speech rehearsed, but at the sight of such loveliness it just flew out of my head."

Cici? she sent.

He is not putting on a display, the terrier answered.

"Oh, dear. I have several speeches to make today," said Cerúlia, turning to humor to cover everyone's embarrassment. "I do hope they won't fly out of my head!"

"I'm sure, Your Majesty, that you are resourceful enough for any occasion," replied the prince.

King Kentros broke in. "Well, Son, if you recall your speech, you can recite it later in the day?"

"No," said Cerúlia with a smile. "I'm afraid there's only one opportunity for pretty speeches. Afterward, we will have to make do with honest talk."

"Honest talk is better anyway," Kemeron agreed.

Kemeron squatted down and called Cici over to him. He petted her with the practiced touch of a man who likes dogs, with firm scratches behind the ears and a direct gaze in her eyes. Cici licked his chin, literally giving her approval.

"Won't you partake of a welcome cup?" Cerúlia offered, and Duke Naven, with a bow, himself carried a silver tray with wine-glasses on it to everyone in the room.

"To years of peace and friendship," Cerúlia offered as a toast.

"To the health of the most-longed-for and most beautiful queen in Ennea Món," said the prince.

"There's a pretty speech!" said the king, arching his brow. "Hear! Hear!"

Percia consulted a little hourglass she wore today as a pendant around her neck.

"Your Majesty . . ." she prompted.

"Ah, yes. Gentlemen, we are due in the Throne Room now," said Cerúlia, and led the way.

Hundreds of Weir citizens—commoners and wealthy burghers, young and old, all dressed in their costliest outfits—filled the two upper balconies and the long benches that had been arranged along the sides of the room. First-time visitors ogled the throne, the Fountain, the gold Dedication Basin, and the catamounts. Her councilors sat in chairs to the side of the throne. When the queen entered through the East Entrance, walking sedately down the wide aisle left open, everyone stood. When she reached the dais, careful to move without haste, Percia helped her arrange her gown and robe and stepped away; then the queen sat, at which point everyone else took their seats.

Amidst all this formal pageantry, Cici caused a small fuss by barking at the catamounts and making little rushes at them.

Cici! sent Cerúlia. *Don't you ever know when to back down? Those big cats could eat you in one bite.*

One doth nay care how big or fierce they be! Regard the cheeky way they hold their tails! But one is pack leader! They must recognize one's precedence.

Catamounts! sent Cerúlia. *Please don't hurt the canine. She is brash, but I do favor her.*

Cici made one more foolhardy rush at the mountain lions. A male stood and growled at her, a growl into which he put all the disdain of a lion for a mouse. To her credit, stouthearted Cici didn't cower or scamper away. She did, however, beat a dignified retreat under the throne.

Councilor Alix caught Cerúlia's eye, and the two of them almost burst out laughing at the dog's antics. The moment helped the queen still her racing heart.

The palace caller knocked three times on the East Entrance with her staff. Then she threw open the double doors.

"Your Majesty, and Ladies and Gentlemen, I have the honor to present to you Our Fellow Citizens, those who unjustly suffered for their loyalty to the realm."

The caller read off names as the people—those who had been imprisoned or a family member who stood in for the deceased—entered in a procession.

It was a gut-wrenching parade. Many of the former prisoners bore the marks of injuries sustained at the hands of Matwyck's Marauders, such as broken noses, missing teeth, or limping gaits. Two people were so crippled that they were carried in on litters. As for the bereaved—who were marked, as customary, by circlets that held gray veils on their foreheads—many were widows, but others looked like mothers or fathers. In two cases, the closest next of kin were young children.

Cerúlia was overwhelmed. Sympathy mixed with anger at these injustices and shame that a Weir government had carried out such atrocities. Once all were assembled, the honorees knelt in front of the dais. She stood.

"Citizens of Weirandale. A government that misuses its authority to oppress its citizens for their thoughts or speech cannot stand. A government that throws citizens in secret jails without public proceedings should never stand. You suffered, unjustly, from such a regime. I beg your forgiveness that I was not here to protect you. I, and the rest of Weirandale"—she looked around at the onlookers—"acknowledge your pain and sorrows and entreat the Nargis Waters to ease your burdens."

Brothers and Sisters of Sorrow, standing discreetly at the sides of the Throne Room, came forward. Each carried a silver cup of Nargis Water that they offered to the assembled victims.

Have any of the wounded been cured? There! He can see through his bad eye again. There! Her expression of pain has eased. There! The little girl's cloud of grief has dissipated; her eyes now sparkle.

Then Lord Marcot rose and addressed everyone in the Throne Room. "'Twas my father, Lord Matwyck, and General Yurgn who bear the greatest responsibility for these injustices. Both of them have already paid with their lives. I have taken these monies from their ill-gotten fortunes in the hopes that, while coin can never recompense, it may ease the burdens you currently face."

Marcot walked among the citizens distributing small pouches filled with golden catamounts. Many of the folk pressed his hand. An older woman kissed his cheek.

After Marcot had distributed his last pouch, the honorees' spokesperson stepped forward. Middle-aged, perhaps a tradesman, he leaned heavily on one crutch.

"Your Majesty." His voice croaked. He stopped, cleared his throat, and started again. "Your Majesty, most of us were imprisoned for speaking aloud our hopes for your safe return. Seeing you sitting on the Nargis Throne, hearing tidings of your setting things to rights all around the realm, why, that is as much a balm to our spirits as the Water and the coin. Welcome home, Your Majesty."

Brother Whitsury nodded to the Abbey Choir, which had been stationed in the rear of the hall on the highest balcony.

Cerúlia stood, as did the rest of the onlookers. The choir sang two hymns, the harmonies wafting down through the Throne Room with unearthly beauty. Then the choir led all in "We Wish You Joy" as the honorees filed out.

The palace caller announced, "This ends the events for the morn. We will reconvene when the bells toll three for this afternoon's program."

The honorees had been invited to midmeal with the queen in the Salon of Queen Cinda, a more intimate space than the Great Ballroom. Vilkit, knowing her preferences now, had arranged mixed tables, so that dukes, duchesses, and councilors were seated at round tables among the citizens. Cerúlia noticed, however, that with his typical cleverness, Vilkit had placed King Kentros next to Councilor Nishtari and Filio Kemeron between Stahlia and Steward Alix.

As for herself, weeks ago Vilkit had devised a system. A footman, Hanks, always stood at the ready to move her chair to another table, so that Cerúlia could rotate among the guests at will, while Ciellō always kept his hands free.

"Percia, will you please take my robe? Hanks, I will start next to the spokesperson."

She thought that the meal would be a somber event, but the honorees would have none of it. Despite their trials, the Nargis Water had put them in a cheerful, even buoyant mood.

Cerúlia had a long talk with a brewer about how hops had fared this season. A widow shyly confessed that her neighbor had come a-courting, and she wanted the queen's advice about whether she should encourage the suit. The man whose sight had been restored wanted to tell her that he had witnessed Queen Cressa's Dedication years ago. All the children in the room were taken with the dogs—the happier little girl had ended up on Fornquit's lap feeding Haki one grain of rice at a time, treats he took with exquisite gentleness and solemnity. Many toasts were drunk to the honorees' health and prosperity, to the queen's health, and even to Marcot's and Percie's health.

As the meal was winding down, Percie stood up and clapped for everyone's attention.

"As many of you know, tonight we will be dancing the Harvest Reel. If any of you would like to practice the steps, I will be leading a class in the ballroom in a few moments. If you feel otherwise inclined, perchance you would like to refresh yourself by a stroll in the East Garden."

No one could leave the room before the queen. Cerúlia stood up; Tilim magically appeared holding out her white robe; and Alix and Vilkit slid in step a few paces behind Ciellō, which meant that they needed a word.

"Chamberlain," said Cerúlia, "my compliments. Everything is going so splendidly. Lord Steward?"

Alix said, "My liege, I wanted you to know that the vessel from the Free States has been sighted, due to dock tonight. Nishtari will play host and greeter. Did your gulls catch any sign of the Lorthers?"

"No, none at all. Pray the Waters that the ship is safe."

"Your Majesty, I hope that without your kin's arrival, tomorrow's festivities will not be anticlimactic for you."

"Tomorrow will be as the Waters will," she said to her steward, and he departed. Vilkit still walked behind her, so he had a private matter to discuss with her.

"Yes, Vilkit?"

"Your Majesty, Filio Kemeron asked a footman to deliver this note to you, and the footman, with wise discretion, brought it to me instead. Do you wish to accept the note, or should I return it?"

Cerúlia stopped in the corridor.

Vilkit coughed. "Your Majesty, this is a very busy day for you. Mayhap you would prefer that I discreetly return the note and inform the prince that you are too occupied right now for such correspondence."

"Ah, Vilkit. That would be perfect. Buy me time, while keeping all options open.

"Oh, and Vilkit, speaking of notes . . ." Cerúlia kept her voice casual. "Please give this to Councilor Nishtari to deliver personally to the Free Staters arriving tonight. 'Tis nothing, just a few words of welcome."

"Of course, Your Majesty," said Vilkit, placing the note in his pocket and giving it a small pat.

A kitchen maid came rushing up to Vilkit babbling about apples, and he rushed away, greatly excited.

Vilkit dashed to the pantry to discover bushels and bushels of apples—the long-awaited shipment had finally arrived from Androvale.

"Borta," he called to the head baker, "they came!"

"I got eyes," said Borta. "Now how we gonna get all of these peeled by tonight?"

"I'll assign you extra hands," he placated her.

Vilkit was so excited that, in an unprecedented lapse, he forgot all about the note to the Free Staters.

The undelivered, unread note in Vilkit's best black waistcoat read:

Commander Thalen—
It gives me great joy to learn that you have safely docked in Cascada.
I have spent my life hiding from enemies of the Nargis Throne.
When I was young I used the name "Wren." When I fled Weirandale,

I adopted the name "Kestrel." When I traveled in Alpetar, I used the name "Finch." When I joined the Raiders, I took the name "Skylark." When I survived the Magi's fireball and recovered in Salubriton, I re-named myself "Phénix," after the bird who rises again from the ashes.

When I claimed the Nargis Throne some moons ago, I also re-claimed my true name.

And it gives me the greatest of pleasures to welcome you and the brave Raiders to the realm of Weirandale as

Cerúlia the Gryphling, Queen of Weirandale

Gryphling

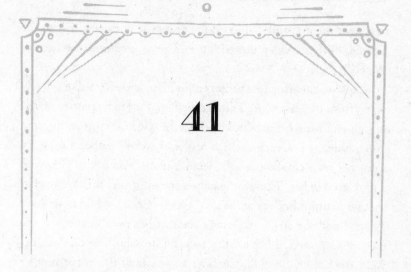

41

Soon enough, the afternoon ceremony began.

The program started with a clarion of trumpets from the upper balcony.

The palace caller announced, "Citizens of Weir, stand in respect for the kin of Queen Cressa's Shield!"

The families of her mother's Shield no longer wore mourning veils because their losses had occurred so long ago. They walked in proudly, if a little awed.

Cerúlia stood. "To serve in the Queen's Shield is a unique responsibility and an unparalleled distinction in Weirandale from the beginning of the monarchy. Should the whole world turn against the queen, her Shield is pledged to protect her to the last. Though all members of such Shields have served valiantly, rarely has a corps been put to this severe test. But in the Days of Treachery, my mother's Shield protected her from would-be assassins in this very palace and stayed by her side until the calamity off the Pellish coast.

"That most of them perished is a tragedy. Almost as distressing is that, up until today, these bravest and most loyal of Weirs have not received the acclaim they deserved. It is thus my deep privilege to convey my gratitude—indeed the gratitude of the realm—to the families of those who followed Queen Cressa even unto the Eternal Waters."

Captain Yanath gave the queen his arm, and she walked slowly down from the dais while Tilim rushed forward to hold up her trailing gown. Yanath introduced her to the kinfolk representing the fallen Shields. For each she had a special word—either a memory from her own childhood, or a detail Yanath, Pontole, or Branwise had relayed to her. Thus, for instance, she informed Bristle's brother that without his bravery at the gate, Queen Cressa would never have escaped and she spoke to Seena's sister of her own memory of the day Seena protected her as they rode on horseback in the hills beyond the palace. She told Clemçon's sister how much her mother relied upon her captain.

And to each family she presented a medal, a replica of Queen Cressa's Nargis Ice Hexagon, made of white gold. Each medal was engraved with the shield's name and the word "Unwavering."

When she finished and returned to the throne, the trumpets played a fanfare, while the onlookers cheered lustily. Yanath escorted the kin of Cressa's Shield to reserved benches.

Next, a mighty tramp of marching feet penetrated from outside the East Entrance. The palace caller announced, "Lord Consort Ambrice commanded a navy brave and true. May I present to all herein the survivors of the battles against the Pellish and the kinfolk of the fallen."

The middle-aged sailors, in their dress uniforms, had obviously practiced their entrance. They put the relatives in the middle of their formation, with sailors linking arms and escorting them on both sides. This phalanx marched into the Throne Room in perfect lockstep. The last rows of mariners held aloft the faded Weir flag from the *Sea Sprite,* the ship on which Queen Cressa had fled Cascada.

The sight was so stirring that the crowd immediately rose on its feet, shouting and cheering. Cerúlia noted that both Yanath and

Wilamara, who had served with these men and women, let their tears stream down their cheeks.

This part of the ceremony was Seamaster Wilamara's show. She called out the names of all the sailors and presented them or their kinfolk with a medal for combat service. Since hundreds of sailors had served, this took hours, but the reactions of the honorees were so varied that the onlookers could not get bored. Sailors shook hands with the seamaster; others knelt to the queen; some boisterously showed off their medal to friends in the crowd; and many family members started sobbing.

After all the names had been called, a quartet of seamasters marched forward. They folded the *Sea Sprite*'s flag with formal and reverent precision and handed it off to Wilamara. The seamaster approached Cerúlia and knelt on one knee.

She called out in a ringing voice, "Your Majesty, you too are the closest kin of a fallen sailor, our noble and much-missed Lord Ambrice. *Sea Sprite* was his first command, and a ship he dearly loved. Will you accept the flag of this vessel as a token of our undying respect for our Lord of the Ships?"

Cerúlia had not been informed that this gesture would be part of the ceremony. The portrait in the Gallery of the Queens and Consorts had brought back long-lost memories of her father. She reached out for the flag and hugged it to her chest.

Does it really smell of sea spray and windy sunshine, or do I just imagine this?

"Huzzah! Huzzah!" shouted all the mariners, many throwing their caps in the air. Then, accompanied by the trumpets in the balcony, they launched into a rowdy rendition of "Where's My Weir Sailor-Boy?"

Cerúlia rose and walked slowly toward the East Entrance, pausing to greet the sailors who made way for her to proceed through their midst. Tilim and Ciellō followed her, matching their pace to hers.

When the sailors reached the last line of their chantey, with all of them shouting, "Back in the bed of his favorite gal!" the trumpets modulated to a minor key. They played the somber "Lamentation for the Lost." Cerúlia timed her walk's progress so that she exited on the last, haunting notes of the lone flute. The lament broke her heart.

Cerúlia strode up the staircase with unseemly haste, almost running. Sensing her distress, her dogs came streaming to her side from varied directions. When she reached her bedchamber, she fought through the lump in her throat to tell Ciellō, "No one. No one may disturb me."

The loneliness of the single flute still echoed in her mind. She threw herself on the bed and wept. She wept for all the losses she'd learned about today; she wept for Clemçon, Bristle, and Seena; she wept for her father and her mother. She wept for the orphaned children, and she wept for herself: the once and always orphaned child who had lost her parents and Wilim and so many dogs and so many friends.

The door opened and closed quickly. Cerúlia looked around, prepared to be furious with Ciellō for allowing anyone to see her in such a state, but it was Percie—the perfect, only person to have near her in her righteous sorrow.

Percie rushed to the bed, shooed the dogs away, and took Cerúlia in her arms, rocking her back and forth.

"Hush now, hush now. We've all been crying, and few of us have as much reason as you do. But come, come, that's enough."

"So much loss, Percie. My own and the nation's. How can I bear it?"

"You bear it because you can't change it. You bear it because it heals everyone else's sorrow to see you standing tall. And me and Mama and everyone—we will help you as much as we can."

"But I need Thalen too!" Cerúlia said through her sobs. "I want to jump on Smoke and ride to the wharf; I want to see the rest of the

Raiders. Percie, I don't even know who survived the last battle with the woros!"

"I know, dear heart, but you can't. All eyes are on you, now especially. How would it look for the queen to gallop off on a secret rendezvous? And wouldn't you be humiliating the Rorthers? One more day, Birdie, one day more."

In a few moments Cerúlia regained control of herself. She washed her face and put cool cloths on her puffy eyes. Percia helped her out of her gown.

"Lie down a spell, Birdie," said Percie. "There's still time yet before you have to dress for the dinner."

"Whaki!" As she lay down, Cerúlia patted the bed next to herself. "Come lie next to me. Percie, will you keep people from bothering me?"

"Ciellō and I will guard the Reception Room door like dragons."

"Good." She sighed, then lifted her head off the pillow, puzzled. "Percie, how did you happen to come? I didn't call you, did I? My Talent has never before stretched to people. . . ."

"No, silly. 'Twas no Magic. Ciellō sent for me," she said as she crossed to the door. "He always knows what you need."

At dinnertime, dressed in the Sunset Gown, with her hair plaited up like a crown, Cerúlia entered the Great Ballroom, where the guests from the day's festivities stood assembled, waiting for her. Nightingales hanging from the Harvest Arch threw themselves into song at her entrance.

Vilkit led her to a seat in between King Kentros and Filio Kemeron, knowing that for her to sit anywhere else tonight would have been seen as a deliberate snub.

Brother Whitsury spoke a benediction to Nargis, pointing out that the fruits of the harvest were due to the sweet Water that had nourished the crops.

Her seatmates had been deeply impressed by the day's events, which spoke to their good hearts. Cerúlia initially had a little difficulty drawing the prince out until she asked him to tell her about Rortherrod. He warmed to this topic, discoursing on the quarries where they cut marble and limestone and their buildings crafted by expert masons. Apparently his castle boasted statues so lifelike that visitors mistook them for people. Horses in Rortherrod had to be from bigger stock, a third again larger than the ones he'd seen in Cascada, in order to pull wagons full of stone.

After a while the queen stopped actually absorbing his descriptions and just watched his face.

He is so animated talking about his home; he loves it with a fierce pride. His hands flex when talking about stonework as if he himself holds a chisel. His eyes are kind.

For the second course, Cerúlia offered her regrets to the Rorthers and moved to sit with the kin of Queen Cressa's Shield. Members of her current shield, including Yanath, Pontole, and Branwise, sat at that table too.

Branwise told a story about how drunk Bristle got when he was elevated to sergeant—so drunk that he couldn't ride and the other shields had to carry him home. Captain Clemçon's sister had brought with her a packet of letters and trinkets that her brother had mailed back to her from Pilagos during the years of the conflicts against the Pellish. She read aloud to the table passages in which the captain praised his troops' courage and steadfastness, and also passages about the queen and Lord Ambrice. The diners at the table, including Cerúlia, hung on every word about their lost loved ones.

"Would you mind sharing those letters, or the parts that aren't personal, with Royal Chronicler Sewel?" Cerúlia requested. "We have no record of those five years, and Clemçon's accounts would help fill in the gaps."

The queen spent the third course amongst the mariners, whose tables proved to be the loudest and jolliest. This choice, however, might have been a mistake, because they kept pouring her more wine.

Then the music started. Tables were pushed back to make room, and Percia, looking splendid in her peach wedding gown with a new pumpkin-colored doublet studded with tiny emeralds, took command of the room, arranging dancers in the proper rows.

By etiquette Cerúlia should have danced the first reel with either King Kentros or the prince, but Seamaster Gourdo, who had both served with her mother and father and been imprisoned by Matwyck's Marauders, invited her to "cut a caper," and his sailors so enthusiastically vouched that he was the fleet's most skilled dancer that she allowed him to lead her to the dance floor.

Gourdo proved to be an excellent partner, leading her so that she never missed a figure or a twirl. She made up for her breach of protocol by dancing the next reel with Filio Kemeron. He hesitated over the steps, whispering, "Please coach me. Don't let me disgrace myself." He had some natural grace, and he tried valiantly. He held her hand and waist with just the right amount of gentleness and firmness, not too intimate or too distant.

She danced a third reel with Shield Branwise. He stepped on her toes and her feet started to hurt, but he glowed with such pride that the discomforts were washed away.

When the dance was over, however, she asked her shield, "Please escort me to Councilor Nishtari. I need to discuss the arrangements for the morrow."

Her councilor for diplomacy had been drinking with the sailors too, so her eyes were a bit unfocused. Cerúlia discussed the order of the presentation of the visitors with her. They had counted on the Lorthers having the place of honor by coming last, but now Cerúlia requested that the Free States Raiders come last.

The Raiders must be in port. There is no note in response to mine? Is he only a few leagues from me tonight? What if he no longer cares for me?

Panic rose in her chest as all the equanimity she'd gained in the morning dissolved and the anxiety of the last few weeks repossessed her. She looked around the room for a distraction. Scores of people danced in couples: sailors with widows; duchesses with former prisoners; Stahlia with Duke Naven; Marcot with Percie; Alix with Wilamara; Tilim with a beautiful girl who was five summers too old for him; Vilkit with a relative of a Queen's Shield. The twirling, laughing dancers offered a rare sight, a vision of the healing and union that Cerúlia had hoped the fest would inspire, but she suddenly felt very alone amongst all this gaiety.

Ciellō's hand gently grasped her elbow. "I wonder, it has been a tiring day for damselle?" he whispered. "I wonder, too much wine, now leaving an aftertaste? What would please damselle?"

"Oh, Ciellō," she exhaled with relief. "I am overheated and agitated. I would like to take a turn in the garden and go to bed. Can I, dare I, slip away? How can I leave without disrupting the dance?"

"Nothing would be easier, damselle," he answered softly. "You just need to follow me in being stealthy. Leave the cloak. Later I fetch it."

They slipped out a side door without fanfare and merely waved to the palace guards who recognized them. When they reached the East Garden, it sat quiet under the yellow harvest moons. Cerúlia kicked off her shoes and walked stocking-foot in the smooth, cool walkways, feeling her pulse return to normal. Owls hooted greetings from the trees, while Whaki lifted his leg on Stahlia's carefully tended flower beds and Cici pranced, aquiver with delight.

"Better now, damselle?" asked Ciellō, breaking the long silence.

"Yes," she sighed.

"You know, Ciellō," she continued absently, grateful that he had rescued her from the Great Ballroom, "*you* never take a day off. You are always . . . just *there*. Don't you want to get away, have a day of leisure?"

"No, damselle."

"Don't be ridiculous. Don't you want to go riding, or sightseeing, or to go practice your fiddle—anything—rather than always shadowing me?" She idly wrapped her hands around a slender tree and twirled her body around it.

"No, damselle." He stood in the moon shadow of a shrub, in his typical pose of relaxation, like a cat always ready to pounce.

His tone is so serious. Does he not trust my Shield? As if his whole life is devoted to me. . . .

Oh, Sweet Waters! Have I been blind to the person who always stands beside me?

Cerúlia came to a dead stop on the path.

"I feel much better," she said with forced brightness. "Let's go in now."

42

Activities did not begin until afternoon, to give everyone a chance to sleep late and to take the pressure off the staff.

Cerúlia had allowed the healer Finzle to mix her a sleeping draught. When she woke she took a long bath; then she sent notes to Filio Kemeron and Percia, asking them to meet her in her closet in the forenoon.

"Have any messages arrived for me?" she asked her servants, but none had been received.

Kiltti dressed her in the Pearl Gown. Cerúlia instructed Geesilla to pull her hair up and back from her face with combs decorated with pearls but to leave the sides and back flowing in loose curls.

She sent her maids away and sat for a moment, fingering the rough, scarred skin on her neck, thinking about pain.

Dogs, she sent, *I have to do something very difficult. I'd like you by my side.*

Cici, who had been lying on a chair, attentively watching her every movement as she dressed, jumped down, wagging her tail. Whaki, who had been dozing in a patch of sunshine, sat up, shook his head, and sniffed the air as if he could smell what troubled her.

Cerúlia crossed to the door to the Reception Room, finding

Ciellō, as always, standing guard before it. A footman and a maid also stood at the ready for any instructions.

She turned to the servants. "I'd like you both to go to my closet. I have a meeting there later this morning. Open the windows, stir the fire, and make the room as fresh and tidy as can be. Don't come back until I give you leave."

"As it pleases Your Majesty." The footman bowed and they departed.

"I need to speak with you," she said to Ciellō, once they had the room to themselves. She stood still, in the middle of the carpet, restraining her hands from fiddling with each other or her skirt. She had wanted to get this interview over with as soon as she had awoken, but she knew it was better to wait until she was fully arrayed in royal garments—her new style of armor.

He inclined his head but said nothing. She gathered her courage.

"Ciellō, you know one day I will marry."

"Of course, damselle." Ciellō's only reaction to what must have been a rather surprising topic was to blink once.

"Whether it be to Filio Kemeron or someone else, one day I *will* wed. I need to produce a daughter for the realm, and I need a husband at my side."

"Of course, damselle." His stance, balanced on both feet, remained completely composed.

"What will it be like for *you,* Ciellō, when I spend time with another man?"

If she hadn't been regarding him so intently, with senses she had trained, she might have missed the flash that passed through his eyes.

Whaki? I sense jealousy and anger.

One doth as well.

And dominance, added Cici.

"I will stand behind you and guard the body," Ciellō said. "Your . . . husband will not guard you as well."

"No," the queen answered. "I don't think such an arrangement is possible or desirable. I have had the blessing of being able to relax and feel safe under your protection for over a year, but that must now come to an end."

"Come to an end? Why, damselle?"

"Because it is not just a sexual spark—you care for me more than a bodyguard should." She tilted her chin up, daring him to deny it.

"Of course, damselle." He smiled his feline smile. "And always will. And one day your husband, he will die, and I will still be here. And you will see me."

"I see you now," Cerúlia answered, and though inside she quailed at the image of Ciellō standing around, waiting for her husband to die, she smiled, trying to convey all the genuine affection she felt for him. "I see your grace, your strength, your good council, and your loyalty. But keeping you beside me would be *using* you in a way I cannot continue. I have been blind to do so for so long."

"And if I want to be 'used' in order to stay close beside you?" He lifted one eyebrow ironically.

"That is an untenable situation that would dishonor both of us."

His eyes flashed again, though he was so in control of his body that he did not move.

"What is dishonorable," his voice came rougher, "is that you yearn for me too. And yet you are too proud to entertain the suit of a Zellish commoner."

"Do you truly think that's the barrier between us?" Cerúlia asked, determined not to get angry.

"What else?" Ciellō shrugged. "Admit, damselle, that if I crossed these few steps and carried you to the bed, you would moan with pleasure."

Cerúlia closed her eyes a moment. She could not deny that a flash of warmth coursed through her at the mere suggestion, but the anger that she'd been determined not to show bubbled up even more strongly. She laid her hand on Whaki's head for strength and opened her eyes.

"Ciellō. Indeed, as you know, I am susceptible to your . . . magnetism. But. I cannot choose a life partner who cares nothing for Weirandale."

Her bodyguard was caught completely off guard by this topic. If he hadn't been so perfectly balanced and poised he might have moved. As it was, his eyebrows shot up.

"Why would I care for this land? It is just a country, like many I have seen. Not even a particularly well-ordered one." His tone softened into a purr. "But if you want to worry over it and its people—during the daytimes—I would not stop you."

"There it is," Cerúlia shot back. "There is the second problem. Your arrogance. *You would not stop me?* You would give me *your permission* to care for my realm? I have Dedicated my life to my realm. Can't you hear yourself, Ciellō?"

"Damselle." He took one step closer. "Don't be *foool-ish*." His voice took on the irritating, patronizing quality she had noted the day they met. "You may wear a pretty bauble, on occasion you surprise me, but you are young and inexperienced. I, an older man, more traveled—"

Cerúlia broke off his sentence. "This audience is at an end." With effort, she regained her self-control. "I am so profoundly grateful for your friendship and your services these last months that I would not end our time together with a quarrel with you.

"As of this moment, you are discharged. I ask that you leave the palace forthwith."

Nostrils flaring, Ciellō took a few deep breaths; he stepped back one step into the spot he had previously occupied.

Although he had just increased the distance between them, Whaki, protectively, moved in front of her leg. Cici yipped once, in warning. Ciellō stared at the dogs as if they, not Cerúlia, had just broken his heart.

"The palace I will leave," Ciellō said quietly. "Once before you 'discharged' me; and soon you discovered your folly—that you need me at your side. That you are in danger without me. Again, I will wait at the Sea Hawk inn until your senses you regain."

Once the door had clicked shut, Cerúlia shook out her skirts and walked back into her bedchamber. Given all that she'd been contending with, perhaps she should forgive herself that she had missed the signs of Ciellō's possessiveness. She suspected that on one level she had noted it since the *Misty Traveler* but had deliberately chosen to overlook the complication because Ciellō was the only person who made her feel, after years of living in fear, entirely safe and protected.

But her selfishness had ended up wounding him, and she berated herself for exploiting his devotion in this manner for so long.

It is past time that I take responsibility, if not literally for my own security—for I will always have shields about me—then for my own sense of safety.

She affixed her dagger to the dress's belt loop.

She rose and took a kerchief to the Queen's Waterfall in her room. She wet the cloth in the flow and then pressed its cool dampness to her temples, throat, and wrists. This was just the beginning of a long and difficult day, a day she'd been praying for and dreading.

Another thought struck her: Had she kept Ciellō beside her because she was insecure about her comeliness? Had she enjoyed having such a man yearn for her? That was an even uglier possibility and she longed to dismiss it outright, but she recognized at least a grain of truth.

In anger at herself, she said out loud to the dogs, "Well, if he is so much more mature and experienced, he should have watched out for his own heart! He should have left me the first time!"

The dogs blinked, and her voice in the empty room sounded childish to her own ears.

Relationships with men—they are just too complicated and messy, she sent to her pack.

Why doth thou not eat? answered Whaki. *A full stomach makes thy tail wag.*

Cerúlia had no better plan of action, so she retrieved her servants and ordered a small tray, which she ate with great care so as not to get a crumb on her gown.

At the appointed time the queen tossed her trailing hair back, squared her shoulders, and went into the Queen's Closet to meet with Filio Kemeron, with Percia as a chaperone. Perchance she should have consulted with her council before speaking to him directly. Undoubtedly Envoy Rakihah would have wished to be in the room. But she had decided that her own marriage was primarily her own business.

And she felt less trepidation treating with the prince directly than she had in talking to Ciellō. Kemeron she had already judged to be a phlegmatic man, unlikely to break out in scenes or reproaches.

After beginning with polite preliminaries, she invited Kemeron to sit across from her at the mahogany table.

"Filio Kemeron, we mentioned 'honest talk' as opposed to courtly compliments. With your permission, I would speak to you openly."

"I would be grateful for this intimacy and trust."

"Please correct me if I am under a misapprehension, but my councilors have speculated whether your visit might be the opening of an intended courtship."

"There is no misapprehension," Kemeron smiled. "That was my father's and my intention, an intention that has turned to certitude upon meeting you."

"I am deeply honored. And I must tell you—however unusual

this may sound from a queen—that though I do not know you well yet, I find myself drawn to you."

He mirrored her seriousness and honesty, "As you must know, I am powerfully attracted to you. Moreover, Your Highness, I believe I could make you happy."

"I believe that you would try your hardest. But we both know that this would be a strategic union, a union intended to bring benefits to both nations."

The prince nodded. "Rorther masons could rebuild your palace better than before. Some of your foundations show shifting. That pond really should be dredged and edged with stone. You'll pardon me for pointing out, but Cascada's cobblestones were poorly laid; we could do much better. The avenue that slopes up from the harbor—it should not be so uneven. We would dig it up and fix its foundation."

Cerúlia tried to interject a word, but Kemeron did not take a breath. She realized that last night at dinner, once she had gotten him started, he had done nearly all the talking too.

"I have heard about statues of queens that stand in some garden. They have been allowed to decay?"

She opened her mouth to respond, but Kemeron continued without pause, "I would work on them myself; I would bring them back to their former glory or even better! I could do that for you, Your Highness, and for your people.

"I know, I know—stonework is not the major point. The major advantage I bring is that Rorther stability could lend strength to a realm that has recently gone through upheaval and insecurity. With a Rorther royal as consort, Weirs would never again have to worry about coups or plotters. Your realm would be protected with all my kingdom's might."

Cerúlia nodded. "I have considered all those advantages, though I didn't know about the cobblestones' deficits."

She continued, "You know, an alliance with Weirandale would

benefit Rortherrod with equal blessings. A Weir queen comes from a fruitful land, where the crops are nourished by Nargis Water. And she comes with a Spirit's grace and endowed with a Talent."

"I did not mean to imply that my realm would be the major donor," said Filio Kemeron, though that is exactly what he had just done. "I am sensible that we would be the recipient of a glorious bounty. And that in you yourself, Rortherrod would gain an unparalleled prize."

Cerúlia didn't particularly enjoy thinking of herself as a prize being bestowed. But she bobbed her head at the compliment.

"Nonetheless, my prince, we must also consider the impediments."

"Impediments? I see only advantages."

"Last night, as you were talking of Rortherrod," she said, "I realized how much you love your country, and how miserable you would be living elsewhere. And you must have learned from yesterday's ceremonies that I will never again leave Weirandale for any period of time."

Kemeron's tawny complexion turned darker, "But you haven't visited yet. Our capital, Feldspar, our redwood forests! I know you would love these treasures. Couldn't we split our time between the two realms? The voyage is not so very long."

"No." Cerúlia's tone grew adamantine. This was nonnegotiable. "Nor could we see each other only rarely. I know myself well enough to admit that I need a husband by my side. My grandmother's marriage was motivated by strategy and it did not survive, and my mother's confidence suffered when she was separated from her husband. I will not make the same errors that they made."

"I see," said Kemeron slowly. "So are you asking me to choose between my country and you?"

"No choice should be made in haste," Cerúlia replied. "No choices are being made today. But there is another problem I wish you to consider. This might prompt you to change your intention."

"Having seen your loveliness, I would never—"

Cerúlia didn't want another compliment, sincere or insincere. She held up her hands to forestall him.

"You must know, Nargis Queens always bear daughters. It is rare that they bear a second child and rarer still that a male child survives. Would you have our daughter rule both Weirandale and Rortherrod? Or were you hoping for a second, male heir for your kingdom? Or would you have your younger brothers' sons inherit the Rorther throne?"

"I had not thought that far in the future, Your Majesty," replied the prince slowly. "You are right, however, that the issue of a successor would be quite important for my realm. Vital, in fact."

"In a marriage made for strategic alliances," Cerúlia remarked, surprised that she had to teach the prince about this topic, "these are the issues that matter most."

"I see," he said, and the room fell silent.

"Your Highness, would you hold my hands?" asked Kemeron.

Cerúlia laid her hands out on the table, and the prince took them in his own. His hands were warm and dry, with calluses from using tools. She'd never liked him as much as she did that moment, holding his hands, trying to dissuade him from wanting to marry her.

"Your Highness, yesterday I found you very beautiful. Today, I find you honest, thoughtful, and so bright that truly, your mind quite dazzles me. You have given me much to ponder."

"Thank you, Kemeron. Wherever Fate may lead us, I wish you joy."

Cerúlia withdrew her hands from his grasp and looked at Percia, who, as chaperone and guard, had been standing silently near the door.

Percia took the hint, looked at her hourglass pendant, and said, "Your Majesty, this afternoon's events are about to commence."

43

Unable to sleep late, Thalen left the Rare Talents Inn, where the Raiders had been lodged. The inn, a large and stately edifice, was located in the center of Cascada, just a short ways down one of the avenues that led to the Courtyard of the Star.

Thalen paced the streets of Weirandale all morning, admiring the white bark trees, half dressed in red, that ran down the medians of the avenues. He let his steps lead him to the Fountain. The intricate patterns, the rainbows arcing in the autumn light, the piece of Nargis Ice mesmerized him. He watched the pilgrims drinking the water and rubbing it on their injuries. He had no cup, but he reached his hands into the spray and caught enough water for several full swallows.

Sweet Water. Nargis Water. There were days in Oromondo when I would have killed for this drink.

He repeated the gesture. Then, on impulse, he leaned into the cascading liquid, allowing the water to douse his head and face.

There, Wareth! I've poured water over my head again. I pray this will help with my wild delusions about the queen. I just hope she's an able monarch, able to maintain this peace, and after this event is over I can go back to the Scolárium with my fantasies and doubts safely chased away.

He sat on the slightly damp ledge, listening to the patter and trying to reason through his situation.

Tutor Helina was starting to grow on him; she was smart and amiable, and she obviously welcomed his attentions. He might never yearn for her the way he had once yearned for Skylark, but that overheated passion might have sprung from the dire circumstances they faced. Helina and he would be compatible with one another because they had such similar interests.

Refreshed, and feeling more grounded and sensible, Thalen headed back to the Rare Talents Inn. His fellow Raiders were already starting to shave and dress. Thalen had invited the quartermasters—Hake, Quinith, and Olet—to come to Cascada, but Hake would not leave the pottery just as it was getting off the ground, Quinith was needed to monitor the recovery progress in the Free States, and Olet did not believe his contribution warranted any fuss.

A Weir councilor, a brown-haired woman named Nishtari of Queen's Harbor, had greeted their ship yesterday. She'd explained that this festival honored many people for many contributions and sacrifices that had occurred during and after the reign of Queen Cressa. This councilor had a polite and professional manner, inspiring confidence. And when she mentioned that in her various travels she had visited both Slagos and Pilagos (where she had once been introduced to Olet), Thalen and Minister Destra had met each other's eyes with a look of relief. This relief had redoubled when Nishtari went on to discuss her multiple trips to Sutterdam and Yosta. There was comfort, arriving in a strange realm, to be welcomed by someone who spoke with respect and familiarity of their homelands.

For the upcoming ceremony, Thalen provided Councilor Nishtari with a parchment listing the names of all the Raiders who had fallen. The fact that his comrades, who had sacrificed their lives, would receive public acclaim was as gratifying as a drink of sweet water to a parched throat.

The order of events provided that "Magistrar Destra of the

Green Isles" precede the Free States Raiders. Councilor Nishtari arrived in an ornate carriage to escort Destra. As Thalen handed her up the steps, Destra patted his cheek and said, "Happy ceremonies are rare occurrences. I'm resolved to enjoy this moment to the fullest. You'd be wise to do so also."

Then three carriages pulled up for the Raiders. As they rattled through the streets, Thalen tried to quiet his thudding heart by looking out the windows at the sights of Cascada. Buildings flashed by his unseeing eyes. His carriage mates were quiet, nervous about the upcoming formalities.

At the palace gate, Nishtari and Destra's carriage stopped as their escort spoke to the guards. The guards then waved the Raiders through, standing at attention. The Nargis Palace, large and resplendent, gleaming white, stood a ways ahead, down a long avenue of nearly bare elms.

The afternoon events began with Chronicler Sewel recounting to the audience how, in Queen Cressa's fight against the Pellish pirates, key allies had come to her aid. Today's celebration was in honor of those whose contributions Weir citizens might not know well enough, but who deserved their utmost gratitude.

My heart is going to smash through my ribs, thought Cerúlia as she tried to maintain composure on the throne.

The palace caller knocked on the door three times. She said, "King Kentros and Filio Kemeron of Rortherrod!"

Followed by an honor guard of Rorther shields, the royals walked down the length of the Throne Room. The onlookers were already familiar with these guests, and they applauded them lustily, drowning out a traditional Rorther anthem played by strings.

Sewel spoke of the ships the Rorthers had sent to help the Allied Fleet. Cerúlia stepped down and thanked them publicly. Kemeron presented her with the shard of the Protection Stone, accompanied by a pretty speech about how he hoped it would always protect the Weir people, and most especially the person of their lovely queen.

"May the bond between our realms always remain strong," said the queen.

"Be it thus and ever so," said the Rorther royalty. And the crowd echoed back to them, "Be it thus and ever so."

Then the palace caller proclaimed, "Minister Destra of the Free States, formerly Magistrar Destra of the Green Isles."

For this event Destra had resumed her Green Isles garb of a spare white gown, her side plait, and a bracelet of green vines. She walked solo down the Throne Room aisle, a small figure with an aura about her. The crowd grew silent, watching her approach. She knelt in front of the queen.

Sewel recounted the facts he had gathered from Seamaster Wilamara: how Magistrar Destra had been the one to suggest the fight against the pirates, how the Allied Fleet had been organized in Pilagos, how throughout the long war she had been ever at the side of Lord Ambrice and Queen Cressa with support, friendship, and wise advice.

Oh, thought Cerúlia. *What dignity and calm. I am so glad my parents had her as an ally.*

"Your Majesty," said Destra, in a quiet voice that still carried, "in my lifetime I have been fortunate to meet three Nargis Queens: Queen Catreena the Strategist, Queen Cressa the Enchanter, and now Queen Cerúlia the Gryphling. One might wonder why Fate has seen fit to entangle my life's journey with that of the Nargis Throne.

"The aid I provided to Queen Cressa was naught; 'twas her own courage and Talent that lifted the predations of the Pellish pirates from the seas.

"I no longer reside in the Green Isles; like you, I have returned from exile to my own homeland, the Free States, in hopes of healing the wounds of troublous times.

"I come before you now with three gifts: the friendship of the Free States; my counsel, should you ever desire it; and *this*." She took off her wrist the green vine bracelet and, kneeling, offered it to Cerúlia.

Cerúlia descended from the dais and spoke quietly to Destra. "The onlookers will not appreciate the preciousness of the gifts you have offered, milady, but I do. Weirandale needs allies; I would feel blessed to have your counsel; and I recognize the vine of Vertia. 'Tis the gift of growth—the pulse of life—for my country and for my person. I am overjoyed to clasp it on my wrist. Later, may we speak together of Gardener?"

She helped Destra rise and impulsively kissed the older woman on the cheek. Though not really understanding what had transpired, the crowd appreciated that their queen honored this foreigner and clapped loudly.

Councilor Nishtari escorted Minister Destra to her seat beside the Rortherrod royalty.

The palace caller announced, "Thalen's Raiders of the Free States."

With Thalen leading the way, they strode into the Throne Room in haphazard order, neither matching their strides into a march nor assuming a military formation.

The first thing Cerúlia took in was how grand they looked. She had never seen any of them in anything other than worn and dirty clothing. They strode with confidence, dressed in straight black coats that came down to the tops of their shining black boots, with silver buttons and no insignia other than armbands of a twisted white-and-black pattern. Their highly polished swords, hanging from black leather belts, were scabbardless; they shone bare against the black fabric. They wore no hats, most of them tying their hair back at the neck in imitation of their commander's style.

The next moment Cerúlia spent casting her eyes over the familiar physiques, noting in one glance who had survived. *There's Wareth! There's Kambey! Dalogun! But oh no! I don't see Gentain or Ooma.*

Thalen and the Raiders advanced down the Throne Room aisle.

Steady, lads, Thalen thought. *If you feel abashed by all these people and that throne, you don't show it. We have faced down woros. We can walk through a crowd with our heads held high.*

Their strong strides had brought them closer to the dais. Cerúlia now could see Thalen's face and his blue eyes.

Oh, Sweet Nargis—save me. For here he stands before me, and again I am lost. Yet he loves me not, or he would have answered my note.

For his part Thalen had gotten close enough that he could discern the queen's face clearly. *Take away the blue hair, that shining pendant, those fancy clothes—*

"YOU'RE ALIVE!" Thalen broke out in a voice strident with both jubilation and fury. "DAMN YOUR EYES, YOU'RE ALIVE!"

"And queen! Queen of Weirandale!" Tristo shouted.

"Skylark!" Wareth roared. "You confounded, lying cur! You—! You bird dung! Do you know how much he's suffered?"

Fedak shouted out, "Skylark. Well, I'll be blowed. How did your hair get blue?"

Pandemonium ensued. The Queen's Shield was alarmed by the lapse that had allowed these men to enter their liege's presence with their swords, and the shouting elicited immediate protective responses. Yanath and several others pulled their swords and rushed in front of the dais. Whaki and Vaki raised their throats in loud howls. Hundreds of onlookers turned to one another with scandalized expressions and confusion.

Thalen held his arms way outstretched from his sides, showing that he had no intent of going for his glittering rapier, while the rest of the Raiders automatically copied his lead. Ignoring the noise and movement, his shock gave way to analysis.

Now I see everything clearly. Why her hair wasn't as yellow as Gunnit's. Why she knew the Weir ballads. Why she could talk to animals. Why she was so smart. Why Nollo and Shyrwin were searching for her. I couldn't find her body because she wasn't dead. All the pieces were there all along. I should have known long ago. How could I have been so stupid? So stupid!

Dogs! Cerúlia commanded. *For Water's sake! Shut up.*

The dogs desisted; the shields paused at the Raiders' pacific gestures, and the moment stretched long. The queen stood and held up her hands for silence.

"Shields, as you were," she ordered. "Commander Thalen and the Raiders would no more injure me than you would. As a general rule, when in doubt, look to the catamounts."

At this direction, everyone in the room looked at the guardians of the Nargis Throne. Two of the mountain lions had continued dozing through all this ruckus; one blinked at the human antics and stretched out more comfortably; the last found the itch on her shoulder much more interesting than the Raiders. With wondering looks, the shields sheathed their swords and returned to their former positions.

Cerf boldly called out into the silence, "Skylark!!! You bloody well owe us an explanation!"

"Indeed I do, Cerf. Actually, I owe an explanation not only to the Raiders but to everyone in this Throne Room and beyond."

Cerúlia took a deep breath. "If everyone will attend, I shall try to dispel this confusion." She held her arms out to the galleries, the Throne Room floor, her councilors, and the Raiders, inviting them all to pay heed.

"On earlier occasions I have told Weirandale that I hid from Lord Matwyck in Androvale until his pursuit got too close, and then I took the fight to my mother's enemies. What I haven't recounted previously is that—under an assumed name and with my hair dyed—I traveled through Alpetar to the heart of Oromondo."

She paused a moment to let the news sink in while everyone in the Throne Room hung on her every word.

"Commander Thalen, standing here before you"—she gestured with her arm and open hand toward his figure—"brilliantly led a troop of the bravest souls I have yet known into the mountain peaks of Oromondo to strike at the underbelly of their stronghold, in hopes of drawing their occupying army out of the Free States. Hawks led me to the Raiders, with whom I joined forces. I did what little I could do to aid them in their fight.

"After a battle, I was captured by Oro forces and held prisoner in Femturan. Most of you have heard about the Femturan Conflagration that killed the Magi in their Octagon? *That fire was the work of these men before you, Thalen's Raiders.* Without their heroism, the Oro army might still be in the Free States, threatening more countries, poised to continue their rampage even into Weirandale.

"Commander Thalen and two other companions succeeded in freeing me from the Femturan cells. But as we were escaping the fire, I was injured and fell into the moat. I was rescued by sea creatures. After a period of recovery and travel, during which I had no way of communicating with my erstwhile comrades in arms, I returned here to Cascada some moons ago to claim the throne. Since that time, as well you know, affairs of state have kept me . . . rather occupied."

A ripple of laughter echoed in the Throne Room amongst onlookers who knew all about recent events in Cascada.

Trying to further lighten the mood, Cerúlia continued, "Hence the Raiders are somewhat . . . surprised to find me alive. And queen. With a new name. And blue hair."

Louder laughter.

During this speech Thalen maintained a stance of stubborn anger, with his legs slightly apart and his hands on his hips. The Raiders again unconsciously mimicked his example.

How dare she shift the credit! She hid herself from us; now she is hiding her true self from her own people.

"You are a bald-faced liar, Skylark, Queen Cerúlia—whoever you are today!" Thalen shouted out. "You didn't aid us 'a little'! Your help was essential. And the fire arrows were your idea! *You are the one who destroyed all the Magi.* I will not take credit that is owed to *you*."

"Commander Thalen!" Cerúlia retorted. "Do you wish our cherished companions to be honored here or not? Because I'll thank you to keep a civil tongue in your mouth! All of you!" Her eyes flashed over the group before her.

"Yes, ma'am," said Dalogun abashedly, going down on one knee. The rest of the Raiders followed suit, except for Thalen, who stood frozen, glaring at her.

She's alive. It's her voice. It's her face. But more has changed than just the long blue hair.

Tristo reached over and tugged at Thalen's coat. Thalen snapped out of his reverie and also knelt.

Cerúlia stepped down from the dais.

"We have many people to honor today—people who perished in this desperate combat, some of whom I lived with for several moons and was proud to call my friends. As I call out the names of the fallen, we will sound the bell in the tower."

Councilor Nishtari had Thalen's list of the Raiders who had died. The queen reached out her hand, taking the parchment from her because she wanted to read it herself. She called out each name, from "Adair" to "Yislan," pausing each time for the bell to sound. Some of the names were new to her; others (such as Gentain) she could hardly get out of her throat. The bell's single chimes echoed in her heart.

Thalen wrenched his thoughts away from the queen and her

mysteries to concentrate on the men and women who had died so that the Free States could be free. He had to concentrate so as not to be bowled over by a gale of grief.

Brother Whitsury stood and offered a prayer to Nargis for the fallen to have been embraced by the Eternal Waters. The audience members bowed their heads, and the Raiders kept kneeling.

After Whitsury finished, Cerúlia walked toward her guests. Councilor Nishtari came forward holding a silver tray with a piece of blue velvet on top. "Arise Tristo of Yosta and receive the queen's gratitude," Cerúlia intoned. She reached onto the tray for a pin of a golden eagle, which she affixed to Tristo's coat. She did this to each of the Raiders in turn, until she got to Thalen.

Thalen's mind churned. *I found her, but I've lost her again. The queen of Weirandale will never care for a shabby history tutor. And if there had been any chance, I have ruined it today with my outbursts. I pride myself on my composure—I've kept my composure in front of woros and enemy generals: how could I have behaved like such a loudmouth lackwit in front of all her people?*

Cerúlia touched his hand. "Arise, Commander Thalen, to receive the queen's gratitude."

He rose to his full height. Her hands were trembling, and she had to reach so high to pin it on his chest. She had difficulty getting the pin to penetrate the stiff, black fabric.

"Forgive me, Your Majesty," he whispered.

"Only if you forgive me, Commander, for deceiving you," she whispered back.

"For playing the fool in this ceremony," he whispered.

"For not finding a way a year ago to send you a message I had survived," she countered. "I sent you a message yesterday. . . ."

"I didn't get it," he protested.

"So I gather," she said with a quiet laugh in her voice.

44

Later, every woman in the Throne Room that day would insist that from the instant she heard the commander and queen quarreling so familiarly, she knew that the two were in love. But that afternoon, Percia was the only person not completely confounded by the scene that had just transpired before them. When the queen left the Throne Room, most of the visitors turned to one another in a babble of consternation.

Stahlia turned to Percia, "What in Ennea—?"

"Sorry, Mama, I must dash," interrupted Percia, actually pushing people aside to get out of the balcony area, lifting up her skirts and sprinting down the hallway to the Royal Wing, searching for her sister.

The queen sat in the Reception Room, one hand on Whaki's head, her whole body trembling slightly. Kiltti and Nana stood to the side, looking at her with concern, but uncertain what to do.

"Oh, Percie," Cerúlia gasped. "Just the right person. Would you oblige me by accompanying me on a stroll in the East Garden?"

"In the East Garden? *Now?* Uh, just let me get my hat and cloak. It'll take a few moments," said Percia.

Slightly more sedately, Percia left the queen's quarters. The honorees and audience were still exiting the Throne Room. Captain Yanath and Tilim had stopped to exchange congratulations with the men in black overcoats, though for the most part the Weirs kept their distances and gave them sidelong glances. Percia spotted a Raider who wasn't quite so hardened in appearance. In fact he was still young, and he had an empty coat sleeve. She walked up to him as unobtrusively as she could and made a little curtsey.

"Sir, I am Lady Percia, the queen's sister. She and I intend to stroll in the East Garden to take the air. Perchance you will pass this information along to your commander?"

The lad looked quite confused, but he said he would do so.

Percia made haste to fetch her hat and wrap. When she returned to the Queen's Chambers, she noticed that Ciellō was not at his post; when she inquired about him, Cerúlia said only, "I'm sure that we will be quite safe in the East Garden today." As they left the Royal Wing, the queen even ordered her Shield to stay behind.

Cerúlia took Percie's arm, and together they walked out toward the garden, a cluster of dogs following around them as a ragged escort. They stopped every few paces to exchange a polite greeting with a guest, but Cerúlia would not be drawn into a long conversation.

Mama was already there, proudly showing off the gardens to Minister Destra, who looked appreciative of every flower. They waved gaily at Percie and Cerúlia and then went back to examining the roses.

The Raiders stood awkwardly together in a little knot near the floral river and statues. Taking care not to head that way directly, but rather to stop and chat with other strollers, Percia led Cerúlia in that direction. The sky was the deepest blue, and the plantings shone with all the care her family had lavished on them.

When they approached, the men bowed politely this time. But her sister rushed over to each of them (except for Commander Thalen) for an informal embrace. The one-armed boy started crying, and a curly-haired man made so free as to twirl her around, laughing in the autumn sunshine.

Cerúlia introduced Percia to each of the Raiders, though Percia caught only a few of the names. Then Percia and Cerúlia seated themselves on a nearby stone bench, and the Raiders arranged themselves in a rough semicircle around them, most squatting on their heels, a few casually stroking the tail-wagging canine corps.

"Where did you go?" Tristo asked. "We dived for you in the moat so many times!"

"A big turtle took me on his back and ferried me away. I don't know how to explain it."

"A turtle!" several voices cried in amazement.

"Where are Eli-anna and Eldie?" Cerúlia asked. "They're not here, but their names weren't on the list—"

"They are hale," the curly-haired man said. "They decided they wanted to return to their kin in Melladrin."

"Hey, how much of the story you told about Sweetmeadow was true?" asked the bald-headed man with an earring. Percie learned surprising things about that blond page boy, Gunnit, and then the commander backtracked to Cerúlia's Wyndton life—and here Percie found herself scrutinized by blue eyes.

Mama and Minister Destra joined the group, interrupting an intense conversation that ricocheted from one country to another with disorienting speed.

"Good. You are getting reacquainted, I see," said Minister Destra.

Percia caught a hint of a knowing smile. "You knew all along," she accused the Minister. "You knew the queen was alive when Commander Thalen didn't; you knew who 'Skylark' was."

Minister Destra turned her soft gray eyes on Percia. "You are correct, my dear. But I never knew about 'Wren.' When your queen was young, she was in *your* keeping and that of your lovely mother's.

Such careful safekeeping. Queen Cressa chose so wisely." Percia felt a surge of pride.

Commander Thalen turned to his countrywoman as if he were going to be wrothful with her for withholding this information, but then he just held his head in his hands.

"Your Majesty, the afternoon ebbs," interjected Mama in an unsubtle hint. "Perchance you need to reenter to attend to your other guests and prepare for this evening?"

"Indeed. There is much too much information to exchange in one afternoon," Cerúlia agreed.

Then she turned to her sister. "Percie, I know the Raiders so well, I could tell you how each holds his reins. But strangely enough, the subject of *dancing* never came up in the midst of the canyons of Oromondo. So I must leave them in your capable hands.

"Teta, will you escort me inside?"

When the queen and her mother departed, Percie stood up. "Tonight at the fest we will all dance the Fountain Reel. I can teach you the steps in a few moments."

"Perfect," said Minister Destra. "Because I want the Raiders to have time to return to their inn to change. I planned their wardrobes with such care, for maximum effect."

While Percia began demonstrating the basic step, she thought, *Minister Destra was responsible for those dashing black outfits? Has she been orchestrating Thalen and Cerúlia's reunion? Does she hold everyone's Fate in her hands?*

45

Wareth couldn't wait to get Thalen alone to discuss the way the world had turned upside down.

"What the fuck!" shouted Kambey as soon as he, Wareth, and the commander had climbed in their return carriage. "She just about gave me a heart attack! If our other losses are going to start jumping out of the bushes, tell me now, so I can keel over and be done with it."

"Did you know?" Wareth asked Thalen, trying to study the face that resolutely gazed out the window.

"It had occurred to me, but I'd dismissed the idea as too far-fetched to be true," said Thalen. "You know what? Peddler once said to me, 'Sometimes I suspect the Spirits have a sense of humor.' I realize now that he was right."

At the Rare Talents Inn, they changed into a second outfit Destra had provided them: black-and-silver waistcoats over white silk shirts with puffed sleeves, accompanied by black trousers that puffed out from their boots accented with a silver stripe. When Wareth had first seen these ensembles, he'd found them too dandyish for the rugged Raiders; now he was glad that he had sumptuous silks to wear in front of the queen and court. The silver stripe made them all look tall.

As the Raiders finished dressing, they all wound up in Thalen's room, the largest in the inn.

"We need to make up for our uncouth behavior earlier," said Thalen. "We will look sharp and act like gentlemen—yes, even you, Kran, can pretend for one night."

"Swords or no?" asked Kambey, fussing with his sleeve to make it puff just perfectly.

"No swords," said Thalen. "They would hamper our dancing."

The men hooted at the thought of dancing, though the queen's sister had made it sound easy and almost fun.

"Do I have to dance?" Jothile asked.

"No," said Tristo, putting a hand on his shoulder. "You don't have to do anything you don't want to do."

"Could I stay here tonight," Jothile said, "instead of going back to there, where everyone is watching us?"

Thalen gave him his full attention. "You could, if you really want to. But the rest of us will be going, and I wonder if the queen would miss you."

Jothile bobbed his head and allowed Cerf to finish fastening his waistcoat.

"The sister is very lovely," Wareth remarked, as he pushed Fedak away from the mirror to pull at his curls to make them lie nicely.

"She's a wedded woman," said Fedak, throwing a towel at him. "Don't start any trouble."

"I'm just saying," replied Wareth, with exaggerated innocence. "Maybe all Weir women are lovely." Again he looked sideways at Thalen, trying to read his thoughts.

"Well, the mother certainly is," said Cerf. Wareth threw the towel at him.

"Well, the queen certainly is," added Dalogun. "My jaw almost dropped to the floor. How did *Skylark* change from that scrawny, quiet pal who you never thought of as a girl—I mean obviously she was a girl, but you never had to worry about that—to someone so, so . . ."

"Breathtaking?" offered Kran.

"Right," said Dalogun. "She stole my breath right out of my chest. We spent hours alongside a queen. What do you think of that? No wonder all the horses adored her."

Wareth purposely did not look at the commander. "She was attractive before too," he said. "More of a quiet beauty, though. And clever."

"Apparently, the prince of Rortherrod has come to court her," said Kran.

Thalen whirled around. *"What?"*

"That's what I heard from a group of folk chatting in the lobby outside the Throne Room," said Kran, oblivious. "They said that the people honored before Destra was called in were Rorther royalty, and that this Filio Kemeron was totally smitten with our bird gal."

"Fellows, don't forget to move the gold pins from your coat to the weskit," Kambey remarked. "They gave us extras too, didn't they? For the others?"

"Yes," said Thalen, pulling himself together. "Councilor Nishtari gave me pins for all the survivors who didn't make the voyage and also ones for any kin we can locate." The commander crossed over to his packing case and pulled out a leather sack, "Dalogun, here. Take one now to give to your parents, for Balogun."

Dalogun blew moist air on the pin and polished it a moment with his sleeve. "Our parents—they'll show this off to everyone in the village. A golden eagle. A gift from the queen of Weirandale, for their son's bravery!"

"As they should, lad," said Cerf.

"Kambey," said Thalen, vigorously rubbing his already-glowing boot, "the queen's little brother is sword crazy. Maybe you could pay special attention to him tonight?"

"Sure," answered their sergeant. "If I'm not too busy dancing with pretty Weir women and showing off my silken duds and fancy stepping." Cerf threw the towel at him but missed. "Earring in or out?" Kambey asked the room, nudging Wareth aside to look in the mirror.

Half the Raiders replied, "In," while the others said, "Out."

Carriages arrived to fetch them and Minister Destra back to the palace. Wareth noticed that Destra had changed into a long waistcoat with a brocade pattern of interlocking circles over a full white skirt.

The Great Ballroom was abuzz with people when they entered. In the center Wareth saw a large fountain of five stacked basins. Two men were proudly demonstrating that if they turned a hand-crank they could pump water up to the top, and then it would flow down over each consecutive basin to the bottom.

The other guests seemed to have lost their wariness of the Raiders now that they no longer wore naked steel. A seamaster brought Wareth a glass of fine wine and engaged him in friendly conversation. Over his glass Wareth noted that Jothile and Dalogun were shyly sticking together; Tristo already had a large group of Weirs laughing; and people were eagerly surrounding the commander for a word with the heroic leader.

When Skylark—the queen, that is—entered, the room fell silent. She now wore a flowing dress of shades of blue. Her blueish hair was held back from her face only with a thin circlet of silver and tumbled down to her shoulders. Everyone bowed.

People sat themselves at round tables with twelve seats. Wareth noted that several of the Raiders had clustered together, but others had dispersed themselves amongst the other guests. Cerf had managed to seat himself at a table with the queen's mother. Thalen sat at a table where several of the diners had amber hair, but he was deep in conversation with a brown-haired young man with a smart face.

Wareth himself was invited by Shield Pontole to share a table that was partly kin of the Queen's Shield, and partly mariners. He asked Pontole, "Who is the commander talking to?"

"Oh, that's our Steward Alix. He was elected by the people as the queen's first councilor. He used to write for the *Cascada News*."

The food was delicious. "Pontole," Wareth muttered to his neighbor, "what are the customs here about second helpings?"

Pontole smiled broadly. "All of you Raiders look a tad gaunt. Let me serve you more. This is Harvest Fest! A time for feasting till your buttons pop!"

"So much of our crop was stolen by the Oros," explained Wareth. "And when we were in Oromondo, many days we survived on thin soup."

"Tell us about your encounters with the enemy," said Shield Pontole.

So Wareth described a few of the skirmishes, enjoying the whole table's attention and respect. In his stories, Codek and other lost Raiders lived again.

The queen started the evening sitting next to Minister Destra. Later she moved in between two red-haired men in rich clothing. Once Wareth saw this pattern, he guessed it was only a matter of time before she moved next to the commander, so he excused himself from his current table to offer whatever emotional support Thalen would accept. When he settled on Thalen's left, the commander did not break off his animated conversation with the steward, but he briefly squeezed Wareth's shoulder.

Servers had taken away the dinner plates and served a sweet. Wareth tried a bite—the pastry was filled with apples and cinnamon custard.

The queen approached their table, so everyone stood up and bowed.

Steward Alix said, "My liege, perhaps you would like my seat next to our honored guest?"

"Thank you, Steward Alix," said the queen. She slipped into the just-vacated chair, and Thalen pushed her chair in.

Once everyone was reseated, however, an awkward silence followed.

"Tell me, Commander Thalen, what happened after I was parted from Tristo, you, and Eli-anna."

Thalen cleared his throat. "We three rode down the coast of Melladrin until we came to a town called Tar's Basin. I'm sorry—I had to sell the horses for ship's passage back to the Green Isles. Even Cinders."

"So Cinders survived the fireball? I didn't know. That's welcome news; she was a lovely filly."

"When we finally got back to the Free States, there were still a few trials ahead. But as you can see, we prevailed."

Wareth interrupted. "We were in a big battle outside of Jutterdam—you should have seen it—uh, Your Majesty. I had to pull him back before he challenged a whole city. Then he and Minister Destra cooked up this trick that made all the Oros surrender."

"Wareth, as usual, overstates my contribution." Thalen again put his hand on Wareth's shoulder. "In the final confrontation, Wareth here made the biggest sacrifice."

"Another time, perchance, you'll tell me the whole story?" said the queen, and her eyes moved from Wareth back to Thalen.

"I'm sure it is not half as interesting as your story about the sea creatures, recovering in Wyeland, and regaining this throne," said Thalen. "I wish that the Raiders had been by your side, to offer any assistance within our power, but I see that you have managed the impossible beautifully."

"Oh, I don't know about beautifully," she replied. "There were *deaths* along the way. I have made grievous mistakes. But in the end, with a great deal of assistance, we managed."

Just then, their conversation was disrupted by a small group of musicians who began tuning up, and by the pretty sister, who ordered all the tables pushed to the sides. Then the sister cajoled the diners to join hands in several concentric rings around the replica Fountain; the rings were formed only of women or only of men. Wareth found himself holding hands with an older man whose name was Fornquit and a slim engraver named Lemle.

The craftsmen made the Fountain flow, and the dance began. Under Lady Percia's direction, the circles danced round the Fountain in opposing directions, then a ring of women dropped hands and moved under the arches formed by the raised arms of men, so that, in a complicated pattern, each ring moved closer and farther away from the flowing water.

Hilarity ensued when people headed the wrong way or missed a step. Finally, everyone ended up more or less back where they started and the dance was completed.

Lady Percia, standing on a chair, called out, "That was truly the worst Fountain Reel I've ever seen. Nargis deserves better! I'll let you take a break, and then we are going to repeat it and do it right this time."

Wareth, like everyone else, groaned and complained, but he also now got the picture of what the dance would be like if performed properly—an intricate pattern around the emblem of Weirandale's Spirit, a dance that was not about any individual's grace or skill, but that celebrated every circle moving in unison. He gulped at a flagon of mead to quench his thirst and looked around for a place to hang his weskit.

Cloaks, robes, doublets, shawls, and scarves now hung like flags on chairs as the guests decided to get serious about the reel. Looking about, he saw the commander tying back his hair, which had come loose. Jothile, in between Fedak and Dalogun, had even joined in and—wonders!—he was the first person who had resumed his place, like a dog overeager to go on a walk.

Lady Percia clapped her hands and they formed up in circles again with new partners. Wareth now held hands with a sailor and a fragile old gentleman named Ryton. The music started. Wareth concentrated, determined not to mess up. Every dancer must have felt the same, because the circles spun, the arches raised and fell, and the circles re-formed much more smoothly. Wareth felt transported by the rhythm and simple beauty of the reel, which made him feel as if they were all ripples in a pond, spreading out and moving in.

When the reel ended, this time everyone broke into applause.

That ended the formalities. The tables were pulled out again, and cheeses and nuts were passed around while wine flowed liberally. The musicians played quietly in the background.

Wareth walked around the room to check on the Raiders he felt protective about. Tristo reported that his missing arm hadn't been a problem while dancing—everyone had graciously held on to his empty sleeve. Dalogun kept gushing about the food and about the fact that the queen had invited him to view her stables tomorrow. Jothile looked nervous and uncomfortable as he always did around strangers, but no more so than usual. From what Wareth could judge, the other guests were patient with Jothile's twitches and frightened glances. And Fedak was also keeping close to their comrade.

"Raider," said a middle-aged uniformed man with a walrus mustache, as he approached Wareth. "I am Captain Athelbern of the palace guard. Would you be so kind as to join our table? We want the chance to hear about your adventures."

Wareth agreed. He was telling the story of the attack on River Road when out of the corner of his eye, he noticed that Thalen had approached the musicians and was conversing with their conductor. Wareth broke off placing cutlery in the position of troops to pay closer attention. One of the players handed Thalen a fife, which Thalen toyed with silently until the musicians finished the air they were playing.

The chatter, laughter, and people moving about covered over the sound of a single fife. The musicians' conductor rapped his wand on a nearby chair, making a sharp noise that asked for quiet.

Thalen began again. Wareth recognized the music, but it took him a few moments to realize that this was the opening of "The Lay of Queen Ciella," the love song Thalen had played on one of their last nights in Emerald Lake Camp. He played to the end of the introduction.

The room hushed.

For a third time, Thalen played the opening of "The Lay of Queen Ciella." Wareth frantically scanned the room for the queen.

Slowly, almost as if compelled, the queen stood and walked close to the musicians.

"Who will sing the echo?" she asked the large and silent hall. A pause ensued while everyone looked around.

"I would be greatly honored," said a man wearing a hexagon pin that had something to do with Queen Cressa's Shield. "At your service, Your Majesty. I am a troubadour from Barston." He crossed to stand next to Queen Cerúlia by the musicians in the front of the room.

The musicians' leader raised his baton, and all the instruments joined the fife, playing the lay's introduction now for a fourth time. When she sang, the queen's voice was weaker than Wareth recalled (though before he'd been standing within paces of her and now she was straining to fill a large room). But what her voice had lost in force or tone, it had gained in emotional quality.

"The Lay of Queen Ciella," Wareth relearned, was about love surviving death. The first time he'd heard it, he'd understood it only in terms of himself and Eldie; now he understood the song as being about all the Raiders and all the Free Staters who had died in the Occupation.

Wareth was ashamed of the tears that began to dribble down his cheeks until he realized that practically everyone in the room was weeping, each for their own losses. They wept for the comrades, husbands, fathers, sons, and daughters they had lost. Many a guest put a hand across their eyes; others covered their faces with their napkins; a few wept on the shoulders of their neighbors.

The queen finished her last verse: *"And I will hear your voice in the murmur of the Waters always."* The troubadour sang the last echo. The room was deadly silent except for the sound of sniffling.

The queen thanked the troubadour, who bowed and retreated to his table, applauded by many claps on the back. The room broke out into excited chatter about how poignant the song was and didn't the queen have a lovely voice and who knew a fearsome raider could play a fife and a hundred other exclamations that allowed the guests to move out of their trances and back into the evening's reality.

Cerúlia took one step to return to her table and then halted because Thalen had set down the fife and reached out to touch her from behind. With a hand on her upper arm he turned her around to face him rather than the hall filled with friends, relatives, and guests.

"I lost you once. I could not survive losing you again," he said. "Don't go away."

"I haven't moved," she said, her eyes searching his face.

"I lost you in Oromondo before—before I could tell you." His words came out in a jumbled rush. "I must tell you. Right now. How much I care for you."

Behind them the musicians struck up a livelier tune that covered up their private conversation. Dimly the two were conscious that quite a few guests had scraped back their chairs to rise and dance again.

"*Who* do you care for?" she asked.

"Whoever you are. You could be a changeling and I'd love that."

"I have already played many roles, and there are others I have yet to assume." Her eyes flicked over her green vine bracelet. "I will always be changing, growing."

Thalen asked, "Do you care for anyone else?"

"I care for many people," Cerúlia said tartly, "but I have never ached for another man the way I ache for you. You'll never find again, under Saulé's sun, someone who feels about you the way I do."

She looked down a moment, fingering his silk shirt cuff. "I've always loved you, Thalen. From the first moment I saw you in Ink Creek Canyon, when the drops of water trickled down your neck." With two fingers she traced the movement on her own neck. "And when I saw—well, you don't really see a mind, but I felt it, I sensed it."

"Don't marry the Filio of Rortherrod," he said, his hand on her arm tightening.

"No, I cannot marry him." She shook her head and continued. "For most of my life I have had to hide my Talents. I cannot wed a man who would have me be *less* than I am. Not Rortherrod, nor any man who needs me to be less so he can be more."

Thalen said, "I bring you nothing: no kingdoms, no riches, no magic. But *I* don't need that; *I* don't want that. All I have to offer is my love, but that love has no limits and imposes none on you."

She searched his face and his eyes. Then she smiled at him—a small smile that grew into the full glow that Thalen had long dreamed of having directed just at him.

Thalen grabbed her with one hand on each side above her waist and lifted her high up into the air, up above his head. She bent to look down at him, her long blue hair making a curtain covering both their faces, her gown and train falling over him, as if she were water and he stood in a waterfall.

Then he slowly lowered her down inch by inch, her body pressed tight against his, her silk gown catching momentarily on his eagle pin, until her face was level with his. Their eyes locked. She entwined her arms around his neck; still holding her off the ground he moved one arm around her waist and another against her back.

Then, they leaned their faces in for the briefest touching of lips.

All conversation in the Great Ballroom had faltered when the commander lifted the queen into the air, and when they embraced the shocked musicians broke off in jarring disarray in the middle of a phrase, but Cerúlia and Thalen heard nothing but a private, sweet melody that lingered in the air around them.

The melody might have been "The Lay of Queen Ciella," but who can say?

46

Cerúlia pulled her face away and whispered to Thalen, "You need to put me down now."

As if setting down a piece of porcelain, Thalen put her down on her feet, though he kept his arm wrapped around her waist. Cerúlia was glad it was there, because she felt so drunk she almost swayed on her feet. She turned around to face the hundreds of shocked guests, at a total loss as to how to handle the situation.

Thank the Waters, Percia saved the day. She jumped back on the chair she'd been using to call the Fountain Reel and shouted, "*That* was just the greatest display of bravery any of us have ever seen! Hooray for Commander Thalen and Queen Cerúlia!"

A pandemonium of cheers, clapping, foot stamping, and loud whistles shook the ballroom. As the noise started to dissipate, Percia mimed violin playing to the musicians and they commenced a loud and lively version of "The Mill Wheel Polka." Percia grabbed Marcot and set off at a fast gallop, as if only wild dancing could capture the room's overflowing emotions. Other couples joined in, trying to weave around the tables, laughing and shouting as more than a few chairs turned over and dishware shattered.

Cerúlia looked up at Thalen. "Can you polka?" she asked.

"Once I read a book about international dance customs," he answered, and biting his lip in concentration, he managed to twirl with her in a circuit of the room. On the third circuit, she nodded toward a door, and they polkaed out of the room into the hallway usually referred to as the Candelabra Corridor.

Behind them the music and gaiety of the party continued unabated; if their absence had been noticed, the guests had politely decided to ignore it. Cerúlia took Thalen's arm, and he matched his long stride to her shorter step. They were followed discreetly by two of the Queen's Shield and more ostentatiously by the canine corps. Whaki and Cici darted in front of them and then looked back, tails wagging and faces expectant, to check that they'd anticipated the walkers' pathway.

"Is there someplace we can talk?" Thalen asked.

"Three hundred and fifty-two rooms." She gestured with both hands at the capacious building surrounding them. "Though seven are under construction." She shuffled through options in her mind as they walked: her closet felt too small, her Reception Room too large, a salon too formal. Prattling like a nervous guide as they passed historic art objects and salons, Cerúlia led him to a room that spoke of her life *before,* and where she thought he might feel comfortable: her old lesson chamber.

The dogs invited themselves inside with the couple, while the shields stationed themselves outside. Discovering that the cold of an autumn night had penetrated the unoccupied room, Thalen immediately set about lighting the fire that lay prepared in the hearth, while Cerúlia walked about igniting the lanterns. The bloom of light revealed books, maps, tables, and stools patiently waiting for Tilim and Ryton to resume their work after the disruption of this festival.

The queen perched herself on Ryton's stool, shivering a little, toying with a stoppered ink bottle, while Thalen leaned against the chimney stone; the dogs finished their nosing around and gathered close to the radiating warmth.

"Aren't you cold?" Thalen asked, breaking the silence between them. "Come near the fire."

"Out of all my hundreds of choices, I may have selected poorly," she admitted. "This was my schoolroom; I see it still has no comfortable chairs, only stools to make inattentive pupils pay attention."

For the first time, Thalen broke out of his thoughts to glance about and survey his surroundings, a small smile starting as his eyes took in books and maps.

"This is where I learned my letters and geography," Cerúlia explained.

"This is where you were a little girl?"

"Yes. Willful and saucy. I'm afraid I plagued my tutor a great deal."

Thalen's smile broadened.

"You're cold." He nodded at the floor in front of the hearth. "We've sat on the ground before. Unless you don't want to risk your gown. . . ."

To prove to him that she wasn't fussy about her finery (though actually she now treasured this outfit above all her possessions combined), she joined him in front of the fireplace and settled herself between Whaki and a deerhound. Thalen sat beside her and crossed his long legs; Cici took advantage of his posture to claim his lap.

"So?" she asked, watching the firelight illuminate the bones of his face, which looked more grim than she remembered.

"I'm trying to adjust to having you beside me," he said. "And there's so much to say, so much to ask, I hardly know where to begin. My thoughts are all tangled up."

"Begin anywhere."

"Tell me again how you disappeared from the moat in Femturan. *A turtle?* This is just too incredible to countenance."

So Cerúlia told him about how Lautan's creatures had rescued her, while Thalen listened without interrupting, staring into her face or into the fire with a contemplative expression, as if his worldview

were being shaken to its core at this tale of a Spirit's deliberate interference in human affairs.

Relating the story made Cerúlia reexperience the pain and fear she
had undergone during this journey. Gradually she realized that Whaki
had begun prodding her left arm with his black nose and uttering
little whines.

She could not change the past, but she had the power to make
the two of them more comfortable tonight in the lesson chamber.
Abruptly, she interrupted herself, rose, and crossed to the doorway.

"Ah, Shield Gatana. Please send a footman. We desire mulled
wine; and have him fetch one of my winter cloaks."

"Right away, Your Majesty," said the shield.

When she closed the door she saw that Thalen had also risen to
his feet.

"Forgive me," he said. "I see now that that was selfish. I needed
to know; I needed to understand how it is that you lived. I've tortured myself endlessly."

Cerúlia stretched her back a little; it had begun to stiffen at the
memory of the pain she had endured.

Noticing, Thalen asked, "Why didn't you ask them for a cushioned chair? You are the queen. A footman could fetch you one—if
you tell me where to search, I'll fetch you one." He looked ready to
spring the length of the palace for her comfort.

She made a circuit of the room, further loosening the cramps in
her muscles; then she came back to stand in front of the flames next
to Thalen.

"I'd rather sit around the fire next to you, as we did before in
Oromondo."

He threw another log on the fire, then stood leaning against the
mantel, his head dipped between his outstretched, bracing arms.

"Is there anything else that you've been torturing yourself about?"
she asked him, reading his mind from the stiffness of his arms.

"Skylark—no, *Cerúlia*—I need to know how you came to be

captured that night. Why didn't you retreat to the rally point? Why weren't you ahead of us, as I thought you'd be?"

She almost laughed. "Do you actually mean, Commander, why did I disobey your direct order and let the Oros take me like a lackwit?"

When he didn't respond, an insight struck her. "You've been angry at me all this time."

"Furious," he said to the fire shadows flickering on the floor beneath him. "It's eaten at me. And now that I know just how badly you were injured—how much you suffered—I'm even angrier." He kept his voice soft and polite, but he couldn't look at her. "This is what has churned over and over in my head: 'She was not supposed to engage in the battle. Skylark, of all the Raiders, should have escaped to the rally point. Why did she put herself in peril?'"

Another silence fell between them, the only noise a log shifting as it burned. Vaki whimpered in his sleep, while Cici vigorously scratched her neck.

Cerúlia had pondered several responses during this moment; the one that escaped her lips was not the most charitable. "I suppose," she said, "the underlying cause lies in the fact that I am a Nargis Queen, and on occasion, for good or ill, I allow my own judgment to dictate my actions, rather than blindly following orders, even from you."

Thalen's shoulders shrank from her blow. The room had grown tolerably warm in the hour or so they had been conversing; she moved to increase the distance between them, choosing to lean her hips against the map table, taking the weight off her back and shoulder with a slanted posture.

When Cerúlia spoke again her voice was softer. "Perchance in your place I would be furious too. Funny, all these months I've missed you, I've grieved for you, but I've never been angry at you. But then I knew what you did not—that what happened did so as much by chance as by anyone's choices.

"But since you need to know, I'll recount the night as best I can."

Cerúlia plunged herself into reliving the Battle of Iron Valley. Midway through her tale, the footman knocked and Thalen answered the door, pouring goblets of wine and draping her cloak over her shoulders. Cerúlia barely registered these changes; she had traveled back to the confused night when Pemphis, revealing himself as a traitor, had tried to kill her; when Cinders had proven too slow; when she had dropped behind to try to stop the wolves from tracking the Raiders; when the woros had torn Nollo's throat and killed the wolfhound Maki; and when she'd lifted her head to discover that Cinders had fled, leaving her with Eldo as Oro soldiers closed in around her.

Trying to dispel the vision of the Oro soldiers climbing the rise, Cerúlia took up the goblet on the map table and drank deep of the warm, spicy wine.

Thalen now sat on the pupil's stool, his long legs stretched out before him. He looked her in the eyes. "You sacrificed yourself to save the Raiders."

"Perchance." She shrugged. "But don't make me out too noble. Maybe everything transpired this way just because Cinders was too slow. Or maybe it was partly my pride—that with all my Talent, those drought damn woros defied me.

"Most things a person does," she said to the dark liquid of the goblet, "they do for several complicated reasons. I'm rarely certain that my motives are pure."

"Yes," said Thalen. "I've learned that too." He took a long drink from the goblet on the table beside him and then straightened up to turn around to face her. "How many times in one day do I need to apologize? I try to think before I act. How many times in one day can I play the muckwit?"

Cerúlia just shook her head, not needing an apology.

"I've often wondered," she asked, changing the subject, "did you care for Eli-anna?"

"No . . . Though later I discovered she ached for me, and that was a pity."

"Unrequited love." Cerúlia spoke as if the words themselves conjured an immensity of power and pain.

"Why did you take up with Adair?" Thalen asked.

"Adair," Cerúlia repeated his name in a lingering tone, twisting her vine bracelet.

Thalen restlessly jumped up, grabbed a poker, and jabbed at a log in the fireplace.

"Commander, you can't be jealous of the dead."

"I can be jealous of anyone I please," he muttered.

"Besides," she said, "you're smart enough to know the answer. You wouldn't pay any attention to me; Adair was charming, and I was so very young and so very lonely. Adair kept saying that we could die any day."

"Did you ever make love to him?"

"No." But she forced herself to answer honestly, "Yet if he had lived, I might have. I know myself now—I am . . . seducible."

The turn of the conversation, or maybe the warm wine, altered the atmosphere in the room.

"That's good to know," said Thalen, grinning at the fire.

Cerúlia straightened herself from her leaning position. "I'm exhausted. Tonight is not the time to tell all the stories. Tonight we should grab what life has to offer. I cannot talk anymore."

She paused, gathering her courage. "Let's go to my bedroom," she said, twisting the green vine bracelet she still wore on her wrist. "That is, if you will."

Thalen looked up from his task with the fire poker. "Are you certain this is what you want?"

She smiled at him.

Thalen banked the fire while she blew out all but one lantern, which she carried with her as she crossed the room and opened the door.

Cerúlia led Thalen to her suite, discovering Kiltti dozing on a chair in the Reception Room, waiting to attend her. The queen had last seen Kiltti dancing the Fountain Reel; she noticed that her hair ribbons had come undone and her upper lip boasted a line of sugar. Around her shoulders lay a lovely, antique silk scarf.

Shaking her shoulder, the queen roused her. "Kiltti, I'm sorry to have kept you so late. You are dismissed for the night; go to bed.

"Shields—and you, canines—thank you for your service today. That will be all. We wish not to be disturbed."

When the door to the Queen's Bedchamber was closed and locked safely behind them, Cerúlia looked around, all at once anxious about its furnishings. Unlike the lesson chamber, this room was warm and softly glowing, but she saw anew the velvet draperies, the silk bedding, the gold gilding around the looking glass, the water feature—would these trappings of wealth and royalty discomfort a potter's son?

Thalen had remained at the doorway, his arms folded over his chest. His glance did not appear to take in the room or its decor; his eyes followed her movements.

Desiring to shed herself of her rich accoutrements, Cerúlia slid off the winter cloak with its fur trim and undid the chain that held her blue train about her, tenderly shaking the ash dust from it and lying it on her dressing table's chair. Then she removed the rings on her fingers and the vine bracelet, placing them on her dressing table. Finally, she took off the silver circlet holding back her hair.

All the while Thalen just studied her intently.

Feeling embarrassed at his scrutiny, she moved to sit on the couch, kicked off her shoes, and stretched her toes.

"Thalen, what are you doing way over there?"

"I'm trying to sort out all the day's events; I'm shutting out the entirety of the rest of Ennea Món; I'm on guard to make sure you don't vanish into smoke."

She patted the upholstery beside her. "Come sit next to me. If you touch me you'll know I'm not a phantom."

At her invitation he crossed the width of the room, sat beside her, and took her hand in one of his. His other hand fingered a ringlet of her hair and then feathered across the back of her neck, just missing the ridged skin from her burn.

Cerúlia held back a gasp of desire. "Thalen, I don't want to shock you—"

"*Now* you are worried about shocking me!"

"No, listen, Thalen. I have scars."

"We all have scars," he said, his index finger now tracing her lips.

"These are different; I was burned." She grabbed his moving hand so that he would attend to her. "You may find them unsightly. Ghastly."

His face grew serious. "If you trust me enough to show me your scars, I will show you mine. Mine are uglier, even if they do not show."

"Do you mean the ones hidden in here?" Cerúlia put her hand on his chest, feeling between the layers of silk that his heart too was beating fast.

He nodded, his eyes dark.

"Nothing you have done or thought or said will make you ugly in my eyes," she told him. "I lived with you every day in Ink Creek and Emerald Lake. I know you too well, Commander Thalen."

"Not as well as you shall by morning," he said, and he leaned his full weight against her, pushing her backward on the couch, and she giggled deep in her throat while a few tears leaked from the sides of her eyes and her body trembled with weariness, relief, and desire.

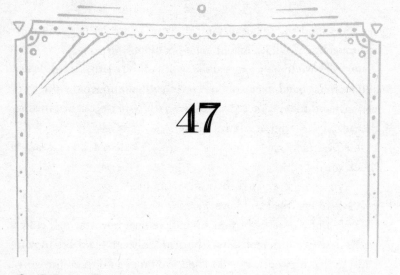

47

On Wave Racer

The night the last clouds finally freed *Wave Racer* and scudded away, the sails sighed with a hint of laughter, and Nithanil, the king-that-was, used his brass astrolabe to measure the change in the constellation the Lorthers called Walrus Tusk. He determined they had been carried south of their course. He suspected too that they'd been pushed to the west—but how far he could only guess at by calculating the hours of the storm.

Strangely enough, however, for such a ferocious test, the ship itself had sustained only minor damage, and the crew's worst injuries were all survivable. But the decks, holds, cabins, and bilge sloshed with seawater; ribbons of kelp had gotten caught on spars, ladders, and poles, and slippery jellyfish and rotting minnows threatened to make the unwary slip. All hands set to more pumping, then vigorous swabbing and cleaning.

They didn't have enough fresh water to wash everything that had gotten dunked in seawater; Iluka festooned the deck with soggy covers and clothing, allowing the material to at least dry out in the sunshine. She wrung out smaller garments and kept fluffing and turning the larger, all while keeping up a steady grumble.

Although her housekeeping was very much in the way of orderly sailing, and her petticoats flapping about compromised the professionalism of his deck, Nithanil ignored her. He plotted a course for Cascada, hoping that Lautan had no more nasty tricks up its seaweed sleeve.

Toward sunset two days after the storm passed, the lookout came sliding down the mast as frantically as a rabbit runs from a hunting pack. "Seamaster, to the west I saw sails—I'm sure of it!—black sails."

"Only the Pellish use black sails," Nithanil noted. "Which way are they headed?"

"They're far off; I couldn't tell."

"Who has the sharpest eyes amongst the crew?" Nithanil asked his first mate.

The mate called over the youngest sailor, who scampered up with Nithanil's own spyglass draped about her neck, in a race against the failing light. As the sky dripped away the last of its glow, she slid down to report.

"Not one ship," she said. "At least twenty, perchance more. They head due north."

Nithanil's mind had already jumped ahead. "An armada. And by their course . . . this is a full-frontal attack on Cascada."

"What can we do?" asked Mikil.

Nithanil didn't answer, but rather turned on his heel and led the way to his chart room. He noted with approval that sailors had already scrubbed the large wooden table, though it still boasted white whirls of salt. Tiny crustaceans had gotten lodged between the planks of the room's wooden floor, making crunching sounds as the men walked about.

The maps, which were always stored in brackets high up the wall and wrapped in oilskin, appeared undisturbed by the storm. Nithanil pointed to the two most relevant charts; a mate grabbed them down and everyone gingerly helped unroll them, discovering that while damp had ruined the edge of one and droplets had penetrated the body of another, both remained readable. The mates placed map weights to keep them flat, while Mikil lit both the overhead oil lamp and a hand lantern for good measure.

Ignoring everyone's impatience, Nithanil studied first one and then the other; Mikil leaned in too, but his father would give up not one inch of his captain's prerogatives: with his hip he shoved his son out of the way.

"We can't do battle twenty to one. And we can't outrun them to give a warning," said Nithanil, calculating aloud. "But we must be converging near the shoals of the Cormorants"—his long finger pointed to a group of rocky isles—"and they'll have to slow and disperse. They don't know the tricky tides there. With Lautan's luck, they'll anchor at night to navigate during the light."

"What good will that do us?" asked the first mate.

"We'll board a laggard and take her over," said Nithanil.

"How will that help?" Mikil asked.

"Not certain," said Nithanil, scratching his beard, which always itched and itched more now when his thinner, aging skin had become inflamed by the weather and salt. "At least we'd be amongst the armada, able to cause a bit of mischief at the right moment, not shadowing behind."

As the men exited the chart room, Nithanil called low, "Son."

"Aye, Sire," said Mikil.

"You're a priest or some such. It's obvious, even to a blasphemous cuss like me, that Lautan has tossed us here to intercept this fleet. See if you can find out what the Old Blowhole has in mind."

So Nithanil ordered *Wave Racer* to put on all sail, paralleling the Pellish ships just out of sight. The Pellish should suspect no mischief this far from land. By the next day all the ships had scattered in the midst of the Cormorants; that night, as he had predicted, the Pellish set anchor.

The Lorther vessel lurked, shielded by the rocky spires of the crags that provided roosts only for birds. Nithanil decided to send Mikil as the head of the boarding party; after all his son had had experience in hand-to-hand with the Pellish during the long campaign for the Green Isles. Mikil took their three longboats and grappling hooks, and set out with muffled oars, rowing around one of the larger isles.

Nithanil would never admit that he was worried, yet instead of turning in, he kept watch on the deck. Iluka insisted on keeping him company, which really meant bothering him.

"Stop scratching," she ordered. "You're making me crazy with your constant scratching. Besides, you keep rubbing off the salve. Let the itch alone or it'll never settle down."

"Hmm," he grunted at her, his hands busily tying knots in a new hank of rope. He'd lost his well-worn knot rope in the storm, and fresh ones always needed a lot of breaking in before they became soft and pliable enough for him.

He spit on the rope a few times to moisten it.

"That's disgusting," Iluka said. "Why don't you use water instead? You, a king, and you've no more manners than a deckhand."

She continued nagging at him. "Don't think you can get away with such tricks when we get to your grand-girl's country! And don't you look daggers at me when I have to remind you of how a gentleman should behave."

Nithanil pretended not to hear her. She moved around the deck—which was tolerably lit by the moons and the stars—clutching at the thicker materials that were still airing, muttering to herself about beating blankets with an oar to "knock the salt out of them." The old man knew that would never work: once you were at sea, everything took on a thick crust of salt. He liked it that way.

He wondered what was happening with the boarding party

and if his son or any of his longtime crew members had been injured.

The knot rope was not allaying his anxieties. When Iluka circled back within arm's reach, he grabbed her waist.

"Stand still. Stay here."

He sent a deckhand for more rope, scraps of leather, and leather-working tools. Iluka had obediently remained rooted to her spot on the deck, possibly wondering if he had Anticipated danger. The old man hadn't meant to frighten her, but he did relish the moment of silence.

When the sailor brought the requested supplies, Nithanil ordered, "Hold up your arms." He wrapped the rope right above her breasts, all around her body, carefully measuring a little slack before he marked it so it wouldn't chafe her but couldn't slip over her shoulders. Then he did the same around her waist.

"Stop tickling me. What you think you're doing, ya old walrus?"

"Hmm," he just grunted in reply, but he moved under the deck lantern with the awl and his dagger to start poking holes in the leather.

"What you making?" Iluka asked. "What does it have to do with me?"

When he didn't reply, she prodded his shoulder.

"A harness," he answered, as if he should be paid for two words.

"A harness? Do you think I'm a horse now? Why would I need a harness?"

"'Cause you're not spry enough to climb down the netting. You'll slip. And you're so heavy you'll capsize the boat." Actually, he couldn't take a chance that she'd fall into the dark water, but he was not about to admit the fact.

"And *you* are spry enough? I'm as spry as you, you old goat!" Her hands were on her hips now, and her voice was loud enough for the watch to overhear. "Besides, why—pray tell—might I need to leave your precious ship and get into a boat? Are we about to sink? I thought you said that *Wave Racer* was the best ship in the navy. . . ."

Nithanil stopped listening to her. Crafting the harness soothed him and allowed his mind to range ahead, and whenever her voice got louder he just manhandled her into the position he needed so he could adjust the fit exactly as he wanted it.

Finally, in the wee hours of the morning, the watch called out, "Captain! Boat returning."

"How many?" Nithanil called out.

"Just the one."

This was either very good or very bad news. Without being aware of what he was doing, his fingers tightened on Iluka's shoulder. She patted his hand and stayed quiet.

The second mate climbed up the net to relay the news that Prince Mikil had remained behind in possession of the Pellish ship, a lightly guarded and crewed supply vessel named *Pexlia's Possession*.

Mikil had taken the Pellish crew totally by surprise and had killed several dozen men before they surrendered.

When Mikil had questioned the captured seamaster he learned that this cargo vessel served an armada of troop ships and war galleys heading to invade Cascada. Lautan's Luck had saved them tonight: if they had chosen another ship they would have faced up to four hundred Oro soldiers. When Mikil's men had examined the cargo they found mostly foodstuffs but also barrel after barrel with warnings written all over them.

With extra inducement the Pellish seamaster had finally identified their contents.

The ship was loaded to the gills with hemlock oil.

"Prince Mikil couldn't get anyone to admit it," said the mate, "but he reckons they were planning to poison the Nargis headwaters."

Nithanil thought about this for a long moment, his mouth finding the idea distasteful. The king-that-was began snapping orders. First, he adjusted *Wave Racer*'s mooring, tethering it in a secure bay, leaving a skeleton crew to take care of his treasured personal vessel. Then, laboriously, the Lorthers transferred all crucial supplies, mariners, and his old biddy in the longboat to *Pexlia's Possession* where Mikil awaited them. Just before sunrise his men assumed the shirts and hats of the Pellish sailors.

The king-that-was couldn't articulate the potential advantages of sailing among the Pellish armada in disguise. He just had a strong feeling of Anticipation that this was where they needed to be if they were to have any hope of assisting his grand-girl.

Cascada Harbor lay a week's journey away.

"Mikil!" ordered his father. "Pour another libation to the Spirit of the Sea and sing your prayers."

Lautan, you crafty old blowhole. Lead on.

48

Cascada

"Your Majesty?" came Nana's voice, waking her up. "There are duties that can't be put off."

"You will wait a few moments," Cerúlia called.

She slid into a night-robe while Thalen dressed himself.

"When will I see you again?" he asked.

"Tonight?"

"I'll wait for a message at the inn."

He kissed her roughly, as a promissory note, and when Cerúlia opened the door to her attendants, he walked out with perfect aplomb.

Geesilla and Nana had brought a tray and a reminder that, taking advantage of the occasion that had gathered so many representatives and rulers, Councilor Nishtari had arranged an informal diplomatic meeting. The queen and her Circle Council were expected in the Nymph Salon in an hour to discuss matters of mutual interest with the Rorthers, Minister Destra, and various envoys.

"There's still no sighting of a Lorther ship?" the queen asked. "The Lorthers were to have been crucial participants at this too."

Receiving a negative, she went to her window and threw it open.

She called to a nearby crow and sent it to summon some seabirds for instructions, though she had little hope that any avian scouts could find her kin's vessel in the vast stretches of the Gray Ocean.

By concentrating on the agenda concerning trade and security that Nishtari had prepared, Cerúlia managed (barely) to shove to the side her embarrassment over last night's display and her own tumult of emotions. Her guests—even King Kentros and Filio Kemeron, who might have had the right to feel aggrieved—aided her by refraining in comment, tone, or gesture from remarking on her liaison. Only Duke Naven took advantage of her discomfiture, and even he kept himself to one bawdy wink.

After a nice midmeal with foreign dignitaries (she would have to thank the kitchen workers), pressing administrative tasks flowed into the afternoon. Cerúlia sent Darzner to Vilkit for a preliminary report on the fest and learned that he had encountered no major difficulties and anticipated that, when totaled, their expenses would end up close to the amount budgeted.

Captain Yanath reported that he had several mariners sleeping in the cells because they had gotten drunk last night and picked a fight with palace guards. Cerúlia shared an exasperated wince with him and told him to deal with them as he thought best.

"I'll talk to Seamaster Wilamara about the appropriate discipline," he said. "There was one other worrisome incident yesterday morning. Two dogs took after a woman trying to enter through the Kitchen Gate."

"A servant or delivery person?"

"The guards on duty said they thought she was nobility because she wore a velvet gown and her hair showed some amber strands. They thought it queer that she sued for entry from the Kitchen Gate. She had a pass from Red Rooster Vineyards that they kept ahold of— it looks on the up-and-up, but Vilkit doesn't know who she could be. Anyways, the two dogs took instant dislike to her; they growled and lunged, and she gave a little scream and ran off into the crowd."

"Do you know which dogs were on duty?"

"Two of the deerhounds."

"I'll see if they remember what alerted them."

"Anyway, she didn't get inside, and we've got our eyes peeled if she comes back."

"Good." Cerúlia nodded absently.

Her steward, Alix, came to her closet to confer about the visitors' schedules: the Rorthers planned to depart tomorrow; Minister Destra had expressed a desire to visit the Abbey of the Waters, and Lord Marcot had offered to escort her and show her a sample of the countryside of the Weir duchies. Seamaster Wilamara had lookouts posted for the Lorther ship, whenever it would arrive.

After conveying this news, Alix, seated across from her, coughed a fake cough.

"If you have something to say, now is the time," Cerúlia said.

"Naven, Nishtari, and I had a private conversation"—*Plink!*— "with the Rorthers about the, uh, situation. We didn't want them to depart angry or humiliated. . . ."

"And?"

"The king expressed a little disappointment and bewilderment, but the prince seemed . . . almost relieved. Filio Kemeron said that he now sees complications between such a match that might not have made it beneficial for either realm."

Cerúlia had been holding her breath; she let it out. "Well done. Keep assuring them how much we desire friendly relations with Rortherrod and that we could not have predicted how events would unfold."

Plink!

Alix made no move to rise. Cerúlia lay down the seal in her hand and raised her brows.

"Forgive me, Your Majesty, but—"

"If you must interfere with my personal life, this is as good a time as any." Cerúlia gritted her teeth.

"I consulted with Chronicler Sewel about the role of the Circle

Council vis-à-vis a queen's—ah—*relations*. He said that most past rulers have been more discreet about such affairs, but we should keep in mind the very unusual nature of your life history and your previous connection with Commander Thalen in a theater of war."

"I'm not sure I approve of your discussing who shares my bed with Sewel"—*Plink!*—"or anyone else."

"Forgive the effrontery. But you must acknowledge that as queen your personal life has ramifications for the realm. And you have no parents to guide you in these matters.

"So Sewel informed me that while the council has no authority over a queen's love affairs—"

"I should think not!"

Alix plunged on, "Should the time come that you"—*Plink!*—"consider marriage, since Queen Cressa is not alive to evaluate the fitness of the match, it would be expected, traditional—at least customary—for you to present your choice to the council."

"The council can tell me whom to marry?"

"Not precisely. But we have a duty to persuade you to think through all the ramifications."

"I see." Cerúlia made her tone neutral.

Plink!

"Your Majesty." Alix shifted a little closer to the edge of his chair. "You must admit that this is reasonable. Weirandale can't have a young, besotted queen run out and marry a striking-looking goose boy."

Instead of angering her, this comparison struck Cerúlia as droll, and she burst out laughing.

"Not, of course, that Commander Thalen—" Alix tried to take back his unfortunate remark, but she waved him off, laughing harder, drowning out the plinks of the Weeping Swan.

When she conquered her mirth, she addressed her steward. "So, in sum, I have the council's permission to welcome the commander into my bed—though you'd prefer this be done discreetly—but not to wed him precipitously?"

Her foot tapped against the carpet a few times. "You may tell your fellow councilors that I will take this all under advisement."

Alix smiled weakly. "Thank you. That is all we ask."

"You are dismissed now," she said, not too gruffly, because much as this presumption grated upon her, her steward had obviously taken no joy in the conversation.

When he left, Cerúlia massaged her forehead, giving way to her fatigue and anxieties. She longed to be alone with Thalen for a moon, to unburden herself of all her secrets, to lay all her uncertainties out for his analysis, and—most of all—to entangle herself in his long limbs. But how could she manage to carve out time for them together, beset as she was by all eyes watching and judging?

"Darzner!" she called to her secretary, who waited outside her door. By the time he entered and offered his services, she knew who could help her.

"Find Lady Percia," she said, "and ask her to attend me."

Two hours later, per Percia's advice and arrangements, the queen's carriage, transporting the sovereign, her sister, and Kiltti, and escorted by a squad of shields, pulled up outside the Rare Talents Inn.

Thalen stood, waiting for her in the courtyard, dressed in the same black coat he had worn when he entered the Throne Room. He opened the carriage door himself, not giving a footman a chance, and stretched out his hand to help her descend.

"How are you?" he asked.

"A little overtired," she admitted, pulling her warm but cumbersome cloak down the steps.

"Lady Percia." Thalen turned to greet her sister as she climbed out lifting her skirts.

"Oh, I'd prefer you just called me 'Percia,'" she smiled, "or even 'Percie,' if you wish."

"Only if you will drop 'Commander' and just call me 'Thalen,'" he responded.

He turned back to help Kiltti, but she had jumped down herself, and dipped him a small curtsey. Whaki leapt out last, sniffing Thalen's leg, recalling his scent, and finding him acceptable.

The party passed through the Rare Talents's tiled foyer and its arched hallway—Percia greeting and thanking the innkeeper so that Cerúlia did not have to pull her attention away from Thalen's profile and the warmth of his arm. Thalen led her to the private dining room in the back of the inn, where they found a vaulted, half-timbered ceiling, a large table lit with many candles, a sideboard bedecked with steaming platters, and the Raiders standing about, waiting for them.

"Well, Your Majesty," said Cerf, after they had risen from their courtesies, "we're awfully honored to have you to ourselves."

Thalen, stepping behind her, lifted off her cloak and its hood, which revealed that underneath the luxurious outer garment of black velvet and fur she wore canvas trousers, a simple linen shirt (whiter and cleaner than all previous incarnations), and a black bodice. Her hair was pinned low on the back of her neck so that at first glance it looked to be cut short.

"Skylark!" Tristo gasped. "You've come back to us!"

"That's the idea," said Cerúlia. "Tonight, I have run away from the palace. I need . . . to be among friends, old friends, good friends, who don't judge my every word or gesture."

"All righty. So, take a load off those tender feet of yours, girl," said Kambey, easily falling into the game and pulling out the chair at the head of the table.

"The victuals here are really quite tasty; shall I fix you a plate?" asked Wareth.

Thalen seated himself beside her, quietly but firmly taking her hand underneath the table, while Fedak and Kran used their best manners to seat Percia and Kiltti. Kiltti tried to pull away to go sit in the kitchen with the other servants, but no one would hear of such a thing, so she sat between Jothile and Fedak, perched on her seat as if Vilkit were going to burst through the door and reprimand her at any moment.

Wareth placed a plate overloaded with food before Cerúlia, while Cerf poured wine all around.

"Is there a traditional Weir toast?" Thalen asked as he stood and lifted his glass.

"May ye never know thirst," Percia supplied.

"We've already known thirst," Tristo said in a dark aside, "and it was awful."

"Ah. That's why it is a great sentiment," Thalen said. "Raiders and guests, may ye never *again* know thirst."

"Or thirst for absent friends," added Cerúlia, her eyes resting first on him and then taking in the rest of the table.

Wareth stood and raised his glass. "And may you always live in freedom!"

The Raiders pounded the table with their fists and drank from their wineglasses.

Between big mouthfuls of food, conversation began to swirl. Cerúlia had so many questions about her friends' escape from Oromondo and their driving the Oros out of the Free States that the Raiders talked over one another, interrupting and correcting, joking and cursing. Percia's eyes grew round with amazement at the tales that unfolded.

Informality ruled. Kran unhooked his waistcoat, which had begun to pull too tightly across his middle; Tristo speared his meat and nibbled off the dagger he held straight up in the air; after a long pull of ale Kiltti belched and everyone applauded. No one seemed to notice when Cerúlia tried to tuck a lock of Thalen's hair back into his leather tie. Whaki circled the table, begging with his big eyes for tidbits, and despite Cerúlia's scolding, everyone gave in. Finally accepting that his belly was full nigh unto bursting, the dog lay down to sleep with his head on Jothile's boot. In rare moments of silence the diners could hear him snoring.

The queen partook of the partridge and greens, ham and corn, bass and squash, sweet cakes and pie, finding it all uncommonly delicious, as if her taste for food had been renewed. Much of her comfort came from Thalen's closeness—if he needed his right hand to eat he moved his leg next to hers so that they were always in contact—but she also relished the easy company of their companions. She leaned back in her chair, feeling the tenseness she habitually carried in her neck drain away.

Fedak and Wareth had started to argue over which meal was worse at the Scoláiríum—midmeal or dinner—when Cerúlia interrupted them.

"You can't leave me, you know," she burst out to the table at large. "You have to stay in Weirandale. You can't ever abandon me." Midway through this presumptuous statement she tried to smile as if she were joking, but her plea's seriousness sounded in everyone's ears.

"I'm your man," said Kambey, without delay, and several others nodded, but Tristo, Wareth, and Jothile first looked to Thalen for his reaction.

Thalen brought up her left hand to his lips and kissed it. "I am yours to command. I will stay or go according to your wishes."

Percia clapped and emitted a little squeal in excitement.

Beaming, Cerúlia waved her fork, pointing at individuals. "Cerf! I need you to take over as palace healer; the person they foisted on me is an aggravating fool. Kambey! My shields could use a weapons master. Dalogun! What about the stables? The rest of you, would you join the Shield? Or really, any position you prefer."

Tristo addressed Thalen. "You ain't never going back to the Free States, are you?"

"Oh, I would go for visits and to help the Scoláiríum," he answered. "But my life lies with Queen Cerúlia as long as she'll have me near her."

"My home is with you," Tristo said slowly, "so if you stay, I stay. But with my arm, I can't be in the Shield; I'd druther stay as your adjutant."

"And if you weren't by my side, who would find my books or maps? I couldn't function without you," Thalen said.

"Wareth?" Cerúlia asked, biting her lower lip.

"To be honest," he answered, "I was bored at the Scoláiríum—all those books and serious, thoughtful faces." He put his chin on his fist, mimicking deep study. "In Cascada exciting things seem to happen every day." He grinned that good-natured, sloppy grin that Cerúlia had always treasured. "And the food's much better here."

Fedak and Kran exchanged looks. "Do you think we could have those fancy uniforms with the blue silk and glowing breastplates like those fellows standing outside the door now?" asked Fedak.

"What? Have you become a dandy so quickly, man?" joked Kran. "I don't care about the uniform, but I must say I find Weir women easy on the eyes." Kran wriggled his eyebrows at Kiltti in a clownish manner, prompting laughter all around.

Cerúlia bounced in her seat as if she were a child given a present.

However, Dalogun's face clouded. "Hold on a tick, everyone. My parents. They've already lost Balogun—I can't desert them while they are still living."

"Of course, Dalogun," Thalen said. "We'll miss you, terribly, but I respect your decision." Cerf squeezed the youth's shoulder.

"I understand," nodded Cerúlia. "We will keep in touch. You may marry and settle down in—?"

"Jígat," he supplied.

"Jígat," she affirmed with her fork. "But I want you to know that the offer will always be open. There will always be a place in the Royal Stables for you, if after your parents pass on you wish to join us. I will send a ship from the Royal Navy just to fetch you."

The people at the table turned to the one Raider who had not yet spoken up.

Jothile's hands began shaking at finding himself the center of attention. The splashes of food around his plate showed that mastering his utensils to eat had already been a trial. He tucked his hands under his armpits to try to quell their movement.

"You don't really want me, Skylark—ah, Your Majesty," he said. "The way I am now, I'm no use to anyone. You're just being gracious."

"Jothile," she said, "we're all injured in different ways. Life is hard enough in normal times, and we've just been through a vicious war. I don't know about what you suffered in the Iron Valley, but clearly you've taken a blow to your psyche. Perchance in time, with Nargis Water, you'll improve; perchance you won't. But Raiders never throw away their injured, and neither do Weirs. Together we would find you a position that is calm and quiet, where you could feel safe. I trust you in a way I trust only a fraction of the people around me: I need your experience and your loyalty. And losing Dalogun already leaves a hole in my heart—don't make it larger."

"You make it awful hard to say no," said Jothile.

"So say yes," urged Wareth, and when Jothile gave a quick nod, the rest of the Raiders shouted and pounded their fists on the table again.

"Commander," Tristo asked, "are you going to direct the queen's army or be her councilor or what?"

Kiltti dared to speak up. "Queen Cressa's consort, Lord Ambrice, he was Lord of the Ships."

"Really?" mused Thalen, looking at Cerúlia. "Your father was a mariner? I'd forgotten that; there's so much I don't know."

He chuckled and shook his head. "Obviously, I'm not a mariner. And I've no hankering to be lord of anything. We haven't had time to discuss this or a thousand other things, Tristo. As Cook would say, we're 'im-pro-vi-sing' moment by moment.

"Speaking of our lack of time together . . ." Thalen used his weight to make his own chair slide away from the table on the wooden floor. "Much as I've delighted in your company"—he nodded his head especially at Percia—"now I am going to claim our queen's undivided attention."

"I thought you'd never ask," Cerúlia said flirtatiously, as he moved her chair so she could rise.

"Percia," she began, "will you—"

"Go!" ordered her sister. "I will see to everything, and I'll send back the carriage and a maid in the morning."

As Cerúlia walked on Thalen's arm to the door she heard a discussion break out behind her as to whether the shields would stay to guard the inn or whether the Raiders would take over their new duties immediately, but she recognized that she didn't need to worry about these arrangements.

In a dignified manner, Thalen escorted her up the Rare Talents's central staircase, passing a sprinkling of servants and guests who looked surprised by her donkey boy garb and blue hair. However, when the couple reached the third floor and realized they were completely alone except for Whaki snuffling the floor, Thalen's pace quickened, and in a moment he was dashing backward down the long hallway pulling both of her hands in his. Cerúlia's hair fell down, and she began laughing like—like a carefree, besotted village girl, running off with her handsome goose boy.

In the morning, she woke to find herself lying in Thalen's arms, staring up at the half-timbered beams of the room's ceiling.

"Good morning," he said.

"Morning." She blinked a few times and rubbed her eyes. Then, marveling at finding him next to her, she buried her head in his chest, luxuriating in his warmth and distinctive scent. He quietly stroked her hair.

She reached her free hand up to tug on his own unruly locks, then picked up a conversation that had gotten dropped the previous night when they'd moved on to more serious business.

"You know," she said into his chest, "the Raiders are the easy ones to broach, because I lived with them for moons. They already knew me. It's going to be harder to introduce you to my Wyndton family. To Teta Stahlia, you might as well have dropped out of Mother Moon."

"Will they like me?" he asked.

"Of course. Percia already does. But prepare yourself for a thorough examination." She raised herself up on one elbow. "And what are we going to do about that hair, Thalen of Sutterdam? It's shorter on one side than the other, and it never stays tied."

"I've noticed that men's hair is kept more formally here."

"In Cascada, though not in the country," she said through a big yawn. "City styles. Courtier primping. It's all so frivolous, but in these moons I've become accustomed to it.

"You know," she continued, "we could wait a while before I take you to visit my family."

"I'd rather not," said Thalen. "I want to get this over with as soon as possible."

The queen sat up, holding the covers to her bare front, and stretched. "I probably need to get back now. I have to see the Rorther party off and check if there's any news about the ship from Lortherrod. I wonder if a maid has arrived yet with a gown and the carriage."

Thalen's hand traced the burn scars on her back as if he were drawing a map.

"I won't be sorry for Filio Kemeron to leave. And I heard your carriage come hours ago."

"Really? I thought you just woke up."

"No. I held still; I wanted you to get as much sleep as possible. Now that you're awake, I'm free."

Thalen leapt out of bed, vigorously splashed around in the basin, and began scavenging his clothes from the floor.

"'Tis very strange," mused Cerúlia, moving more slowly, "to consider that I do have blood kin. A grandfather and two half uncles. I don't know how to feel about my 'real family' versus the family that raised me." She tugged ineffectually at the bed cover, wanting to pull it loose and wrap it around herself for warmth and modesty. "I do hope no harm has come to them."

With only trousers and one boot on, Thalen interrupted his own toilette to detach the cover and drape it around her. As he finished tucking a corner about her upper chest, he kissed her on the top of her head.

"Families are always complicated, even when you're raised with your own kin. The fierceness of the love also creates hurts and rivalries, all mixed up."

He sat down to pull on his second boot. "I'm going out for a walk so your maid can fuss over you." Through the shirt that he was pulling on over his head he said, "If Jothile is awake, I want to follow up on your suggestion and take him to the Fountain."

"Don't be disappointed," cautioned Cerúlia. "The Waters are capricious: they healed Percia's leg but did nothing for my burns. And take all the Raiders; you never know whom the Waters will heal. Even if the Waters don't heal you, just drinking at the Fountain tends to raise everyone's spirits."

Grabbing his cloak, he asked, "You'll send a message later?"

"Aye, Commander," she responded, mock-saluting. He grinned and ducked out the door.

Once she was washed, dressed, and coiffed as befitted her station, Cerúlia returned to take up the duties of a busy day at the palace. She had Darzner write to Stahlia, informing her mother that she planned to bring a guest to West Cottage for family dinner that evening. Then, reluctantly, she turned to her schedule of meetings and consultations.

* * *

A light rain had wet the streets by the time the carriage brought Cerúlia, Marcot, and Percia to Stahlia's brick house. Covered lanterns flared a welcome at the top of the stoop, but Tilim answered the door with a cat-in-cream grin on his face.

"Mama's been in the worst flurry all day," he confided. "She wouldn't take anything Vilkit offered from the kitchens except wine and ale. She kept Tovalie hopping to the markets. And she made me take a bath even though it's three days early."

"Really, Cerúlia," Stahlia said as she joined them in the front room, her brown face glowing red from bending over the stove, "you are most inconsiderate! You could have given me more notice."

"Now, Teta," replied Cerúlia, "you know that I would have happily dined on bread and drippings. If you wanted to show off your cookery, that's on you." She softened her words with a quick hug. "Besides, if I'd kept Commander Thalen to myself one moment longer, you'd have railed at me for hiding him from you."

"Mama," said Percie, always the peacemaker between them, "she's probably right."

"Of course she's right," said Stahlia, "but that doesn't mean I haven't panicked all day long. Bringing this man to our house without even a by-your-leave!"

"Teta, he's important to me."

"Well, obviously, but who is he really?"

They didn't have time for more confidences, because Thalen himself (Cerúlia noticed he'd gotten his hair tended to by a barber) knocked on the front door.

He presented Stahlia a gift of a beautifully fashioned ceramic milk jug. They had just finished all their greetings and reintroductions when Lemle stuck his head in the front door.

"Hey, sorry, am I late? I got a note that a man—not just anybody, mind you, but the hero of three continents—was going to be drawn and quartered here tonight, and I'm eager to watch the show."

"Stop letting in the rain, Lem, and wipe your boots," Stahlia answered.

"Good evening, Your Majesty," continued Lemle, with a bow, not suppressed in the least by Stahlia's cross tone. "You're looking distinctly radiant this evening."

"*Lem-le,*" Cerúlia warned him.

"What?" he answered, all innocence. "That yellow silk makes you look like a flash of spring on this gloomy day. And the scarlet doublet hints at passionate depths. Doesn't she look lovely?" he asked everybody with a glint in his eyes.

"Sister," said Marcot, "would you like me to murder him now or wait until later?"

Once they gathered at the table, Stahlia, predictably, started the cross-examination first, insisting on hearing everything about Thalen's background and how he was raised. He tried to turn the conversation from pottery to tapestries, from Sutterdam to Wyndton, but she would have none of it and so he gave in, laying down his fork and knife, letting her chicken dish grow cold, and relating all the essential information about his family, his education, and how he had become involved in the fight against the Oro Occupation.

Under the table, Cerúlia reached for his hand when he spoke of the deaths of his brother and mother and the injuries suffered by his eldest brother and his father.

"Forgive me, Commander," said Stahlia, "for making you speak of such painful things. I feel protective of my daughter, and you've been sprung on us so suddenly. . . ."

"No offense taken," Thalen answered. "I expect you to be at least as protective as a mountain lion, if not more."

This brought a smile to Stahlia's face, and Tilim broadened it by making scratching motions in the air and "Grr" noises.

"Enough, Tilim," said Percia. "But what about your remaining family in Sutterdam? If you stay in Cascada, won't you miss them? Don't they need you?"

Thalen had tried to eat a few mouthfuls during the respite, so they had to wait until he swallowed and drank a sip of ale.

"Not every family is as close as yours, Percie. Or maybe—once, when my mother was alive, when we boys were young, we were as tightly bonded. But if I think about our past, it wasn't just the war and our losses. . . . I started to drift away once I left for the Scoláiríum. Their life revolved so around Sutterdam Pottery, and I grew to have interests they didn't share."

Marcot, perhaps because he sympathized with a man being judged by the Wyndton family, engaged Thalen in a long conversation about the Scoláiríum, sharing his own mother's interest in raising education levels in Weirandale. Cerúlia wished Darzner were present to take notes; here was yet another area of Weir society she needed to prioritize.

Tilim had been impatiently waiting his turn. "You're wearing your rapier again, Commander. Can I see it?"

"It's not mine, lad. Only borrowed for a time." Thalen stood to pull Quinith's grandfather's rapier out of its scabbard and told the story of how he came to carry it. "Truly, Tilim, I am not one of the better fencers amongst the Raiders. I started learning the skill too late. Because of my long reach I've become barely passable. Actually, though, I'd prefer not to wear a weapon and never again be involved in killing.

"However, whenever I am in the queen's presence I will wear arms. Just in case my meager skill can offer her protection."

"What a beaut this is! Marcot! Look at the jewels in the pommel!" Tilim said, turning the sword over in the light. "Does it have a name?"

"I think that Quinith's grandfather named it. But I never have. It's just steel, Tilim. Just a tool."

"Don't worry, Commander," Tilim said. "One day I'll be captain of Queen Cerúlia's Shield, and I'll protect you both so you don't have to."

"Put it away now," said Stahlia. "You'll knock over the pitcher. Of course you didn't know, Commander, but there's a house rule—no swords at the table."

As Tovalie served the sweet, Lemle, who'd been quietly absorbing the conversation, spoke up. "Begging your pardon—Commander, Cerúlia—but there's something I need to settle. Will it bother you that she's the queen and you merely the consort? All sorts of honors and attention go to the ruler in Weirandale, much less to her husband."

"You mean the consorts are only valuable as studs to provide princellas?" Thalen laughed. "Actually, I'd be honored to be regarded as a worthy breeding prospect!"

When the table's laughter subsided, Thalen said, "But let's be clear: no one has yet asked me to assume that role."

Although Thalen wouldn't look at Cerúlia, he squeezed her hand under the table.

"He's only been here three days!" said Cerúlia defensively. "Everybody. *Stop rushing us.*"

"Who's rushing?" Stahlia said under her breath, and the queen had to admit to herself that she had rushed into Thalen's arms, rushed to secure the Raiders, and now had rushed to bring him into her family.

But I have waited so long.

Thalen was still speaking. "No, Lemle, I do not crave the limelight. In fact, often I hate dragging this reputation around. I prefer the quiet of my books. When I left Latham I was writing an essay on Oromondo beliefs; I would gladly miss the next ten banquets to work on it. However, should Cerúlia ever need me, nothing would make me happier than to be by her side or offer counsel."

By the time Tovalie brought out nuts and Stahlia offered her brandy bottle, the family had switched from grilling Thalen to telling him stories about Cerúlia when she was little: how meek she pretended to be and how shy, and how she had never sung for *them*, not even once.

Thalen ate up these stories, turning around to study Cerúlia.

"Was it hard, hiding all that—that *Talent* under a barrel?"

"Not really," she answered. "After all, Water takes the shape of its container. And I'd been told that my life and their lives depended on how good I was as a playactor.

"They are all a confounded nuisance," she said, her half-affectionate, half-scolding glance circling the table, "but I didn't want to be responsible for anything happening to any one of them."

Stahlia winced. Cerúlia read the thought that flashed across her foster mother's mind: that despite her best efforts at concealment, Wilim had died protecting her.

"I'm so sorry, Teta," she said in a miserable tone.

"That's what fathers do. And it wasn't just for you, Birdie," Stahlia answered her, speaking as if the two of them were alone in the room. "It was to protect the rest of us too. And the realm itself."

Her foster mother smashed a walnut shell. "But you've got to be the best queen ever, to balance his sacrifice."

"So many have sacrificed, Teta," Cerúlia remonstrated. "That's what this festival was about. Don't think I'm not trying. I'm trying, every day."

Lemle whispered, "The Spirits giveth and taketh away."

Probably wanting to spare their guest more exposure to family heartache, Marcot cleared his throat and stood up. "What a lovely meal, Mother Stahlia. You don't mind, do you, if I show your visitor your workroom and loom? I'm sure Commander Thalen will want to see your drawing of Cerúlia and the Catamounts."

49

Cascada to Vittorine

When Thalen accompanied the queen's party back to the palace after the dinner, Cerúlia's secretary, a pudgy-faced man she introduced as Darzner, was waiting for her in the Reception Room.

"Your Majesty, I so regret to disturb you, but there's been a messenger with a note that appears urgent."

With a sigh, Cerúlia reached for the paper, skimmed it, and then handed it to Thalen. He read:

Your Majesty—

Reports have reached me of the wonderful celebrations in Cascada. How I wish that I had been well enough to attend!

Unfortunately, the healers have just left me with numerous dire predictions.

Is it possible that with the festivities concluded, you would do an old man the honor of a short visit?

My chamberlain is staying in Cascada, waiting for your answer. If your party could accompany him to my

Vittorine manor in two days' time, you would fulfill my fondest and last desire.

Master Belcazar, former councilor to Queen Cressa

Cerúlia told Thalen what she had learned from Sewel's *Chronicle of Queen Cressa* about Belcazar being the only councilor who aided her mother.

"In fact, I think you could say that he saved my mother's life and mine."

"Then you have to go," he said, "though I can hardly bear to be parted from you."

"Why don't we all go?" said Cerúlia. "Your Raiders—even Minister Destra—might enjoy seeing a little more of Weirandale before winter sets in. We can ride straight to Belcazar's estate, and then on the way back take a more roundabout route. On our return we could visit the Abbey of the Waters on Nargis Mountain."

She turned to Darzner. "First thing in the morning, start making arrangements."

"Very well, Your Majesty." The secretary left.

Thalen followed Cerúlia into her bedroom and locked the door behind him.

When he turned around, she was right in front of him, tugging at his clothes. "I need to examine your wounds from that dissection in West Cottage."

"Just scratches," he said. "I like your family. I imagine I'll like them more when they trust me."

"You know what I like?" she asked. "I like the idea of having my way with you in a tent."

In the morning, Thalen joined the queen as she sent for Belcazar's man, a mild, elderly chamberlain who gave his name as Gruber. He was overjoyed to learn that the queen had decided to accept the invitation. He recovered from the news of the enlarged party quickly; what appeared most important to him was that they leave on the morrow.

"Otherwise, Your Majesty, I fear it will be too late."

So the palace went into a small uproar, planning for a royal journey. Thalen left Cerúlia's capable people to their arrangements and went to find the Raiders. He warned them to get their gear together and took them up to the Royal Stables to choose mounts. As much as they had been enjoying the hospitality of Cascada, a sightseeing journey appealed to all.

Everyone joked around in high spirits. Jothile had shown no outward improvement from his drink of Nargis Water. But Tristo had confessed to Cerf (who relayed the news to Thalen) that the near-constant pain he had quietly endured in the arm that was no longer there had magically eased.

That evening, Thalen dined alone with Minister Destra. He had barely seen her since their arrival in Cascada, and she wanted to discuss all the things she'd gathered from her diplomatic meetings. Thalen found a certain respite in this impersonal discussion of administrative organization, elections of stewards, and systems of currency exchanges.

When a note arrived at the Rare Talents saying that Cerúlia was so busy clearing her schedule for the journey and making provisions for her absence that she could not see him until the morning of their departure, Thalen was disappointed. But he recognized that a little distance, not to mention more sleep, would be beneficial for them both.

An entourage of forty-two shields, Raiders, and servants, accompanied by six dogs, gathered around the royal carriage carrying the queen and Minister Destra, breathing out white clouds in the cold morning air. A second, larger but less luxurious conveyance had been loaded with supplies, two cooks, and one maid each for the queen and minister.

Belcazar's chamberlain began fretting about the delay getting started; Thalen reassured him that once Destra and Cerúlia got away from all of Vilkit's and Nana's ministrations, he knew them both to be travelers who could set a good pace.

Captain Yanath drew Thalen to the side.

"Cici doesn't like that man. She yapped at him."

"What?" asked Thalen, confused. "What man? Who's Cici?"

"The littlest dog—she's the most attuned to people's emotions. She would have attacked Chamberlain Gruber if she sensed he was actually a threat to the queen. I pulled him aside and searched him thoroughly; he's not carrying any weapon. But Cici has made it clear she doesn't like him. She's picking up something about him."

"Tension about his master's health?"

"Could be. Or could be he's lying about something. In the last moons, I've learned to trust the dogs. I thought you'd want to know."

"Indeed. Thank you." Thalen had seen Cerúlia, tucked in under fur rugs, chatting with Destra. "If the dog is really worried, she'll tell the queen. If she doesn't, let's leave it alone unless you get more definite information. She looks happy today, and I hate to worry her."

Yanath nodded. "That's why I told you instead."

Finally, they got underway. Thalen rode amidst the Raiders on a smooth-gaited mare that the heavyset stableman had recommended. The expedition made its way through city neighborhoods and then struck the High Road, which at first was dotted with homes and businesses where people halted their activities and gaped at the royal carriage, but that gradually gave way to farms and rolling hills. As the hours passed by, Thalen mused about dozens of topics, including how the Fountain chose whom to succor, how hard it would be to let Dalogun return to Jígat on his own, whether he could set up a branch of the Scoláiríum in Cascada, and whether Cerúlia found his lovemaking awkward or satisfying.

He meant to be watching out for any unusual events, but Wareth had to rouse him from his reverie with a quick whistle and a pointing hand. "Look! A hawk."

The hawk circled down slowly, landing with its talons on the carriage ledge nearest the queen. Thalen found the sharp beak so close to her face a disquieting image, but Cerúlia conversed amiably with the raptor for a few moments, then stroked the back of its head and neck. It flew off, and Cerúlia continued her conversation with Destra as if nothing had happened. But Thalen, who was now able to read her expressions more accurately, saw confusion warring with unease.

When they stopped for a late midmeal at the Riverine Rest, a large roadside tavern that an advance servant had alerted to their upcoming arrival, he gave his horse to Tristo to water and approached the carriage.

"Ah! Commander." Cerúlia smiled as he helped her descend. "Minister, why don't you go in by the fire? I'm a little stiff from just sitting still. I imagine Commander Thalen will do me the service of walking with me a moment to stretch my legs."

"I'd be delighted. Which direction shall we go?"

"Um." She cast around. "Let's walk into this field across the road. See those hay stooks? In Wyndton I helped with the harvesting. I want to show you how heavy they are."

Once on the other side of the very ordinary hay bale where they couldn't be observed, he asked, "Raider, what news from your bird?" in his best commander voice.

"Thalen, it's so queer, I wonder if the hawk may have made a mistake. He said that a seagull told him of sighting a flotilla of black-sailed ships heading into the Bay of Cinda from the south."

"Black sails would be Pellish, but your mother destroyed the Pellish fleet nearly a decade ago."

"That's why I need to go back to gather better information. I'd like you to lead the procession onward—I will catch up with you once I've untangled this mystery. I'll take Smoke—he's so fast—and rejoin you, probably before you get to Councilor Belcazar's."

"You're not going off alone. We'll all turn back. Or at least let me go with you."

"That would be rude to Destra and Belcazar. And few horses can keep up with Smoke."

She ran a finger across his frown. "Look. You can confer with Yanath and choose one Raider and one shield each as my guardians. I'll take the deerhounds and Whaki too, because they might be able to keep up, and leave you just Vaki and Cici."

"Cici doesn't trust Belcazar's man."

"Really?" She sighed and shivered a little. "Then try to keep my departure from him as long as you can."

Thalen was putting the pieces together. "Let's think about this. All that rush and insistence on getting you out of Cascada, just as black sails draw close. Could this be a coincidence? Surely not. Something untoward might be planned. Maybe there's an ambush on the road ahead."

"But we don't know yet if the hawk's message is accurate," said Cerúlia. "Bird to bird can get garbled, especially across species. I have to send out more seabirds and be the one to confer with each directly.

"And if there's a plot in progress, Belcazar might be being held hostage by people who know that I could not refuse his plea. Perchance he needs to be rescued? That is why I wish you to continue. But be careful."

"Of course I'll be careful," he said, pushing her back into the bale of hay, capturing her with one arm on each side. "One way to be careful is to make everyone think that we came out here for another reason." He kissed her until she started having trouble catching her breath, and then he sprinkled a bit of hay in her hair.

"Now I know you'll ride back posthaste," he said.

Cerúlia and he walked back to the tavern hand in hand. Belcazar's man, fortunately, was already inside by the fire, while Captain Yanath and several of the Raiders lingered outside tending the horses and watching out for the queen.

When Cerúlia bent down to converse with her canine corps, Thalen spoke to Yanath, who decided on a shield named Pontole, while Thalen chose Fedak, as a swifter rider than either Kambey or Kran and almost as good a swordsman. He sent Tristo inside to make sure that Chamberlain Gruber was occupied, and asked Dalogun to get three horses ready for a sprint.

"Go inside and act normal," said Cerúlia. "Say I decided I needed a quiet rest in the carriage. I'll catch up with you soon—really, you have no idea how fast Smoke is when I give him permission to fly."

"May I kiss you good luck?"

"In front of all these people?" she mocked him.

So he kissed her one more time and then strode into the building, full of false heartiness, knocking mugs and chairs about to cover the sound of hoofbeats.

The trip continued throughout the cold afternoon. The next likely stopping point was a village called The Crossing, along the High Road. The travelers reached it once the moons had been out for over an hour. When they disembarked at the two small inns that had prepared to receive the royal party, the chamberlain noticed that the queen was missing.

He turned on Thalen in the small common room. "But, but my orders, I was to—I have to bring the queen tomorrow."

"Unfortunately, she was called away," Thalen said with narrowed eyes. "She will return when she can. Why is it so crucial that she appear in Vittorine tomorrow?"

"My master wishes to see her desperately. The healers have given him only days to live!" Gruber repeated.

Thalen and Captain Yanath exchanged looks, but neither of them had the stomach to force the full truth out of the frightened, elderly man.

Yanath turned on his heel, and Thalen followed him into the entryway.

"I'm going to post extra sentries tonight," the captain told him, "armored."

"Good. Let's all turn in early. The sooner we get to this councilor's manor and make sure he's all right, the sooner we can head back to Cascada and the queen."

When he returned to the common room, he almost bumped into Destra, who had her long white skirt gathered up in her hands.

"Ah, Commander," she said. "I'm fatigued from the journey. You set a lively pace! The innkeep has said my room is prepared. Mabbie will bring me some supper and I'm going to bed. One never knows what challenges Fate has in store; best to be prepared."

Cerúlia did not rejoin the party in the night.

Pushing their horses hard, the expedition reached the turnoff to Belcazar's estate, called Pineywoods, just after midday. It was a handsome, two-story, white stone building backed by a stand of towering green-black pines that stretched up the hill behind it. The whole would have presented a picture especially pleasing to the eye—because the barn, walkway, fences, and other outbuildings had been situated with great care to fit the landscape—but the estate wore an air of dishevelment: the shrubs had gotten scraggly, and the glass-paned windows wore a coat of grime. A dozen men sauntered in the yard, but Thalen could tell at a glance that they were not ordinary workers; their posture and their clothing didn't fit either household staff or field hands.

When these men approached the riders to take their horses, Vaki started growling at them.

"I see them, dog. Don't cause a ruckus," Thalen said, hoping the creature understood him.

Thalen rode his horse next to Captain Yanath's at the hitching fence and crossed under his mare's belly, undoing the cinch, so that he and Yanath were hidden between the horses from general sight.

"Matwyck's Marauders, I'll wager," Yanath mouthed. "Thugs, mercenaries who worked for Regent Matwyck."

"How many?" Thalen whispered.

"Could be the missing fifty."

"I only count twelve." Thalen answered.

"Movement in the barn," Yanath whispered, as he patted his horse's rump.

An elderly lady, drawn and bloodless under her caramel complexion, appeared in a mended silk gown, waiting at the front door with a stirrup cup.

"Gentlefolk, I am Master Belcazar's wife, Engeliqua. We are delighted that you have arrived."

Destra spoke for the group. "Queen Cerúlia has been detained, but she believes she will rejoin us soon."

"I just heard this from Chamberlain Gruber," said Engeliqua stiffly. "We are so disappointed. May I offer you a drink after your long, cold journey?"

Cici trotted over and whined at the hostess.

"It would please me if you would leave the dogs outside," Engeliqua said. "Also, we weren't expecting quite so many guards. Your men will be comfortable on the lawn? We will serve them from a spit out here; we started a fire, and we have plenty of ale."

"Come along, chaps," said one of the Marauders dressed as a stableman, putting his arm with false friendliness over Dalogun's shoulder. Most of the hungry Raiders and shields started drifting toward the wooden trestles visible to the side of the manse, but Thalen managed to catch Kambey's and Wareth's eyes and convey a warning. Kambey nonchalantly ran a hand down his own chest from neck to belt; if Thalen read the gesture aright his sword master was pointing out that the Marauders wore no breastplates.

Apparently, Tristo was determined that Thalen not disappear inside this house without him. He ran up to the doorway. "I am the Commander's adjutant," he told the lady with his most winning smile. "I stand by his side."

"Not today. You may go with the female servants"—she nodded her head at Mabbie and Geesilla—"to the kitchen. My man will show you the way." So Tristo unwillingly allowed himself to be led around the back.

Cerf stepped forward. "Madam, I am Queen Cerúlia's healer. Perhaps I can be of service to your husband."

"Oh, I don't think so," said Engeliqua. "The other healers have quite given him up."

"You'd be surprised," said Thalen, "at Cerf's special skills. Were I Councilor Belcazar, I would want the very best of the medical profession attending me."

Engeliqua ungraciously inclined her head toward Cerf. So four of them entered the front door: Captain Yanath (who knew Councilor Belcazar from Queen Cressa's days), Destra (who took all this strangeness with poise), Cerf, and Thalen.

The lady of the house led them into a washing room where a maid poured hot water into basins for them to scrub off the road dust and brushed off their clothes.

"Gentlemen, wouldn't you be more comfortable without your swords?" she asked with downcast eyes.

"No," said Thalen.

When they emerged, Engeliqua led them to a room with a vaulted roof that doubled as a sitting room and a dining salon. A fire burned in a stone hearth; the rug lying before it boasted scattered small burns and scorch marks.

A man with amber hair, nearly seventy summers old, awaited them near the fire in a wheeled chair with blankets spread over his legs. One half of his facial muscles drooped, causing the left eye to tear and the left half of his mouth to drool a bit.

One glance substantiated that the man was unwell. But he had loads of flesh on his bones.

Captain Yanath came forward. "The last time I saw you, Councilor, was on the quay, near *Sea Sprite* that fateful night. I grieve not to see you on your feet."

"Yanath, is it? Aye, I'd heard that the queen named you captain of her New Shield. Congratulations. Of course, we still miss Captain Clemçon, don't we? Ah, *there* was a formidable man." His speech was slurred.

Because the comment was pitched so ambiguously, Thalen couldn't tell whether it conveyed sorrow for the lost captain or was a deliberate insult to Yanath.

"We shall always miss Captain Clemçon," responded Yanath. He continued, "I should like to introduce my companions: this is Minister Destra, a visiting dignitary from the Free States; Commander Thalen of Thalen's Raiders; and Master Cerf, the new palace healer."

Councilor Belcazar took each hand in turn and eyed the guests up and down, but offered no polite remarks.

His hand is plump and warm.

Madam Engeliqua gestured to the polished table, which was prepared for midmeal.

"You must be hungry after your journey. Pray, won't you be seated?" She wheeled Belcazar's chair to the head, placing Destra on Belcazar's right and Thalen on his left. Cerf sat next to Thalen, and Yanath next to Destra, with the mistress at the foot of the table.

She rang a bell, which brought in two burly footmen in ill-fitting uniforms who poured wine and water and started gracelessly passing around platters of pickled onions and cucumbers.

Destra allowed Yanath to seat her as if she had no misgivings about arriving at the home of a "dying" man who was actually well enough to join them at the table with pickled tasties.

"Such lovely porcelain," she said to her hostess, admiring the pattern of multicolored rings that decorated the white plate. "Beautiful.

It calls to the mind the Fountain Reel. I do so admire a nice setting. It makes the food taste better, doesn't it? How long has this service been in your family?"

Madam Engeliqua opened her mouth to reply.

"I'd like to offer a toast," Councilor Belcazar interrupted, "to my honored guests."

Destra held up her glass, cutting him off with a gracious smile. "I'd like to offer a toast in return, Councilor. To those who remain faithful when all around are faithless."

Everyone held up his or her glass. Yanath was just about to drink when Destra's musical tones forestalled him.

"Before we drink, however," Destra said, "I'm sure you will indulge me: it's a time-honored custom of the Free States that we exchange glasses at the table."

Thalen took in a breath. Destra had just invented this "time-honored" custom—she didn't need any warning.

Destra continued, "I believe this practice goes back to King Siga's day, when treachery and poisonings were rife, but we have kept it as a sign of friendship and trust. So, if you will just exchange glasses with me"—she took Belcazar's glass out of his hand and replaced it with her own—"and your lovely wife with Captain Yanath"—Yanath followed her lead—"we can all set to this very tasty-looking repast."

Belcazar pretended to sniff the wine. "Oh, bah! Wine steward, this cask has gone bad. Nobody drink it. Let me send for a fresh cask." He put his glass back on the table with a gesture of disdain.

An elderly (authentic?) servant moved forward to reclaim the glasses, but halted midstep when Thalen rose, drew his rapier, and pointed its tip at the host's throat. "I'm afraid we must decline all food and drink at this table. Poison ruins our appetites, as does being enticed into a trap. Councilor, I await your explanation."

Belcazar yanked back from Thalen's sword point, but it was

really Cerf's dagger—now held across his wife's throat—that riveted his eyes.

"'Zar," said Madam Engeliqua, tears starting as her hand patted her lower neck. "'Zar—I'm *bleeding*."

"Never fear, madam," said Cerf. "Just a trickle. I know how far I can cut. Your skin is on the thin side, but your windpipe will be just where everyone else's lies."

"Leave her be," Belcazar ordered hoarsely.

Three more "footmen" rushed through the doorway. All five grabbed swords that had been stashed behind a curtain and started circling round the table to come at Cerf and Thalen from behind.

"Tell your men to stop and lay down their arms, or we'll kill you," said Thalen.

"They don't care if you kill me. They aren't my men," said Belcazar slurring.

"I was afraid of that."

The false footmen smirked and launched their attack. Yanath sprang into action, parrying and slashing. Thalen was able to knock a weapon out of one enemy's hand. Cerf had substituted his sword for his dagger and engaged with an assailant. The two leaned together, straining, swords crossed.

Yanath, the mightiest fencer in the room, had already engaged another attacker. Thalen grabbed a platter at random off the table, ignoring the food that went flying, using it as a shield. Pressing forward with the platter and his rapier, he backed a Marauder into the wall and stabbed deep into the man's groin more than once. When he looked around he saw that a second man had set upon Cerf, who was bleeding and giving ground. Thalen clunked the nearer man over the head with the metal platter, satisfied to see his antagonist drop like a stone, and Cerf used the distraction to give the first false footman a deep, disabling slash.

In just moments, injured men lay bleeding and moaning on the floor. Thalen took stock. Madam Engeliqua had backed herself into a corner, cowering beside a carved sideboard. Destra still sat calmly at the table, her hands in her lap, as if bloodshed and flying onions were an everyday occurrence. Noise from outside in the yard and deeper within the household indicated that other members of their party were now under assault. Yanath bolted in the direction of the front door and his men outside. Cerf pressed a napkin to his own wound and called to Thalen, "Going to the kitchen!"

But Thalen couldn't leave the room without answers about the threat to Cerúlia. "What is going on here?" he asked, just keeping his voice under control.

"'Zar! You fool! What have you done to us?" whimpered Madam Engeliqua.

Belcazar roared, pushing away the blankets on his legs and standing up. He grabbed a short sword that had been hidden by the blankets, taking a wild swipe in Thalen's direction.

Thalen slapped Belcazar's left knee very hard with the side of his rapier, causing the elderly man to topple first against his wheeled chair, which rolled away, and then to the floor.

"I have no more time to play your games. I thought you were on the queen's side. Why did you try to kill us?"

"Why?" sputtered Belcazar, propping himself up on his elbows. *"Why? Why* was I exiled out here to the countryside, forgotten and abandoned by everyone who counts? *Why* did Matwyck kill my older son and spoil my daughter's match?"

"Don't listen to him, I beg you!" Engeliqua cried out.

"*Why* should Cerúlia waltz back into the realm and enjoy adulation and riches?" said Belcazar.

Engeliqua took two steps forward, holding out her hands. "He had a stroke six years ago! Since then, he's not been himself. He used to be a good man, a thoughtful man.

"General Yurgn began visiting, pouring his venom in his ear," Engeliqua babbled on. She started to sob. "Then, in the summer, after the general died, Burgn rode up. He left those guards here; they run my household; they've eaten all my stores.

"Burgn said that if we enticed *her* here exactly when commanded, my husband would be restored to his former stature and more.

"I told him he shouldn't; I told him!" She stamped her foot and pointed to the man flopped on the floor. "Rash, addled old fool, stewing in bitterness."

"You were trying to poison the queen?" Thalen asked.

Without a shadow of remorse, the old man boasted, "While she struggled for air I would tell her what a trusting little twit her mother was. Helping a Nargis Queen ruined my family."

Thalen regarded the incapacitated figure on the floor. He wanted to kill him, but what purpose would that serve? And what if his twisted plan came from a mind twisted by his stroke?

One of the wounded false footmen on the floor started to try to gather himself on all fours. Destra grabbed her beautiful plate and smashed it over his head.

With effort Thalen controlled his fury at Belcazar. "Destra! Grab a weapon and keep an eye on them and the injured guards." Thalen ran to join the battle raging outside.

Oaths, screams, and growls filled the air, along with the clatter of swords.

The Marauders were husky men who enjoyed cruelty; they were accustomed to pushing around unarmed and frightened civilians. But they had no great fencing skills, and they had never fought disciplined, experienced soldiers. So even though the Marauders had a numerical advantage, the palace group had made headway.

Thalen rushed up behind a man who was in the midst of exchanging blows with Dalogun; Thalen stabbed him deep in the buttocks with his rapier's sharp point. His antagonist screamed, dropped his weapon, and bolted away from the pain. When Thalen whirled around he found himself momentarily engaged in fighting off two swordsmen simultaneously: the first one used his sword like a pickaxe, with wild overhead blows, and the second stumbled over his own big feet as he advanced. Thalen desperately parried several thrusts from opposite directions; then his rapier opened the clumsy one's leg from groin to knee, while Jothile, coming out of nowhere, his sword flashing with his former speed and confidence, snuck in under Pickaxe's flailing arms and sliced his throat.

The dogs pitched in—Cici by biting through the back of men's ankles, the hound by sinking his teeth into calves. Tristo and Cerf burst out from the back of the house, racing forward with swords drawn, with Mabbie, Destra's maid, behind them, a cleaver in one hand and an iron skillet in the other. The Queen's Shield, protected by their breastplates and helms, pressed the Marauders relentlessly.

An attacker knocked Kran's sword from his hand, so Kran picked up the plank of wood resting on supports that had been set up as a sitting bench. The big Raider wielded this long plank almost like a scythe, knocking over a group of Marauders as if they were but a gaggle of ducks.

Thalen's stomach rebelled at the sight of so much blood and death.

He leapt onto the wooden trestle table and blew a piercing whistle through the thumb and middle finger of his left hand. Everyone looked up at him.

The excitement pouring through him made Thalen want to shout, but he knew the advantages of quiet.

"Marauders," he said with control. "You have failed at your task. The queen isn't even present to fall to your plot. Inside, five of your fellows are down."

"Two more in the kitchen!" shouted Cerf.

"If you wish to live to see tomorrow," Thalen continued, "drop your weapons and sit on your hands."

A long pause ensued as the Marauders looked at one another and glanced around at their injured, dying, or dead comrades. Each was loath to look craven.

Captain Yanath walked up to the foe standing closest to him. Very deliberately, he grabbed the man's wrist and pried the sword from his hand. Then he pushed on the man's shoulder until the man bent his knees and sat. One by one, the others complied.

As always after a skirmish, Thalen's first thought was for his men. Kran thrashed on the grass like a wounded stag. Thalen ran to him; his hand encircling Kran's broad back immediately grew slick with hot blood. At some point during the battle, he must have taken a thrust from behind, and swinging the plank had ripped the wound deeper. Thalen bent on the ground on one knee and held his friend in his arms as, wordlessly, Kran bled out and his eyes turned glassy.

Laying the body down gently, Thalen stood up and inventoried the others. Dalogun had taken an injury in his foot; Kambey—whose wounds weren't as serious—already had the boy laying down and a tourniquet on his ankle. Wareth was squatting in front of Jothile, holding his shoulders as the latter vomited on the grass.

Cerf was bleeding from multiple slashes but his two hands braced about his knee.

"How bad?" Thalen asked him.

"Fuck!" said Cerf, squinting at his own wounds. "I'll need stitching." He reached for his commander's arm and nodded toward the one upright bench. Thalen helped him cover the grass as Cerf limped and cursed.

"What is it?" Thalen asked, for he saw no rent in Cerf's trousers.

"Drought damn shattered kneecap," said Cerf through clenched teeth. "A villain in the kitchen smacked me with a poker.

"Get my saddlebag and tell everyone to lay the wounded on this table. This time I'll work sitting down."

Crossing to Cerf's horse, Thalen noticed that many of the bodies laying lifeless on the blood-soaked grass wore the livery of palace servants because the Marauders had attacked unarmed and untrained civilians first. Fury flamed even higher inside him when he spotted several shields carrying the flopped figure of the queen's maid Geesilla onto the table as Cerf's most urgent case.

When Thalen sprinted back with the saddlebag, Cerf rummaged through it frantically, finding a small bottle of milk of the poppy. While Thalen tied a bandage tightly around Cerf's knee and padded a slash in his neck and tied a strip to keep it in place, the healer took a controlled sip. Cerf then roared to Mabbie, who stood nearby wringing her hands, "Fetch hot water and bandages. This woman is dying."

Looking about, Thalen next tried to judge how the Queen's Shield had fared. Most were on their feet, disarming and tying up Marauders. Two sprawled on the greensward in the indignity of death: a female shield and an older man with a broken nose.

Captain Yanath sat clasping that man's hand in two of his own.

Thalen touched Yanath's shoulder, and the captain roused himself and rose to a standing position. "Branwise was my friend for over twenty years," he said. "You wouldn't know it to look at him now, but when he joined the Shield at eighteen summers, he was gorgeous. The first time I saw him, light was at his back. He looked just like— exactly like—a hero out of ballads. Strong, invincible. Now a miserable old sot, not fast enough against scum like these here.

"You fuckin' miserable old sot," Yanath cursed at the prone figure. "Drought damn your eyes, to leave me now."

"I'm sorry," said Thalen, trying to make the statement sound less inadequate. Then, getting to business, he prompted, "Wounded on the table there. You brought a healer?"

"Aye. Mirja." Yanath's gaze flicked over the dead female shield sprawled paces distant. "That's not her. I'll get Mirja started."

Satisfied that the most urgent cases would be dealt with, Thalen walked to a well in the middle of the yard, winched up a bucket, and started washing the blood and gore off his arms.

Destra appeared at his side with a jar of soap and a mug of coffee for when he'd finished.

Both the water and the coffee called him back to himself, pulling his mind away from the image of Kran's vacant eyes.

"Commander, why did the queen return to Cascada?" Destra asked.

Thalen told her about the hawk's message.

"Someone wanted her out of Cascada and dead, *today*. If you were planning on breaching Cascada's harbor, isn't that what you'd want?" she asked.

"I figured that out myself!" Thalen snapped, angry at Destra for implying he was stupid, but angrier at himself for leading them into this trap and for letting Cerúlia ride off only lightly guarded. He drew in a breath. "Which is why I am leaving you and the captain to care for our wounded and clean up here. I'm riding back to Cascada as soon as I can get ready.

"Tristo," Thalen shouted. "Where the devil are you? I need you to see to that mare I've been riding."

"You'll also need food for the journey," Destra said with no trace of pique. "I'll raid their pantry."

Wareth joined him at the well bucket.

"I'm coming with you, 'Mander," he said.

"Aren't you hurt?" Thalen asked, pointing at the blood trickling down the side of Wareth's face.

"About as much as you." Wareth pointed to Thalen's bleeding knuckles and the shallow slash across his waist where a sword tip had caught him. He washed Thalen's cut and hand in fresh water and hollered for unguent and bandages, which a shield fetched for them.

Thalen blotted and inspected the scalp gash leaking blood into Wareth's curls, then wrapped together his friend's sprained or broken fingers. When he finished, he asked, "How is Jothile?"

"He's upset is all; there's not a scratch on him. Somehow he's got his speed and skill back—fuckin' saved me from a bastard just about to skewer me."

"Hmm," Thalen grunted. "So maybe the Fountain did him some good we couldn't see."

"Why do little things hurt so much?" Wareth asked, staring at his hands. "I swear my fingers throb as much as that lance in my back in Oromondo."

"Hold your hand upright so the blood doesn't flow down to your fingers and make them swell. You were so drunk on milk of the poppy you just don't remember the pain from the lance."

Tristo's face was a mass of swelling bruises, and his lips were torn and bleeding—perhaps from a collision with a heavy fist and sword guard—but the boy just wiped the blood out of his eyes as he prepared the horses and fed and watered the dogs.

The sun was lowering on the horizon and the air was cooling by the time two horses, two dogs, and two Raiders were ready to ride.

"Don't kill the hostages," Thalen shouted to Yanath across the yard.

"Now whyever would we do that?" replied the captain. "We're not bloody barbarians."

"We'll see you in Cascada," Thalen, his foot in his stirrup, called down to Destra.

"Aye," she said. "If Fate be willing."

Thalen had started to trot away when Destra ran after him, desperately calling, "Thalen! Wait!" He pulled up his mare.

"Thalen, keep in mind. It takes Three Spirits to defeat any One."

50

SeaWidow Cliff

Sending Pontole and Fedak to escort her back to the palace showed sense and caution, but Cerúlia burned with impatience. Their horses kept pace with Smoke for the first league only because she held her gelding in check. Then their mounts began to tire and lag, while her anxiety over the hawk's message amplified. She hoped to get back before dark, before all the diurnal birds retired for the night.

Accordingly, disregarding her guards' shouts of outrage, the queen pulled out in front and gave Smoke his freedom. When she reached the crests of small hills on the High Road, she reined in to make Smoke breathe, turned around, and waved her arm at the small figures behind her to demonstrate that she was fine. But the shortness of the autumn daylight undermined the queen's chance of reaching bird informants in time, and soon made it impossible for her to reassure the furious men behind her.

Nevertheless, she galloped on, slowing Smoke only for brief spells of rest. The cold wind chafed her cheeks and made her eyes water, her shoulder ached, and she recalled that she had not eaten at the inn she left behind. Cerúlia's legs and gown grew damp from

Smoke's sweat, and occasionally great gobs of saliva foam flew back at her.

Do you tire? she asked Smoke as, two hours later, he began to clatter on the cobblestones of the outskirts of Cascada.

One never gets to run like this. Being pent up in a field makes one rage. This is one's talent, and using one's talent feels right, the horse responded, though he acknowledged hunger and thirst.

Due to obstacles, Smoke was forced to moderate his pace as he approached the center of the city. Cerúlia was assailed by a not-quite-graspable memory of doing this once before: riding Smoke fast through the cold autumn air of the city at night, pedestrians shouting alarms and getting out of the way.

At an even slower canter she turned him into the avenue that led to the Arrival Gate. As soon as she saw in the torchlight that the gate was closed for the night, she began shouting like a wild woman, "'Tis the Queen—open the Gate! 'Tis the Queen—raise the Gate!" The guards sprang to the winch. Both she and the horse had to duck their heads, but they made it through without stopping to wait, which would have felt intolerable in her state of anxiety.

At the formal palace entrance, she slid off her winded mount. "Walk him for at least an hour," she said to the stableman who, mis-buttoning his waistcoat, ran out to take Smoke's head.

Turning briefly from the height of the entrance steps, she noted that the palace and the city lay peaceful except for the dust she herself had caused. She allowed herself to hope that the hawk's message had been in error. In which case she might look like a lackwit for this mad dash, but she'd prefer to suffer embarrassment than have the city suffer assault.

Footmen opened the door for her, shocked to see the queen back alone, and in such a bedraggled state. Cerúlia caught the subdued hum of the palace; no doubt the staff was enjoying a quiet night after all the festivities.

"There're some guards and dogs coming on behind me. They'll be worn out and need care," she said, as if this explained everything.

"Very good, Your Majesty. We will watch for them."

"Food, a bath, and my Circle Council, in that order—but all with dispatch," she said to the footman.

"Very good, Your Majesty."

She rushed toward the Royal Stair, too apprehensive to move sedately, even though her own fatigue made her leg muscles shake. Her eyes blinked to adjust from the night's darkness to the flicker of wall torches lighting the palace at night.

She saw Nana standing on the top step almost in a trance, twisting her hands in her apron, her face vacant. Cerúlia paused, struck by Nana's odd pose and the slight shimmer in the air about her.

When Nana saw her, the light came back on in her eyes and she called out, "Oh, thank the Waters, you've returned!"

And Cerúlia knew with certainty that Cascada was under attack.

To their credit, none of the councilors panicked when the queen met with them briefly that night.

Wilamara started counting up ships and sailors currently in port in Cascada. By pressing into service any of the mustered-out mariners who had just been honored but lingered about celebrating, she calculated she could manage a rough blockade of the harbor.

"That will only buy the city a few hours," she said. "Our ships can't hold back a whole fleet. There is going to be a battle—a bloody battle—on the streets of Cascada. Send for the Ice Pikemen and the cavalry."

"Indeed, we must," Cerúlia agreed. "But given General Yurgn's long influence over them, can we trust them? Will they fight the invaders or welcome them?"

"We have no choice," said Steward Alix, already writing the order and dispatching it.

Marcot and Naven had started plans for evacuating women and children from the city. They would immediately requisition every cart, carriage, and horse, pony, mule, or donkey to be had.

"Where will you send them?" asked Cerúlia.

"To the inland duchies. The invaders might rampage, but at least they would find fewer citizens right at hand. The Pellish want easy plunder—they won't travel far from the coast."

"But if easy plunder is what they desire most, why have they traveled the length of the continents to strike *us*?"

No one had an answer.

After they all snatched a few hours of sleep, they met again, an hour after dawn, in the Circle Chamber.

"Councilors," said the queen, "I've talked with the original gull. Birds can't count, but as far as I can determine she saw more than twenty black-sailed ships and war galleys. There is no longer any doubt that Pellish are upon us—we estimate that they will arrive in two days.

"None of the measures we discussed will save Cascada from a terrible invasion. I don't want to slow down the Pellish ships nor hide our citizens. I want to stop this before they come ashore.

"Why do we have no towers, no chain, and no trebuchets? Why is it that our harbor is so completely open to the sea, so defenseless?"

"You could ask Chronicler Sewel about ancient history," said Duke Naven. "As far as I know, we've had raids along the coast and once an invasion in Maritima, but Nargis has always protected the city through the queens' Talents."

All the councilors lifted their heads from the lists they were drawing up.

"Could you order birds to drop fire arrows, like in Femturan?" asked Nishtari.

"I thought of that. But that worked because the birds only had to fly a short ways holding the arrow. Flying out to sea—the arrows would burn their claws and the birds would drop them. No, we need a threat that comes from the sea itself."

"You can't whip up a storm, can you?" asked Duke Naven.

"No, no. Nothing like that. My Talent only extends to animals and birds."

"Sea creatures?" asked Steward Alix.

"I've talked to dolphins in the past when they came up to the surface. But I don't see how dolphins could stop a Pellish armada."

"What about whales? Could whales sink a ship?" asked Marcot. Cerúlia startled. "*Are* there whales close by?"

Wilamara spoke about the body of water, fifty leagues wide, that separated the Western and Eastern Duchies. "The Bay of Cinda is a summer feeding ground for humpbacks, blues—"

"And the little ones," Nishtari said. "I'm so rattled words escape me. What are they called? Pilots. Travelers climb to the top of Sea-Widow Cliff to watch the whales spout!"

"But they leave in late autumn for warmer climes," Wilamara continued. "What if they've already left?"

The queen bolted out of her seat. "That's where I'm going—SeaWidow Cliff. That's my command post for now. Proceed with the rest of your plans as a fallback, but pray the Waters that whales still linger close by, that they hear me and agree to obey my requests."

She took the first horse the stablemen offered, leaving her guards and other attendants to follow as best they could. The climb up Sea-Widow Cliff, just north of the harbor, consisted of a narrow footpath, braced in worn spots by logs or stones, that wound through sparse tree cover of now-barren deciduous species. She leaned against the horse's neck, letting it pick its own footing.

Dismounting, Cerúlia realized that in the moons since her return she should have made time to visit one of Cascada's most famous attractions. At the top, one came out on a flat hilltop, about as large as Nymph Salon. An ancient stone lighthouse (which queen built it and why, she couldn't recall) stood near the edge, no longer kept lit but serviceable as shelter from the wind that whipped so strongly on the bluff. A short trail—dirt hard-packed by the pacing of women waiting for their sailors or tourists seeing the view—stretched along the hem of the drop-off in front of the lighthouse, with tumbled slabs of rock leading to wave-pummeled boulders in the water. In front of her she saw league upon league of open water, sparkling; behind her the city and the palace's white towers stretched placidly in a normal midmorning. Below to her right, down a steep drop-off, she saw the harbor, already swarming with activity whipped up by Wilamara.

Some fishing boats bobbed in the waters outside the harbor, searching their normal haul. She strained her eyes to the southeast, but she could not make out any large sails—black or otherwise.

Gulls. Attend me.

First one, then five, then dozens, hundreds of seagulls within range of her call fluttered to the ground at her feet.

She sent her numberless scouts out to look for the Pellish fleet. Then she scanned the Bay of Cinda below, looking for any sign of whales.

By this time, people from the palace caught up with her, bringing all the things that in her haste she had overlooked, such as food, a warmer cloak, a spyglass, a stool, boys and girls to serve as messengers (including Tilim), and palace guards to protect her. Kiltti reported that her canine corps was too sapped by yesterday's wild dash to attend her. The dogs were footsore and spent.

Cerúlia was scanning the Bay of Cinda with the spyglass when a flock of large gray pelicans, their striated wings barely counterbalancing their big beaks and throats so they looked ungainly in flight, beat its way to the top of SeaWidow Cliff.

The leader of this flock, waddling on its webbed feet a little closer, staring with button black eyes, asked the queen, *Why did thee snub us ones, in favor of those screeching garbage eaters?*

Marquise of the Marine, Cerúlia improvised a flattering sobriquet, *I did not know you were nigh. Do you have information for me?*

Us ones always keep watch on these waters. We have kept watch for years and years. One's mother kept watch, her mother, her mother, her mother, her mother, one's sisters, one's cousins, one's aunts, one's brothers, one's uncles—

Cerúlia had no patience for this litany and she held up her hands. *Forgive my slight. I was ignorant. I have not spent enough time here at the coastline. What have any of you seen?*

Ships. Many ships. A few of the men toss fish to us. With sails the color of mussel shells. Mussels are very tasty. Not as tasty as—

Tell me about the men on the ships.

The pelican flapped her wings huffily; Cerúlia guessed that she hadn't seen or hadn't paid any attention to the sailors.

Another of her flock waddled forward a few steps. *White-haired men on the deck, playing with shiny sticks.*

Are you sure you saw white hair?

As white as screechy garbage eaters.

"Tilim," Cerúlia called behind her, in a careful tone. "Step forward and slowly pull your sword. Easy now."

The boy did as he was bid. The pelicans took several steps backward as he approached, but they did not fly off the cliff.

Shiny sticks like this? Cerúlia prodded.

The pelicans all bobbed their heads on their long necks.

Have you seen any whales? Have they all left the Bay of Cinda?

What is a whale? asked the marquise. *Is it good to eat? Does it toss the fish?*

Cerúlia tried to explain about whales, but pelicans paid no attention to marine life they couldn't consume. She wanted to send this flock back to scout the ships again, but the birds grew huffy when they heard she had already sent a flock of gulls. So she thanked them for their scouting and dismissed them.

"Tilim, I need you to ride back to the palace with a message. Tell my councilors that the ships are not bringing Pellish to *raid us*—they are bringing Oros, who intend to *invade us*."

For hours Cerúlia sat on the stool, scanning the waters below her, looking for whale spouts. She couldn't send a message to the whole vast ocean; she needed a specific creature. The sunlight made the water look cheerful, but it defeated her vision, and until a page took off her own hair leather and offered it to the queen, her loose hair kept blowing in her face. Kiltti started a fire in the lighthouse hearth and warmed up the food that Vilkit had sent.

Finally, far off, Cerúlia saw spray that gushed higher than the swell and a shadow that flicked underwater.

Whale, can you hear me? If you hear me, swim closer to land and blow air three times.

Moments elapsed. Cerúlia's nails dug into her own palms.

Then, much closer to shore: three spouts. But it must be a small creature, merely a pilot, nothing like what Cerúlia needed.

Ah, sent Cerúlia. *Thank you, whale. I need your help and the help of any other whales within a day's swim of here. Please, please, will you gather all the whales?*

A whale's thoughts sounded different to the queen than those of a bird or land animals. Rather muffled, bubbly, and inflected on rising or falling notes.

Dun-no. One's pod? One's podlings swim nigh.

All the pods of all the whales. Are you a pilot whale? I'm told you swim with big whales, the queer-shaped ones and blue ones.

Dun-nooo. Lau-tan rules us, not Narrr-gis. One hears thee, but dun-noooo whales follow thee-eee.

Indeed, I know about Lautan's dominion. Once, in southern waters, I heard whales sing "Beloved of Lautan." I believe that Nargis and I are also "Beloved of Lautan."

The juvenile pilot whale was distracted by this story. *Dun-*

nooooo. Did they have the right tune in the southern waters? Let one sing it for thee now—ow—ow.

Pilot, please! Time presses. Could you search for other whales? Have they left on their winter journey?

Dun-nooo. Some have; some have noo-whoa-whoa. The whale spouted dramatically and flapped its tail in the water. *Dun-nooo. Dun-nooo. Dun-nooo.* Then it sped off.

Cerúlia hoped that it had gone to gather other whales, but it might have just decided it didn't like the conversation. She scanned the sea to the southwest again, wondering how much time they had left, what had happened in Vittorine, and how preparations proceeded in the city.

"Begging your pardon, Your Majesty, this woman says she has information of utmost importance."

Whirling around, she saw that one of the guards stood on top of the cliffside path next to a well-dressed, middle-aged woman, with hair elaborately coiffed in a high style on top of her head.

"Can't you take this to someone else?" Cerúlia said.

"She says she knows about the Pellish ships," said the guard.

"Really." Cerúlia frowned and then addressed the unfamiliar lady. "Who are you? And how do you come by this information?"

"My information is for your ears only," she said, from her deep curtsey. "Your Majesty, may I approach?"

Impatiently, the queen beckoned her to move forward. When the lady had moved within three paces of the queen, the guard, with automatic protectiveness, called out, "That's close enough!" He then turned to talk to another figure, a shadow that had appeared from the footpath.

"Those ships are in communication with Weirs, with people who wish your death," the stranger said in a low tone.

"Communication? But how?"

"They use trained petrels." She took another half step forward.

"Trained petrels . . ." The queen recalled that she had once read something about such messengers. "How do you know this? State your name."

"I am Clovadorska of Riverine, Your Majesty." The wind pulled at her elaborate hairstyle and she tried to pat it back in place.

"Clovadorska of Riverine, how do you know about these petrels and Weir traitors?"

"You don't even recognize the name, do you?" the woman asked the queen softly.

"No, I don't think that I've heard it before. Tell me, what is your connection?"

"The Pellish have been sending us messages for three moons, updating us on the armada's progress, so we can coordinate our timing."

Too late, Cerúlia realized her danger. Instinctively she took a half step back. She couldn't retreat far—the cliff fell away right behind her. Her right hand grabbed her dagger but the woman stood just too far away for a lunge.

Clovadorska hadn't been smoothing her hair; she'd pulled out something hidden within its high stack. She now brought this object (it was cylindrical, hollow black wood) up to her mouth.

"I've thought of you so often," she said, her voice now charged with repressed ferocity. "And you've never even heard of me! I want you to know my name. I am the widow of Captain Lurgn. Your mother was responsible for my husband's death."

As the woman raised her poison blowdart to her lips, Cerúlia dived to the ground and rolled. Since her would-be assassin could easily pivot to adjust her aim, this desperate movement would not have saved her life, but it bought the queen an extra half tick—and in that instant she heard a faint whoosh of air, a thud, and a cry. A bloody dagger point suddenly appeared, poking right out of Clovadorska's heart.

The woman collapsed to the ground, dropping her weapon.

When she fell, she revealed the person behind her who had just joined the gathering on the cliff top. It was Ciellō.

People rushed to the queen with exclamations and cries of fear, helped her to her feet, and dusted off her clothing. While she was so engaged she saw Ciellō retrieve his dagger, wipe off the blood on his victim's velvets, examine the blowdart, and toss it into the sea.

A little shaky on her feet, Cerúlia turned to him.

Ciellō sketched a bow, keeping a self-satisfied grin off his lips, though it sparkled in his eyes.

"Damselle, I hear there is trouble from invaders. Quick as the wind, I come. You see, your man Ciellō, he is invaluable."

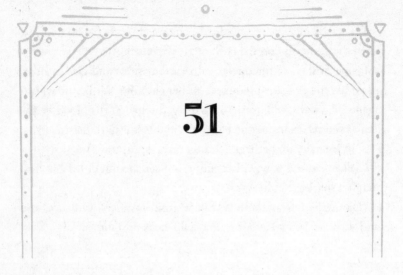

51

Cascada

Dust etched the lines of their faces by the time that Thalen and Wareth reached the palace's Arrival Gate, in the late morning, two days after the skirmish at Belcazar's estate.

They had pushed themselves hard, changing horses at inns along the route, snatching a few hours of shallow sleep while new mounts were readied, but traveling at night had slowed their progress. Thalen was hounded by apprehension over Cerúlia's safety and over what might be transpiring in Cascada.

Cici, cradled in front of Wareth, demonstrated an enviable ability to sleep in the saddle; Vaki, the larger hunting dog, loped most of the distance at their side, but to give him a break Thalen hoisted him up in front of himself; the dog had leaned back against his chest, slobbering into his cloak and providing a constant chorus of ragged pants into his ear.

Throughout this journey, as much as his fatigue and dread allowed, Thalen reviewed everything he had ever read about sea battles and assaults on harbor cities. Unfortunately, he found his internal library barely covered the field.

All in all, they made good time until the riders found that they no longer had the High Road to themselves. As they drew close to Cascada, first a carriage passed them, then two wagons, and then more carts. Within minutes their passageway was blocked by a procession of motley vehicles, all filled to the brim with women and children being borne away from the capital city.

Thalen shook his head at the familiar sight. Wareth led the way into the fields on the side of the road, out of the path of the refugees; this strategy worked well enough until they reached a major crossing of a second road coming in from the south. There the Raiders discovered squads of cavalry, carts carrying gear, and—in the distance—platoons of foot soldiers, all trying to head into the city just as civilians attempted to flee. Despite the soldiers' orders and curses and the civilians' protests and wails, both the road and its verge became so congested that no one could move.

"Wareth!" Thalen called.

"Keep your hat on. I see," Wareth yelled back. "Follow me." And he led their mounts across a harvested field, away from the crowds. Cutting cross-country posed little danger here, because it was not as if one could lose the capital city—the white towers of the palace glinted in the sun before them.

Once they reached the metropolis itself every street swarmed with people frantically loading carts or beasts with household goods, filling water bags at wells, or carrying dull implements to smithies to be sharpened. More than once Wareth chose a turning, only to decide against it and find another where their progress would be less impeded.

Finally, they cantered up Arrival Avenue. The metal barrier at the gate was closed. Four palace guardsmen, warily holding out pikes, halted the begrimed riders.

"State your business," said the officer on duty.

"I am Commander Thalen of Sutterdam. I need to see the queen urgently."

"Ah! I recognize you," said the officer. "And those dogs I would know anywhere. Herself is not in residence."

"Where is she?"

The guard hesitated, as if deciding whether or not to give Thalen this information.

"For Water's sake, Sergeant, that's the commander of the Raiders," burst out one of the guards. "Mebbe he can help."

"Shut up, you," the sergeant growled, then turned to the horsemen. "She's on top of SeaWidow Cliff—the cliff that overlooks the sea and the harbor. I'll send a soldier with you as guide. Expect security up there to be tight."

"Here, take this dog, will you? He's all in and needs tending," Thalen asked, and willing hands reached up to grab Vaki. Other soldiers reached for Cici. She snapped at the guards, missing their fingers by a pinch.

"Huh. Well, better just leave this one be," Wareth said.

A palace guard mounted a tethered horse. He carried a Weir flag on a pole, and this, the Raiders found, magically cleaved the way through the crowds on the street—everyone dashed to get out of their way. Soon their tired horses labored up a steep path near the harbor. Wareth silently pointed out that the path showed signs of recent heavy use: scores of hoofprints in both directions and a handful of the support beams knocked out of true.

Just below the crown of the hill, a thick ring of white-sashed guards barred their passage.

"Halt!" these soldiers commanded.

Their escort spoke to his comrades. "I'm bringing these two Raiders to the queen."

"I don't care if you're bringing the king of Agfador," said the sergeant. "My orders are that no one goes cliffside with a weapon. No one. Dismount so that we can pat you down."

"What's the reason for all this?" asked Thalen, complying, but with a stab of disquiet. "Has something happened?"

No one answered him. Thalen turned over his rapier and dagger, while Wareth did the same.

"You can leave your horses here; we'll take care of them. Everyone hikes the rest of the way."

Wareth gave the terrier a lift from the horse's saddle to the ground. Yipping excitedly, she ran ahead of them up the steep dirt path.

As they climbed the last paces to the top of the cliff, Thalen tried—pretty much in vain—to wipe the dust off his face and clothes and retie his hair in his hair leather.

When the path allowed him to see over the crest, Thalen discerned several groups of people clustered about—pages, maids, the queen's secretary, and the queen herself—standing near the edge, overlooking the ocean.

"Commander!" A male voice interrupted Thalen's wave of relief that she appeared uninjured.

"Fedak!" shouted Wareth. Fedak and Shield Pontole were standing guard, with weapons drawn, one on each side at the top of the path.

"Damn, it's good to see you," said Fedak. "We've been worried, Commander, about what was happening in Vittorine."

"There was a bit of a scrap," Thalen said, his mind and eyes elsewhere.

"But you're all right. And Wareth!!" Fedak shook Wareth's hands in two of his own.

"Easy on the fingers," Wareth said, wincing.

Thalen addressed the shield. "Your Captain Yanath was unscathed too. There were a few injuries—but let's not go into that now. Why this much security around the queen?"

"An assassination attempt," Shield Pontole answered. "Spoiled just in the nick by her personal bodyguard—see that man with the strange hair? That's Ciellō. I don't know where he's been the last few days, but he was always at her side before the festival, and by the grace of the Waters he appeared in time to kill the traitor who tried to kill the queen."

Alerted by the terrier pawing her skirts and the sound of their voices, Cerúlia turned in their direction. She wore her warm black cloak against the wind. Someone (it must have been Fedak) had given her a Raider black-and-white armband to use as a headband to keep the wind from blowing her hair in her face. Thalen wanted— he expected—her to come rushing into his arms, but she didn't; her face brightened and she took two steps forward, then halted.

"Commander!" she called.

Taking his cue from her formality, Thalen strode forward and bowed. "Your Majesty. I returned as soon as I uncovered that the visit was a trap to lure you out of town."

"Please rise. And my mother's councilor?"

"Belcazar was not actually a hostage, though a gang of Marauders were using him as bait. He's not on his deathbed either; he should live long enough to face your justice."

"Do you know who set the plot in motion?"

"The name I heard was 'Burgn.'"

"That makes sense." She looked at the man with braided hair who stood two steps behind her.

"Commander, three moons ago, I assassinated the head of the family—one of the key members of the coup against my mother, General Yurgn. I did not even consider that we needed to destroy all his kin. Burgn, his son, fled before we captured the general's manse, as did the widow of another son. That woman tried to kill me yesterday with a poison dart. I realize now that allowing the family to escape was a grave mistake. We should have followed and hunted them all down when we had a chance."

"Hatred can corrode a whole family," Thalen remarked, "and we all know about the desire for vengeance. But do not blame yourself; if letting them escape was an error, it is better to err on the side of thinking well of others. Should you have killed Marcot because of *his* father?"

"Of course not!" she answered, and some of the cloud on her face lifted. "Well. Through luck and skill I survived their plot—and so did you. Are you injured? Presently we must face a bigger threat: we are about to be invaded by an armada. My birds have confirmed this."

"Pellish ships?"

"Aye, but they transport Oro soldiers. This is not a raiding party. They bring an occupation force."

"In point of fact, I would hazard their goal is not to occupy Weirandale," said Thalen, "but to *sack* Cascada, to enact revenge for the Femturan Conflagration. And to put an end to the line of Nargis Queens, as we destroyed the Magi."

The bodyguard snorted through his nose.

"Ah. I don't believe the two of you have met," said Cerúlia. "Commander Thalen, for my voyage home from Wyeland, I hired a bodyguard. Ciellō of Zellia saved my life yesterday morning." She grinned. "He believes that no harm can come to me as long as he is nigh."

She turned to the man behind her. "Ciellō, I spent half a year with the Free States Raiders in Oromondo. The commander and I . . . grew close. Together Commander Thalen and I burned Femturan to the ground; that is actually how I sustained the injuries that brought me to Salubriton." She had been holding her cloak closed against the wind with her hands about chest-high; she let go of the fabric and interlaced her fingers together. "A few days ago, at Harvest Fest, we were reunited."

Almost overcome with gratitude to this man who had saved Cerúlia, Thalen moved forward to clasp his hand, but the Zellishman gave him a stiff but respectful half bow, so he followed in kind.

"Sir," said Thalen, "I—we—are forever in your debt."

"I didn't save the queen for you," said Ciellō.

"Of course not," said Thalen, drawing back half a step in bewilderment. "But I can be grateful just the same."

An uncomfortable silence fell. The bodyguard inclined his head in Thalen's direction.

"Well, Commander," said the queen, with a dismissive wave of her hand, "let's put General Yurgn's cursed family aside and consider our current quandary: the defense of the city."

She led Thalen to a plank of wood held up between two supports near the cliff edge. On it, weighted down with stones against the wind, sat a map of Cascada Harbor and the city.

Thalen shoved other worries to the side and turned his full attention to studying the map. Then he walked around the lighthouse as far as the path would take him to the south, surveying the harbor itself. He wheeled around and followed the path as far as it led to the north; then, he returned to the map table where Cerúlia stood, her shoulders hunched against the wind, her face tense with worry.

"As you've undoubtedly figured out, Your Majesty, you have an open harbor, with no defensive fortifications. Much too late to miss them now. And what are your plans?"

"I have summoned all the whales in the Bay of Cinda. Like birds, whales don't count, but as far as I can tell about thirty are swimming toward us now. However, most are smaller pilots, incapable of sinking a full-size ship. I believe I only have six blue whales and eight humpbacks. And three of those are juveniles, so their fighting power might be limited. In fact, their mothers will insist the calves stay out of the fray."

"Will they obey you?"

"I'm not certain. Today, the ones nearby"—she pointed out into the sea—"are more interested in singing different songs and new verses to me, but I hope that tomorrow they'll settle down to business."

"And you will have the whales . . . ?"

"Ram, strike with their tails, breach from underneath—anything they can do to stave in or upend the Pellish ships."

"Where will they accost them?"

Cerúlia pointed to an area outside of the harbor, deep enough for the biggest blue whale. "Once the invaders are inside the harbor area where we have some shoals, the whales would find it tricky to maneuver or build up speed."

Thalen picked up a quill and drew an oblong in the waters of the map. "This will be your first line of defense—the line of whales. Don't spend all your forces at once; keep a number in reserve for the battle's twists and turns.

"So, say they succeed in sinking some of the ships," Thalen thought aloud. "The Pellish sailors might be able to manage, but the Oros—especially if they don't get their breastplates off—they'll drown. Oros don't swim."

Cerúlia nodded. "The pilot whales are supposed to tip over any small boats carrying enemies. Our second major line of defense will be the ships that Seamaster Wilamara is readying. She is making a cordon of all the ships currently docked; we don't have very many, and most are just fishing boats. But we do have one war galley, *Queen Carra,* and Wilamara will put her most experienced seamaster, a veteran from the Green Isles, in command."

"Where will the cordon be?" Thalen asked.

Cerúlia drew a line on the map. "She's been keeping me up-to-date on which ship she plans to place where, but I don't understand the advantages or disadvantages. You'll confer with her?"

"If you like. And her ships will have archers?"

"Yes. With fire arrows."

"Right." Thalen nodded. "So let's think this through. Surely, the armada will send its warships first to shatter our defenses and keep its troop carriers in reserve. So if attackers escape the whales and others bull through the seamaster's cordon—then what?"

"Then they will dock in the harbor, and we will have to fight them on the quay. I've called in the Ice Pikemen and the Catamount Cavalry."

Thalen walked back to the harbor overlook again, and Wareth, who had been standing idly about nearby, joined him, pointing at the layout of the quay.

"They'd run into each other; it would be a fuckin' mess," Wareth said.

"Of course. I see it too." In a louder voice, he said to the queen, "No cavalry on the quay."

Thalen returned to the map table. "Besides, were I your enemy, once I saw that the harbor had a flotilla guarding it, I would flank it. I would send ships to dock north and south and march my troops in overland. Are you absolutely certain they haven't done so already?"

"The birds have reported no landings as of yet," said Cerúlia, "but I didn't think that they might try this once the battle starts."

"So, I would station your cavalry here and here, to protect your flanks," Thalen marked on the map, "depending upon where on the coastline the devils can pull close to shore. Can we get good information from locals who know about all possible landing sites?"

"I'm sure we can. And I can post birds to watch the coastline."

"Archery is going to be key here," Thalen said, studying the map. "Fortunately, we'll have plenty of high positions with cover and clean sight lines in the buildings that surround the harbor."

Cerúlia rested her hand on his forearm. Her touch was more than casual, but less than a caress.

"Do we have a chance?" she asked.

"You haven't told me: When will the fleet arrive?"

"Tomorrow. Midmorning is what we calculate."

Thalen repressed a wince at the time frame, but answered her truthfully. "Time is not on our side. But several things have already broken in our favor. Your enemies expect you to be dead; they hoped to catch us unawares; and they know nothing about your whales. So, yes, we have a chance."

"Thalen, will you assume command of my forces? I don't know my Weir officers, but even if I did, I'd rather entrust this to you."

Thalen wanted to object that he'd never commanded more than two dozen men (well, except for the Battle of Jutterdam—did that count?) and that he was a foreigner in her land. Why would her people follow him? But he could not deny that he had developed a talent for strategy. And he had the queen's trust. Besides, he had learned not to protest when responsibilities were thrust at him.

He sank down on one knee. "Your Majesty, I am yours to command."

Cerúlia looked around to all the retainers on the cliffside. "Commander Thalen is in charge. Pass the word that this is my direct order."

"Your Majesty, he should have an escort of flag bearers," called Shield Pontole from his position guarding the trailhead. "Then everyone will know who he is, see, and also it's easier for messengers to spot him."

"Thank you, Shield. You will see that this happens right away."

"May I requisition Fedak and Wareth from this cliff top?" Thalen asked Cerúlia. "I'll have need of them."

"Yes. With Ciellō and the dogs, I am as safe as I need to be. I will stay here; though it is a climb to send me messages, I find it easier to confer with the whales and the birds from this vantage."

"You'll stay here all night?" Thalen asked.

"Kiltti made me a pallet in the lighthouse last night. I slept a little. Tonight I will sleep"—she shrugged—"as much as I can sleep. I have slept rough before."

Thalen smiled at her reference to their past.

"One more order, Raider Wareth and Commander Thalen. Get your wounds"—their grimy bandages apparently had not escaped her notice—"looked at by a healer before you do anything else. You're no good to Cascada if you fever. Food and sleep too, as soon as you can.

"Not that I care about you two; no, not at all." Her lips formed a teasing smile, and light crept back into her eyes. "But because your judgment will be impaired if you don't."

"Of course." Thalen whirled around. "With your permission . . ." He was already in motion, already planning the agenda of his conference with the seamasters and the captains of the cavalry and pikemen. Already desperately wishing he had Kran by his side to supervise the building of barricades, and Captain Yanath's advice.

As he hurried down the slope toward their weapons and horses, flanked by Wareth and Fedak, Thalen realized that he'd neither kissed her nor said goodbye. He paused, wanting to run back, and then redoubled his pace downhill. Focusing on the battle ahead was the best way to contribute to her safety.

And if he was the one to perish?

Well, at least he had known love.

52

The massive Pellish fleet with its black sails approached the perfect half moon of Cascada Harbor on a chill day in autumn. The wind stretched their sheets taut, and with the tide also in their favor, the ships flew forward. Those observers perched on SeaWidow Cliff spotted the tops of the first masts in early morning, and as they kept watching, mouths agape, more and more sails rose above the horizon, arrayed in a chevron.

Since this was the first time ever that an enemy fleet had threatened this peaceful harbor, the scene would have made a stirring composition for one of Stahlia's tapestries, if she had been standing on SeaWidow Cliff to sketch it. She was not there. Although she and Percia had refused to flee the capital (no matter how much Marcot implored them), they also had no place amongst the combatants. With great reluctance, Marcot left them in West Cottage, with only Lemle as an inadequate guardian. Stahlia occupied herself by working on "Cerúlia and the Catamounts" while singing "The Lay of Queen Callindra"; Lemle set aside his late uncle's sword and joined Percia in starting to prepare a celebratory feast, hoping that their confidence would demonstrate to Nargis how much they trusted the Spirit to shelter the realm.

* * *

On *Pexlia's Passion,* a troop ship, General Sumroth finished one more letter to Zea and tucked it into the chest in his cabin. This long voyage had kept him away from her for too long: in order to maintain secrecy and to stop for water and provisions at less-populated ports, they had sailed around the west side of the continent and up the Ribbon, thus totally bypassing the Free States and the Green Isles.

The general strode on deck to watch the shore of Weirandale as the ships neared. With his spyglass Sumroth could see the Ice held aloft by the Nargis Fountain. But Oro Protectors would not be deterred by a pretty piece of frozen water.

Admiral Hixario had determined the order of attack. The six war galleys, each with sixty oars on a side, would strike first to establish a beachhead. Hixario spoke glowingly about the fighting skills of his oarsmen; these were freemen, well paid with Oro gold. The fleet also used galley slaves to row, but since slaves could not be counted on in a battle, they kept these in the cargo and troop transport ships in the rear, closely supervised by guards.

The Pellish admiral, a veteran of the War for the Green Isles, had high hopes for the new weapons mounted on the front of his galleys—weapons not available during the contest against the Allies more than a decade earlier. The "striker" resembled an enormous crossbow; when cranked to tension it sent a spear-like missile with such force that its steel-tipped point could punch through a hull. The Pellish also had a slingshot device designed by Smithy (in which Sumroth placed more faith). The Pellish named this "the lobber." What made the lobber uniquely deadly was not its design but its ammunition, also fabricated to Smithy's instruction: earthenware balls, which would shatter on impact, filled with white phosphorus.

Sumroth's soldiers had grumbled over the tedious task of collecting aurochs urine, then distilling and drying the residue; but the powder that remained glowed white when exposed to air. Sumroth had seen a demonstration of its usefulness as a weapon; on contact, phosphorus would eat through the wood of a barn or straight through the body of an aurochs. The Pellish mariners were wary of using the lobber, however, because if winds blew the white cloud back at them, they could suffer terrible burns.

After Hixario and his sailors cleared the harbor of defenses, Sumroth would send his troops ashore in "swifts"—shallow, twelve-oar-to-a-side transport boats. If events transpired according to plan, the Witch Queen would already be dead at that point, which would be a pity, since Sumroth would like to kill her personally. He reminded himself that those seabirds the Pellish used, those petrels, had not relayed messages that the assassination attempts had succeeded, so he might still have an opportunity to dispatch her with his own hands. Either way, the general intended to take her scalp of blue hair back to Femturan to show his people that he had wrought their vengeance and lifted the destructive blights.

Vengeance would also win Sumroth the indisputable right to govern. He would lead his people back into the Land and have himself declared king. On the long voyage, he drew in the margins of his letters little sketches of crowns with gold-and-ruby flames. Mayhap Smithy would forge one.

And to make up for his long absence, he would cut a lock of the blue hair and have it fashioned into a ring for Queen Zea.

From her perch on SeaWidow Cliff, Cerúlia sent her last instructions to the whales. A large blue bull had appointed himself Leader of the Pods. The queen had no choice but to leave the timing and targets to him. In return for their assistance, she promised to have a song composed about the whales' heroic deeds today. Many tedious hours were wasted as the whales argued about how the song should start; they ultimately decided on:

Smash them, crash them,
Drop them in the Sea!
Foes of Nargis
Are foes of We.

Cerúlia spared a moment to glance around at her hilltop retinue. Shield Pontole and Shield Gatana stood as sentries at the spot where the narrow path crested the cliff edge. The queen had learned her lesson from yesterday, when she had not had her canine corps protecting her; all six dogs attended her today. The deerhounds and Vaki patrolled the hillside, continually on alert for intruders, while Whaki sat near the edge of the drop-off and Cici slept curled in a ball inside the lighthouse where it was warmer. Darzner stood, quills at the ready, at the map and message table; Ciellō shadowed Cerúlia's movements, always a pace behind her, scanning everyone and everything, only rarely looking out to sea. Kiltti tended a fire in the shelter of the lighthouse, trying to keep a kettle of coffee warm.

Due to her ability to use birds, the queen didn't need any messengers, but six horses—one for each person on the cliff top, saddled and at the ready—bunched together for warmth as far away as they could get from the cliff edge.

The wind blew fiercely, ruffling the short grasses, making her cloak billow around her, and pushing Whaki's ears straight behind him as if he were the figurehead of a vessel named SeaWidow Cliff.

Seamaster Wilamara had given her longtime colleague, Seamaster Gourdo, the command of the *Queen Carra,* the only Weir war galley currently berthed in Cascada Harbor, crewed by fifty oars on a side and gleaming with blue-and-silver paint. Gourdo was no longer spry, because his captivity in a Weir jail had drained away the last of his youth, but he was seasoned and valiant. Wilamara tucked two other fighting ships—thirty-oar-per-side galliots—temporarily out of sight:

one hidden between wharfs and the other maintaining its position in the lee of a merchant ship. She herself set up her command station, complete with flagmen and a trumpeter, on the largest fishing boat available, named by its owner *The Big Catch*. The owner had a younger brother who'd named his own fishing boat *The Little Catch*. If their plans worked, *The Little Catch* would serve as a decoy, leading a Pellish war galley aground on the shoal close to the mouth of the harbor.

In addition to the three fighting ships, she had three passenger/ merchant cogs and seven sizeable fishing boats at her disposal— that is, if one didn't count all the tiny rowboats that dotted Cascada Harbor. Commander Thalen had asked her what she planned to do with those; she kept twenty of the sturdiest and best-crewed as lifeboats to rescue any of her sailors. He said he had a plan for the rest, so she turned the others over to him for whatever he had in mind.

Her trumpeter was staring off into space as she strode the deck. Wilamara kicked his boot.

"Look alive," she said.

"Yes, ma'am," he answered.

Nithanil and Mikil stood at the helm of the trailing ship of the Pellish armada, *Pexlia's Possession,* scanning ahead. Iluka sat comfortably on a large coiled-up rope, darning a sock to give herself something useful to do.

As his fingernails dug at his itchy skin, Nithanil, standing near the wheel, muttered, "Lautan. What's a few cross words between old comrades? That was a mighty storm you threw at me. I have given my son to serve you; I would happily trade my own life if you see fit to help Cressa's daughter."

At the same time, Mikil stared into the gray-green depths at the ship's stern, praying and pouring in a libation of wine. *Lautan the Munificent, you have helped the Nargis Heir before. You brought us here, to this battle; you must have a plan for us. I will just rest in faith.*

* * *

Nana sat on the ledge of the Fountain in the Courtyard of the Star. Probably she should have stayed out of the way in her little room in the palace, but she hadn't wanted to wait through this ordeal alone. Her friends in the kitchens were in a frenzy, baking loaves stuffed with meats and cheeses; Hiccuth had lent his services to a cavalry troop north of Cascada; Cerúlia and her retinue stood on SeaWidow Cliff; and staying behind, alone and in suspense, was intolerable.

All around her, people bustled with frantic energy, since the courtyard—as a universally known, large open area in the middle of the city—had become a rendezvous point for troops, supplies, and healers. Across the way from where she currently sat, Councilors Alix, Nishtari, and Fornquit had set a canopy up over a table they used as a rally point. The councilors tried to cope with the myriad of concerns that city dwellers pressed upon them, such as last-minute evacuations or an outbreak of looting of abandoned businesses. Several people holding wailing children congregated in front of the table, arguing frantically. Nana worried whether the orphans that she had often fed had found a way to leave the city.

Brother Whitsury weaved his way through columns of foot soldiers and archers moving in diverse directions and sat beside her.

"How are you?" he asked.

Nana shrugged. "I'm too old for this, Whitsury. I was already old when assassins invaded the palace, I was old when my darling perished, and I was old when Cerúlia returned. I'm tired, Whit; I'm burned down to the fag end of a candle. I can't face more trouble, more death."

"I understand," said Brother Whitsury in his sympathetic manner, though, wise as he was in the ways of sorrow, even he couldn't comprehend Nana's burden, because he didn't know she served as Nargis's Agent.

"We'll just sit quietly here, shall we?" he said. "Look, I brought a cup and snagged a loaf of bread. We'll sit and sip Nargis Water and say the five prayers. Like the old friends we are. And soon enough this day, and whatever it will bring, will pass overhead. And then, together, we'll face whatever tomorrow may bring."

Destra, Fate's Spinner, was trapped leagues away from the crisis in Belcazar's estate, supervising the care of the shields and Raiders wounded in the attack by Matwyck's Marauders. She wished she had rushed back to Cascada with Thalen a few days ago; she chafed at being sidelined and helpless.

Sitting alone at the long table, she finished her cup of tisane. Idly, she stared at the ring of leaves clinging around the bottom of the cup. In the pattern, all at once she *saw* a scene from far away—not a detailed picture as in Saulė's mirror, but an outline of forms and volumes. Dark-sailed ships and pikemen clashed with riders and archers. A battle about to crash against the shore, with death reaping an abundant harvest.

If she were on the scene in Cascada, could she use her talent at negotiation to forestall this calamity?

Well, she wasn't there to try. So instead, Destra attempted to persuade Mìngyùn to become involved in this conflict.

You abandoned the people of Iga when you found them too petty and grasping to be worthy of your favor, she argued. *Hasn't the Free Staters' selflessness throughout the Occupation caused you to reevaluate their worth? Did you not see Thalen—one of your people—spare the life of the wretched old man who lured him into an ambush? Wasn't that nobly done?*

Hush, Spinner. Your human affections are just noise, signifying nothing. I have not decided. I will watch how the day unfolds.

Thalen had learned from Duke Naven that the cavalry and foot had been under General Yurgn's influence and the new government had not yet made it a priority to test their loyalty or skills. When he met with their officers in the common room of a seaside tavern last night, he asked basic questions about their training, equipment, and numbers, but he found it impossible to evaluate either the leaders or the soldiers on such rushed acquaintance.

Uncertain about the competence of the leaders of the Catamount Cavalry, he sent Wareth to the north of the city with a company of one hundred and fifty riders; Fedak to the south with another group; and kept a third, under Marcot's command, in reserve, ready to ride in either direction should Cerúlia's birds bring news that the enemy was attempting to flank the harbor.

With his whole heart, Thalen longed for Mellie archers. He didn't know the skills or nerves of the three hundred Weir bowmen, wielding an assortment of bows, that had been turned over to him. He would swap the whole lot of them for Eldie, Eli-anna, Telbein, Eldo, and a few more of their kin. Still, he placed the men and women strategically in buildings and on rooftops overlooking the quay. The Oros, he surmised, would not have archers in their ranks, but what about their Pellish allies?

"This is madness," he complained to Duke Naven, who kept dogging his heels. "I don't know these soldiers or their capabilities, and the queen doesn't completely trust her own troops. How can I lead them into battle? I'm fighting with one hand tied behind my back."

"Look," said the duke, "we're all doing things we've never done before. I guarantee that none of these soldiers has ever defended Cascada before. I'll wager you can trust them to do their best. Put your trust in them, and they'll put their trust in you."

Captain Athelbern, the head of the palace guard (who admitted he'd never swung a sword outside of the practice yard, but who appeared levelheaded and organized), came to Thalen, begging to be useful. Thalen put him in charge of citizens who were also eager to lend their mite. Athelbern instructed them to build barricades to block the major avenues that led into the city proper; though Thalen hoped that the Oros would never penetrate that far off the quay, if they did, he needed to slow them down and keep them from scattering or hiding.

Chamberlain Vilkit removed a major worry by taking over the task of supplying victuals and water to the troops who massed in carefully positioned squads.

The hours had been so busy that Thalen couldn't recall who had brought him the Weir hat. Someone had borrowed (or stolen) the hat of a previous consort for him to wear. It was black with tall feathers dyed cerulean blue, obviously designed to help soldiers spot him from a distance. Thalen settled it on his head, pleased that it fit well enough and that it had a tie in the back to keep it from being blown off.

The Harbormaster Hut was centrally located on the quay, and it had good sight lines of the whole area. Thalen decided to make it his command post, flying flags that symbolized headquarters. He had men pile crates behind the building so he could get to the roof for an even better view of the action. Tilim and other messenger girls and boys, mounted on good horses, waited near at hand.

The commander reminded himself to send Cerúlia's brother on an errand removed from the fray as soon as fighting engaged. He might not be able to save the city; he might even fail at defending her; but he should be able to keep alive one boy on a good horse.

The wind, the current, and Pellish oars combined to carry the ships toward them at frightening speed. With her naked eye Cerúlia could now discern thousands of Oro soldiers arrayed on the decks; clear autumn light sparkled off their armor. The Oros banged their metal gauntlets against their breastplates, making a rhythmic clank that echoed off the quay's stone buildings and the cliff that rose on the north side.

Cerúlia muttered, "So many! How did they get so many vessels?"

Ciellō cursed under his breath. "They bought half a dozen from the Zellish. See the ones with the figureheads of Ghibli, with the long feathers sweeping down their prows? How much coin did ship merchants of my country rake in selling our ships to those heathens?"

He snorted with anger, but he counted out loud to Darzner, "Six war galleys, five galliots, fourteen troop carriers, and three cargo ships. And so many swifts, at least three dozen."

"What's a swift?" asked Darzner.

"It's a shallow boat, a landing craft. It has twelve oars per side. It is used to transport troops between ships or to beach them."

Darzner wrote these figures down and slipped the paper into a leather holder. The queen tied the holder to the leg of a seagull.

Take this first to the Harbormaster Hut, and then to the fishing boat flying blue flags, she instructed her avian messenger.

Still well outside the harbor, the invaders rearranged themselves so that the six war galleys pulled into a line in front of the other ships. They brought down their sails so that they had more precise control over their movement. Their flags—the Pellish Crossed Oars and the Oro Fire Mountains—whipped on their masts.

Without fanfare or signal, the Battle of Cascada Harbor began when the blue whale, the Leader of the Pods, swam underneath one of the Pellish war galleys and then breached, lifting the port side of the ship completely out of the water. Pellish oarsmen tumbled about like skittles, all losing their oars and two dozen falling overboard.

A tick later, three humpbacks converged on a second war galley, ramming it from opposite sides. The shallow keel cracked with a report that could be heard across the water. While the sailors on the first ship scrambled to recover, the second was a lost cause—it was already sinking.

The whales, singing *"Smash 'em, crash 'em"* to one another, turned their attention to a third war galley. Noting what had happened to their comrades, these mariners had moments to prepare. Their oars could not outrun the whales, who could, if necessary, put on bursts of speed twice as fast as the ships, but the sailors could fight back with their weapons. With their striker they fired one bolt after another, missing their targets, who streaked by underwater. A blue jostled them and then threw two-thirds of his body out of the water, hoisting his enormous weight on the stern end, upending the galley so that its prow lifted nearly vertical. Most of the Pellish sailors tumbled into the sea, and those who managed to hold on were knocked senseless or broke bones in the overwhelming crash that ensued when the ship slammed back into the surface of the water.

However, while the whales concentrated on attacking the third galley, the fourth ship, *Pexlia's Power,* maneuvered neatly and came up behind them unnoticed. A striker bolt hit a blue whale near its eye, turning the sea black with its blood.

Cerúlia heard the animal's cry of pain and distress. She realized that the other whales had lost their focus.

Oh! How terrible. But no! Don't retreat. You should get angry! Attack the next ship!

The first galley, *Pexlia's Pride,* which had not sustained a devastating blow, had by now, even with only a partial crew, pulled into waters too shallow for the whales, as had the fourth. Galleys five and six rowed toward the shore in tandem, almost out of the big creatures' territory. The whales attacked, but without coordination; so their random bumps splintered wood but sank neither.

When the Leader of the Pods next breached, the Pellish sailors peering into the clear water had anticipated his location well; they hit him with a grenado volleyed by the lobber. The explosion of trails of white smoke looked strange and frightening from SeaWidow Cliff, but this appearance didn't accurately convey the degree of pain the missile inflicted. As the whale's agony assailed Cerúlia through her connection to his mind, she closed her eyes, covered her ears, crouched, and shrunk in on herself.

A small cloud of the smoke blew forward, threatening to blind a score of the Pellish sailors who rowed on the starboard side—the men leapt off the galley to hide and wash in seawater, and the ship circled back around to pick them up.

In horror and disarray, the blues and humpbacks retreated eastward, deeper into the Bay of Cinda, and broke off communication with the queen. Cerúlia still felt a connection to the more numerous, but smaller, pilot whales. When Kiltti helped her rise, she began to cajole these allies, urging them to stay in the battle.

Seamaster Gourdo ordered *Queen Carra*'s rowers to aim straight into the first war galley that entered the harbor. The Pellish sailors had not recovered enough oars to maneuver out of the way, and with a shuddering crash *Queen Carra*'s ram penetrated deep into the flank of the Pellish ship, ripping it asunder. Instead of boarding this injured vessel, Gourdo ordered, "Reverse!" and the rowers tried to disentangle themselves from the debris to get in position for the next galley—the uninjured fourth ship, *Pexlia's Power,* which came flying at them at the speed of one hundred and twenty oars.

The *Power* hit *Queen Carra* before the latter could completely straighten out; thus the Pellish ram—a wicked hook—smashed through *Queen Carra*'s side, disabling the Weir ship. Grappling hooks flew in both directions as Weir and Pellish sailors abandoned their oars for hand-to-hand combat on canted, wet decks washed by waves. Gourdo, sword in hand, headed for the man wearing the seamaster's uniform. He blocked a cutlass swing from a sailor and, leaping onto a bench, stabbed the next Pellishman in the torso. But as he tried to jump to the next bench, he slipped and fell.

"Captain!" one of his sailors cried.

The Weir mariners couldn't cut their way to his side in time. Pellish cutlasses rained down on Gourdo.

Meanwhile, two Weir fishing boats set their tillers to collide with the slower, damaged, fifth Pellish war galley. At the last moment, the Weir seamasters lit the oil-soaked straw they had piled everywhere. Their crafts burst into flames while the sailors dived for the seawater, leaving the burning torpedoes to collide with the enemy.

The Little Catch presented itself to the sixth war galley as easy prey. The Pellish seamaster took the bait, adjusting his course to ram the small, ignominious craft, which now fled before his might. *The Little Catch* had been chosen for this "broken-wing snare" because it had a particularly shallow draft. It skimmed over the rocks of the shoal, leading the war galley on until—with a harrowing grinding noise—the highest peaks of the underwater rocks ripped the galley's keel to shreds.

In revenge, the Pellish sent a grenado at *The Little Catch,* and it burst into a cloud of white smoke.

Yet, when the Pellish sailors of the run-aground galley tried to evacuate into the swifts that converged close by, pilot whales upended the shallow craft. In fury the Pellish sailors swung their oars at the pilots, but these blows hit wave tops instead of the whales, who, chortling, ducked down at the last instant.

From her lookout point, Cerúlia saw three smaller Pellish fighting ships—"galliots" with only twenty oarsmen on a side—and three troop carriers break course and turn north, paralleling the coastline. She realized that this contingent was attempting to flank the main attack. She tied a warning note to the foot of a hawk, sent the bird to the northern contingent of cavalry, and ordered a flock of gulls to shadow their movements closely.

When she turned back to the battle before her, she saw that *Queen*

Carra had sunk, and the oarsmen of *Pexlia's Power* had regained their places. Two Weir craft—a fishing boat and a merchant ship—tried to throw themselves in its path, raining arrows down on the rowers from their vantage point on higher decks.

The first civilian vessel took mortal blows when the Pellish penetrated its hull several times with bolts from a striker.

The second had its prow sheared away by the Pellish ram.

Nothing now prevented that galley from reaching the quay.

Smoke from burning ships made the scene below the queen more chaotic and difficult to comprehend. Cerúlia thought she spotted Weir rowboats plucking countrymen out of the water.

Despite the Weirs' brave efforts, one war galley, two galliots, and thirteen troop carriers still menaced the city. The queen desperately hoped that Seamaster Wilamara had more tricks up her sleeve, but she turned her own thoughts back to the whales to see if she could rally them to the cause.

"Fuck!" said Wilamara to her longtime trumpeter, when she saw that none of her efforts would halt *Pexlia's Power.*

"Yes, ma'am," said the trumpeter, an unexcitable man.

"Well, Commander Thalen, you'll have to deal with this one," she said aloud, shaking off the galley as just a distraction.

Wilamara focused on the two enemy galliots that now skimmed the waves into the harbor, and the large, if less maneuverable, troop carriers behind them. She had kept her two galliots hidden in reserve; now she had her trumpeter call them into the fray. From opposite sides of the harbor each one engaged with an enemy vessel of similar size: grappling hooks arched in both directions. Hand-to-hand battles raged across their decks; oarsmen were pushed overboard or perished from stab wounds. Wilamara strained to discern who had the upper hand. One conflict might be going the way of the Weirs, but the Pellish decidedly had the upper hand on the second mess of smashed timber bobbing precariously up and down on the waves.

The entangled galliots were inside the arms of the harbor, but the troop carriers hovered just outside when the queen succeeded in persuading the humpbacks to rejoin the battle. The humpbacks pounded one of the troop ships repeatedly, determined to break holes in its keel. People aboard threw casks or weapons down on the whales, but these just made the humpbacks more determined.

"Yes!" shouted Wilamara, hitting her fist into her other palm as she saw wooden beams on at least one vessel stave in.

"Indeed, ma'am," said her trumpeter.

From the deck of the cargo ship *Pexlia's Possession,* lagging a bit behind the other vessels, Mikil watched the beginning moves of the battle with anxiety.

"Sire, we must act—now!" Mikil urged.

"Hold your piss, boy! Haven't you noticed that I've closed the distance?"

Nithanil had been catching the wind and issuing fussy orders to the teams of long oars so as to pull ever closer to the other cargo ship that lingered behind warships.

Wearing the uniforms of the Pellish sailors they had captured, smiling, waving, and miming the need to converse, the Lorthers brought their ship alongside the other cargo vessel—lettering named it *Pexlia's Plentitude*—which, like theirs, had twelve, three-person oars on a side. The *Plentitude*'s crew stowed their oars and let the *Possession* approach without suspicion.

Without suspicion, at least, until the Lorthers threw their grappling hooks over the *Plentitude*'s railing and gave a synchronized, mighty heave as their own oars—with one more half stroke—rammed their ship into the side of their enemy's vessel with a bone-jarring *ka-thump.*

Mikil was the first to jump over the water churning between the ships, his sword already drawn from its scabbard, the Lorther sailors following his lead. The stunned Pellish mariners did not have time to grab their bows while Lorther archers rained arrows wherever they could be assured of not striking their own men; indeed, the Pellish barely had a chance to reach for their cutlasses. Mikil managed to be everywhere, slashing as if this was his one chance to make up for all his mistakes and take vengeance for all the Lorthers killed by the Magi a decade ago. Men fell before his sword, if not quite like grass before a scythe, then at least like reeds before a knife—resisting, but in the end being hacked down.

Ultimately, Mikil's trail of blood came to a halt when a desperate Pellish rower smacked him in the head with a bucket.

By then the Pellish remaining alive had surrendered. Nithanil crossed over a gangplank to *Pexlia's Plentitude,* where the cries of his men brought him to Mikil's side. Nithanil stared at his son lying prostrate. "Water!" he ordered, kneeling beside Mikil, his lips moving in an unvoiced prayer. He waited with his hands reaching upward until a Lorther passed him a full bucket of seawater. He doused his son's unconscious form: first a small splash, and then a deluge of all the liquid that remained. After a wait that seemed forever, Mikil opened his eyes, stirred to wipe his face, and groaned.

Satisfied that his son still lived, Nithanil stood tall. He looked around at their captives. With a flourish, he removed his hat, displaying his gray braid to the Pellish crew, who couldn't fathom why one of their "own" crews had attacked them.

"Not exactly what you expected, eh? We been right there on your aft starboard for nearly a week, and you shitwits never noticed."

Nithanil didn't need to crow over his ruse more than once. "All right, now," he said to a captured mate. "We found some surprises on board that ship yonder. Not just the usual shipboard fare. *You* got any surprises in store here?"

Unlike their captured cargo ship, the *Plentitude* was not ferrying casks of hemlock juice. But just belowdecks it did have several large barrels tightly lashed to the side of the hull. When sailors took off their tops, the Lorthers discovered earthenware balls floating in water.

"What are these?" Nithanil asked the Pellish mate.

"Those are grenadoes for the lobber," he answered, looking uneasy when Nithanil picked one up.

Noise and rustle made Nithanil look toward the ladder. Mikil came to join them, his clothes dripping with water turned lightly pink from all the Pellish blood that had sprayed on him.

"Explain," his son said to the mate.

"Very dangerous things, those grenadoes—if that gets hot or you drop it, we're all dead. The war galleys have this big slingshot," the mate said, miming the motion with his two hands, "that hurls these grenadoes. They break open, and the stuff inside them burns through flesh and wood. Burns a man's eyes or his lungs. We keep these extras here, out of the way of accidents."

Mikil said, "Sire, let me feel how heavy they are." Nithanil passed him the ball; carefully, Mikil held it in two hands, judging its weight. "Too heavy for birds," he pronounced, disappointed.

Nithanil and Mikil climbed back topside; Mikil swayed on one of the ladder steps, but his father put his hand out and steadied him. Nithanil appraised Mikil's eyes and color; he figured he'd do well enough in fresh air.

"Now what, Sire?" Mikil asked Nithanil as they both squinted into the confused smoke and battle raging in front of them.

"Now . . ." Nithanil scratched the itchy beard rash on his neck. "Now, you take this sow—she's damaged but she'll stay afloat—and I'll take the one with my old biddy on it, and we'll move up behind that last troop carrier there, from port and starboard, with fire arrows. Now that we have two, we can close on her from both directions."

"Aye, aye, Captain," said Mikil.

"Son, time to run up the Trident flag. Strike fear into those sons of bitches."

"Aye, Captain." Mikil smiled grimly. "The Lorthers have arrived."

Sumroth could do nothing to affect the naval battle, and he had given his orders to the fifth- and sixth-flamers on each ship long ago. So instead of focusing on which vessel was sunk or saved, he used his spyglass to survey the harbor defenders. He paused over the Harbormaster Hut, noting its flags. He considered all of the taller and more substantial buildings behind the quay area, but he didn't find what he sought.

If she still lives, she will be close by.

A rush of seagulls flying together caught his eye, and he followed them with his glass as they landed on the top of the cliff that loomed north of the harbor. People stood there. People in Weir uniforms. He took the glass down from his face and tried again to focus it.

Ah! Blue hair!

It was impossible for him to judge whether this was the same girl he had captured after the Battle of Iron Valley—he couldn't distinguish features well enough. But the blue hair was unmistakable. Sumroth was overjoyed that she had escaped all the earlier assassination attempts. He pumped his fist in the air and almost crowed with delight.

Thalen saw *Pexlia's Power* pause just outside of Weir bow range in the waters lapping against the quay, its oars holding its position. The Pellish sailors rearranged themselves—only half the men now manned oars, while others readied crossbows and fussed with their munitions in the prow. Were they planning to send those balls of white devilment into the quay to burn or panic Thalen's forces?

The commander motioned to his trumpeter, who blew the predetermined cadence.

At the signal, the Weir archers Thalen had entrusted with the difficult task of lying still all morning in the casually arrayed and anchored rowboats threw off the tarps or sacking that disguised them, lit their prepared fire arrows, aimed, and let them fly at *Pexlia's Power*. Many flew wide, the archers' aim disturbed by their boats' rocking surface or their nerves, but several hit various parts of the enemy ship. The water-soaked wood did not immediately catch fire, but the Pellish sailors had to stop their preparations to fight the flames, and while they worked to extinguish those threats more and more fire arrows hit the vessel.

Then one of the Pellish sailors shouted something Thalen couldn't hear, and men started diving off the vessel.

"They're afraid that their grenadoes will rupture in the fire," Naven commented with more insight than Thalen would have credited the man.

Ultimately, *Pexlia's Power* didn't flame over—the water-soaked wood wouldn't catch no matter how many times the archers' burning bolts struck it. But Thalen didn't care, because now he had its crew weaponless and swimming for their lives.

He watched through his spyglass, discovering the Pellish were strong swimmers. A group of six swam in tandem to the closest rowboat. They massed on one side, rocked the craft a few times, and then with a mighty effort overturned it, sending the Weir archer into the water. Thalen saw several arms holding daggers reach up above the surface. Then the Pellish sailors flipped the boat back right-side up, climbed in one by one, and thus repurposed it as their own lifeboat.

Thalen couldn't help but admire their teamwork and skill. Luckily, several of his Weir archers in nearby rowboats drew closer and began peppering the enemy craft with arrows. And all over the harbor, the men and women who had waited all morning for their part of the battle pursued swimmers; a few, the more humane ones, rescued captives, but most—rendered cruel by their fear—clubbed wildly with their oars until their enemies sank under the water.

Looking up to survey the whole field of battle, Thalen realized that although the whales and Wilamara's ad hoc navy had performed nobly, all they had actually accomplished was to blunt the threat from Pellish sailors. The bigger menace—the Oro troop ships—now bore down upon the defenders, and he had no more surprise tactics left.

53

The troop ships, stretched in one formidable line, entered Cascada Harbor in a simultaneous onslaught.

They didn't, however, make even progress toward the quay. The water now was full of obstacles—principally the smashed or burning carcasses of other ships—which the seamasters had to navigate around with care. The vessel the humpbacks had bashed began to take on water and sink. And the sails of another ship, originally in the rear of the pack, burst into flames—flames that in this case, since the high deck was drier and easier to light, spread.

The Weir merchant ships that had been pressed into service put themselves in the way of the invaders. Sailors loosed arrows down from the rigging, but the Pellish vessels returned fire with their big striker, puncturing their hulls. As the Weir sailors rushed to man their pumps, the troop ships brushed past them.

"Time to go," Wilamara ordered her trumpeter.

"Yes, ma'am," he said. He jumped feetfirst, holding his trumpet high above his head, and she felt relieved at the sight of a lifeboat heading for the glint of his metal instrument. Then she aimed *The Big Catch* at one of the troop ships and dashed around the boat, lighting the piles of oil-soaked straw. She waited to see these piles burst into flames; then, coughing, she climbed up on the side and dived into the water.

But her sacrifice was for naught; the fishing boat got caught up on a Pellish ram sticking out of the water like the long finger of a corpse. *The Big Catch* burned itself out without harming any of the incoming vessels.

Thus, nine troop ships—carrying, Thalen quickly calculated, at least three thousand Oro soldiers—used their long oars to weave around all obstacles, set their anchors, and began disgorging their men into swifts.

Although this process took nearly an hour, Thalen watched it unfold helplessly, knowing that nothing he could do would forestall the coming landings. Through a spyglass he examined the Oros; for this battle they wore nearly full armor; they'd covered their heads, chests, backs, and shoulders. For mobility they left their arms and legs free, but he saw that once they settled in the flat swifts, they strapped on thigh protectors and pulled on their gauntlets.

The Oros' allies, the Pellish, wore no armor. But they wore something worse—bows and full quivers. Each swift was protected by a brace of Pellish archers who sat forward with bows of yew.

"Tilim!" The name came out of Thalen's throat more forcefully than he intended. He swallowed to regain control of his voice. "Ride to the cliff and tell Her Majesty that I sent Marcot's cavalry north to bolster Wareth's company. I'd like a report from her birds when they engage the Oros to help me decide where to commit the last of the cavalry. I've pulled them closer in, so they can go in any direction."

Duke Naven returned from a last tour of the Weir positions.

"How are the archers and foot holding up?" Thalen asked.

"Nervous," said the duke. "But ready. And I found a warehouse for captives. And the navy has been plucking a lot of their men from the water, and Alix has set up a healers' area back that way for their hurts." He continued, as if reassuring himself, "I'm sure they'll pull

out Wilamara. Did you see that dive? Forty years on that woman
if she's a day, and she arched out into the water like a porpoise. I'm
sure she's all right."

Thalen was not listening; he was measuring the distance to when
the landing craft would be in range. "Here they come," he said. He
ordered his nearby trumpeter, "Sound 'Fire at will.'" The notes, repeated five times, echoed. The Weir archers rose from where they
lay, concealed in buildings and on rooftops, and fired volley after
volley at the approaching craft. Where their arrows hit the wood
of the swifts, they penetrated and vibrated, but most of those that
struck the Oros bounced off of their armor without causing significant injury. Thalen cursed softly, wishing for Mellie archers capable
of hitting those elusive flashes of skin, or even for repeating crossbows that could punch through the steel.

The Pellish archers in the swifts returned fire, forcing the Weir
bowmen to duck down and take cover.

"Shoot the archers, you damn idiots!" Thalen shouted, and soon
enough his archers figured this out for themselves. Many of the Pellish guardians were killed or wounded.

Thalen ordered his force to continue the barrage of archery as
the swifts began beaching or tying up; he hoped that as the Oros
disgorged, his bowmen would be able to aim at unprotected areas.
Perhaps a few dozen more enemy took hurts, but not enough to
make a difference.

Timing was crucial. "Now!" Thalen ordered. "Call out the infantry!" The trumpeter blew the signals to cease archery and un-
leash the foot soldiers that had waited, massed in squads of twenty
in the shelter of the quay buildings, out of sight of any Pellish archers. Like their antagonists, Weir pikemen wore a breastplate and
helm; they wielded halberds, and their officers had swords.

The Weirs came running out, shouting, eager to engage. No one
could have hoped for more spirit and bravery. They hacked at men
caught between the landing craft and solid footing, killing them,

maiming them, and pushing them back into the water. But while they clustered around one craft, other swifts landed, unimpeded. And whenever the Oros were able to gain the surface of the quay securely and then engage the Weir infantry, Thalen could tell at a glance that the Oros were stronger and more skilled fighters. Weirs began to die—first by tens, then by scores.

And while his infantry was engaged in fighting the men from the landing craft, the troop ships used their long oars in skilled choreography to bring themselves up to piers at the north and south ends of the quay. Once docked, they began to disgorge all the men who hadn't fit in the swifts, which was hundreds, or a thousand, more soldiers.

Through galloping messengers, Thalen redeployed his archery squads to attack the ships while they docked. Arrows bit deep into the backs of enemy legs as they scrambled down the rigging. He had also kept companies of infantry in reserve; he sent these, running double-time, to meet the new threat. His troops crashed into the enemies' pikes with verve. But the Weirs were no match.

Naven hissed, "A handful of our men are fleeing up the alleyways! Drought damn them!"

A few dozen Oros pursued their enemy into city streets. Thalen had to hope that the barricades would hold both those who were retreating and those who chased them.

For the most part, however, the fresh Oro infantrymen formed disciplined pike squares and began, inexorably, to converge on the middle of the quay. Their plan was to surround the Weir fighters.

Thalen's mind reeled at the prospect of another Rout.

Recalling the battle outside of Sutterdam, he knew it had been lost not only because of numbers but because of faulty tactics. The quay area had turned into pandemonium. Where—in all this mayhem—was the Oro general?

Finally, Thalen spotted a cluster of red helmet feathers on a wide pier to his left, close to the north edge of the harbor.

"Give me your horse," he shouted to a messenger nervously waiting behind the Harbormaster Hut. Naven copied his action, grabbing a horse's reins from a girl, turning her to face the city, and giving her a strong push toward cover.

"Weirs! Follow me! Follow me!" Thalen called. A squad of twenty pikemen heard his cries and formed up around the horses.

Sumroth had landed on one of the last swifts and had set up his command post on the widest of the wooden piers, just where it met the solid quay, near the north end of the harbor and the tall cliff that was his goal. Of course he could have stayed out of the fray on the troop ship, as Admiral Hixario had done, but that was not his way. He hadn't traveled all these leagues to keep his sword clean.

His flagmen gave signals for his men to drive the Weirs before them from both ends of the quay; eventually they would encircle the bastards. Those magicked whales had been a nasty surprise, and the ragtag navy had put up a staunch fight, but now the tide had turned. And the sixth-flamer in charge of the flanking action up the coast should have also disembarked by now, and should be moving in a pincer movement toward the harbor.

As soon as these defenders were swept away, he would redeploy his troops to encircle that cliff.

Above the other noises, Sumroth heard a welcome sound: his men were singing as they took down their enemies.

From the top of SeaWidow Cliff, Cerúlia watched the battle buffeted by alternating waves of hope and despair. Her eye had been drawn by movement at the back of the armada: two ships drawing very close together. When she next looked back at them, she was astonished to see the Lorther flag, the Walrus Trident against a gray background, flying from their masts.

"Look! Look!" she shouted to Darzner, grabbing his elbow. "Do you see?"

"What am I looking for?"

"The Lorther flag on the two rear ships!"

Darzner peered through the spyglass she had handed him, trying to get his bearings. "Yes! I see it too!"

Cerúlia drew in a breath. "It could be a trick. Write a note. 'Identify yourself.' Those two are the only ones left where whales could reach them, but if they're really Lorther . . ."

She dispatched the note attached to a pelican leg.

A seagull returned with news concerning the Oro detachment that was attempting to flank the city. They had pulled in to a small sandy beach of a small fisherman's village just north of Cascada.

"That's Clam Diggers Cove," Darzner explained in a rush. "I used to swim there as a child. The water is plenty deep for them to dock, but then they have to climb these sandy dunes. After the dunes, they'll hit a narrow dirt road that passes between foothills."

Cerúlia questioned the gull and learned that the Weir cavalry companies had positioned themselves to waylay the enemy soldiers on the dunes and then to lure them into an ambush.

"Halt!" cried Shield Pontole's voice from the crest of SeaWidow Cliff, where he and Shield Gatana stood guard.

"It's me! It's Tilim!"

Tilim was allowed to proceed; he gave the queen Thalen's message about the third group of cavalry.

Ciellō had been remarkably silent, even for him, as the battle raged below them. Now he spoke. "Damselle, you must use that last cavalry company as escort for your escape."

"What?" The queen wheeled on him.

"You need to flee the city. You have your horse." He pointed at Smoke. "Staying is foolishness. The enemy, she does not have horses.

You on the fast horse—a company of cavalry as shields—you could get to safety."

"And leave my city and people to be sacked? And leave everyone I love to be killed or captured?"

Ciellō shrugged. "Lots of people are dying today."

A horrible thought passed through Cerúlia's mind: *Is Ciellō hoping that Thalen will die?*

She stared at him aghast. As if reading her suspicion, a shadow passed over his face and he shifted his gaze to the side.

A pelican, its large wings making a breeze that scattered papers, interrupted their confrontation by flying right on top of the map table. It had something attached to its leg. Darzner detached it and handed the note to the queen.

Shrimpella! Sorry we missed the festival! Could pelicans drop grenadoes? We captured crates full.

Heart soaring, Cerúlia knew that no Oro could mimic her uncle's tone. She pondered the issue he raised: could pelicans carry and release those explosive missiles?

Pelican, can you carry a heavy thing in your beak?

One carries big mackerel.

But these balls are not good to eat. What I mean is: could you carry it, not swallow it, drop it where I tell you, and fly away quickly?

The pelican turned its head this way and that, looking at her with his small black eyes. She sensed his reluctance and she knew that delivering grenadoes would be dangerous for the birds.

But every moment, people on the quay below her perished.

Pelicans within range of my thought, I Command you to come to this cliff top for instructions.

While she waited for the birds to gather, she looked down on the struggle on the quay.

"*Oh!*" she cried. "No! Thalen! What are you doing!"

Following her gaze, Ciellō also stared intently at the scene below.

Then, without a word, he sprinted from her side, mounted Smoke in a single vault, and headed down the path at a gallop.

The queen closed her eyes and desperately cast about, trying to think of what additional help her Talent could provide.

Hoping that the horses would just intimidate men into dodging, Thalen refused to engage with any of the skirmishes between himself and the red plumed helmets; he, Naven, and the brave squad of pikemen just weaved, pushed, and butted a path toward their objective. They succeeded in getting close enough to the Oro command post to discern that a score of elite men-at-arms formed a protective knot around a cluster of high-ranking officers, flagmen, and a trumpeter standing on the land end of a wharf.

Now Thalen and his followers had no choice but to engage in hand-to-hand combat. Standing up in the stirrups of his horse, he used his rapier to slash necks or pierce the small opening at the men's elbows. The Weir pikemen accompanying him flung themselves at the line of halberds, their spears thrusting, crossing with pikes of their enemies, being beaten back.

From his perch high on the horse, out of the corner of his eye, Thalen thought he saw a rider dashing toward the same wharf at a speed so fantastic that hardened soldiers from both armies dived to get out of the way. But before he could focus on the horse and rider, the general's guard began a charge to drive away these pesky attackers. An Oro blade succeeded in slashing the throat of Thalen's own mount, and he had to jump off and scramble just to stay on his feet. The Weir infantryman to the left of him was decapitated by the axe of a pike, while just to his right another Weir took a point deep into his groin. While the Oro tried to pull his weapon out of the dying Weir pikeman, Thalen's rapier flashed, opening the artery in the back of his leg.

The head of an Oro's halberd had broken off but refusing to

give in, the soldier wielded what was left like a quarterstaff. He struck Thalen's arm with the wooden handle so smartly Thalen lost sensation. His rapier went flying and disappeared from view. He fell back a few steps, cradling his numbed forearm.

"Weirs!" Thalen shouted. "We must get through; we must try again! Men, follow me!!"

Duke Naven, who was still ahorse, echoed, "Forward! Forward!" as he led the third sortie. Just as the Weirs charged the line, a flock of seagulls swooped down from the sky, shrieking, clawing, and pecking at the faces of the ring of Oro Protectors. In the chaos of beating wings and cursing men throwing up their arms to ward off the birds, Thalen managed to slip between two enemies.

Their attention drawn by the unexpected bird attack, the Oro command officers standing on the pier all stared open-mouthed in his direction, their swords already gripped in their hands.

Although he'd managed to reach his objective, Thalen had no weapon but his mind.

In his loudest, most commander-like voice, he called out, "*Who is in charge here?*"

Six Oro officers, with tall red plumes on their helmets, just looked at him as if he were a madman.

Facing shoreward, these Oros did not notice what Thalen saw: the queen's bodyguard, Ciellō, dripping, had climbed from the water onto the seaward end of the wharf, his dagger in his teeth. At all costs, Thalen had to keep these men focused on himself.

General Sumroth could not stop himself from taking credit for this daring, brilliant invasion—an invasion on the verge of success.

"I am!" he barked. "You address Sumroth the First, the new king of Oromondo. I will take your queen's blue scalp back to the Land. All her evil witch tricks with whales and these fucking birds will amount to nothing."

Although the clamor of the battlefield rose all around them, Thalen concentrated so intently on the tall man in front of him, it seemed as if they stood alone in a cone of silence. With a great effort, Thalen steadied his voice. "Are you really a king?" he asked, looking the general straight in the eyes. "You look vaguely familiar to me. Actually, yes!—*I know you!* That scar near your chin! That was me. You're the coward who hid in a Magi's cloak and played games with sick wolves, are you not? That worked out very well for the Land of Asswipes, didn't it?"

"YOU!!!" roared Sumroth, in his fury not noticing that the fifth-flamer to his left had fallen to Ciellō's dagger across his throat. Simultaneously, dozens of birds had massed upon his two flagmen, who tried to bat them away with their flags and, when that didn't work, dropped their flags and crouched down on the pier in an attempt to protect their faces with their hands. The trumpeter, similarly besieged, swiped at the birds with his instrument.

"*You* invaded the Land and burned our Worship Citadels?" Faster than Thalen anticipated, Sumroth's giant two-handed sword cleaved the air. It would have cleaved his head if Thalen hadn't shrunk back just in time. He couldn't retreat far; as it was, he had bumped into the back of an Oro pikeman preoccupied with holding off the determined Weir foot soldiers who persevered, despite their heavy losses, with Naven urging them forward. Thalen sidled a few steps to his left. He longed for a weapon. Anything to hold in his hands. Desperately, he took off his fancy hat and held it in front of himself.

Sumroth recovered from his swing in a flash and kept his eyes glued on Thalen, who purposely did not break the connection. Thalen continued moving, edging a touch forward, moving left, then moving right. He waved the hat about. The general watched him as a snake watches a mouse. A seagull dared to perch on Sumroth's shoulder; he shook it off like a fly.

In the intensity of his concentration on his prey, Sumroth didn't pay heed to the fact that the birds now mobbed the fourth-flamer beside him on the pier, beating their wings in his face, trying to peck his eyes, and biting at the back of his bare legs. The Oro swept them off his legs and mangled several with sword slashes. But the more he killed, the more flew, cawing, into his face. Two perched on his helmet, fiercely gripping the metal with their claws, their open wings covering his eyes, despite his attempts to shake them off.

And outside the cordon of elite guards, the Weir infantrymen pressed one more attack on soldiers distracted by vicious birds.

"Who are *you*?" the general bellowed over the caws and shrieks around them.

"Who am I?" answered Thalen, shifting to the right a step, his hands outstretched, balancing his weight on both feet, ready to spring in any direction. "A Free Stater. A student." He waved his hat about in a pitiful attempt at distraction. "The Oros killed my mother, Jerinda, and my brother Harthen. *They* were heroes. But me? I am nobody." He moved a step to the left, crouching. "Truly, I am nobody."

"How did a nobody sneak into the Land?" Sumroth's body effortlessly followed Thalen's little movements. "How did you escape? Did *you* burn down Femturan?"

"General *Some Rot,* did you say? Really, it's a long story," Thalen answered. He paused his weaving to airily wave his hand holding the hat, trying to copy Adair's insouciance. Then he stood still and tall, keeping his eyes far from Ciellō, trying to show only bravado. "Now, if you'll surrender, I promise to satisfy your curiosity and relate every detail."

"You will burn in the Eternal Flames, heathen," said Sumroth, "and in moments I will kill the blue-haired witch on the cliff top." He settled himself into an attack stance, one knee braced forward, the great sword held high above his head, with the tip pointed backward. Several birds fluttered to land on that sword, but he shook them off. Thalen prepared himself to die. He surely would have died from Sumroth's tremendous blow . . . except that in the last instant before the sword slashed forward, Ciellō's knife buried itself deep in the back of Sumroth's bare muscular neck with enough force to sever his spine.

Sumroth's sword fell with a crash from his paralyzed arms, and the man tumbled down after it.

Light-headed at his near escape, Thalen braced his hands on his knees and put his head down.

"Foolishness, to risk your own life thus," Ciellō hissed at his ear, "but clever. You give me the glory of killing all her enemies?"

It took Thalen a moment to straighten up and glance at the dead littering the pier. "There's no glory in killing, Ciellō. Sometimes it is necessary, but it is never glorious."

Sumroth had fallen to the boards of the wooden wharf. He could not move his chest to breathe. But with the little air he had left in his brain, his last thoughts flew to Zea.

Ciellō and Thalen returned to the battle; the bodyguard drew his sword from his scabbard and attacked the nearest enemy with lightning speed, barely halting as he took on new combatants. Thalen picked up the great sword that the Oro general had dropped. It was too heavy for him; he was untrained in its use; and he felt as if he moved through molasses. So he put his back against Ciellō's and just used the weapon to block strikes from Oro halberds—his only aim to keep Ciellō safe from attacks from his rear. Occasionally, Ciellō's back recoiled into his, but the Zellishman fought on.

An explosion and then a chorus of yells made everyone look out into the water. One of the anchored troop ships had a cloud of white smoke and sparks billowing above it, and the Pellish sailors aboard were jumping into the water in frantic haste. A flock of five pelicans flew over another of these vessels and dropped small, dark balls. In an instant, that ship too had thin white ribbons sparking from it.

And then . . . the battle shifted, as if all the playing pieces were suddenly in new positions, or rather, as if the whole board had been kicked over.

Certainly, seeing their ships destroyed would strike fear into the hearts of the Oro soldiers. Certainly, when they looked to Command, the pikemen would be worried by the missing flags. Certainly, the birds joining the fray contributed: by the minute hundreds more seagulls attacked Oro soldiers, getting in their way, obscuring their vision, frightening them with their bewitched single-mindedness. But the instantaneous sapping of the will to fight affected all the Oro Protectors so thoroughly and so instantaneously, Thalen wondered if there could be a magical explanation.

Heartened, the exhausted, blood-soaked Weirs gathered their last reserves of strength.

Three Pellish ships began scrambling with their large oars to turn around and flee the harbor. One of these had special lanterns shining in the front, and particularly large Pellish flags of the Crossed Oars flew from its mast. Again, pelicans hovered over a ship and dropped their deadly cargo.

Seeing their admiral's ship try to flee and end up exploding was too much. Oro soldiers began throwing down their weapons and surrendering. First just a few, and then hundreds. Only the general's elite guard fought on.

Thalen was revolted by the blood and death around him. With the last reserves of his strength he jumped onto a crate, raised the great sword high in the air on a trembling arm, and shouted, "Halt this loss of life! Lay down your weapons and surrender!"

The nearby fighters took stock of their situation. Then, one by one, their swords clattered on the stone quay.

Breathing hard, Thalen climbed down from the crate. Ciellō, a few paces away, had slumped to his knees. Thalen thought he was just winded and walked over to give him a hand up. That was when he saw the multiple wounds Ciellō had sustained—thigh, chest, arms. Blood gushed out of the Zellishman's skin everywhere. Thalen groped with his fingers to find the arteries to press them closed. But Ciellō fell over on his side.

Thalen leaned close. "Hold on, just a little while. Healers—"

"Tell her . . ." Ciellō said, his voice surprisingly forceful. "Tell her . . . I wish her . . . never to be lonely. And you, Commander . . . May the wind always be at your back."

Ciellō struggled to cup his own hands close to his mouth. He blew his last breath into them, his hands falling empty to the blood-slicked stone.

Wareth left Marcot and the Catamount Cavalry officers to deal with the wounded and their Oro captives from the battle north of the city. Accompanied by two riders, he rode back to tell Thalen that they'd vanquished the contingent they had faced. His broken fingers, which had had a rough day, hurt like blazes, and he tried to rest them on his shoulder.

When he reached the harbor, he could read at a glance that the Weirs had prevailed here too and were in the early stages of caring for the wounded and rounding up captives.

Looking about, he recognized the messenger boy on a nice horse. "Hey! Tilim! Where's the commander?"

"He's in the Harbormaster Hut. Follow me."

When they dismounted they had to wait a moment while Thalen finished giving instructions to a man in the uniform of the palace guard. Finally, the man saluted and left to carry out his duties.

"'Mander," said Tilim, "the queen says that the last two boats— see those, flying the Lorther flag?" The boy pointed. "They are truly Lorthers. She wants to make sure that you don't attack them and they are clear to dock."

Thalen raised his head to gaze over the water in surprise. "Ah. Good." He shook his head, trying to clear his muddled mind. "Look, you take all the messengers hereabouts and spread the word. Decide on which two piers they should use and set men to clearing and securing them."

"Me?" said Tilim, shocked to receive such an important assignment.

"Yes, *you*. Get along now."

Thalen turned to Wareth, who opened his lips, but whose words Thalen forestalled. "Sorry, Wareth. I already heard the news. Her birds, you know, watched the whole battle. The archers hiding in the dunes was a nice touch, and then enticing the foot forward into that ambush."

"I should have known," said Wareth, glum at not being able to relay his triumph. "We might have lost more men if the enemy hadn't all suddenly lost heart. Here too?"

"Yes."

"You hurt?"

"No," said Thalen. "Once again, we survived."

He took a step out of the hut to motion at all the bodies on the quay. "Why do some live while others perish? It's so unfair. Even to them." He meant the enemy. "Young men, most of them . . ." He staggered, and his eyes filled with tears.

Wareth grabbed him to keep him from falling. "Come on, 'Mander," he said. "Plenty of capable Weirs about to do the mopping up. You're all in. Neither of us has really slept in I-don't-know-when."

Wareth called to the Weir riders who had accompanied him. "I'm taking the commander back to the Rare Talents Inn. That's where he'll be if anyone needs him, but if you bother him about nonsense I'll cut out your gizzard and toast it for fastbreak."

Smoke trotted back up to SeaWidow Cliff because that's where She was. The trot cooled him off a little from his full-speed sprint. She was kneeling on the ground. He nuzzled the back of her neck to tell her he had returned, but She paid no attention to him.

The smallest canine stalked forward with her face turned up; Smoke touched her tiny black nose with his muzzle.

She is busy now, said the tiny canine. *She is thanking the airborne ones and the marine ones.*

Smoke didn't know anything about those other beasts, but since canines often seemed to be in the queen's confidence, he accepted the explanation. He snorted through his nose.

A man who smelled of metal patted Smoke and looked him over. Smoke suffered the attention because the man had a familiar scent. Besides, She kept him near her.

"That was some dash, Smoke," the man said. "Never dreamt that even you could go so fast. How about some water?"

The man filled a bucket with water, and Smoke drank thankfully, because his throat felt raw from his sprint and irritated by a whiff of something sharp and burning in the air. The water was soft, wet, and so soothing. By pushing his nose deep in the bucket he washed the bad air out of his nostrils.

When he finished, She was standing upright. She patted his nose once.

Well done, Smoke. Your speed saved the day.

She said to the man who had just watered him, "Pour a clean basin of water, Pontole. And everyone, gather round. We need to thank Nargis and pray for Home, Health, Safety, Comradeship, and the Future of the Realm."

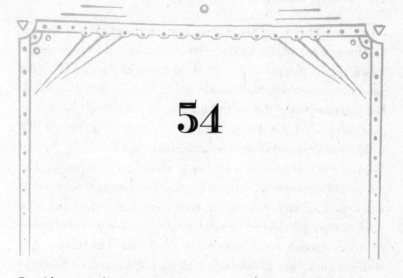

54

Considerate as always, Marcot had sent a messenger to West Cottage in the late afternoon to tell Stahlia and her family that the battle was over and the Weirs had triumphed. Forgetting all about their half-prepared meal, Percie, Tovalie, and Lemle ran to the quayside to see if they could succor the wounded.

Stahlia decided not to go. The thought of all the blood and gore sickened her. She would finish the stew, add the potatoes at the right time, set the bread for its second rise, and prepare an apple pudding. Her kin would be hungry when they returned.

Perchance I'm a shirker. But they also serve who feed the warriors and the healers.

When she could think of nothing more to do, she sat alone at the long table in the autumn dusk, rubbing the tension in her aching neck, picking crumbs off the table, and thinking of Wilim.

Wilim, could you ever have imagined all these things happening to our little family? Could we ever have foreseen the way the threads of our lives would have woven into this larger tapestry?

When did this all start? Could it have been her vow to serve Nargis after the Fountain healed Percia?

Flickering motion and the noises of carriage wheels and baying dogs startled her from her reverie. The queen herself had arrived. Stahlia was deeply pleased that after such an ordeal Cerúlia sought solace not in the palace but at West Cottage. As Cerúlia came running in the door, Stahlia held her at arm's length to examine her: her face looked drawn and her blue hair had pulled out of its plait and snarled, but the creased and dirty military-style outfit that Editha had designed showed no bloodstains.

And she had brought with her a whole parcel of people. The cranky old man with a thin gray braid and surprisingly warm smile was *Cerúlia's grandfather,* and the competent, heavyset woman who started helping Stahlia set refreshments on the table turned out to be his wife—though not actually his wedded wife. The middle-aged man cracking jokes, in dashing but blood- and sea-stained silks, was almost Cerúlia's uncle, but not quite.

Stahlia gave up trying to puzzle out the relationships and just concentrated on offering washcloths, basins of warm water, chairs, and tankards while she weaved around the dogs that kept getting underfoot until she thought to set out bowls of water and food for them in the kitchen.

They settled the old king in Stahlia's most comfortable chair. Stahlia noticed Cerúlia's eyes sparkling with an overexcited brightness.

"Shrimpella," said the almost-uncle, Prince Mikil. "Let me feast my eyes on you." He grabbed both her hands and held her in front of himself. "Can you forgive me for not recognizing you on *Island Dreamer?* You can't know how much and how often I've rued my blindness."

"Nothing to forgive," said Cerúlia. "You saved my life out of disinterested kindness. How are Arlettie and Gilboy? They were so good to me."

"Arlettie, well Arlettie—"

"Here, Cressa's girl," the grandfather interrupted. "I have a little gift for you." He handed her a small box he carried inside a pouch tied by a string to his neck. She opened it and showed it around. The box contained the most beautiful broach Stahlia had ever seen: a dolphin made out of silver and blue sapphires. When Cerúlia pinned it on her collar, the old man shone brighter than all the lanterns.

"Oh, my Shrimpella!" said the uncle, embracing Cerúlia. "You look so much like your mother! To see you hale and sparkling! Would that your mother could see through my eyes!"

"Can we talk about her someday soon? I'm so eager to hear about her, and you knew her best."

"That would gladden my heart," said the uncle.

Then Stahlia's own family surged in, returning from the nursing stations. After jumbled introductions all around, Stahlia pulled Percia and Lemle downstairs into the kitchen to question them privately.

"Was it bad?" Stahlia asked.

Percie answered, "Not that bad for me; I just wrapped broken limbs. And Tilim's friends in the Shield kept him running errands, not working in the healers' tents after all. Tovalie decided to stay, to roll more bandages. Lem, though—Lem volunteered to hold the hands of the dying."

Lemle's face had lost its healthy nutmeg color, and his eyes lacked focus. Stahlia gently smoothed his hair and poured him a glass of wine. He put the glass down and came into her arms for a hug.

"The toughest and kindest of them all," she whispered to him. "I mean it, now. No one else is strong enough to do what you did."

When they rejoined the others upstairs, the half uncle confessed that his head was hurting from a bad blow he'd taken earlier. Food was ready, and food would help everyone. A knock on the front door revealed servants dropping off baskets of pies, bread, and wine sent along by Chamberlain Vilkit. The family crowded round the table to eat. Stahlia did not have enough chairs, so Tilim, Lemle, and Iluka leaned against the wall.

Just as they were starting on the sweets, another knock on the door came from Marcot, who said the situation was well enough in hand that he could take a break. Percia ran into his arms with relief. Before Stahlia could close the door after her son-in-marriage, Commander Thalen and his close friend Raider Wareth, freshly washed, walked up the steps.

Stahlia had never before believed that this enormous house could be too small, but right now it overflowed with people.

"Goodness, do you think we should move this gathering to the palace?" she asked.

"No, no. I want to be here," said Cerúlia. "Come sit, Commander— you must be starving."

Several people jumped up to give Thalen their chair with exclamations about how whatever he had done had "saved the city." Stahlia couldn't follow the jumbled explanations about battle strategy, but that was partially because she turned a deaf ear—she didn't want to picture the deadly peril they had all just undergone.

She noticed that Thalen had ended up seating himself beside Cerúlia and that under the table the two of them held hands.

The sight of young sweethearts together always makes me miss you more, Wilim. These young folks think that love is their very own invention.

Well, every time it happens it seems like a miracle.

Marcot poured wine all around. "To our queen, Commander Thalen, King Nithanil, Prince Mikil, and our magnificent victory!"

Cerúlia raised her glass. "To the help of the whales and the gulls and pelicans. Without them, we never would have won the day."

"To my Cressa," the grandfather said, looking down into his glass. "Gone but never forgotten."

Prince Mikil added, "To Lautan the Munificent, who cares even for shrimps such as us."

Percia added, "To my mother, the best cook in Weirandale." This brought a chorus of laughter and requests for second or third helpings.

"You are going to have to tell us everything, Shrimpella," said the uncle. "How you escaped capture, how you survived your injuries. How you won this battle. Your strength amazes me."

"Strength? Often I have felt so weak," said Cerúlia. "But an old friend of mine would say that my roots got a start in good soil: here, with my mother, father, and Nana; and then in Wyndton, where I was transplanted and nurtured by my second family."

Feeling restive, Stahlia carried a stack of dishes down to the kitchen. She leaned against a table, finding her shoulders shaking and her eyes wet. Looking around upstairs just now she had experienced such a stab of loss. Both girls were complete and grown; they'd found love (and now, new blood family connections); they no longer needed her. And Tilim! So long as he had a swordsman around him, the boy would be content. The three might love her still in a muted manner, but this affection was just the long trailing echo of children's all-encompassing love for the one who cared for them. She felt so lonely without Wilim.

She cried harder, ashamed that in the midst of this national emergency, she had turned inward to a personal and selfish grief.

"Mother Stahlia?" said Marcot at the door, catching her sobbing into her apron. Marcot, who had probably never carried a dirty dish before in his whole life, had followed her with another load.

"Oh, but it's been a day," said Stahlia, waving away his concern with her hands.

Marcot put down the plates he carried and drew her into a hug.

"A day of tension and sorrow, which brings out all our other heartaches," he said. Stahlia leaned against his shoulder a moment, soaking in warmth and comfort, and giving some in return to the young man who had lost a mother he dearly loved.

As the evening progressed and everyone's hunger slackened, the guests spoke reverently of the people taken from them. Seamaster Gourdo had fallen and Duke Naven too. Stahlia was heartsick to hear about Naven, but comforted to hear tales of his unexpected and impressive battle courage.

They prayed for Nargis to take their souls to the Eternal Waters.

Cerúlia stood and raised her glass. "Ciellō of Zellia, who will live in my heart forever."

"Ciellō too!" Percia cried. "Oh, no! That's awful!"

"Worse," said Commander Thalen, "he died after saving me."

Stahlia found herself reaching across the table to pat the commander's hand. "Sometimes," she said, thinking of Wilim, "bighearted people forfeit themselves to protect others. If we grieve over this too much, we lose sight of the important part. You have to accept their actions as their choice, or you dishonor their sacrifice."

The queen raised a tearstained face. "Wise as always, Teta."

They all drank to Ciellō's honor.

Then her rascal Tilim, who had drunk too much wine, launched into a long tale about everything he had seen and done from his perch on top of Indigo.

Nithanil of Lortherrod rapped on the table for quiet. "I am an old man," he said, "and old men can't *wait around*. We might dive the depths any moment. You two"—he pointed at Cerúlia and Commander Thalen, whose shoulders touched—"look mighty cozy there."

"Oh, hush, you old buffoon!" said the almost-wife. "Remember your manners. Don't start trouble, now."

"I will not hush!" He banged on the table. "I am that woman's closest blood kin, and I demand to know: When is the wedding?"

Cerúlia sat up straight and spoke with clipped anger. "Grandfather, Weirs have our own customs. We do not allow our lives to be ruled by patriarchs"—she softened her tone as she continued—"no matter how glad we may be about being reunited."

"Well?" Thalen asked Cerúlia, ignoring the testy exchange to concentrate on the subject that had been raised. "I am yours to command. Name the hour."

"If you must press me, what about tomorrow at noon?" she whispered, staring into his blue eyes.

"Water's sakes, Birdie! Not tomorrow!" Stahlia cried, allowing all the stress of the past days to burst forth. "What kind of malarkey is in your head? Give us all a chance to recover. A royal wedding can't just be thrown together in a rush. I'd hate to think I raised such a thoughtless young woman!"

"Mama," said Tilim with his devil grin, "I think she's joking."

"Indeed," answered Cerúlia, winking at Stahlia. "We can wait *two* days." This struck most everyone as remarkably funny, and such laughter ensued that Lemle choked on his ale and Wareth had to pound him on the back and all the dogs started barking in excitement. And Thalen kissed Cerúlia's hand and then her forehead.

"That's fine. That's fine," said the almost-uncle, rubbing his forehead with both palms. "You know, I drank a bit of wine, but it hasn't exactly helped my head; I'm going outside for a breath of air."

The others returned to talk about a wedding, but Stahlia kept her eye on Prince Mikil out the window. He waved to the guards and walked a few paces, one hand on each side of his head. When he staggered a bit, she started to rise. By the time Stahlia flung open the doorway, he had vomited copiously in the grass; by the time she reached his side, his lips had gone bloodless and his eyes rolled back. By the time she screamed for help, he had gone limp in her arms as she sought to hold him up. By the time everyone huddled round with advice and concern, he was gone.

Cerúlia rushed outside and took the body from her, sitting on the dark, cold grass, holding Mikil's head in her lap, stroking his forehead and gray temples. Guards had gathered with torches. Inside the cottage, the grandfather wailed as if his heart had been torn out of him. Stahlia knelt so close, her hand pressed on her daughter's shoulder, she may have been the only one who heard her girl softly singing an unfamiliar song with a repeated chorus of "Beloved of Lautan."

PART
FOUR

*Reign of Queen Cerúlia,
Year 2*

SUMMER

55

Moot Table

Peddler looked around Moot Table, registering new participants since the Agents' last meeting. He saw a new Sailor—a woman this time; a new Water Bearer—a young boy; and a new Gardener—a man in his prime. Peddler sighed, knowing that the former Agents had passed on. He wasn't surprised about losing the former Gardener, who had leaned like a gnarled tree about to fall, but he would miss him.

Pozhar, Ghibli, 'Chamen, and Restaurà were represented by the same humans as the last time the Agents had gathered. And he recognized Spinner, whom he had met in the flesh as Magistrar Destra in the Garden in Slagos. Her gossamer cape floated about her.

Healer spoke. "I believe it was you, Spinner, who called this meeting?"

"Aye," she replied. "That I did. Mìngyùn sent me with this offer."

She stepped into the middle of the flat rock.

"For hundreds of years Oromondo and Weirandale have been at war. Most of this conflict stems from deep friction and ancient grudges between the two nations. But the recent hostilities have been exacerbated by the blights and food shortages in Oromondo. These blights have intensified the rivalries, leading to open warfare and much loss of life.

"Oromondo believes that the Weirs are responsible for the blights. To the contrary: Pozhar's people have brought this catastrophe on themselves by polluting their own water with toxic minerals from their mines."

"You lie!" shouted Smithy, instantly defensive.

"Please, hear me out," Spinner entreated. "It does no harm just to listen."

"Of course no one deliberately caused this pollution. Pozhar and Pozhar's people had no way of knowing that disturbing these metals would lead to their dispersal in the water. And in their search for a reason for their suffering, of course it was totally understandable that they would blame their ancient enemy."

Mason scrunched up his face, deep in thought. "Everyone thinks that rocks are rocks. No one pays attention to how very different they are. Smithy, your mountains are volcanic—and the years of lava and ash on top . . ."

Peddler had always thought of Mason as rather dull and stolid; he realized that he may have underestimated his colleague.

"In hopes of lessening the tensions and earning peace for future generations," Spinner continued, "the greatest minds in Weirandale and the Free States have worked on solutions to this pollution. Water Bearer?"

As she ceded the floor, the young boy stepped forward, rainbows spilling wildly from his bowl because he held it in one hand. "Smithy, I have here a gift from the people of Nargis to the people of Pozhar." He held up a small sack in his free hand. "This contains a compound that you can mix in your contaminated water. If you then pour the water through a filter before allowing people or animals to drink, the filter will catch the toxic metals. The water will be sweet and healthy.

Your people and your livestock—or at least those that are not already sick—will thrive."

Peddler held his breath and stroked his beard braids. Would Smithy accept the gift?

The new Water Bearer intuited how much this offer injured Smithy's pride. The boy went down on one knee, put down his bowl, bent his face to the ground, and held the sack out in a supplicating manner.

Smithy grabbed the sack suspiciously, opened it, and peered inside. "How do I know that this is not poison?"

Water Bearer answered, "Your land is poisoned now. You know this, though you push away the knowledge. We beg you to sample this solution."

"Why would your people do this for Oromondo? Why would you not pursue conquest while we are weak and hungry?"

"Nargis desires no conquest."

Healer added, "An illness anywhere threatens the health of people everywhere."

Smithy's eyes still squinted in suspicion.

The new Gardener stepped forward. "Smithy, I hear your crops and trees crying out in distress. Wouldn't it be grand to have lush fields again?"

"Wait," Mason interrupted with authority. "The soil in the fields will hold on to the poisons for a long time even if the water runs pure now. Don't make promises the earth can't deliver. Also, Smithy, you may need to permanently close down many of your mines so as not to pollute more water sources. Is Oromondo prepared to do this?"

Peddler could tell that Smithy found Mason's warnings and caution more convincing than Gardener's grand vision.

Pozhar's Agent hefted the sack in his hand, considering.

"What does Nargis want in return? Will you expect a fortune in jewels for more of this compound? And you, Spinner—we invaded

Mìngyùn's ancestral homeland. What will you demand of us? Reparations?"

Spinner answered first. "Peace. Peace is what we desire."

The young Water Bearer stood up in the center of Moot Table, now holding his bowl steadily. "We do have a price, but it is not riches. In return for this gift, we ask that you renounce your long-held aim of killing the Nargis Queens."

No one spoke further. Always impatient at long meetings (because Ghibli was the Spirit of restlessness), Hunter took off her hat and began combing the long feather with her fingers as she puffed air through her cheeks. Smithy paced, tapping his fire tongs absently against his boot. Peddler became aware of the waves crashing on the rocky isle's edge and heard the bells in his own hair and beard making a small tinkle. Since he could think of nothing to add that would help the situation, he kept his mouth shut.

After the silence grew awkwardly long, the new Gardener, however, sank down on his knees and stretched his arms out in entreaty. "Won't you agree, my friend, we should always reach for life, life in all its bounty and richness!"

Gardener's humility made an impression. Very grudgingly, Smithy said, "We will try this compound and filtration. We make no promises."

"Will your fires warm the people when it is cold and illness threatens?" Healer asked.

Smithy made no reply.

EPILOGUE

*Reign of Queen Cerúlia,
Year 6*

WINTER

Cascada

Cerúlia and Thalen's daughter, Catalina, had her father's blue eyes and her mother's blue hair. At three summers she was a thriving toddler with fat caramel-colored cheeks—never fretful, though truth be told, occasionally willful.

Peace between Oromondo and Weirandale had prevailed since the Battle of Cascada Harbor. Cerúlia and her consort, Lord of the Scholars, were free to concentrate on the improvements they wanted to make domestically, such as founding a branch of the Scoláiríum and upgrading under schools.

Then a grippe epidemic struck the country. Waves of grippe periodically swept Weirandale in the winters: ofttimes mild, occasionally severe. Sometimes they sickened mostly the elderly, or the middle-aged, or the young. Sometimes they spread slowly, sometimes rapidly. The people generally found there was little to do but endure and wait for the eventual triumph of spring over winter.

This year, the grippe spread rapidly, harvesting nearly all of those unfortunate enough to be afflicted. And it struck the most precious segment of the Weir population: the children. The Weirs named it "Reaper of Babes." Shrieks of heartbroken mothers pierced the night air of every neighborhood, rich or poor. Cerf and the other healers tried every remedy they knew, but each day carts carrying tiny shrouded figures rumbled down the streets. Thalen worked feverishly and fruitlessly in his new laboratory, trying to discover a cure.

Frantic parents thronged the Courtyard of the Star, fighting one another for Nargis Water. When the Waters helped one sick child but did nothing for another, desperate citizens turned on one another in envy and rage. Queen Cerúlia had to station guards around the Fountain to keep order. These were the darkest of days.

The queen wanted to send Princella Catalina to the Eastern Duchies, but Lord Thalen pointed out that reports of outbreaks there were as grave as in the capital.

Then the Reaper snuck into the palace itself. Percia and Marcot's two sons, Parkier and Larkeen, fell ill. Cerúlia could do nothing but support her distraught sister.

With Nargis Water, Parkier rallied; but Larkeen, the four-summers boy, was failing. Cerf did not expect him to last the night.

Tilim had been dispatched to the Princella's Bedchamber. He was vainly trying to distract and entertain her while the adults of her circle were so preoccupied and distraught. Jothile, her usual nurseryman, had had to be dismissed for the evening because he was too upset to tend his charge.

"Come on, Catalina. Stop playing with your food and finish your supper. Eat that nice apple," he said.

"Jo-Jo peels my apples," she replied, so Tilim impatiently took out his knife. The apple was slick and he wasn't attentive; his knife slipped and cut his own thumb.

"Blast!" he muttered, sticking his bleeding thumb in his mouth.

"What happened?" asked Catalina, climbing up on her chair to grab at Tilim's arm. "Did you get an ouchie? Let me see."

She tugged Tilim's thumb out of his mouth and looked at the small bleeding gash. "Does it hurt?" she asked with wonder.

"Of course it hurts, silly."

Catalina touched the wound with her index finger. The wound closed as if the knife had never touched it.

Heartbeat quickening, Tilim looked at the princella closely. "Have you ever done that before?"

She casually tugged on the apple in his hand. "Finish."

"Catalina, look at me. Have you ever cured a cut before?"

"Yeah," she said.

"What else can you do?" he asked. "If I burn myself, can you cure that too?"

"I want apple," she said, now single-minded about the food she had refused earlier.

Tilim finished peeling the apple and cut it into slices. Then he went over to the fireplace, took a deep breath, and put his hand in the flames.

"Oh, Sweet Waters!" he screamed at the pain, tears filling his eyes. Catalina rushed up from her small-sized table, overturning her chair, ran to Tilim, touched his hand, and removed the burn. Tilim felt faint from the instant relief.

He got down on his knees to look her in the eyes, holding her shoulders in his hands too tightly. "Catalina, have you—or Jo-Jo—ever felt *ill*: you know, your head hurts, your throat hurts, your nose gets all clogged, and you feel really hot or really cold?"

Catalina nodded and took another bite of her apple.

"Are you able to make that go away too?"

The princella nodded.

"Catalina, this is so serious. Are you certain?"

She nodded gravely, unable to speak because of the slices she kept stuffing in her mouth.

Tilim picked her up with his arm around the back of her upper thighs and started running down the hallways, shouting at people in his path, "Make way! Make way!"

When he got to Marcot and Percia's suite, he saw that Percie sat in the common room, her head in her hands, weeping, while his mother rubbed her shoulders and Cerúlia sat on her other side, gripping her thigh.

When Cerúlia realized that Tilim carried Catalina against his chest, she sprang up in alarm.

"Tilim, what are you doing? No, no! You can't take her in there!!!"

When he didn't even pause at her command, Cerúlia pulled out her dagger. Tilim didn't quite believe that his sister would stab him, but he rushed even faster into his nephew's dim bedchamber. Marcot sat next to the bed, his face frozen in misery, holding Larkeen's hand. The boy's breath came in ragged gasps.

As Tilim dropped the princella down on Larkeen's bed Cerúlia and his other kinfolk crowded together at the doorway.

Catalina crawled up the bed covers until she sat beside Larkeen, dropping bits of apple out of her chubby hands. Then she patted her cousin on the forehead, crooning softly. "Lar-keen, Lar-keen." Little bits of chewed apple sprayed about. "They won't let you play with me. Don't you feel good? Go away, ouchie. Larkeen and me want to play.

"Lar-keen, Lar-keen. Don't you want to play with me?"

Immediately, Larkeen's breath steadied. Catalina watched him, still chewing, with a saucy grin on her face. A few moments later he opened his eyes.

"Why are you sitting on my arm, Little Lina?" he asked. "You're heavy—slide off, will ya?" Rubbing his eyes, Larkeen noticed the crowd of breathless adults. "I'm awful hungry. Could I have apple fritters?"

As Percia and Marcot embraced their son and promised him he could have anything in the Nine Realms he wanted to eat, Cerúlia picked up Catalina and twirled her round and round with glee.

"Find Chronicler Sewel this instant!" she ordered the room in general. "This princella must have her Definition! 'Catalina the Healer'!

"Sweetie, can you cure other children?" the queen was asking, but Tilim had taken her order personally and dashed out of the room. He ran through the palace hallways singing to the tapestries, the portraits, and anyone passing by:

> *When danger through the realm may reach,*
> *The Nargis Nymph allots to each,*
> *A Talent for the Times.*

APPENDIX ONE

CHARACTERS AND
PLACES IN ENNEA MÓN

The Spirits

'Chamen, Spirit of Stone
   Agent "Mason," chosen realm, Rortherrod
Ghibli, Spirit of the Wind
   Agent "Hunter," chooses no country
Lautan, Spirit of the Sea, "the Munificent"
   Agent "Sailor" (unnamed, then Mikil), chosen realm, Lortherrod
Mìngyùn, Spirit of Fate
   Agent "Spinner" (Destra)
Nargis, Spirit of Fresh Water
   Agent "Water Bearer" (Tiklok, then Nana), chosen realm,
   Weirandale
Pozhar, Spirit of Fire
   Agent "Smithy," chosen realm, Oromondo
Restaurà, Spirit of Sleep and Health
   Agent "Healer" (Myrnah), chosen realm, Wyeland
Saulė, Spirit of the Sun

Agent "Peddler" (Gunnit is agent-in-waiting), chosen realm, Alpetar

Vertia, Spirit of Growth

Agent "Gardener," chosen realm, the Green Isles

In Weirandale

THE EIGHT WESTERN DUCHIES (WEST TO EAST)

Northvale

Prairyvale

Woodsdale

Lakevale

Maritima—includes city of Queen's Harbor

Riverine—includes Cascada

Crenovale

Vittorine

THE THREE EASTERN DUCHIES ACROSS THE BAY OF CINDA (WEST TO EAST)

Androvale—contains Gulltown (port city) and Wyndton (country village)

Patenroux

Bailiwick—Barston (major city)

THE FORMER GENERATION ON THE THRONE

Queen Catreena the Strategist (deceased)

Consort: King Nithanil of Lortherrod (abdicated)

THE ROYALS

Queen Cressa the Enchanter (deceased)

Consort: Ambrice, Lord of the Ships (deceased)

Cerúlia, the princella

PEOPLE IN CASCADA, THE CAPITAL CITY

Bakilai, Lorther envoy

Editha, head of Editha's Exceptional Garments for People of Quality

Lemle, friend of the family from rural Wyndton

Judiciaries (unnamed)

Mistress Stahlia, Cerúlia's foster mother, a weaver

Percia, the queen's foster sister

Lord Marcot, son of the former Lord Regent, married to Percia

Tilim, the queen's foster brother

Rakihah, Rorther envoy

Tovalie, servant at West Cottage

Brother Whitsury, a Brother of Sorrow

AT THE PALACE

Athelbern, sergeant of the palace guard who becomes captain

Jadwinga, sergeant of the palace guard

Tade, sergeant of the palace guard

Besi, the head cook

Borta, baker

Ciellō, Cerúlia's personal bodyguard, from Zellia

Darzner, Cerúlia's secretary

Geesilla, a hair maid

Hiccuth, a stableman

Kiltti, a room maid

Nana, Water Bearer, the queen's former nursemaid

Sewel, royal chronicler

Vilkit, chamberlain of the palace

The New Queen's Shield

Captain Yanath, former shield to Queen Cressa

Sergeant Pontole, former shield to Queen Cressa

Branwise, former shield to Queen Cressa

Gatana, hired by Yanath

Mirja, healer, shield

Conspirators against Queen Cerúlia
At the Palace

Duke Inrick, from Crenovale

Lord Regent Matwyck

> Duchette Lolethia, his fiancée (deceased)
> Duchess Felethia, Lolethia's mother
> Murgn, captain of the Marauders, nephew to General Yurgn

Prigent, former councilor and treasurer

> Vanilina, his mistress

In Riverine

General Yurgn, head of the armed forces and former councilor

> Burgn, son
> Clovadorska, daughter-in-law, widow of deceased son Lurgn
> Yurgenia, daughter
> Cosmas, a manservant

In Vittorine

Belcazar, former councilor of Queen Cressa

> Engeliqua, wife
> Chamberlain Gruber

QUEEN CERÚLIA'S COUNCILORS

Alix, Steward, former reporter for the *Cascada News*

Fornquit, a cheese wholesaler

Lord Marcot, son of Matwyck the Usurper

Naven, Duke of Androvale

Nishtari, specializes in diplomacy

Wilamara, also seamaster

*The Alliance of Free States, once a unified country
called "Iga," now four smaller nation states*

Fígat—contains Latham and the Scoláiríum

Jígat—contains Jutterdam

Vígat—contains Sutterdam

Wígat—contains Yosta

SUTTERDAM (SECOND-LARGEST CITY)

Hartling, a potter and owner of a thriving pottery business

> Norling, Hartling's older sister
>
> Hake, his oldest son
>
> Pallia, Hake's girlfriend, a candlemaker
>
> Fordana, a servant girl

JUTTERDAM

Bellishia, captain of the city watch

Minister Destra, formerly Magistrar Destra of the Green Isles,
    Agent of Mìngyùn

Hulia, a tavern owner, once a member of the Defiance

Quinith, former student of the Scoláiríum

The Scoláiríum of the Free States

Located in the town of Latham, reached by ferry from Trout's Landing

Rector Meakey

Andreata, tutor of Ancient Languages

Irinia, tutor of Earth and Water

Granilton, tutor of History (deceased)

      Graville, his son (deceased)

Helina, tutor of Poetry

Hyllidore, porter for the Scoláiríum

Setty, widow in Latham

Wrillier, innkeep in Latham

Alnum, Oro deserter

Unvelder, Oro deserter

Surviving Members of the Raiders

Commander Thalen

Cerf, a healer

Dalogun, surviving twin

Fedak, cavalry

Jothile, cavalry

Kambey, weapons master

Kran, swordsman

Tristo, Thalen's adjutant, formerly a street orphan from Yosta

Wareth, cavalry scout

Lortherrod: capital city Liddlecup, castle Tidewater Keep

King Nithanil, abdicated and twice widowed

      Iluka, his common-law wife

King Rikil, the current king
>   wife and two sons

Prince Mikil
>   Arlettie, wife, originally from the Green Isles
>   Gilboy, adopted

Alpetar

Peddler, Agent of Saulė

Dewpepper, a beekeeper, sister to hostler Culpepper

Gunnit, an apprentice

Smithy, Agent of Pozhar, now living in Camp Ruby

Zea, wife of General Sumroth, now living in Camp Topaz

Rortherrod

King Kentros

Filio Kemeron

Appendix Two

Notable Historic Queens of Weirandale in Chronological Order

Cayla the Foremother

Carra the Royal

Chista the Builder

Cayleethia the Artist

Carlina the Gryphling

Charmana the Fighter

Cinda the Conqueror

Chyneza the Wise

Crylinda the Fertile

Cashala the Enchanter

Catorie the Swimmer

Ciella the Patient

Cenika the Protector

Chanta the Musical

Carmena the Perseverant

Callindra the Faithful

Cymena the Proud

Chella the Kind

Crilisa the Just

ACKNOWLEDGMENTS

In the years that I worked on this series I incurred debts, large and small, to those who guided, helped, and encouraged me.

I am grateful to Vassar College, which has always valued creative pursuits on an equal plane with traditional scholarship, for travel funds and the William R. Kenan Jr. Endowed Chair.

Throughout the drafting, Lt. Colonel Sean Sculley, Academy Professor and Chief of the American History Division at West Point, generously shared his military, historical, strategic, and sailing expertise. (I drew specialized information from Angus Konstam's *Renaissance War Galley, 1470–1590* and Sean McGrail's *Ancient Boats in North-West Europe*.)

Professors Kirsten Menking and Jeff Walker of Vassar's Earth Science Department led me away from grievous errors concerning world-building.

Stefan Ekman, Professor of English at the University of Gothenburg, took the time to share his unique knowledge regarding fantasy maps.

Professor Leslie Dunn of Vassar's English Department, a Shakespeare scholar, studied my poetry with the seriousness and skill she applies to more exalted works.

Professor Darrell James, who teaches stage combat in Drama, showed me his swords and taught me about their use.

I was fortunate indeed to find Penelope Duus, Vassar '17, who was trained in cartography. She started the map of Ennea Món when she was a senior and has patiently, loyally tweaked it for years. For the final corrections I am grateful to Amy Laughlin of Vassar's Academic Computing office.

A professional editor, Linda Branham, critiqued the first fifty pages. Friends who read drafts—in whole or in part—provided comments and encouragement that kept my roots watered. Thank you for your time, Fred Chromey, Joanne Davies, Madelynn Meigs '18, and Molly Shanley. Feedback from Madeline Kozloff, Daniel Kozloff, Bobbie Lucas '16, and Dawn Freer came at particularly timely moments or was particularly influential.

I tapped Theodore Lechterman for his knowledge of the Levelers (the historical analogue of the Parity Party) and his linguistic skills. Tom Racek '18, captain of the fencing team, helped me choreograph some of the fight scenes.

Rather late in my writing process I was lucky to find a writing partner with whom I exchanged manuscripts. The fantasy author James E. Graham provided irreplaceable assistance by reading nearly all of the series and filling the margins with passionate comments.

Others were kind and patient in giving a novice advice about how to publish in a new field, including Susan Chang (Tor), Alicia Condon (Kensington), Diana Frost (Macmillan), and Eddie Gamarra (The Gotham Group). Without their guidance these manuscripts might never have been published.

My husband, Robert Lechterman, supported me in this endeavor as selflessly as he has throughout our life together. Without him, the appliances would have just stayed broken and I would have subsisted on frozen fish sticks.

Martha Millard—my original agent at Sterling Lord Literistic—

knew and delighted in the fact that she was changing my life when she pursued me as a client and sold the series. She has retired and I shall miss her, but Nell Pierce of SLL has now ably filled her shoes.

At Tor my manuscripts fell into the hands of Rafal Gibek (production editor) and Deanna Hoak (copy editor), who saved me from myself.

My editor, Jennifer Gunnels of Tor, took a leap of faith on a nontraditional debut author, a four-volume series, and a rapid publication schedule. She also found the balance between corralling me when I wandered astray and giving me freedom. "You really need to research X," she would advise, and I would obediently get busy. Other times, when I fretted over whether I should change something, she'd remind me, "It's *your* book, Sarah."

It is my book, Jen, but in a larger sense it belongs to everyone mentioned here, to a dozen others who offered a hand, not to mention to the books, films, and teachers who formed me. Except the mistakes and infelicities, which pool around my feet, mewling like attention-mongering kittens—those poor things are mine own.